The Athelings by Margaret Oliphant

Or, The Three Gifts

In Three Volumes

Margaret Oliphant Wilson was born on April 4th, 1828 to Francis W. Wilson, a clerk, and Margaret Oliphant, at Wallyford, near Musselburgh, East Lothian.

Her youth was spent in establishing a writing style and by 1849 she had her first novel published: Passages in the Life of Mrs. Margaret Maitland.

Two years later, in 1851 Caleb Field was published and also an invitation gained to contribute to Blackwood's Magazine; the beginning of a lifelong business relationship.

In May 1852, Margaret married her cousin, Frank Wilson Oliphant. Their marriage produced six children but, tragically, three died in infancy. When her husband developed signs of the dreaded consumption (tuberculosis) they moved to Florence, and then to Rome where, sadly, he died.

Margaret was naturally devastated but was also now left without support and only her income from writing to support the family. She returned to England and took up the burden of supporting her three remaining children by her literary activity.

Her incredible and prolific work rate increased both her commercial reputation and the size of her reading audience. Tragedy struck again in January 1864 when her only remaining daughter, Maggie, died.

In 1866 she settled at Windsor to be closer to her sons, who were being educated at near-by Eton School.

For more than thirty years she pursued a varied literary career but family life continued to bring problems. Cyril Francis, her eldest son, died in 1890. The younger son, Francis, who she nicknamed 'Cecco', died in 1894.

With the last of her children now lost to her, she had little further interest in life. Her health steadily and inexorably declined.

Margaret Oliphant Wilson Oliphant died at the age of 69 in Wimbledon on 20th June 1897. She is buried in Eton beside her sons.

Index of Contents

VOLUME I

CHAPTER I

IN THE STREET

One of them is very pretty—you can see that at a glance: under the simple bonnet, and through the thin little veil, which throws no cloud upon its beauty, shines the sweetest girl's face imaginable. It is only eighteen years old, and not at all of the heroical cast, but it brightens like a passing sunbeam through all the sombre line of passengers, and along the dull background of this ordinary street. There is no resisting that sweet unconscious influence: people smile when they pass her, unawares; it is a natural homage paid involuntarily to the young, sweet, innocent loveliness, unconscious of its own power. People have smiled upon her all her days; she thinks it is because everybody is amiable, and seeks no further for a cause.

The other one is not very pretty; she is twenty: she is taller, paler, not so bright of natural expression, yet as far from being commonplace as can be conceived. They are dressed entirely alike, thriftily dressed in brown merino, with little cloaks exact to the same pattern, and bonnets, of which every bow of ribbon outside, and every little pink rosebud within, is a complete fac-simile of its sister bud and bow. They have little paper-parcels in their hands each of them; they are about the same height, and not much different in age; and to see these twin figures, so entirely resembling each other, passing along at the same inconsistent youthful pace, now rapid and now lingering, you would scarcely be prepared for the characteristic difference in their looks and in their minds.

It is a spring afternoon, cheery but cold, and lamps and shop-windows are already beginning to shine through the ruddy twilight. This is a suburban street, with shops here and there, and sombre lines of houses between. The houses are all graced with "front gardens," strips of ground enriched with a few smoky evergreens, and flower-plots ignorant of flowers; and the shops are of a highly miscellaneous character, adapted to the wants of the locality. Vast London roars and travails far away to the west and to the south. This is Islington, a mercantile and clerkish suburb. The people on the omnibuses—and all the omnibuses are top-heavy with outside passengers—are people from the City; and at this time in the afternoon, as a general principle, everybody is going home.

The two sisters, by a common consent, come to a sudden pause: it is before a toy-shop; and it is easy to discover by the discussion which follows that there are certain smaller people who form an important part of the household at home.

"Take this, Agnes," says the beautiful sister; "see how pretty! and they could both play with this; but only Bell would care for the doll."

"It is Bell's turn," said Agnes; "Beau had the last one. This we could dress ourselves, for I know mamma has a piece over of their last new frocks. The blue eyes are the best. Stand at the door, Marian, and look for my father, till I buy it; but tell me first which they will like best."

This was not an easy question. The sisters made a long and anxious survey of the window, varied by occasional glances behind them "to see if papa was coming," and concluded by a rapid decision on Agnes's part in favour of one of the ugliest of the dolls. But still Papa did not come; and the girls were proceeding on their way with the doll, a soft and shapeless parcel, added to their former burdens, when a rapid step came up behind them, and a clumsy boy plunged upon the shoulder of the elder.

"Oh, Charlie!" exclaimed Agnes in an aggrieved but undoubting tone. She did not need to look round. This big young brother was unmistakable in his salutations.

"I say, my father's past," said Charlie. "Won't he be pleased to find you two girls out? What do you wander about so late for? it's getting dark. I call that foolish, when you might be out, if you pleased, all the day."

"My boy, you do not know anything about it," said the elder sister with dignity; "and you shall go by yourself if you do not walk quietly. There! people are looking at us; they never looked at us till you came."

"Charlie is so handsome," said Marian laughing, as they all turned a corner, and, emancipated from the public observation, ran along the quiet street, a straggling group, one now pressing before, and now lagging behind. This big boy, however, so far from being handsome, was strikingly the opposite. He had large, loose, ill-compacted limbs, like most young animals of a large growth, and a face which might be called clever, powerful, or good-humoured, but certainly was, without any dispute, ugly. He was of dark complexion, had natural furrows in his brow, and a mouth, wide with fun and happy temper at the present moment, which could close with indomitable obstinacy when occasion served. No fashion could have made Charlie Atheling fashionable; but his plain apparel looked so much plainer and coarser than his sisters', that it had neither neatness nor grace to redeem its homeliness. He was seventeen, tall, big, and somewhat clumsy, as unlike as possible to the girls, who had a degree of natural and simple gracefulness not very common in their sphere. Charlie's masculine development was unequivocal; he was a thorough boy now, and would be a manful man.

"Charlie, boy, have you been thinking?" asked Agnes suddenly, as the three once more relapsed into a sober pace, and pursued their homeward way together. There was the faintest quiver of ridicule in the elder sister's voice, and Marian looked up for the answer with a smile. The young gentleman gave some portentous hitches of his broad shoulders, twisted his brow into ominous puckers, set his teeth—and at last burst out with indignation and unrestrained vehemence—

"Have I been thinking?—to be sure! but I can't make anything of it, if I think for ever."

"You are worse than a woman, Charlie," said the pretty Marian; "you never can make up your mind."

"Stuff!" cried the big boy loudly; "it isn't making up my mind, it's thinking what will do. You girls know nothing about it. I can't see that one thing's better than another, for my part. One man succeeds and another man's a failure, and yet the one's as good a fellow and as clever to work as the other. I don't know what it means."

"So I suppose you will end with being misanthropical and doing nothing," said Agnes; "and all Charlie Atheling's big intentions will burst, like Beau's soap-bubbles. I would not have that."

"I won't have that, and so you know very well," said Charlie, who was by no means indisposed for a quarrel. "You are always aggravating, you girls—as if you knew anything about it! I'll tell you what; I don't mind how it is, but I'm a man to be something, as sure as I live."

"You are not a man at all, poor little Charlie—you are only a boy," said Marian.

"And we are none of us so sure to live that we should swear by it," said Agnes. "If you are to be something, you should speak better sense than that."

"Oh, a nice pair of tutors you are!" cried Master Charlie. "I'm bigger than the two of you put together—and I'm a man. You may be as envious as you like, but you cannot alter that."

Now, though the girls laughed, and with great contempt scouted the idea of being envious, it is not to be denied that some small morsel of envy concerning masculine privileges lay in the elder sister's heart. It was said at home that Agnes was clever—this was her distinction in the family; and Agnes, having a far-away perception of the fact, greatly longed for some share of those wonderful imaginary advantages which "opened all the world," as she herself said, to a man's ambition; she coloured a little with involuntary excitement, while Marian's sweet and merry laughter still rang in her ear. Marian could afford to laugh—for this beautiful child was neither clever nor ambitious, and had, in all circumstances, the sweetest faculty of content.

"Well, Charlie, a man can do anything," said Agnes; "we are obliged to put up with trifles. If I were a man, I should be content with nothing less than the greatest—I know that!"

"Stuff!" answered the big boy once more; "you may romance about it as you like, but I know better. Who is to care whether you are content or not? You must be only what you can, if you were the greatest hero in the world."

"I do not know, for my part, what you are talking of," said Marian. "Is this all about what you are going to do, Charlie, and because you cannot make up your mind whether you will be a clerk in papa's office, or go to old Mr Foggo's to learn to be a lawyer? I don't see what heroes have to do with it either one way or other. You ought to go to your business quietly, and be content. Why should you be better than papa?"

The question was unanswerable. Charlie hitched his great shoulders, and made marvellous faces, but replied nothing. Agnes went on steadily in a temporary abstraction; Marian ran on in advance. The street was only half-built—one of those quietest of surburban streets which are to be found only in the outskirts of great towns. The solitary little houses, some quite apart, some in pairs—detached and semi-detached, according to the proper description—stood in genteel retirement within low walls and miniature shrubberies. There was nothing ever to be seen in this stillest of inhabited places—therefore it was called Bellevue: and the inhabitants veiled their parlour windows behind walls and boarded railings, lest their privacy should be invaded by the vulgar vision of butcher, or baker, or green-grocer's boy. Other eyes than those of the aforesaid professional people never disturbed the composure of Laurel Cottage and Myrtle Cottage, Elmtree Lodge and Halcyon House—wherefore the last new house had a higher wall and a closer railing than any of its predecessors; and it was edifying to observe everybody's virtuous resolution to see nothing where there was visibly nothing to see.

At the end of this closed-up and secluded place, one light, shining from an unshuttered window, made a gleam of cheerfulness through the respectable gloom. Here you could see shadows large and small moving upon the white blind—could see the candles shifted about, and the sudden reddening of the stirred fire. A wayfarer, when by chance there was one, could scarcely fail to pause with a momentary sentiment of neighbourship and kindness opposite this shining window. It was the only evidence in the darkness of warm and busy human life. This was the home of the three young Athelings—as yet the centre and boundary of all their pleasures, and almost all their desires.

CHAPTER II

HOME

The house is old for this locality—larger than this family could have afforded, had it been in better condition,—a cheap house out of repair. It is impossible to see what is the condition of the little garden before the door; but the bushes are somewhat straggling, and wave their long arms about in the rising wind. There is a window on either side of the door, and the house is but two stories high: it is the most commonplace of houses, perfectly comfortable and uninteresting, so far as one may judge from without. Inside, the little hall is merely a passage, with a door on either side, a long row of pegs fastened against the wall, and a strip of brightly-painted oil-cloth on the floor. The parlour door is open—there are but two candles, yet the place is bright; and in it is the lighted window which shines so cheerily into the silent street. The father sits by the fire in the only easy-chair which this apartment boasts; the mother moves about on sundry nameless errands, of which she herself could scarcely give a just explanation; yet somehow that comfortable figure passing in and out through light and shadow adds an additional charm to the warmth and comfort of the place. Two little children are playing on the rug before the fire—very little children, twins scarcely two years old—one of them caressing the slippered foot of Mr Atheling, the other seated upon a great paper book full of little pictures, which serves at once as amusement for the little mind, and repose for the chubby little frame. They are rosy, ruddy, merry imps, as ever brightened a fireside; and it is hard to believe they are of the same family as Charlie and Agnes and Marian. For there is a woeful gap between the elder and the younger children of this house—an interval of heavy, tardy, melancholy years, the records of which are written, many names, upon one gravestone, and upon the hearts of these two cheerful people, among their children at their own hearth. They have lived through their day of visitation, and come again into the light beyond; but it is easy to understand the peculiar tenderness with which father and mother bend over these last little children—angels of consolation—and how everything in the house yields to the pretty childish caprice of little Bell and little Beau.

Yes, of course, you have found it out: everybody finds it out at the first glance; everybody returns to it with unfailing criticism. To tell the truth, the house is a very cheap house, being so large a one. Had it been in good order, the Athelings could never have pretended to such a "desirable family residence" as this house in Bellevue; and so you perceive this room has been papered by Charlie and the girls and Mrs Atheling. It is a very pretty paper, and was a great bargain; but unfortunately it is not matched—one-half of the pattern, in two or three places, is hopelessly divorced from the other half. They were very zealous, these amateur workpeople, but they were not born paperhangers, and, with the best intentions in the world, have drawn the walls awry. At the time Mrs Atheling was extremely mortified, and Agnes overcome with humiliation; but Charlie and Marian thought it very good fun; Papa burst into shouts of laughter; Bell and Beau chorused lustily, and at length even the unfortunate managers of the work forgave themselves. It never was altered, because a new paper is an important consideration where so many new frocks, coats, and bonnets are perpetually wanting: everybody became accustomed to it; it was an unfailing source of family witticism; and Mrs Atheling came to find so much relaxation from her other cares in the constant mental effort to piece together the disjointed pattern, that even to her there was consolation in this dire and lamentable failure. Few strangers came into the family-room, but every visitor who by chance entered it, with true human perversity turned his eyes from the comfort and neatness of the apartment, and from the bright faces of its occupants, to note the flowers and arabesques of the pretty paper, wandering all astray over this unfortunate wall.

Yet it was a pretty scene—with Marian's beautiful face at one side of the table, and the bright intelligence of Agnes at the other—the rosy children on the rug, the father reposing from his day's labour, the mother busy with her sweet familiar never-ending cares; even Charlie, ugly and characteristic, added to the family completeness. The head of the house was only a clerk in a merchant's office, with a modest stipend of two hundred pounds a-year. All the necessities of the family, young and old, had to be supplied out of this humble income. You may suppose there was not much over, and that the household chancellor of the exchequer had enough to do, even when assisted by that standing committee with which she consulted solemnly over every little outlay. The committee was prudent, but it was not infallible. Agnes, the leading member, had extravagant notions. Marian, more careful, had still a weakness for ribbons and household embellishments, bright and clean and new. Sometimes the committee en permanence was abruptly dismissed by its indignant president, charged with revolutionary sentiments, and a total ignorance of sound financial principles. Now and then there occurred a monetary crisis. On the whole, however, the domestic kingdom was wisely governed, and the seven Athelings, parents and children, lived and prospered, found it possible to have even holiday dresses, and books from the circulating library, ribbons for the girls, and toys for the babies, out of their two hundred pounds a-year.

Tea was on the table; yet the first thing to be done was to open out the little paper parcels, which proved to contain enclosures no less important than those very ribbons, which the finance committee had this morning decided upon as indispensable. Mrs Atheling unrolled them carefully, and held them out to the light. She shook her head; they had undertaken this serious responsibility all by themselves, these rash imprudent girls.

"Now, mamma, what do you think? I told you we could choose them; and the man said they were half as dear again six months ago," cried the triumphant Marian.

Again Mrs Atheling shook her head. "My dears," said the careful mother, "how do you think such a colour as this can last till June?"

This solemn question somewhat appalled the youthful purchasers. "It is a very pretty colour, mamma," said Agnes, doubtfully.

"So it is," said the candid critic; "but you know it will fade directly. I always told you so. It is only fit for people who have a dozen bonnets, and can afford to change them. I am quite surprised at you, girls; you ought to have known a great deal better. Of course the colour will fly directly: the first sunny day will make an end of that. But I cannot help it, you know; and, faded or not faded, it must do till June."

The girls exchanged glances of discomfiture. "Till June!" said Agnes; "and it is only March now. Well, one never knows what may happen before June."

This was but indifferent consolation, but it brought Charlie to the table to twist the unfortunate ribbon, and let loose his opinion. "They ought to wear wide-awakes. That's what they ought to have," said Charlie. "Who cares for all that trumpery? not old Foggo, I'm sure, nor Miss Willsie; and they are all the people we ever see."

"Hold your peace, Charlie," said Mrs Atheling, "and don't say old Foggo, you rude boy. He is the best friend you have, and a real gentleman; and what would your papa do with such a set of children about him, if Mr Foggo did not drop in now and then for some sensible conversation. It will be a long time before you try to make yourself company for papa."

"Foggo is not so philanthropical, Mary," said Papa, for the first time interposing; "he has an eye to something else than sensible conversation. However, be quiet and sit down, you set of children, and let us have some tea."

The ribbons accordingly were lifted away, and placed in a heap upon a much-used work-table which stood in the window. The kettle sang by the fire. The tea was made. Into two small chairs of wickerwork, raised upon high stilts to reach the table, were hoisted Bell and Beau. The talk of these small interlocutors had all this time been incessant, but untranslatable. It was the unanimous opinion of the family Atheling that you could "make out every word" spoken by these little personages, and that they were quite remarkable in their intelligibility; yet there were difficulties in the way, and everybody had not leisure for the close study of this peculiar language, nor the abstract attention necessary for a proper comprehension of all its happy sayings. So Bell and Beau, to the general public, were but a merry little chorus to the family drama, interrupting nothing, and being interrupted by nobody. Like crickets and singing-birds, and all musical creatures, their happy din grew louder as the conversation rose; but there was not one member of this loving circle who objected to have his voice drowned in the jubilant uproar of those sweet small voices, the unceasing music of this happy house.

After tea, it was Marian's "turn," as it appeared, to put the little orchestra to bed. It was well for the little cheeks that they were made of a more elastic material than those saintly shrines and reliquaries which pious pilgrims wore away with kissing; and Charlie, mounting one upon each shoulder, carried the small couple up-stairs. It was touching to see the universal submission to these infants: the house had been very sad before they came, and these twin blossoms had ushered into a second summer the bereaved and heavy household life.

When Bell and Beau were satisfactorily asleep and disposed of, Mrs Atheling sat down to her sewing, as is the wont of exemplary mothers. Papa found his occupation in a newspaper, from which now and then he read a scrap of news aloud. Charlie, busy about some solitary study, built himself round with books at a side-table. Agnes and Marian, with great zeal and some excitement, laid their heads together over the trimming of their bonnets. The ribbon was very pretty, though it was unprofitable; perhaps in their secret hearts these girls liked it the better for its unthrifty delicacy, but they were too "well brought up" to own to any such perverse feeling. At any rate, they were very much concerned about their pretty occupation, and tried a hundred different fashions before they decided upon the plainest and oldest fashion of all. They had taste enough to make their plain little straw-bonnets very pretty to look at, but were no more skilled in millinery than in paperhanging, and timid of venturing upon anything new. The night flew on to all of them in these quiet businesses; and Time went more heavily through many a festive and courtly place than he did through this little parlour, where there was no attempt at pleasure-making. When the bonnets were finished, it had grown late. Mr Foggo had not come this night for any sensible conversation; neither had Agnes been tempted to join Charlie at the side-table, where lay a miscellaneous collection of papers, packed within an overflowing blotting-book, her indisputable property. Agnes had other ambition than concerned the trimming of bonnets, and had spoiled more paper in her day than the paper of this parlour wall; but we pause till the morning to exhibit the gift of Agnes Atheling, how it was regarded, and what it was.

CHAPTER III

AGNES

Dearest friend! most courteous reader! suspend your judgment. It was not her fault. This poor child had no more blame in the matter than Marian had for her beauty, which was equally involuntary. Agnes Atheling was not wise; she had no particular gift for conversation, and none whatever for logic; no accomplishments, and not a very great deal of information. To tell the truth, while it was easy enough to discover what she had not, it was somewhat difficult to make out precisely what she had to distinguish her from other people. She was a good girl, but by no means a model one; full of impatiences, resentments, and despairs now and then, as well as of hopes, jubilant and glorious, and a vague but grand ambition. She herself knew herself quite as little as anybody else did; for consciousness of power and prescience of fame, if these are signs of genius, did not belong to Agnes. Yet genius, in some kind and degree, certainly did belong to her, for the girl had that strange faculty of expression which is as independent of education, knowledge, or culture as any wandering angel. When she had anything to say (upon paper), she said it with so much grace and beauty of language, that Mr Atheling's old correspondents puzzled and shook their grey heads over it, charmed and astonished without knowing why, and afterwards declared to each other that Atheling must be a clever fellow, though they had never discovered it before; and a clever fellow he must have been indeed, could he have clothed these plain sober sentiments of his in such a radiant investiture of fancy and youth. For Agnes was the letter-writer of the household, and in her young sincerity, and with her visionary delight in all things beautiful, was not content to make a dutiful inquiry, on her mother's part, for an old ailing country aunt, or to convey a bit of city gossip to some clerkish contemporary of her father's, without induing the humdrum subject with such a glow and glory of expression that the original proprietors of the sentiment scarcely knew it in its dazzling gear. She had been letting her pearls and her diamonds drop from her lips after this fashion, with the prodigality of a young spendthrift—only astonishing the respectable people who were on letter-writing terms with Mr and Mrs Atheling—for two or three years past. But time only strengthened the natural bent of this young creature, to whom Providence had given, almost her sole dower, that gift of speech which is so often withheld from those who have the fullest and highest opportunity for its exercise. Agnes, poor girl! young, inexperienced, and uninstructed, had not much wisdom to communicate to the world—not much of anything, indeed, save the vague and splendid dreams—the variable, impossible, and inconsistent speculations of youth; but she had the gift, and with the gift she had the sweet spontaneous impulse which made it a delight. They were proud of her at home. Mr and Mrs Atheling, with the tenderest exultation, rejoiced over Marian, who was pretty, and Agnes, who was clever; yet, loving these two still more than they admired them, they by no means realised the fact that the one had beauty and the other genius of a rare and unusual kind. We are even obliged to confess that at times their mother had compunctions, and doubted whether Agnes, a poor man's daughter, and like to be a poor man's wife, ought to be permitted so much time over that overflowing blotting-book. Mrs Atheling, when her own ambition and pride in her child did not move her otherwise, pondered much whether it would not be wiser to teach the girls dress-making or some other practical occupation, "for they may not marry; and if anything should happen to William or me!—as of course we are growing old, and will not live for ever," she said to herself in her tender and anxious heart. But the girls had not yet learned dress-making, in spite of Mrs Atheling's fears; and though Marian could "cut out" as well as her mother, and Agnes, more humble, worked with her needle to the universal admiration, no speculations as to "setting them up in business" had entered the parental brain. So Agnes continued at the side-table, sometimes writing very rapidly and badly, sometimes copying out with the most elaborate care and delicacy—copying out even a second time, if by accident or misfortune a single blot came upon the well-beloved page. This occupation alternated with all manner of domestic occupations. The young writer was as far from being an abstracted personage as it is possible to conceive; and from the momentous matter of the household finances to the dressing of the doll, and the childish play of Bell and Beau, nothing came amiss to the incipient author. With this sweet stream of common life around her, you may be sure her genius did her very little harm.

And when all the domestic affairs were over—when Mr Atheling had finished his newspaper, and Mrs Atheling put aside her work-basket, and Mr Foggo was out of the way—then Papa was wont to look over his shoulder to his eldest child. "You may read some of your nonsense, if you like, Agnes," said the household head; and it was Agnes's custom upon this invitation, though not without a due degree of coyness, to gather up her papers, draw her chair into the corner, and read what she had written. Before Agnes began, Mrs Atheling invariably stretched out her hand for her work-basket, and was invariably rebuked by her husband; but Marian's white hands rustled on unreproved, and Charlie sat still at his grammar. It was popularly reported in the family that Charlie kept on steadily learning his verbs even while he listened to Agnes's story. He said so himself, who was the best authority; but we by no means pledge ourselves to the truth of the statement.

And so the young romance was read: there was some criticism, but more approval; and in reality none of them knew what to think of it, any more than the youthful author did. They were too closely concerned to be cool judges, and, full of interest and admiration as they were, could not quite overcome the oddness and novelty of the idea that "our Agnes" might possibly one day be famous, and write for the world. Mr Atheling himself, who was most inclined to be critical, had the strangest confusion of feelings upon this subject, marvelling much within himself whether "the child" really had this singular endowment, or if it was only their own partial judgment which magnified her powers. The family father could come to no satisfactory conclusion upon the subject, but still smiled at himself, and wondered, when his daughter's story brought tears to his eyes, or sympathy or indignation to his heart. It moved him without dispute,—it moved Mamma there, hastily rubbing out the moisture from the corner of her eyes. Even Charlie was disturbed over his grammar. "Yes," said Mr Atheling, "but then you see she belongs to us; and though all this certainly never could have come into my head, yet it is natural I should sympathise with it; but it is a very different thing when you think of the world."

So it was, as different a thing as possible; for the world had no anxious love to sharpen its criticism—did not care a straw whether the young writer was eloquent or nonsensical; and just in proportion to its indifference was like to be the leniency of its judgment. These good people did not think of that; they made wonderful account of their own partiality, but never reckoned upon that hypercritical eye of love which will not be content with a questionable excellence; and so they pondered and marvelled with an excitement half amusing and half solemn. What would other people think?—what would be the judgment of the world?

As for Agnes, she was as much amused as the rest at the thought of being "an author," and laughed, with her bright eyes running over, at this grand anticipation; for she was too young and too inexperienced to see more than a delightful novelty and unusualness in her possible fame. In the mean time she was more interested in what she was about than in the result of it, and pleased herself with the turn of her pretty sentences, and the admirable orderliness of her manuscript; for she was only a girl.

CHAPTER IV

MARIAN

Marian Atheling had as little choice in respect to her particular endowment as her sister had; less, indeed, for it cost her nothing—not an hour's thought or a moment's exertion. She could not help shining forth so fair and sweet upon the sober background of this family life; she could not help charming every stranger who looked into her sweet eyes. She was of no particular "style" of beauty, so far as we are aware; she was even of no distinct complexion of loveliness, but wavered with the sweetest shade of uncertainty between dark and fair, tall and little. For hers was not the beauty of genius—it was not exalted and heroical expression—it was not tragic force or eloquence of features; it was something less distinct and more subtle even than these. Hair that caught the sunshine, and brightened under its glow; eyes which laughed a sweet response of light before the fair eyelids fell over them in that sweet inconsistent mingling of frankness and shyness which is the very charm of girlhood; cheeks as soft and bloomy and fragrant as any flower,—these seemed but the appropriate language in which alone this innocent, radiant, beautiful youth could find fit expression. For beauty of expression belonged to Marian as well as more obvious beauties; there was an entire sweet harmony between the language and the sentiment of nature upon this occasion. The face would have been beautiful still, had its possessor been a fool or discontented; as it was, being only the lovely exponent of a heart as pure, happy, and serene as heart could be, the face was perfect. Criticism had nothing to do with an effect so sudden and magical: this young face shone and brightened like a sunbeam, touching the hearts of those it beamed upon. Mere admiration was scarcely the sentiment with which people looked at her; it was pure tenderness, pleasure, unexpected delight, which made the chance passengers in the street smile as they passed her by. Their hearts warmed to this fair thing of God's making—they "blessed her unaware." Eighteen years old, and possessed of this rare gift, Marian still did not know what rude admiration was, though she went out day by day alone and undefended, and would not have faltered at going anywhere, if her mother bade or necessity called. She knew nothing of those stares and impertinent annoyances which fastidious ladies sometimes complained of, and of which she had read in books. Marian asserted roundly, and with unhesitating confidence, that "it was complete nonsense"—"it was not true;" and went upon her mother's errands through all the Islingtonian streets as safely as any heroine ever went through ambuscades and prisons. She believed in lovers and knights of romance vaguely, but fervently,—believed even, we confess, in the melodramatic men who carry off fair ladies, and also in disguised princes and Lords of Burleigh; but knew nothing whatever, in her own most innocent and limited experience, of any love but the love of home. And Marian had heard of bad men and bad women,—nay, knew, in Agnes's story, the most impossible and short-sighted of villains—a true rascal of romance, whose snares were made on purpose for discovery,—but had no more fear of such than she had of lions or tigers, the Gunpowder Plot, or the Spanish Inquisition. Safe as among her lawful vassals, this young girl went and came—safe as in a citadel, dwelt in her father's house, untempted, untroubled, in the most complete and thorough security. So far as she had come upon the sunny and flowery way of her young life, her beauty had been no gift of peril to Marian, and she had no fear of what was to come.

And no one is to suppose that Mrs Atheling's small means were strained to do honour to, or "set off," her pretty daughter. These good people, though they loved much to see their children happy and well esteemed, had no idea of any such unnecessary efforts; and Marian shone out of her brown merino frock, and her little pink rosebuds, as sweetly as ever shone a princess in the purple and pall of her high estate. Mrs Atheling thought Marian "would look well in anything," in the pride of her heart, as she pinched the bit of white lace round Marian's neck when Mr Foggo and Miss Willsie were coming to tea. It was indeed the general opinion of the household, and that other people shared it was sufficiently proved by the fact that Miss Willsie herself begged for a pattern of that very little collar, which was so becoming. Marian gave the pattern with the greatest alacrity, yet protested that Miss Willsie had many collars a great deal prettier—which indeed was very true.

And Marian was her mother's zealous assistant in all household occupations—not more willing, but with more execution and practical power than Agnes, who, by dint of a hasty anxiety for perfection, made an intolerable amount of blunders. Marian was more matter-of-fact, and knew better what she could do; she was constantly busy, morning and night, keeping always in hand some morsel of fancy-work, with which to occupy herself at irregular times after the ordinary work was over. Agnes also had bits of fancy-work in hand; but the difference herein between the two sisters was this, that Marian finished her pretty things, while Agnes's uncompleted enterprises were always turning up in some old drawer or work-table, and were never brought to a conclusion. Marian made collars for her mother, frills for Bell and Beau, and a very fine purse for Charlie; which Charlie, having nothing to put in the same, rejected disdainfully: but it was a very rare thing indeed for Agnes to come to an end of any such labour. With Marian, too, lay the honour of far superior accuracy and precision in the important particular of "cutting out." These differences furthered the appropriate division of labour, and the household work made happy progress under their united hands.

To this we have only to add, that Marian Atheling was merry without being witty, and intelligent without being clever. She, too, was a good girl; but she also had her faults: she was sometimes saucy, very often self-willed, yet had fortunately thus far shown a sensible perception of cases which were beyond her own power of settling. She had the greatest interest in Agnes's story-telling, but was extremely impatient to know the end before the beginning, which the hapless young author was not always in circumstances to tell; and Marian made countless suggestions, interfering arbitrarily and vexatiously with the providence of fiction, and desiring all sorts of impossible rewards and punishments. But Marian's was no quiet or superficial criticism: how she burned with indignation at that poor unbelievable villain!—how she triumphed when all the good people put him down!—with what entire and fervid interest she entered into everybody's fortune! It was worth while being present at one of these family readings, if only to see the flutter and tumult of sympathies which greeted the tale.

And we will not deny that Marian had possibly a far-off idea that she was pretty—an idea just so indistinct and distant as to cause a momentary blush and sparkle—a momentary flutter, half of pleasure and half of shame, when it chanced to glide across her young unburdened heart; but of her beauty and its influence this innocent girl had honestly no conception. Everybody smiled upon her everywhere. Even Mr Foggo's grave and saturnine countenance slowly brightened when her sweet face shone upon him. Marian did not suppose that these smiles had anything to do with her; she went upon her way with a joyous young belief in the goodness of everybody, except the aforesaid impossible people, who were unspeakably black, beyond anything that ever was painted, to the simple imagination of Marian. She had no great principle of abstract benevolence to make her charitable; she was strongly in favour of the instant and overwhelming punishment of all these imaginary criminals; but for the rest of the world, Marian looked them all in the face, frank and shy and sweet, with her beautiful eyes. She was content to offer that small right hand of kindliest fellowship, guileless and unsuspecting, to them all.

CHAPTER V

CHARLIE

This big boy was about as far from being handsome as any ordinary imagination could conceive: his large loose limbs, his big features, his swarthy complexion, though they were rather uglier in their present development than they were likely to be when their possessor was full-grown and a man, could never, by any chance, gain him the moderate credit of good looks. He was not handsome emphatically, and yet there never was a more expressive face: that great furrowed brow of his went up in ripples and waves of laughter when the young gentleman was so minded, and descended in rolls of cloud when there was occasion for such a change. His mouth was not a pretty mouth: the soft curve of Cupid's bow, the proud Napoleonic curl, were as different as you could suppose from the indomitable and graceless upper-lip of Charlie Atheling. Yet when that obstinate feature came down in fixed and steady impenetrability, a more emphatic expression never sat on the haughtiest curve of Greece. He was a tolerably good boy, but he had his foible. Charlie, we are grieved to say, was obstinate—marvellously obstinate, unpersuadable, and beyond the reach of reasoning. If anything could have made this propensity justifiable—as nothing could possibly make it more provoking—it was, that the big boy was very often in the right. Time after time, by force of circumstances, everybody else was driven to give in to him: whether it really was by means of astute and secret calculation of all the chances of the question, nobody could tell; but every one knew how often Charlie's opinion was confirmed by the course of events, and how very seldom his odd penetration was deceived. This, as a natural consequence, made everybody very hot and very resentful who happened to disagree with Charlie, and caused a great amount of jubilation and triumph in the house on those occasions, unfrequent as they were, when his boyish infallibility was proved in the wrong.

Yet Charlie was not clever. The household could come to no satisfactory conclusion upon this subject. He did not get on with his moderate studies either quicker or better than any ordinary boy of his years. He had no special turn for literature either, though he did not disdain Peter Simple and Midshipman Easy. These renowned productions of genius held the highest place at present in that remote corner of Charlie's interest which was reserved for the fine arts; but we are obliged to confess that this big boy had wonderfully bad taste in general, and could not at all appreciate the higher excellences of art. Besides all this, no inducement whatever could tempt Charlie to the writing of the briefest letter, or to any exercise of his powers of composition, if any such powers belonged to him. No, he could not be clever—and yet—

They did not quite like to give up the question, the mother and sisters. They indulged in the loftiest flights of ambition for him, as heaven-aspiring, and built on as slender a foundation, as any bean-stalk of romance. They endeavoured greatly, with much anxiety and care, to make him clever, and to make him ambitious, after their own model; but this obstinate and self-willed individual was not to be coerced. So far as this matter went, Charlie had a certain affectionate contempt for them all, with their feminine fancies and imaginations. He said only "Stuff!" when he listened to the grand projects of the girls, and to Agnes's flush of enthusiastic confidence touching that whole unconquered world which was open to "a man!" Charlie hitched his great shoulders, frowned down upon her with all the furrows of his brow, laughed aloud, and went off to his grammar. This same grammar he worked at with his usual obstinate steadiness. He had not a morsel of liking for "his studies;" but he "went in" at them doggedly, just as he might have broken stones or hewed wood, had that been a needful process. Nobody ever does know the secret of anybody else's character till life and time have evolved the same; so it is not wonderful that these good people were a little puzzled about Charlie, and did not quite know how to dispose of their obstinate big boy.

Charlie himself, however, we are glad to say, was sometimes moved to take his sisters into his confidence. They knew that some ambition did stir within that Titanic boyish frame. They were in the secret of the great discussion which was at present going on in the breast of Charlie, whose whole thoughts, to tell the truth, were employed about the momentous question—What he was to be? There was not a very wide choice in his power. He was not seduced by the red coat and the black coat, like the ass of the problem. The syrens of wealth and fame did not sing in his ears, to tempt him to one course or another. He had two homely possibilities before him—a this, and a that. He had a stout intention to be something, and no such ignoble sentiment as content found place in Charlie's heart; wherefore long, animated, and doubtful was the self-controversy. Do not smile, good youth, at Charlie's two chances—they are small in comparison of yours, but they were the only chances visible to him; the one was the merchant's office over which Mr Atheling presided—head clerk, with his two hundred pounds a-year; the other was, grandiloquently—by the girls, not by Charlie—called the law; meaning thereby, however, only the solicitor's office, the lawful empire and domain of Mr Foggo. Between these two legitimate and likely regions for making a fortune, the lad wavered with a most doubtful and inquiring mind. His introduction to each was equally good; for Mr Atheling was confidential and trusted, and Mr Foggo, as a mysterious rumour went, was not only most entirely trusted and confidential, but even in secret a partner in the concern. Wherefore long and painful were the ruminations of Charlie, and marvellous the balance which he made of precedent and example. Let nobody suppose, however, that this question was discussed in idleness. Charlie all this time was actually in the office of Messrs Cash, Ledger, and Co., his father's employers. He was there on a probationary and experimental footing, but he was very far from making up his mind to remain. It was an extremely difficult argument, although carried on solely in the deep invisible caverns of the young aspirant's mind.

The same question, however, was also current in the family, and remained undecided by the household parliament. With much less intense and personal earnestness, "everybody" went over the for and against, and contrasted the different chances. Charlie listened, but made no sign. When he had made up his own mind, the young gentleman proposed to himself to signify his decision publicly, and win over this committee of the whole house to his view of the question. In the mean time he reserved what he had to say; but so far, it is certain that Mr Foggo appeared more tempting than Mr Atheling. The family father had been twenty or thirty years at this business of his, and his income was two hundred pounds—

"that would not do for me," said Charlie; whereas Mr Foggo's income, position, and circumstances were alike a mystery, and might be anything. This had considerable influence in the argument, but was not conclusive; for successful merchants were indisputably more numerous than successful lawyers, and Charlie was not aware how high a lawyer who was only an attorney could reach, and had his doubts upon the subject. In the mean time, however, pending the settlement of this momentous question, Charlie worked at two grammars instead of one, and put all his force to his study. Force was the only word which could express the characteristic power of this boy, if even that can give a sufficient idea of it. He had no love for his French or for his Latin, yet learned his verbs with a manful obstinacy worthy all honour; and it is not easy to define what was the special gift of Charlie. It was not a describable thing, separate from his character, like beauty or like genius—it was his character, intimate and not to be distinguished from himself.

CHAPTER VI

PAPA AND MAMMA

The father of this family, as we have already said, was a clerk in a merchant's office, with a salary of two hundred pounds a-year. He was a man of fifty, with very moderate abilities, but character unimpeachable—a perfect type of his class—steadily marching on in his common routine—doing all his duties without pretension—somewhat given to laying down the law in respect to business—and holding a very grand opinion of the importance of commerce in general, and of the marvellous undertakings of London in particular. Yet this good man was not entirely circumscribed by his "office." He had that native spring of life and healthfulness in him which belongs to those who have been born in, and never have forgotten, the country. The country, most expressive of titles!—he had always kept in his recollection the fragrance of the ploughed soil, the rustle of the growing grass; so, though he lived in Islington, and had his office in the City, he was not a Cockney—a happy and most enviable distinction. His wife, too, was country born and country bred; and two ancestral houses, humble enough, yet standing always among the trees and fields, belonged to the imagination of their children. This was a great matter—for the roses on her grandmother's cottage-wall bloomed perpetually in the fancy of Agnes; and Marian and Charlie knew the wood where Papa once went a-nutting, as well as—though with a more ideal perception than, Papa himself had known it. Even little Bell and Beau knew of a store of secret primroses blooming for ever on a fairy bank, where their mother long ago, in the days of her distant far-off childhood, had seen them blow, and taken them into her heart. Happy primroses, that never faded! for all the children of this house had dreamed and gathered them in handfuls, yet there they were for ever. It was strange how this link of connection with the far-off rural life refined the fancy of these children; it gave them a region of romance, into which they could escape at all times. They did not know its coarser features, and they found refuge in it from the native vulgarity of their own surroundings. Happy effect to all imaginative people, of some ideal and unknown land.

The history of the family was a very common one. Two-and-twenty years ago, William Atheling and Mary Ellis had ventured to marry, having only a very small income, limited prospects, and all the indescribable hopes and chances of youth. Then had come the children, joy, toil, and lamentation—then the way of life had opened up upon them, step by step; and they had fainted, and found it weary, yet, helpless and patient, had toiled on. They never had a chance, these good people, of running away from their fate. If such a desperate thought ever came to them, it must have been dismissed at once, being hopeless; and they stood at their post under the heavy but needful compulsion of ordinary duties, living through many a heartbreak, bearing many a bereavement—voiceless souls, uttering no outcry except to the ear of God. Now they had lived through their day of visitation. God had removed the cloud from their heads and the terror from their heart: their own youth was over, but the youth of their children, full of hopes and possibilities still brighter than their own had been, rejoiced these patient hearts; and the warm little hands of the twin babies, children of their old age, led them along with delight and hopefulness upon their own unwearying way. Such was the family story; it was a story of life, very full, almost overflowing with the greatest and first emotions of humanity, but it was not what people call eventful. The private record, like the family register, brimmed over with those first makings and foundations of history, births and deaths; but few vicissitudes of fortune, little success and little calamity, fell upon the head of the good man whose highest prosperity was this two hundred pounds a-year. And so now they reckoned themselves in very comfortable circumstances, and were disturbed by nothing but hopes and doubts about the prospects of the children—hopes full of brightness present and visible, doubts that were almost as good as hope.

There was but one circumstance of romance in the simple chronicle. Long ago—the children did not exactly know when, or how, or in what manner—Mr Atheling did somebody an extraordinary and mysterious benefit. Papa was sometimes moved to tell them of it in a general way, sheltering himself under vague and wide descriptions. The story was of a young man, handsome, gay, and extravagant, of rank far superior to Mr Atheling's—of how he fell into dissipation, and was tempted to crime—and how at the very crisis "I happened to be in the way, and got hold of him, and showed him the real state of the case; how I heard what he was going to do, and of course would betray him; and how, even if he could do it, it would be certain ruin, disgrace, and misery. That was the whole matter," said Mr Atheling—and his affectionate audience listened with awe and a mysterious interest, very eager to know something more definite of the whole matter than this concise account of it, yet knowing that all interrogation was vain. It was popularly suspected that Mamma knew the full particulars of this bit of romance, but Mamma was as impervious to questions as the other head of the house. There was also a second fytte to this story, telling how Mr Atheling himself undertook the venture of revealing his hapless hero's misfortunes to the said hero's elder brother, a very grand and exalted personage; how the great man, shocked, and in terror for the family honour, immediately delivered the culprit, and sent him abroad. "Then he offered me money," said Mr Atheling quietly. This was the climax of the tale, at which everybody was expected to be indignant; and very indignant, accordingly, everybody was.

Yet there was a wonderful excitement in the thought that this hero of Papa's adventure was now, as Papa intimated, a man of note in the world—that they themselves unwittingly read his name in the papers sometimes, and that other people spoke of him to Mr Atheling as a public character, little dreaming of the early connection between them. How strange it was!—but no entreaty and no persecution could prevail upon Papa to disclose his name. "Suppose we should meet him some time!" exclaimed Agnes, whose imagination sometimes fired with the thought of reaching that delightful world of society where people always spoke of books, and genius was the highest nobility—a world often met with in novels. "If you did," said Mr Atheling, "it will be all the better for you to know nothing about this," and so the controversy always ended; for in this matter at least, firm as the most scrupulous old knight of romance, Papa stood on his honour.

As for the good and tender mother of this house, she had no story to tell. The girls, it is true, knew about her girlish companions very nearly as well as if these, now most sober and middle-aged personages, had been playmates of their own; they knew the names of the pigeons in the old dovecote, the history of the old dog, the number of the apples on the great apple-tree; also they had a kindly recollection of one old lover of Mamma's, concerning whom they were shy to ask further than she was pleased to reveal. But all Mrs Atheling's history was since her marriage: she had been but a young girl with an untouched heart before that grand event, which introduced her, in her own person, to the unquiet ways of life; and her recollections chiefly turned upon the times "when we lived in— Street,"—"when we took that new house in the terrace,"—"when we came to Bellevue." This Bellevue residence was a great point in the eyes of Mrs Atheling. She herself had always kept her original weakness for gentility, and to live in a street where there was no straight line of commonplace houses, but only villas, detached and semi-detached, and where every house had a name to itself, was no small step in advance—particularly as the house was really cheap, really large, as such houses go, and had only the slight disadvantage of being out of repair. Mrs Atheling lamed her most serviceable finger with attempts at carpentry, and knocked her own knuckles with misdirected hammering, yet succeeded in various shifts that answered very well, and produced that grand chef-d'œuvre of paperhanging which made more amusement than any professional decoration ever made, and was just as comfortable. So the good mother was extremely well pleased with her house. She was not above the ambition of calling it either Atheling Lodge, or Hawthorn Cottage, but it was very hard to make a family decision upon the prettiest name; so the house of the Athelings, with its eccentric garden, its active occupants, and its cheery parlour-window, was still only Number Ten, Bellevue.

And there in the summer sunshine, and in the wintry dawning, at eight o'clock, Mr Atheling took his seat at the table, said grace, and breakfasted; from thence at nine to a moment, well brushed and buttoned, the good man went upon his daily warfare to the City. There all the day long the pretty twins played, the mother exercised her careful housewifery, the sweet face of Marian shone like a sunbeam, and the fancies of Agnes wove themselves into separate and real life. All the day long the sun shone in at the parlour window upon a thrifty and well-worn carpet, which all his efforts could not spoil, and dazzled the eyes of Bell and Beau, and troubled the heart of Mamma finding out spots of dust, and suspicions of cobwebs which had escaped her own detection. And when the day was done, and richer people were thinking of dinner, once more, punctual to a moment, came the well-known step on the gravel, and the well-known summons at the door; for at six o'clock Mr Atheling came home to his cheerful tea-table, as contented and respectable a householder, as happy a father, as was in England. And after tea came the newspaper and Mr Foggo; and after Mr Foggo came the readings of Agnes; and so the family said good-night, and slept and rested, to rise again on the next morning to just such another day. Nothing interrupted this happy uniformity; nothing broke in upon the calm and kindly usage of these familiar hours. Mrs Atheling had a mighty deal of thinking to do, by reason of her small income; now and then the girls were obliged to consent to be disappointed of some favourite project of their own—and sometimes even Papa, in a wilful fit of self-denial, refused himself for a few nights his favourite newspaper; but these were but passing shadows upon the general content. Through all these long winter evenings, the one lighted window of this family room brightened the gloomy gentility of Bellevue, and imparted something of heart and kindness to the dull and mossy suburban street. They "kept no company," as the neighbours said. That was not so much the fault of the Athelings, as the simple fact that there was little company to keep; but they warmed the old heart of old Mr Foggo, and kept that singular personage on speaking terms with humanity; and day by day, and night by night, lived their frank life before their little world, a family life of love, activity, and cheerfulness, as bright to look at as their happy open parlour-window among the closed-up retirements of this genteel little street.

CHAPTER VII

THE FIRST WORK

"Now," said Agnes, throwing down her pen with a cry of triumph—"now, look here, everybody—it is done at last."

And, indeed, there it was upon the fair and legible page, in Agnes's best and clearest handwriting, "The End." She had written it with girlish delight, and importance worthy the occasion; and with admiring eyes Mamma and Marian looked upon the momentous words—The End! So now it was no longer in progress, to be smiled and wondered over, but an actual thing, accomplished and complete, out of anybody's power to check or to alter. The three came together to look at it with a little awe. It was actually finished—out of hand—an entire and single production. The last chapter was to be read in the family committee to-night—and then? They held their breath in sudden excitement. What was to be done with the Book, which could be smiled at no longer? That momentous question would have to be settled to-night.

So they piled it up solemnly, sheet by sheet, upon the side-table. Such a manuscript! Happy the printer into whose fortunate hands fell this unparalleled copy! And we are grieved to confess that, for the whole afternoon thereafter, Agnes Atheling was about as idle as it is possible even for a happy girl to be. No one but a girl could have attained to such a delightful eminence of doing nothing! She was somewhat unsettled, we admit, and quite uncontrollable,—dancing about everywhere, making her presence known by involuntary outbursts of singing and sweet laughter; but sterner lips than Mamma's would have hesitated to rebuke that fresh and spontaneous delight. It was not so much that she was glad to be done, or was relieved by the conclusion of her self-appointed labour. She did not, indeed, quite know what made her so happy. Like all primal gladness, it was involuntary and unexplainable; and the event of the day, vaguely exciting and exhilarating on its own account, was novel enough to supply that fresh breeze of excitement and change which is so pleasant always to the free heart of youth.

Then came all the usual routine of the evening—everything in its appointed time—from Susan, who brought the tea-tray, to Mr Foggo. And Mr Foggo stayed long, and was somewhat prosy. Agnes and Marian, for this one night, were sadly tired of the old gentleman, and bade him a very hasty and abrupt good-night when at last he took his departure. Even then, with a perverse inclination, Papa clung to his newspaper. The chances were much in favour of Agnes's dignified and stately withdrawal from an audience which showed so little eagerness for what she had to bestow upon them; but Marian, who was as much excited as Agnes, interposed. "Papa, Agnes is done—finished—done with her story—do you hear me, papa?" cried Marian in his ear, shaking him by the shoulder to give emphasis to her words— "she is going to read the last chapter, if you would lay down that stupid paper—do you hear, papa?"

Papa heard, but kept his finger at his place, and read steadily in spite of this interposition. "Be quiet, child," said the good Mr Atheling; but the child was not in the humour to be quiet. So after a few minutes, fairly persecuted out of his paper, Papa gave in, and threw it down; and the household circle closed round the fireside, and Agnes lifted her last chapter; but what that last chapter was, we are unable to tell, without infringing upon the privacy of Number Ten, Bellevue.

It was satisfactory—that was the great matter: everybody was satisfied with the annihilation of the impossible villain and the triumph of all the good people—and everybody concurred in thinking that the winding-up was as nearly perfect as it was in the nature of mortal winding-up to be. The MS. accordingly was laid aside, crowned with applauses and laurels;—then there was a pause of solemn consideration— the wise heads of the house held their peace and pondered. Marian, who was not wise, but only excited and impatient, broke the silence with her own eager, sincere, and unsolicited opinion; and this was the advice of Marian to the family committee of the whole house: "Mamma, I will tell you what ought to be done. It ought to be taken to somebody to-morrow, and published every month, like Dickens and Thackeray. It is quite as good! Everybody would read it, and Agnes would be a great author. I am quite sure that is the way."

At which speech Charlie whistled a very long "whew!" in a very low under-tone; for Mamma had very particular notions on the subject of "good-breeding," and kept careful watch over the "manners" even of this big boy.

"Like Dickens and Thackeray! Marian!" cried Agnes in horror; and then everybody laughed—partly because it was the grandest and most magnificent nonsense to place the young author upon this astonishing level, partly because it was so very funny to think of "our Agnes" sharing in ever so small a degree the fame of names like these.

"Not quite that," said Papa, slowly and doubtfully, "yet I think somebody might publish it. The question is, whom we should take it to. I think I ought to consult Foggo."

"Mr Foggo is not a literary man, papa," said Agnes, somewhat resentfully. She did not quite choose to receive this old gentleman, who thought her a child, into her confidence.

"Foggo knows a little of everything,—he has a wonderful head for business," said Mr Atheling. "As for a literary man, we do not know such a person, Agnes; and I can't see what better we should be if we did. Depend upon it, business is everything. If they think they can make money by this story of yours, they will take it, but not otherwise; for, of course, people trade in books as they trade in cotton, and are not a bit more generous in one than another, take my word for that."

"Very well, my dear," said Mamma, roused to assert her dignity, "but we do not wish any one to be generous to Agnes—of course not!—that would be out of the question; and nobody, you know, could look at that book without feeling sure of everybody else liking it. Why, William, it is so natural! You may speak of Thackeray and Dickens as you like; I know they are very clever—but I am sure I never read anything of theirs like that scene—that last scene with Helen and her mother. I feel as if I had been present there my own self."

Which was not so very wonderful after all, seeing that the mother in Agnes's book was but a delicate, shy, half-conscious sketch of this dearest mother of her own.

"I think it ought to be taken to somebody to-morrow," repeated Marian stoutly, "and published every month with pictures. How strange it would be to read in the newspapers how everybody wondered about the new book, and who wrote it!—such fun!—for nobody but us would know."

Agnes all this time remained very silent, receiving everybody's opinion—and Charlie also locked up his wisdom in his own breast. There was a pause, for Papa, feeling that his supreme opinion was urgently called for, took time to ponder upon it, and was rather afraid of giving a deliverance. The silence, however, was broken by the abrupt intervention, when nobody expected it, of the big boy.

"Make it up into a parcel," said Master Charlie with business-like distinctness, "and look in the papers what name you'll send it to, and I'll take it to-morrow."

This was so sudden, startling, and decisive, that the audience were electrified. Mr Atheling looked blankly in his son's face; the young gentleman had completely cut the ground from under the feet of his papa. After all, let any one advise or reason, or argue the point at his pleasure, this was the only practical conclusion to come at. Charlie stopped the full-tide of the family argument; they might have gone on till midnight discussing and wondering; but the big boy made it up into a parcel, and finished it on the spot. After that they all commenced a most ignorant and innocent discussion concerning "the trade;" these good people knew nothing whatever of that much contemned and long-suffering race who publish books. Two ideal types of them were present to the minds of the present speculators. One was that most fatal and fictitious savage, the Giant Despair of an oppressed literature, who sits in his den for ever grinding the bones of those dismal unforgettable hacks of Grub Street, whose memory clings unchangeably to their profession; the other was that bland and genial imagination, equally fictitious, the author's friend—he who brings the neglected genius into the full sunshine of fame and prosperity, seeking only the immortality of such a connection with the immortal. If one could only know which of these names in the newspapers belonged to this last wonder of nature! This discussion concerning people of whom absolutely nothing but the names were known to the disputants, was a very comical argument; and it was not concluded when eleven o'clock struck loudly on the kitchen clock, and Susan, very slumbrous, and somewhat resentful, appeared at the door to see if anything was wanted. Everybody rose immediately, as Susan intended they should, with guilt and confusion: eleven o'clock! the innocent family were ashamed of themselves.

And this little room up-stairs, as you do not need to be told, is the bower of Agnes and of Marian. There are two small white beds in it, white and fair and simple, draped with the purest dimity, and covered with the whitest coverlids. If Agnes, by chance or in haste—and Agnes is very often "in a great hurry"—should leave her share of the apartment in a less orderly condition than became a young lady's room, Marian never yielded to such a temptation. Marian was the completest woman in all her simple likings; their little mirror, their dressing-table, everything which would bear such fresh and inexpensive decoration, was draped with pretty muslin, the work of these pretty fingers. And there hung their little shelf of books over Agnes's head, and here upon the table was their Bible. Yet in spite of the quiet night settling towards midnight—in spite of the unbroken stillness of Bellevue, where every candle was extinguished, and all the world at rest, the girls could not subdue all at once their eager anticipations, hopes, and wondering. Marian let down all her beautiful hair over her shoulders, and pretended to brush it, looking all the time out of the shining veil, and throwing the half-curled locks from her face, when something occurred to her bearing upon the subject. Agnes, with both her hands supporting her forehead, leaned over the table with downcast eyes—seeing nothing, thinking nothing, with a faint glow on her soft cheek, and a vague excitement at her heart. Happy hearts! it was so easy to stir them to this sweet tumult of hope and fancy; and so small a reason was sufficient to wake these pure imaginations to all-indefinite glory and delight.

CHAPTER VIII

CHARLIE'S ENTERPRISE

It was made into a parcel, duly packed and tied up; not in a delicate wrapper, or with pretty ribbons, as perhaps the affectionate regard of Agnes might have suggested, but in the commonest and most matter-of-fact parcel imaginable. But by that time it began to be debated whether Charlie, after all, was a sufficiently dignified messenger. He was only a boy—that was not to be disputed; and Mrs Atheling did not think him at all remarkable for his "manners," and Papa doubted whether he was able to manage a matter of business. But, then, who could go?—not the girls certainly, and not their mother, who was somewhat timid out of her own house. Mr Atheling could not leave his office; and really, after all their objections, there was nobody but Charlie, unless it was Mr Foggo, whom Agnes would by no means consent to employ. So they brushed their big boy, as carefully as Moses Primrose was brushed before he went to the fair, and gave him strict injunctions to look as grave, as sensible, and as old as possible. All these commands Charlie received with perfect coolness, hoisting his parcel under his arm, and remaining entirely unmoved by the excitement around him. "I know well enough—don't be afraid," said Charlie; and he strode off like a young ogre, carrying Agnes's fortune under his arm. They all went to the window to look after him with some alarm and some hope; but though they were troubled for his youth, his abruptness, and his want of "manners," there was exhilaration in the steady ring of Charlie's manful foot, and his own entire and undoubting confidence. On he went, a boyish giant, to throw down that slender gage and challenge of the young genius to all the world. Meanwhile they returned to their private occupations, this little group of women, excited, doubtful, much expecting, marvelling over and over again what Mr Burlington would say. Such an eminence of lofty criticism and censorship these good people recognised in the position of Mr Burlington! He seemed to hold in his hands the universal key which opened everything: fame, honour, and reward, at that moment, appeared to these simple minds to be mere vassals of his pleasure; and all the balance of the future, as Agnes fancied, lay in the doubtful chance whether he was propitious or unpropitious. Simple imaginations! Mr Burlington, at that moment taking off his top-coat, and placing his easy-chair where no draught could reach it, was about as innocent of literature as Charlie Atheling himself.

But Charlie, who had to go to "the office" after he fulfilled his mission, could not come home till the evening; so they had to be patient in spite of themselves. The ordinary occupations of the day in Bellevue were not very novel, nor very interesting. Mrs Atheling had ambition, and aimed at gentility; so, of course, they had a piano. The girls had learned a very little music; and Marian and Agnes, when they were out of humour, or disinclined for serious occupation, or melancholy (for they were melancholy sometimes in the "prodigal excess" of their youth and happiness), were wont to bethink themselves of the much-neglected "practising," and spend a stray hour upon it with most inconsistent and variable zeal. This day there was a great deal of "practising"—indeed, these wayward girls divided their whole time between the piano and the garden, which was another recognised safety-valve. Mamma had not the heart to chide them; instead of that, her face brightened to hear the musical young voices, the low sweet laughter, the echo of their flying feet through the house and on the garden paths. As she sat at her work in her snug sitting-room, with Bell and Beau playing at her feet, and Agnes and Marian playing too, as truly, and with as pure and spontaneous delight, Mrs Atheling was very happy. She did not say a word that any one could hear—but God knew the atmosphere of unspoken and unspeakable gratitude, which was the very breath of this good woman's heart.

When their messenger came home, though he came earlier than Papa, and there was full opportunity to interrogate him—Charlie, we are grieved to say, was not very satisfactory in his communications. "Yes," said Charlie, "I saw him: I don't know if it was the head-man: of course, I asked for Mr Burlington—and he took the parcel—that's all."

"That's all?—you little savage!" cried Marian, who was not half as big as Charlie. "Did he say he would be glad to have it? Did he ask who had written it? What did he say?"

"Are you sure it was Mr Burlington?" said Agnes. "Did he look pleased? What do you think he thought? What did you say to him? Charlie, boy, tell us what you said?"

"I won't tell you a word, if you press upon me like that," said the big boy. "Sit down and be quiet. Mother, make them sit down. I don't know if it was Mr Burlington; I don't think it was: it was a washy man, that never could have been head of that place. He took the papers, and made a face at me, and said, 'Are they your own?' I said 'No' plain enough; and then he looked at the first page, and said they must be left. So I left them. Well, what was a man to do? Of course, that is all."

"What do you mean by making a face at you, boy?" said the watchful mother. "I do trust, Charlie, my dear, you were careful how to behave, and did not make any of your faces at him."

"Oh, it was only a smile," said Charlie, with again a grotesque imitation. "'Are they your own?'— meaning I was just a boy to be laughed at, you know—I should think so! As if I could not make an end of half-a-dozen like him."

"Don't brag, Charlie," said Marian, "and don't be angry about the gentleman, you silly boy; he always must have something on his mind different from a lad like you."

Charlie laughed with grim satisfaction. "He hasn't a great deal on his mind, that chap," said the big boy; "but I wouldn't be him, set up there for no end but reading rubbish—not for—five hundred a-year."

Now, we beg to explain that five hundred a-year was a perfectly magnificent income to the imagination of Bellevue. Charlie could not think at the moment of any greater inducement.

"Reading rubbish! And he has Agnes's book to read!" cried Marian. That was indeed an overpowering anti-climax.

"Yes, but how did he look? Do you think he was pleased? And will it be sure to come to Mr Burlington safe?" said Agnes. Agnes could not help having a secret impression that there might be some plot against this book of hers, and that everybody knew how important it was.

"Why, he looked—as other people look who have nothing to say," said Charlie; "and I had nothing to say—so we got on together. And he said it looked original—much he could tell from the first page! And so, of course, I came away—they're to write when they've read it over. I tell you, that's all. I don't believe it was Mr Burlington; but it was the man that does that sort of thing, and so it was all the same."

This was the substance of Charlie's report. He could not be prevailed upon to describe how this important critic looked, or if he was pleased, or anything about him. He was a washy man, Charlie said; but the obstinate boy would not even explain what washy meant, so they had to leave the question in the hands of time to bring elucidation to it. They were by no means patient; many and oft-repeated were the attacks upon Charlie—many the wonderings over the omnipotent personage who had the power of this decision in his keeping; but in the mean time, and for sundry days and weeks following, these hasty girls had to wait, and to be content.

CHAPTER IX

A DECISION

"I've been thinking," said Charlie Atheling slowly. Having made this preface, the big boy paused: it was his manner of opening an important subject, to which the greater part of his cogitations were directed. His sisters came close to him immediately, half-embracing this great fellow in their united arms, and waiting for his communication. It was the twilight of an April evening, soft and calm. There were no stars in the sky—no sky even, except an occasional break of clear deep heavenly blue through the shadowy misty shapes of clouds, crowding upon each other over the whole arch of heaven. The long boughs of the lilac-bushes rustled in the night wind with all their young soft leaves—the prim outline of the poplar was ruffled with brown buds, and low on the dark soil at its feet was a faint golden lustre of primroses. Everything was as still—not as death, for its deadly calm never exists in nature; but as life, breathing, hushing, sleeping in that sweet season, when the grass is growing and the bud unfolding, all the night and all the day. Even here, in this suburban garden, with the great Babel muffling its voices faintly in the far distance, you could hear, if you listened, that secret rustle of growth and renewing which belongs to the sweet spring. Even here, in this colourless soft light, you could see the earth opening her unwearied bosom, with a passive grateful sweetness, to the inspiring touch of heaven. The brown soil was moist with April showers, and the young leaves glistened faintly with blobs of dew. Very different from the noonday hope was this hope of twilight; but not less hopeful in its silent operations, its sweet sighs, its soft tears, and the heart that stirred within it, in the dark, like a startled bird.

These three young figures, closely grouped together, which you could see only in outline against the faint horizon and the misty sky, were as good a human rendering as could be made of the unexpressed sentiment of the season and the night—they too were growing, with a sweet involuntary progression, up to their life, and to their fate. They stood upon the threshold of the world innocent adventurers, fearing no evil; and it was hard to believe that these hopeful neophytes could ever be made into toil-worn, care-hardened people of the world by any sum of hardships or of years.

"I've been thinking;"—all this time Charlie Atheling had added nothing to his first remarkable statement, and we are compelled to admit that the conclusion which he now gave forth did not seem to justify the solemnity of the delivery—"yes, I've made up my mind; I'll go to old Foggo and the law."

"And why, Charlie, why?"

Charlie was not much given to rendering a reason.

"Never mind the why," he said, abruptly; "that's best. There's old Foggo himself, now; nobody can reckon his income, or make a balance just what he is and what he has, and all about him, as people could do with us. We are plain nobodies, and people know it at a glance. My father has five children and two hundred a-year—whereas old Foggo, you see—"

"I don't see—I do not believe it!" cried Marian, impatiently. "Do you mean to say, you bad boy, that Mr Foggo is better than papa—my father? Why, he has mamma, and Bell and Beau, and all of us: if anything ailed him, we should break our hearts. Mr Foggo has only Miss Willsie: he is an old man, and snuffs, and does not care for anybody: do you call that better than papa?"

But Charlie only laughed. Certain it was that this lad had not the remotest intention of setting up Mr Foggo as his model of happiness. Indeed, nobody quite knew what Charlie's ideal was; but the boy, spite of his practical nature, had a true boyish liking for that margin of uncertainty which made it possible to surmise some unknown power or greatness even in the person of this ancient lawyer's clerk. Few lads, we believe, among the range of those who have to make their own fortune, are satisfied at their outset to decide upon being "no better than papa."

"Well," said Agnes, with consideration, "I should not like Charlie to be just like papa. Papa can do nothing but keep us all—so many children—and he never can be anything more than he is now. But Charlie—Charlie is quite a different person. I wish he could be something great."

"Agnes—don't! it is such nonsense!" cried Marian. "Is there anything great in old Mr Foggo's office? He is a poor old man, I think, living all by himself with Miss Willsie. I had rather be Susan in our house, than be mistress in Mr Foggo's: and how could he make Charlie anything great?"

"Stuff!" said Charlie; "nobody wants to be made; that's a man's own business. Now, you just be quiet with your romancing, you girls. I'll tell you what, though, there's one man I think I'd like to be—and I suppose you call him great—I'd like to be Rajah Brooke."

"Oh, Charlie! and hang people!" cried Marian.

"Not people—only pirates," said the big boy: "wouldn't I string them up too! Yes, if that would please you, Agnes, I'd like to be Rajah Brooke."

"Then why, Charlie," exclaimed Agnes—"why do you go to Mr Foggo's office? A merchant may have a chance for such a thing—but a lawyer! Charlie, boy, what do you mean?"

"Never mind," said Charlie; "your Brookes and your Layards and such people don't begin by being merchants' clerks. I know better: they have birth and education, and all that, and get the start of everybody, and then they make a row about it. I don't see, for my part," said the young gentleman meditatively, "what it is but chance. A man may succeed, or a man may fail, and it's neither much to his credit nor his blame. It is a very odd thing, and I can't understand it—a man may work all his life, and never be the better for it. It's chance, and nothing more, so far as I can see."

"Hush, Charlie—say Providence," said Agnes, anxiously.

"Well, I don't know—it's very odd," answered the big boy.

Whereupon there began two brief but earnest lectures for the good of Charlie's mind, and the improvement of his sentiments. The girls were much disturbed by their brother's heterodoxy; they assaulted him vehemently with the enthusiastic eagerness of the young faith which had never been tried, and would not comprehend any questioning. Chance! when the very sparrows could not fall to the ground—The bright face of Agnes Atheling flushed almost into positive beauty; she asked indignantly, with a trembling voice and tears in her eyes, how Mamma could have endured to live if it had not been God who did it? Charlie, rough as he was, could not withstand an appeal like this: he muttered something hastily under his breath about success in business being a very different thing from that, and was indisputably overawed and vanquished. This allusion made them all very silent for a time, and the young bright eyes involuntarily glanced upward where the pure faint stars were gleaming out one by one among the vapoury hosts of cloud. Strangely touching was the solemnity of this link, not to be broken, which connected the family far down upon the homely bosom of the toilsome earth with yonder blessed children in the skies. Marian, saying nothing, wiped some tears silently from the beautiful eyes which turned such a wistful, wondering, longing look to the uncommunicating heaven.

Charlie, though you could scarcely see him in the darkness, worked those heavy furrows of his brow, and frowned fiercely upon himself. The long branches came sweeping towards them, swayed by the night wind; up in the east rose the pale spring moon, pensive, with a misty halo like a saint. The aspect of the night was changed; instead of the soft brown gloaming, there was broad silvery light and heavy masses of shadow over sky and soil—an instant change all brought about by the rising of the moon. As swift an alteration had passed upon the mood of these young speculators. They went in silently, full of thought—not so sad but that they could brighten to the fireside brightness, yet more meditative than was their wont; even Charlie—for there was a warm heart within the clumsy form of this big boy!

CHAPTER X

MR FOGGO

They went in very sedately out of the darkness, their eyes dazzled with the sudden light. Bell and Beau were safely disposed of for the night, and on the side-table, beside Charlie's two grammars and Agnes's blotting-book, now nearly empty, lay the newspaper of Papa; for the usual visitor was installed in the usual place at the fireside, opposite Mr Atheling. Good companion, it is time you should see the friend of the family: there he was.

And there also, it must be confessed, was a certain faint yet expressive fragrance, which delicately intimated to one sense at least, before he made his appearance, the coming of Mr Foggo. We will not affirm that it was lundyfoot—our own private impression, indeed, is strongly in favour of black rappee—but the thing was indisputable, whatever might be the species. He was a large brown man, full of folds and wrinkles; folds in his brown waistcoat, where secret little sprinklings of snuff, scarcely perceptible, lay undisturbed and secure; wrinkles, long and forcible, about his mouth; folds under his eyelids, deep lines upon his brow. There was not a morsel of smooth surface visible anywhere even in his hands, which were traced all over with perceptible veins and sinews, like a geographical exercise. Mr Foggo wore a wig, which could not by any means be complimented with the same title as Mr Pendennis's "'ead of 'air." He was between fifty and sixty, a genuine old bachelor, perfectly satisfied with his own dry and unlovely existence. Yet we may suppose it was something in Mr Foggo's favour, the frequency of his visits here. He sat by the fireside with the home-air of one who knows that this chair is called his, and that he belongs to the household circle, and turned to look at the young people, as they entered, with a familiar yet critical eye. He was friendly enough, now and then, to deliver little rebukes and remonstrances, and was never complimentary, even to Marian; which may be explained, perhaps, when we say that he was a Scotsman—a north-country Scotsman—with "peculiarities" in his pronunciation, and very distinct opinions of his own. How he came to win his way into the very heart of this family, we are not able to explain; but there he was, and there Mr Foggo had been, summer and winter, for nearly half-a-score of years.

He was now an institution, recognised and respected. No one dreamt of investigating his claims—possession was the whole law in his case, his charter and legal standing-ground; and the young commonwealth recognised as undoubtingly the place of Mr Foggo as they did the natural throne and pre-eminence of Papa and Mamma.

"For my part," said Mr Foggo, who, it seemed, was in the midst of what Mrs Atheling called a "sensible conversation,"—and Mr Foggo spoke slowly, and with a certain methodical dignity,—"for my part, I see little in the art of politics, but just withholding as long as ye can, and giving as little as ye may; for a statesman, ye perceive, be he Radical or Tory, must ever consent to be a stout Conservative when he gets the upper hand. It's in the nature of things—it's like father and son—it's the primitive principle of government, if ye take my opinion. So I am never sanguine myself about a new ministry keeping its word. How should it keep its word? Making measures and opposing them are two as different things as can be. There's father and son, a standing example: the young man is the people and the old man is the government,—the lad spurs on and presses, the greybeard holds in and restrains."

"Ah, Foggo! all very well to talk," said Mr Atheling; "but men should keep their word, government or no government—that's what I say. Do you mean to tell me that a father would cheat his son with promises? No! no! no! Your excuses won't do for me."

"And as for speaking of the father and son, as if it was natural they should be opposed to each other, I am surprised at you, Mr Foggo," said Mrs Atheling, with emphatic disapproval. "There's my Charlie, now, a wilful boy; but do you think he would set his face against anything his papa or I might say?"

"Charlie," said Mr Foggo, with a twinkle of the grey-brown eye which shone clear and keen under folds of eyelid and thickets of eyebrow, "is an uncommon boy. I'm speaking of the general principle, not of exceptional cases. No! men and measures are well enough to make a noise or an election about; but to go against the first grand rule is not in the nature of man."

"Yes, yes!" said Mr Atheling, impatiently; "but I tell you he's broken his word—that's what I say—told a lie, neither more nor less. Do you mean to tell me that any general principle will excuse a man for breaking his promises? I challenge your philosophy for that."

"When ye accept promises that it's not in the nature of things a man can keep, ye must even be content with the alternative," said Mr Foggo.

"Oh! away with your nature of things!" cried Papa, who was unusually excited and vehement,— "scarcely civil," as Mrs Atheling assured him in her private reproof. "It's the nature of the man, that's what's wrong. False in youth, false in age,—if I had known!"

"Crooked ways are ill to get clear of," said Mr Foggo oracularly. "What's that you're about, Charlie, my boy? Take you my advice, lad, and never be a public man."

"A public man! I wish public men had just as much sense," said Mrs Atheling in an indignant under-tone. This good couple, like a great many other excellent people, were pleased to note how all the national businesses were mismanaged, and what miserable 'prentice-hands of pilots held the helm of State.

"I grant you it would not be overmuch for them," said Mr Foggo; "and speaking of government, Mrs Atheling, Willsie is in trouble again."

"I am very sorry," exclaimed Mrs Atheling, with instant interest. "Dear me, I thought this was such a likely person. You remember what I said to you, Agnes, whenever I saw her. She looked so neat and handy, I thought her quite the thing for Miss Willsie. What has she done?"

"Something like the Secretary of State for the Home Department," said Mr Foggo,—"made promises which could not be kept while she was on trial, and broke them when she took office. Shall I send the silly thing away?"

"Oh, Mr Foggo! Miss Willsie was so pleased with her last week—she could do so many things—she has so much good in her," cried Marian; "and then you can't tell—you have not tried her long enough—don't send her away!"

"She is so pretty, Mr Foggo," said Agnes.

Mr Foggo chuckled, thinking, not of Miss Willsie's maid-servant, but of the Secretary of State. Papa looked at him across the fireplace wrathfully. What the reason was, nobody could tell; but Papa was visibly angry, and in a most unamiable state of mind: he said "Tush!" with an impatient gesture, in answer to the chuckle of his opponent. Mr Atheling was really not at all polite to his friend and guest.

But we presume Mr Foggo was not sensitive—he only chuckled the more, and took a pinch of snuff. The snuff-box was a ponderous silver one, with an inscription on the lid, and always revealed itself most distinctly, in shape at least, within the brown waistcoat-pocket of its owner. As he enjoyed this refreshment, the odour diffused itself more distinctly through the apartment, and a powdery thin shower fell from Mr Foggo's huge brown fingers. Susan's cat, if she comes early to the parlour, will undoubtedly be seized with many sneezes to-morrow.

But Marian, who was innocently unconscious of any double meaning, continued to plead earnestly for Miss Willsie's maid. "Yes, Mr Foggo, she is so pretty," said Marian, "and so neat, and smiles. I am sure Miss Willsie herself would be grieved after, if she sent her away. Let mamma speak to Miss Willsie, Mr Foggo. She smiles as if she could not help it. I am sure she is good. Do not let Miss Willsie send her away."

"Willsie is like the public—she is never content with her servants," said Mr Foggo. "Where's all the poetry to-night? no ink upon Agnes's finger! I don't understand that."

"I never write poetry, Mr Foggo," said Agnes, with superb disdain. Agnes was extremely annoyed by Mr Foggo's half-knowledge of her authorship. The old gentleman took her for one of the young ladies who write verses, she thought; and for this most amiable and numerous sisterhood, the young genius, in her present mood, had a considerable disdain.

"And ink on her finger! You never saw ink on Agnes's finger—you know you never did!" cried the indignant Marian. "If she did write poetry, it is no harm; and I know very well you only mean to tease her: but it is wrong to say what never was true."

Mr Foggo rose, diffusing on every side another puff of his peculiar element. "When I have quarrelled with everybody, I reckon it is about time to go home," said Mr Foggo. "Charlie, step across with me, and get some nonsense-verses Willsie has been reading, for the girls. Keep in the same mind, Agnes, and never write poetry—it's a mystery; no man should meddle with it till he's forty—that's my opinion—and then there would be as few poets as there are Secretaries of State."

"Secretaries of State!" exclaimed Papa, restraining his vehemence, however, till Mr Foggo was fairly gone, and out of hearing—and then Mr Atheling made a pause. You could not suppose that his next observation had any reference to this indignant exclamation; it was so oddly out of connection that even the girls smiled to each other. "I tell you what, Mary, a man should not be led by fantastic notions—a man should never do anything that does not come directly in his way," said Mr Atheling, and he pushed his grizzled hair back from his brow with heat and excitement. It was an ordinary saying enough, not much to be marvelled at. What did Papa mean?

"Then, papa, nothing generous would ever be done in the world," said Marian, who, somewhat excited by Mr Foggo, was quite ready for an argument on any subject, or with any person.

"But things that have to be done always come in people's way," said Agnes; "is not that true? I am sure, when you read people's lives, the thing they have to do seems to pursue them; and even if they do not want it, they cannot help themselves. Papa, is not that true?"

"Ay, ay—hush, children," said Mr Atheling, vaguely; "I am busy—speak to your mother."

They spoke to their mother, but not of this subject. They spoke of Miss Willsie's new maid, and conspired together to hinder her going away; and then they marvelled somewhat over the book which Charlie was to bring home. Mr Foggo and his maiden sister lived in Bellevue, in one of the villas semi-detached, which Miss Willsie had named Killiecrankie Lodge, yet Charlie was some time absent. "He is talking to Mr Foggo, instead of bringing our book," said Marian, pouting with her pretty lips. Papa and Mamma had each of them settled into a brown study—a very brown study, to judge from appearances. The fire was low—the lights looked dim. Neither of the girls were doing anything, save waiting on Charlie. They were half disposed to be peevish. "It is not too late; come and practise for half an hour, Agnes," said Marian, suddenly. Mrs Atheling was too much occupied to suggest, as she usually did, that the music would wake Bell and Beau: they stole away from the family apartment unchidden and undetained, and, lighting another candle, entered the genteel and solemn darkness of the best room. You have not been in the best room; let us enter with due dignity this reserved and sacred apartment, which very few people ever enter, and listen to the music which nobody ever hears.

CHAPTER XI

THE BEST ROOM

The music, we are grieved to say, was not at all worth listening to—it would not have disturbed Bell and Beau had the two little beds been on the top of the piano. Though Marian with a careless hand ran over three or four notes, the momentary sound did not disturb the brown study of Mrs Atheling, and scarcely roused Susan, nodding and dozing, as she mended stockings by the kitchen fire. We are afraid this same practising was often an excuse for half an hour's idleness and dreaming. Sweet idleness! happy visions! for it certainly was so to-night.

The best room was of the same size exactly as the family sitting-room, but looked larger by means of looking prim, chill, and uninhabited—and it was by no means crowded with furniture. The piano in one corner and a large old-fashioned table in another, with a big leaf of black and bright mahogany folded down, were the only considerable articles in the room, and the wall looked very blank with its array of chairs. The sofa inclined towards the unlighted fire, and the round table stood before it; but you could not delude yourself into the idea that this at any time could be the family hearth. Mrs Atheling "kept no company;" so, like other good people in the same condition, she religiously preserved and kept in order the company-room; and it was a comfort to her heart to recollect that in this roomy house there was always an orderly place where strangers could be shown into, although the said strangers never came.

The one candle had been placed drearily among the little coloured glass vases on the mantel-shelf; but the moonlight shone broad and full into the window, and, pouring its rays over the whole visible scene without, made something grand and solemn even of this genteel and silent Bellevue. The tranquil whiteness on these humble roofs—the distinctness with which one branch here and there, detached and taken possession of by the light, marked out its half-developed buds against the sky—the strange magic which made that faint ascending streak of smoke the ethereal plaything of these moonbeams—and the intense blackness of the shadow, deep as though it fell from one of the pyramids, of these homely garden-walls—made a wonderful and striking picture of a scene which had not one remarkable feature of its own; and the solitary figure crossing the road, all enshrined and hallowed in this silvery glory, but itself so dark and undistinguishable, was like a figure in a vision—an emblematic and symbolical appearance, entering like a picture to the spectator's memory. The two girls stood looking out, with their arms entwined, and their fair heads close together, as is the wont of such companions, watching the wayfarer, whose weary footstep was inaudible in the great hush and whisper of the night.

"I always fancy one might see ghosts in moonlight," said Marian, under her breath. Certainly that solitary passenger, with all the silvered folds of his dress, and the gliding and noiseless motion of his progress, was not entirely unlike one.

"He looks like a man in a parable," said Agnes, in the same tone. "One could think he was gliding away mysteriously to do something wrong. See, now, he has gone into the shadow. I cannot see him at all—he has quite disappeared—it is so black. Ah! I shall think he is always standing there, looking over at us, and plotting something. I wish Charlie would come home—how long he is!"

"Who would plot anything against us?" said innocent Marian, with her fearless smile. "People do not have enemies now as they used to have—at least not common people. I wish he would come out again, though, out of that darkness. I wonder what sort of man he could be."

But Agnes was no longer following the man; her eye was wandering vaguely over the pale illumination of the sky. "I wonder what will happen to us all?" said Agnes, with a sigh—sweet sigh of girlish thought that knew no care! "I think we are all beginning now, Marian, every one of us. I wonder what will happen—Charlie and all?"

"Oh, I can tell you," said Marian; "and you first of all, because you are the eldest. We shall all be famous, Agnes, every one of us; all because of you."

"Oh, hush!" cried Agnes, a smile and a flush and a sudden brightness running over all her face; "but suppose it should be so, you know, Marian—only suppose it for our own pleasure—what a delight it would be! It might help Charlie on better than anything; and then what we could do for Bell and Beau! Of course it is nonsense," said Agnes, with a low laugh and a sigh of excitement, "but how pleasant it would be!"

"It is not nonsense at all; I think it is quite certain," said Marian; "but then people would seek you out, and you would have to go and visit them—great people—clever people. Would it not be odd to hear real ladies and gentlemen talking in company as they talk in books?"

"I wonder if they do," said Agnes, doubtfully. "And then to meet people whom we have heard of all our lives—perhaps Bulwer even!—perhaps Tennyson! Oh, Marian!"

"And to know they were very glad to meet you," exclaimed the sister dreamer, with another low laugh of absolute pleasure: that was very near the climax of all imaginable honours—and for very awe and delight the young visionaries held their breath.

"And I think now," said Marian, after a little interval, "that perhaps it is better Charlie should be a lawyer, for he would have so little at first in papa's office, and he never could get on, more than papa; and you would not like to leave all the rest of us behind you, Agnes? I know you would not. But I hope Charlie will never grow like Mr Foggo, so old and solitary; to be poor would be better than that."

"Then I could be Miss Willsie," said Agnes, "and we should live in a little square house, with two bits of lawn and two fir-trees; but I think we would not call it Killiecrankie Lodge."

Over this felicitous prospect there was a great deal of very quiet laughing—laughing as sweet and as irrepressible as any other natural music, but certainly not evidencing any very serious purpose on the part of either of the young sisters to follow the example of Miss Willsie. They had so little thought, in their fair unconscious youth, of all the long array of years and changes which lay between their sweet estate and that of the restless kind old lady, the mistress of Mr Foggo's little square house.

"And then, for me—what should I do?" said Marian. There were smiles hiding in every line of this young beautiful face, curving the pretty eyebrow, moving the soft lip, shining shy and bright in the sweet eyes. No anxiety—not the shadow of a shade—had ever crossed this young girl's imagination touching her future lot. It was as rosy as the west and the south, and the cheeks of Maud in Mr Tennyson's poem. She had no thought of investigating it too closely; it was all as bright as a summer day to Marian, and she was ready to spend all her smiles upon the prediction, whether it was ill or well.

"Then I suppose you must be married, May. I see nothing else for you," said Agnes, "for there could not possibly be two Miss Willsies; but I should like to see, in a fairy glass, who my other brother was to be. He must be clever, Marian, and it would be very pleasant if he could be rich, and I suppose he ought to be handsome too."

"Oh, Agnes! handsome of course, first of all!" cried Marian, laughing, "nobody but you would put that last."

"But then I rather like ugly people, especially if they are clever," said Agnes; "there is Charlie, for example. If he was very ugly, what an odd couple you would be!—he ought to be ugly for a balance— and very witty and very pleasant, and ready to do anything for you, May. Then if he were only rich, and you could have a carriage, and be a great lady, I think I should be quite content."

"Hush, Agnes! mamma will hear you—and now there is Charlie with a book," said Marian. "Look! he is quite as mysterious in the moonlight as the other man—only Charlie could never be like a ghost—and I wonder what the book is. Come, Agnes, open the door."

This was the conclusion of the half-hour's practising; they made grievously little progress with their music, yet it was by no means an unpleasant half-hour.

CHAPTER XII

A SERIOUS QUESTION

Mrs Atheling has been calling upon Miss Willsie, partly to intercede for Hannah, the pretty maid, partly on a neighbourly errand of ordinary gossip and kindliness; but in decided excitement and agitation of mind Mamma has come home. It is easy to perceive this as she hurries up-stairs to take off her shawl and bonnet; very easy to notice the fact, as, absent and preoccupied, she comes down again. Bell and Beau are in the kitchen, and the kitchen-door is open. Bell has Susan's cat, who is very like to scratch her, hugged close in her chubby arms. Beau hovers so near the fire, on which there is no guard, that his mother would think him doomed did she see him; but—it is true, although it is almost unbelievable— Mamma actually passes the open kitchen-door without observing either Bell or Beau!

The apples of her eye! Mrs Atheling has surely something very important to occupy her thoughts; and now she takes her usual chair, but does not attempt to find her work-basket. What can possibly have happened to Mamma?

The girls have not to wait very long in uncertainty. The good mother speaks, though she does not distinctly address either of them. "They want a lad like Charlie in Mr Foggo's office," said Mrs Atheling. "I knew that, and that Charlie could have the place; but they also want an articled clerk."

"An articled clerk!—what is that, mamma?" said Agnes, eagerly.

To tell the truth, Mrs Atheling did not very well know what it was, but she knew it was "something superior," and that was enough for her motherly ambition.

"Well, my dear, it is a gentleman," said Mrs Atheling, "and of course there must be far greater opportunities of learning. It is a superior thing altogether, I believe. Now, being such old friends, I should think Mr Foggo might get them to take a very small premium. Such a thing for Charlie! I am sure we could all pinch for a year or two to give him a beginning like that!"

"Would it be much better, mamma?" said Marian. They had left what they were doing to come closer about her, pursuing their eager interrogations. Marian sat down upon a stool on the rug where the fire-light brightened her hair and reddened her cheek at its pleasure. Agnes stood on the opposite side of the hearth, looking down upon the other interlocutors. They were impatient to hear all that Mrs Atheling had heard, and perfectly ready to jump to an unanimous opinion.

"Better, my dear!" said Mrs Atheling—"just as much better as a young man learning to be a master can be better than one who is only a servant. Then, you know, it would give Charlie standing, and get him friends of a higher class. I think it would be positively a sin to neglect such an opportunity; we might never all our lives hear of anything like it again."

"And how did you hear of it, mamma?" said Marian. Marian had quite a genius for asking questions.

"I heard of it from Miss Willsie, my love. It was entirely by accident. She was telling me of an articled pupil they had at the office, who had gone all wrong, poor fellow, in consequence of—; but I can tell you that another time. And then she said they wanted one now, and then it flashed upon me just like an inspiration. I was quite agitated. I do really declare to you, girls, I thought it was Providence; and I believe, if we only were bold enough to do it in faith, God would provide the means; and I feel sure it would be the making of Charlie. I think so indeed."

"I wonder what he would say himself?" said Agnes; for not even Mrs Atheling knew so well as Agnes did the immovable determination, when he had settled upon anything, of this obstinate big boy.

"We will speak of it to-night, and see what your papa says, and I would not mind even mentioning it to Mr Foggo," said Mrs Atheling: "we have not very much to spare, yet I think we could all spare something for Charlie's sake; we must have it fully discussed to-night."

This made, for the time, a conclusion of the subject, since Mrs Atheling, having unburthened her mind to her daughters, immediately discovered the absence of the children, rebuked the girls for suffering them to stray, and set out to bring them back without delay. Marian sat musing before the fire, scorching her pretty cheek with the greatest equanimity. Agnes threw herself into Papa's easy-chair. Both hurried off immediately into delightful speculations touching Charlie—a lawyer and a gentleman; and already in their secret hearts both of these rash girls began to entertain the utmost contempt for the commonplace name of clerk.

We are afraid Mr Atheling's tea was made very hurriedly that night. He could not get peace to finish his third cup, that excellent papa: they persecuted him out of his ordinary play with Bell and Beau; his invariable study of the newspaper. He could by no means make out the cause of the commotion. "Not another story finished already, Agnes?" said the perplexed head of the house. He began to think it would be something rather alarming if they succeeded each other like this.

"Now, my dears, sit down, and do not make a noise with your work, I beg of you. I have something to say to your papa," said Mrs Atheling, with state and solemnity.

Whereupon Papa involuntarily put himself on his defence; he had not the slightest idea what could be amiss, but he recognised the gravity of the preamble. "What is the matter, Mary?" cried poor Mr Atheling. He could not tell what he had done to deserve this.

"My dear, I want to speak about Charlie," said Mrs Atheling, becoming now less dignified, and showing a little agitation. "I went to call on Miss Willsie to-day, partly about Hannah, partly for other things; and Miss Willsie told me, William, that besides the youth's place which we thought would do for Charlie, there was in Mr Foggo's office a vacancy for an articled clerk."

Mrs Atheling paused, out of breath. She did not often make long speeches, nor had she frequently before originated and led a great movement like this, so she showed fully as much excitement as the occasion required. Papa listened with composure and a little surprise, relieved to find that he was not on his trial. Charlie pricked his big red ears, as he sat at his grammar, but made no other sign; while the girls, altogether suspending their work, drew their chairs closer, and with a kindred excitement eagerly followed every word and gesture of Mamma.

"And you must see, William," said Mrs Atheling, rapidly, "what a great advantage it would be to Charlie, if he could enter the office like a gentleman. Of course, I know he would get no salary; but we could go on very well for a year or two as we are doing—quite as well as before, certainly; and I have no doubt Mr Foggo could persuade them to be content with a very small premium; and then think of the advantage to Charlie, my dear!"

"Premium! no salary!—get on for a year or two! Are you dreaming, Mary?" exclaimed Mr Atheling. "Why, this is a perfect craze, my dear. Charlie an articled clerk in Foggo's office! it is pure nonsense. You don't mean to say such a thought has ever taken possession of you. I could understand the girls, if it was their notion—but, Mary! you!"

"And why not me?" said Mamma, somewhat angry for the moment. "Who is so anxious as me for my boy? I know what our income is, and what it can do exactly to a penny, William—a great deal better than you do, my dear; and of course it would be my business to draw in our expenses accordingly; and the girls would give up anything for Charlie's sake. And then, except Beau, who is so little, and will not want anything much done for him for many a year—he is our only boy, William. It was not always so," said the good mother, checking a great sob which had nearly stopped her voice—"it was not always so— but there is only Charlie left of all of them; and except little Beau, the son of our old age, he is our only boy!"

She paused now, because she could not help it; and for the same reason her husband was very slow to answer. All-prevailing was this woman's argument; it was very near impossible to say the gentlest Nay to anything thus pleaded in the name of the dead.

"But, my dear, we cannot do it," said Mr Atheling very quietly. The good man would have given his right hand at that moment to be able to procure this pleasure for the faithful mother of those fair boys who were in heaven.

"We could do it if we tried, William," said Mrs Atheling, recovering herself slowly. Her husband shook his head, pondered, shook his head again.

"It would be injustice to the other children," he said at last. "We could not keep Charlie like a gentleman without injuring the rest. I am surprised you do not think of that."

"But the rest of us are glad to be injured," cried Agnes, coming to her mother's aid; "and then I may have something by-and-by, and Charlie could get on so much better. I am sure you must see all the advantages, papa."

"And we can't be injured either, for we shall just be as we are," said Marian, "only a little more economical; and I am sure, papa, if it is so great a virtue to be thrifty, as you and Mr Foggo say, you ought to be more anxious than we are about this for Charlie; and you would, if you carried out your principles—and you must submit. I know we shall succeed at last."

"If it is a conspiracy, I give in," said Mr Atheling. "Of course you must mulct yourselves if you have made up your minds to it. I protest against suffering your thrift myself, and I won't have any more economy in respect to Bell and Beau. But do your will, Mary—I don't interfere. A conspiracy is too much for me."

"Mother!" said Charlie—all this time there had been nothing visible of the big boy, except the aforesaid red ears; now he put down his grammar and came forward, with some invisible wind working much among the furrows of his brow—"just hear what I've got to say. This won't do—I'm not a gentleman, you know; what's the good of making me like one?—of course I mean," said Charlie, somewhat hotly, in a parenthesis, as Agnes's eyes flashed upon him, "not a gentleman, so far as being idle and having plenty of money goes;—I've got to work for my bread. Suppose I was articled, at the end of my time I should have to work for my bread all the same. What is the difference? It's only making a sham for two years, or three years, or whatever the time might be. I don't want to go against what anybody says, but you wouldn't make a sham of me, would you, mother? Let me go in my proper place—like what I'll have to be, all my life; then if I rise you will be pleased; and if I don't rise, still nobody will be able to say I have come down. I can't be like a gentleman's son, doing nothing. Let me be myself, mother—the best thing for me."

Charlie said scarcely any more that night, though much was said on every side around; but Charlie was the conqueror.

CHAPTER XIII

KILLIECRANKIE LODGE

Killiecrankie Lodge held a dignified position in this genteel locality: it stood at the end of the road, looking down and superintending Bellevue. Three square houses, all duly walled and gardened, made the apex and conclusion of this suburban retirement. The right-hand one was called Buena Vista House; the left-hand one was Green View Cottage, and in the centre stood the lodge of Killiecrankie. The lodge was not so jealously private as its neighbours: in the upper part of the door in the wall was an open iron railing, through which the curious passenger might gain a beatific glimpse of Miss Willsie's wallflowers, and of the clean white steps by which you ascended to the house-door. The corresponding loopholes at the outer entrance of Green View and Buena Vista were carefully boarded; so the house of Mr Foggo had the sole distinction of an open eye.

Within the wall was a paved path leading to the house, with a square bit of lawn on either side, each containing in its centre a very small round flower-plot and a minute fir-tree. These were the pine forests of the Islingtonian Killiecrankie; but there were better things within the brief enclosure. The borders round about on every side were full of wallflowers—double wallflower, streaked wallflower, yellow wallflower, brown wallflower—every variety under the sun. This was the sole remarkable instance of taste displayed by Miss Willsie; but it gave a delicate tone of fragrance to the whole atmosphere of Bellevue.

This is a great day at Killiecrankie Lodge. It is the end of April now, and already the days are long, and the sun himself stays up till after tea, and throws a slanting golden beam over the daylight table. Miss Willsie, herself presiding, is slightly heated. She says, "Bless me, it's like July!" as she sets down upon the tray her heavy silver teapot. Miss Willsie is not half as tall as her brother, but makes up the difference in another direction. She is stout, though she is so restlessly active. Her face is full of wavering little lines and dimples, though she is an old lady; and there are the funniest indentations possible in her round chin and cheeks. You would fancy a laugh was always hiding in those crevices. Alas! Hannah knows better. You should see how Miss Willsie can frown!

But the old lady is in grand costume to-night; she has her brown satin dress on, her immense cairngorm brooch, her overwhelming blue turban. This sublime head-dress has an effect of awe upon the company; no one was prepared for such a degree of grandeur, and the visitors consequently are not quite at their ease. These visitors are rather numerous for a Bellevue tea-party. There is Mr Richards from Buena Vista, Mrs Tavistock from Woburn Lodge, and Mr Gray, the other Scotch inhabitant, from Gowanbrae; and there is likewise Mr Foggo Silas Endicott, Miss Willsie's American nephew, and her Scotch nephew, Harry Oswald; and besides all this worshipful company, there are all the Athelings—all except Bell and Beau, left, with many cautions, in the hands of Susan, over whom, in fear and self-reproach, trembles already the heart of Mamma.

"So he would not hear of it—he was not blate!" said Miss Willsie. "My brother never had the like in his office—that I tell you; and there's no good mother at home to do as much for Harry. Chairles, lad, you'll find out better some time. If there's one thing I do not like, it's a wilful boy!"

"But I can scarcely call him wilful either," said Mrs Atheling, hastily. "He is very reasonable, Miss Willsie; he gives his meaning—it is not out of opposition. He has always a good reason for what he does—he is a very reasonable boy."

"And if there's one thing I object to," said Miss Willsie, "it's the assurance of these monkeys with their reasons. When we were young, we were ill bairns, doubtless, like other folk; but if I had dared to make my excuses, pity me! There is Harry, now, will set up his face to me as grand as a Lord of Session; and Marian this very last night making her argument about these two spoiled babies of yours, as if she knew better than me! Misbehaviour's natural to youth. I can put up with that, but I cannot away with their reasons. Such things are not for me."

"Very true—so true, Miss Willsie," said Mrs Tavistock, who was a sentimental and sighing widow. "There is my niece, quite an example. I am sadly nervous, you know; and that rude girl will 'prove' to me, as she calls it, that no thief could get into the house, though I know they try the back-kitchen window every night."

"If there's one thing I'm against," said Miss Willsie, solemnly, "it's that foolish fright about thieves— thieves! Bless me, what would the ragamuffins do here? A man may be a robber, but that's no to say he's an idiot; and a wise man would never put his life or his freedom in jeopardy for what he could get in Bellevue."

Mrs Tavistock was no match for Miss Willsie, so she prudently abstained from a rejoinder. A large old china basin full of wallflowers stood under a grim portrait, and between a couple of huge old silver candlesticks upon the mantelpiece; Miss Willsie's ancient tea-service, at present glittering upon the table, was valuable and massive silver: nowhere else in Bellevue was there so much "plate" as in Killiecrankie Lodge; and this was perfectly well known to the nervous widow. "I am sure I wonder at your courage, Miss Willsie; but then you have a gentleman in the house, which makes a great difference," said Mrs Tavistock, woefully. Mrs Tavistock was one of those proper and conscientious ladies who make a profession of their widowhood, and are perpetually executing a moral suttee to the edification of all beholders. "I was never nervous before. Ah, nobody knows what a difference it makes to me!"

"Young folk are a troublesome handful. Where are the girls—what are they doing with Harry?" said Miss Willsie. "Harry's a lad for any kind of antics, but you'll no see Foggo demeaning himself. Foggo writes poems and letters to the papers: they tell me that in his own country he's a very rising young man."

"He looks intellectual. What a pleasure, Miss Willsie, to you!" said the widow, with delightful sympathy.

"If there's one thing I like worse than another, it's your writing young men," said Miss Willsie, vehemently. "I lighted on a paper this very day, that the young leasing-maker had gotten from America, and what do you think I saw therein, but just a long account—everything about us—of my brother and me. My brother Robert Foggo, as decent a man as there is in the three kingdoms—and me! What do you think of that, Mrs Atheling?—even Harry in it, and the wallflowers! If it had not been for my brother, he never should have set foot in this house again."

"Oh dear, how interesting!" said the widow. Mrs Tavistock turned her eyes to the other end of the room almost with excitement. She had not the least objection, for her own part, in the full pomp of sables and sentiment, to figure at full length in the Mississippi Gazette.

"And what was it for?" said Mrs Atheling, innocently; "for I thought it was only remarkable people that even the Americans put in the papers. Was it simply to annoy you?"

"Me!—do you think a lad like yon could trouble me?" exclaimed Miss Willsie. "He says, 'All the scenes through which he has passed will be interesting to his readers.' That's in a grand note he sent me this morning—the impertinent boy! My poor Harry, though he's often in mischief, and my brother thinks him unsteady—I would not give his little finger for half-a-dozen lads like yon."

"But Harry is doing well now, Miss Willsie?" said Mrs Atheling. There was a faint emphasis on the now which proved that Harry had not always done well.

"Ay," said Miss Willsie, drily; "and so Chairles has settled to his business—that's aye a comfort. If there's one thing that troubles me, it is to see young folk growing up in idleness; I pity them, now, that are genteel and have daughters. What are you going to do, Mrs Atheling, with these girls of yours?"

Mrs Atheling's eyes sought them out with fond yet not untroubled observation. There was Marian's beautiful head before the other window, looking as if it had arrested and detained the sunbeams, long ago departed in the west; and there was Agnes, graceful, animated, and intelligent, watching, with an affectionate and only half-conscious admiration, her sister's beauty. Their mother smiled to herself and sighed. Even her anxiety, looking at them thus, was but another name for delight.

"Agnes," said Marian at the other window, half whispering, half aloud—"Agnes! Harry says Mr Endicott has published a book."

With a slight start and a slight blush Agnes turned round. Mr Foggo S. Endicott was tall, very thin, had an extremely lofty mien, and a pair of spectacles. He was eight-and-twenty, whiskerless, sallow, and by no means handsome: he held his thin head very high, and delivered his sentiments into the air when he spoke, but rarely bent from his altitude to address any one in particular. But he heard the whisper in a moment: in his very elbows, as you stood behind him, you could see the sudden consciousness. He perceived, though he did not look at her, the eager, bright, blushing, half-reverential glance of Agnes, and, conscious to his very finger-points, raised his thin head to its fullest elevation, and pretended not to hear.

Agnes blushed: it was with sudden interest, curiosity, reverence, made more personal and exciting by her own venture. Nothing had been heard yet of this venture, though it was nearly a month since Charlie took it to Mr Burlington, and the young genius looked with humble and earnest attention upon one who really had been permitted to make his utterance to the ear of all the world. He had published a book; he was a real genuine printed author. The lips of Agnes parted with a quick breath of eagerness; she looked up at him with a blush on her cheek, and a light in her eye. A thrill of wonder and excitement came over her: would people by-and-by regard herself in the same light?

"Oh, Mr Endicott!—is it poems?" said Agnes, shyly, and with a deepening colour. The simple girl was almost as much embarrassed asking him about his book, as if she had been asking about the Transatlantic lady of this Yankee young gentleman's love.

"Oh!" said Mr Endicott, discovering suddenly that she addressed him—"yes. Did you speak to me?—poems?—ah! some little fugitive matters, to be sure. One has no right to refuse to publish, when everybody comes to know that one does such things."

"Refuse?—no, indeed; I think not," said Agnes, in spite of herself feeling very much humbled, and speaking very low. This was so elevated a view of the matter, and her own was so commonplace a one, that the poor girl was completely crestfallen. She so anxious to get into print; and this bonâ fide author, doubtless so very much her superior, explaining how he submitted, and could not help himself! Agnes was entirely put down.

"Yes, really one ought not to keep everything for one's own private enjoyment," said the magnanimous Mr Endicott, speaking very high up into the air with his cadenced voice. "I do not approve of too much reserve on the part of an author myself."

"And what are they about, Mr Endicott?" asked Marian, with respect, but by no means so reverentially as Agnes. Mr Endicott actually looked at Marian; perhaps it was because of her very prosaic and improper question, perhaps for the sake of the beautiful face.

"About!" said the poet, with benignant disdain. "No, I don't approve of narrative poetry; it's after the time. My sonnets are experiences. I live them before I write them; that is the true secret of poetry in our enlightened days."

Agnes listened, much impressed and cast down. She was far too simple to perceive how much superior her natural bright impulse, spontaneous and effusive, was to this sublime concentration. Agnes all her life long had never lived a sonnet; but she was so sincere and single-minded herself, that, at the first moment of hearing it, she received all this nonsense with unhesitating faith. For she had not yet learned to believe in the possibility of anybody, save villains in books, saying anything which they did not thoroughly hold as true.

So Agnes retired a little from the conversation. The young genius began to take herself to task, and was much humiliated by the contrast. Why had she written that famous story, now lying storm-stayed in the hands of Mr Burlington? Partly to please herself—partly to please Mamma—partly because she could not help it. There was no grand motive in the whole matter. Agnes looked with reverence at Mr

Endicott, and sat down in a corner. She would have been completely conquered if the sublime American had been content to hold his peace.

But this was the last thing which occurred to Mr Endicott. He continued his utterances, and the discouraged girl began to smile. She was no judge of character, but she began to be able to distinguish nonsense when she heard it. This was very grand nonsense on the first time of hearing, and Agnes and Marian, we are obliged to confess, were somewhat annoyed when Mamma made a movement of departure. They kept very early hours in Bellevue, and before ten o'clock all Miss Willsie's guests had said good-night to Killiecrankie Lodge.

CHAPTER XIV

THE HOUSE OF FOGGO

It was ten o'clock, and now only this little family circle was left in the Lodge of Killiecrankie. Miss Willsie, with one of the big silver candlesticks drawn so very close that her blue turban trembled, and stood in jeopardy, read the Times; Mr Foggo sat in his armchair, doing nothing save contemplating the other light in the other candlestick; and at the unoccupied sides of the table, between the seniors, were the two young men.

These nephews did not live at Killiecrankie Lodge; but Miss Willsie, who was very careful, and a notable manager, considered it would be unsafe for "the boys" to go home to their lodgings at so late an hour as this—so her invitations always included a night's lodging; and the kind and arbitrary little woman was not accustomed to be disobeyed. Yet "the boys" found it dull, we confess. Mr Foggo was not pleased with Harry, and by no means "took" to Endicott. Miss Willsie could not deny herself her evening's reading. They yawned at each other, these unfortunate young men, and with a glance of mutual jealousy thought of Marian Atheling. It was strange to see how dull and disenchanted this place looked when the beautiful face that brightened it was gone.

So Mr Foggo S. Endicott took from his pocket his own paper, the Mississippi Gazette, and Harry possessed himself of the half of Miss Willsie's Times. It was odd to observe the difference between them even in manner and attitude. Harry bent half over the table, with his hands thrust up into the thick masses of his curling hair; the American sat perfectly upright, lifting his thin broadsheet to the height of his spectacles, and reading loftily his own lucubrations. You could scarcely see the handsome face of Harry as he hung over his half of the paper, partly reading, partly dreaming over certain fond fancies of his own; but you could not only see the lofty lineaments of Foggo, which were not at all handsome, but also could perceive at a glance that he had "a remarkable profile," and silently called your attention to it. Unfortunately, nobody in the present company was at all concerned about the profile of Mr Endicott. That philosophical young gentleman, notwithstanding, read his "Letter from England" in his best manner, and demeaned himself as loftily as if he were a "portrait of a distinguished literary gentleman" in an American museum. What more could any man do?

Meanwhile Mr Foggo sat in his armchair steadily regarding the candle before him. He loved conversation, but he was not talkative, especially in his own house. Sometimes the old man's acute eyes glanced from under his shaggy brow with a momentary keenness towards Harry—sometimes they shot across the table a momentary sparkle of grim contempt; but to make out from Mr Foggo's face what Mr

Foggo was thinking, was about the vainest enterprise in the world. It was different with his sister: Miss Willsie's well-complexioned countenance changed and varied like the sky. You could pursue her sudden flashes of satisfaction, resentment, compassion, and injury into all her dimples, as easily as you could follow the clouds over the heavens. Nor was it by her looks alone that you could discover the fluctuating sympathies of Miss Willsie. Short, abrupt, hasty exclamations, broke from her perpetually. "The vagabond!—to think of that!" "Ay, that's right now; I thought there was something in him." "Bless me—such a story!" After this manner ran on her unconscious comments. She was a considerable politician, and this was an interesting debate; and you could very soon make out by her continual observations the political opinions of the mistress of Killiecrankie. She was a desperate Tory, and at the same moment the most direful and unconstitutional of Radicals. With a hereditary respect she applauded the sentiments of the old country-party, and clung to every institution with the pertinacity of a martyr; yet with the same breath, and the most delightful inconsistency, was vehement and enthusiastic in favour of the wildest schemes of reform; which, we suppose, is as much as to say that Miss Willsie was a very feminine politician, the most unreasonable of optimists, and had the sublimest contempt for all practical considerations when she had convinced herself that anything was right.

"I knew it!" cried Miss Willsie, with a burst of triumph; "he's out, and every one disowning him—a mean crew, big and little! If there's one thing I hate, it's setting a man forward to tell an untruth, and then letting him bear all the blame!"

"He's got his lawful deserts," said Mr Foggo. This gentleman, more learned than his sister, took a very philosophical view of public matters, and acknowledged no particular leaning to any "party" in his general interest in the affairs of state.

"I never can find out now," said Miss Willsie suddenly, "what the like of Mr Atheling can have to do with this man—a lord and a great person, and an officer of state—but his eye kindles up at the name of him, as if it was the name of a friend. There cannot be ill-will unless there is acquaintance, that's my opinion; and an ill-will at this lord I am sure Mr Atheling has."

"They come from the same countryside," said Mr Foggo; "when they were lads they knew each other."

"And who is this Mr Atheling?" said Endicott, speaking for the first time. "I have a letter of introduction to Viscount Winterbourne myself. His son, the Honourable George Rivers, travelled in the States a year or two since, and I mean to see him by-and-by; but who is Mr Atheling, to know an English Secretary of State?"

"He's Cash and Ledger's chief clerk," said Mr Foggo, very laconically, looking with a steady eye at the candlestick, and bestowing as little attention upon his questioner as his questioner did upon him.

"Marvellous! in this country!" said the American; but Mr Endicott belonged to that young America which is mightily respectful of the old country. He thought it vulgar to do too much republicanism. He only heightened the zest of his admiration now and then by a refined little sneer.

"In this country! Where did ye ever see such a country, I would like to know?" cried Miss Willsie. "If it was but for your own small concerns, you ought to be thankful; for London itself will keep ye in writing this many a day. If there's one thing I cannot bear, it's ingratitude! I'm a long-suffering person myself; but that, I grant, gets the better of me."

"Mr Atheling, I suppose, has not many lords in his acquaintance," said Harry Oswald, looking up from his paper. "Endicott is right enough, aunt; he is not quite in the rank for that; he has better—" said Harry, something lowering his voice; "I would rather know myself welcome at the Athelings' than in any other house in England."

This was said with a little enthusiasm, and brought the rising colour to Harry Oswald's brow. His cousin looked at him, with a curl of his thin lip and a somewhat malignant eye. Miss Willsie looked at him hastily, with a quick impatient nod of her head, and a most rapid and emphatic frown. Finally, Mr Foggo lifted to the young man's face his acute and steady eye.

"Keep to your physic, Harry," said Mr Foggo. The hapless Harry did not meet the glance, but he understood the tone.

"Well, uncle, well," said Harry hastily, raising his eyes; "but a man cannot always keep to physic. There are more things in the world than drugs and lancets. A man must have some margin for his thoughts."

Again Miss Willsie gave the culprit a nod and a frown, saying as plain as telegraphic communication ever said, "I am your friend, but this is not the time to plead." Again Mr Endicott surveyed his cousin with a vague impulse of malice and of rivalry. Harry Oswald plunged down again on his paper, and was no more heard of that night.

CHAPTER XV

THE PROPOSAL

"I suppose we are not going to hear anything about it. It is very hard," said Agnes disconsolately. "I am sure it is so easy to show a little courtesy. Mr Burlington surely might have written to let us know."

"But, my dear, how can we tell?" said Mrs Atheling; "he may be ill, or he may be out of town, or he may have trouble in his family. It is very difficult to judge another person—and you don't know what may have happened; he may be coming here himself, for aught we know."

"Well, I think it is very hard," said Marian; "I wish we only could publish it ourselves. What is the good of a publisher? They are only cruel to everybody, and grow rich themselves; it is always so in books."

"He might surely have written at least," repeated Agnes. These young malcontents were extremely dissatisfied, and not at all content with Mrs Atheling's explanation that he might be ill, or out of town, or have trouble in his family. Whatever extenuating circumstances there might be, it was clear that Mr Burlington had not behaved properly, or with the regard for other people's feelings which Agnes concluded to be the only true mark of a gentleman. Even the conversation of last night, and the state and greatness of Mr Endicott, stimulated the impatience of the girls. "It is not for the book so much, as for the uncertainty," Agnes said, as she disconsolately took out her sewing; but in fact it was just because they had so much certainty, and so little change and commotion in their life, that they longed so much for the excitement and novelty of this new event.

They were very dull this afternoon, and everything out of doors sympathised with their dulness. It was a wet day—a hopeless, heavy, persevering, not-to-be-mended day of rain. The clouds hung low and leaden over the wet world; the air was clogged and dull with moisture, only lightened now and then by an impatient shrewish gust, which threw the small raindrops like so many prickles full into your face. The long branches of the lilacs blew about wildly with a sudden commotion, when one of these gusts came upon them, like a group of heroines throwing up their arms in a tragic appeal to heaven. The primroses, pale and drooping, sullied their cheeks with the wet soil; hour after hour, with the most sullen and dismal obstinacy, the rain rained down upon the cowering earth; not a sound was in Bellevue save the trickle of the water, a perfect stream, running strong and full down the little channel on either side the street. It was in vain to go to the window, where not a single passenger—not a baker's boy, nor a maid on pattens, nobody but the milkman in his waterproof-coat—hurrying along, a peripatetic fountain, with little jets of water pouring from his hat, his cape, and his pails—was visible through the whole dreary afternoon. It is possible to endure a wet morning—easy enough to put up with a wet night; but they must have indeed high spirits and pleasurable occupations who manage to keep their patience and their cheerfulness through the sullen and dogged monotony of a wet afternoon.

So everybody had a poke at the fire, which had gone out twice to-day already, and was maliciously looking for another opportunity of going out again; every person here present snapped her thread and lost her needle; every one, even, each for a single moment, found Bell and Beau in her way. You may suppose, this being the case, how very dismal the circumstances must have been. But suddenly everybody started—the outer gate swung open—an audible footstep came towards the door! Fairest of readers, a word with you! If you are given to morning-calls, and love to be welcomed, make your visits on a wet day!

It was not a visitor, however welcome—better than that—ecstatic sound! it was the postman—the postman, drenched and sullen, hiding his crimson glories under an oilskin cape; and it was a letter, solemn and mysterious, in an unknown hand—a big blue letter, addressed to Miss Atheling. With trembling fingers Agnes opened it, taking, with awe and apprehension, out of the big blue envelope, a blue and big enclosure and a little note. The paper fell to the ground, and was seized upon by Marian. The excited girl sprang up with it, almost upsetting Bell and Beau. "It is in print! Memorandum of an agreement—oh, mamma!" cried Marian, holding up the dangerous instrument. Agnes sat down immediately in her chair, quite hushed for the instant. It was an actual reality, Mr Burlington's letter—and a veritable proposal—not for herself, but for her book.

The girls, we are obliged to confess, were slightly out of their wits for about an hour after this memorable arrival. Even Mrs Atheling was excited, and Bell and Beau ran about the room in unwitting exhilaration, shouting at the top of their small sweet shrill voices, and tumbling over each other unreproved. The good mother, to tell the truth, would have liked to cry a little, if she could have managed it, and was much moved, and disposed to take this, not as a mere matter of business, but as a tender office of friendship and esteem on the part of the unconscious Mr Burlington. Mrs Atheling could not help fancying that somehow this wonderful chance had happened to Agnes because she was "a good girl."

And until Papa and Charlie came home they were not very particular about the conditions of the agreement; the event itself was the thing which moved them: it quickened the slow pace of this dull afternoon to the most extraordinary celerity; the moments flew now which had lagged with such obstinate dreariness before the coming of that postman; and all the delight and astonishment of the first moment remained to be gone over again at the home-coming of Papa.

And Mr Atheling, good man, was almost as much disturbed for the moment as his wife. At first he was incredulous—then he laughed, but the laugh was extremely unsteady in its sound—then he read over the paper with great care, steadily resisting the constant interruptions of Agnes and Marian, who persecuted him with their questions, "What do you think of it, papa?" before the excellent papa had time to think at all. Finally, Mr Atheling laughed again with more composure, and spread out upon the table the important "Memorandum of Agreement." "Sign it, Agnes," said Papa; "it seems all right, and quite business-like, so far as I can see. She's not twenty-one, yet—I don't suppose it's legal—that child! Sign it, Agnes."

This was by no means what Papa was expected to say; yet Agnes, with excitement, got her blotting-book and her pen. This innocent family were as anxious that Agnes's autograph should be well written as if it had been intended for a specimen of caligraphy, instead of the signature to a legal document; nor was the young author herself less concerned; and she made sure of the pen, and steadied her hand conscientiously before she wrote that pretty "Agnes Atheling," which put the other ugly printer-like handwriting completely to shame. And now it was done—there was a momentary pause of solemn silence, not disturbed even by Bell and Beau.

"So this is the beginning of Agnes's fortune," said Mr Atheling. "Now Mary, and all of you, don't be excited; every book does not succeed because it finds a publisher; and you must not place your expectations too high; for you know Agnes knows nothing of the world."

It was very good to say "don't be excited," when Mr Atheling himself was entirely oblivious of his newspaper, indifferent to his tea, and actually did not hear the familiar knock of Mr Foggo at the outer door.

"And these half profits, papa, I wonder what they will be," said Agnes, glad to take up something tangible in this vague delight.

"Oh, something very considerable," said Papa, forgetting his own caution. "I should not wonder if the publisher made a great deal of money by it: they know what they're about. Get up and get me my slippers, you little rascals. When Agnes comes into her fortune, what a paradise of toys for Bell and Beau!"

But the door opened, and Mr Foggo came in like a big brown cloud. There was no concealing from him the printed paper—no hiding the overflowings of the family content. So Agnes and Marian hurried off for half an hour's practising, and then put the twins to bed, and gossiped over the fire in the little nursery. What a pleasant night it was!

CHAPTER XVI

FAMILY EXCITEMENT

It would be impossible to describe, after that first beginning, the pleasant interest and excitement kept up in this family concerning the fortune of Agnes. All kinds of vague and delightful magnificences floated in the minds of the two girls: guesses of prodigious sums of money and unimaginable honours were constantly hazarded by Marian; and Agnes, though she laughed at, and professed to disbelieve, these splendid imaginations, was, beyond all controversy, greatly influenced by them. The house held up its head, and began to dream of fame and greatness. Even Mr Atheling, in a trance of exalted and exulting fancy, went down self-absorbed through the busy moving streets, and scarcely noticed the steady current of the Islingtonian public setting in strong for the City. Even Mamma, going about her household business, had something visionary in her eye; she saw a long way beyond to-day's little cares and difficulties—the grand distant lights of the future streaming down on the fair heads of her two girls. It was not possible, at least in the mother's fancy, to separate these two who were so closely united. No one in the house, indeed, could recognise Agnes without Marian, or Marian without Agnes; and this new fortune belonged to both.

And then there followed all those indefinite but glorious adjuncts involved in this beginning of fate—society, friends, a class of people, as those good dreamers supposed, more able to understand and appreciate the simple and modest refinement of these young minds;—all the world was to be moved by this one book—everybody was to render homage—all society to be disturbed with eagerness. Mr Atheling adjured the family not to raise their expectations too high, yet raised his own to the most magnificent level of unlikely greatness. Mrs Atheling had generous compunctions of mind as she looked at the ribbons already half faded. Agnes now was in a very different position from her who made the unthrifty purchase of a colour which would not bear the sun. Mamma held a very solemn synod in her own mind, and was half resolved to buy new ones upon her own responsibility. But then there was something shabby in building upon an expectation which as yet was so indefinite. And we are glad to say there was so much sobriety and good sense in the house of the Athelings, despite their glorious anticipations, that the ribbons of Agnes and Marian, though they began to fulfil Mrs Atheling's prediction, still steadily did their duty, and bade fair to last out their appointed time.

This was a very pleasant time to the whole household. Their position, their comfort, their external circumstances, were in no respect changed, yet everything was brightened and radiant in an overflow of hope. There was neither ill nor sickness nor sorrow to mar the enjoyment; everything at this period was going well with them, to whom many a day and many a year had gone full heavily. They were not aware themselves of their present happiness; they were all looking eagerly forward, bent upon a future which was to be so much superior to to-day, and none dreamed how little pleasure was to be got out of the realisation, in comparison with the delight they all took in the hope. They could afford so well to laugh at all their homely difficulties—to make jokes upon Mamma's grave looks as she discovered an extravagant shilling or two in the household accounts—or found out that Susan had been wasteful in the kitchen. It was so odd, so funny, to contrast these minute cares with the golden age which was to come.

And then the plans and secret intentions, the wonderful committees which sat in profound retirement; Marian plotting with Mamma what Agnes should have when she came into her fortune, and Agnes advising, with the same infallible authority, for the advantage of Marian. The vast and ambitious project of the girls for going to the country—the country or the sea-side—some one, they did not care which, of those beautiful unknown beatific regions out of London, which were to them all fairyland and countries of magic. We suppose nobody ever did enjoy the sea breezes as Agnes and Marian Atheling, in their little white bed-chamber, enjoyed the imaginary gale upon the imaginary sands, which they could perceive brightening the cheek of Mamma, and tossing about the curls of the twin-babies, at any moment of any night or day. This was to be the grand triumph of the time when Agnes came into her fortune, though even Mamma as yet had not heard of the project; but already it was a greater pleasure to the girls than any real visit to any real sea-side in this visible earth ever could be.

And then there began to come, dropping in at all hours, from the earliest post in the morning to the last startling delivery at nine o'clock at night, packets of printed papers—the proof-sheets of this astonishing book. You are not to suppose that those proofs needed much correcting—Agnes's manuscript was far too daintily written for that; yet every one read them with the utmost care and attention, and Papa made little crosses in pencil on the margin when he came to a doubtful word. Everybody read them, not once only, but sometimes twice, or even three times over—everybody but Charlie, who eat them up with his bread and butter at tea, did not say a word on the subject, and never looked at them again. All Bellevue resounded with the knocks of that incessant postman at Number Ten. Public opinion was divided on the subject. Some people said the Athelings had been extravagant, and were now suffering under a very Egyptian plague, a hailstorm of bills; others, more charitable, had private information that both the Miss Athelings were going to be married, and believed this continual dropping to be a carnival shower of flowers and bonbons, the love-letters of the affianced bridegrooms; but nobody supposed that the unconscious and innocent postman stood a respectable deputy for the little Beelzebub, to whose sooty hands of natural right should have been committed the custody of those fair and uncorrectable sheets. Sometimes, indeed, this sable emissary made a hasty and half-visible appearance in his own proper person, with one startling knock, as loud, but more solemn than the postman—"That's the Devil!" said Charlie, with unexpected animation, the second time this emphatic sound was heard; and Susan refused point-blank to open the door.

How carefully these sheets were corrected! how punctually they were returned!—with what conscientious care and earnestness the young author attended to all the requirements of printer and publisher! There was something amusing, yet something touching as well, in the sincere and natural humbleness of these simple people. Whatever they said, they could not help thinking that some secret spring of kindness had moved Mr Burlington; that somehow this unconscious gentleman, most innocent of any such intention, meant to do them all a favour. And moved by the influence of this amiable delusion, Agnes was scrupulously attentive to all the suggestions of the publisher. Mr Burlington himself was somewhat amused by his new writer's obedience, but doubtful, and did not half understand it; for it is not always easy to comprehend downright and simple sincerity. But the young author went on upon her guileless way, taking no particular thought of her own motives; and on with her every step went all the family, excited and unanimous. To her belonged the special joy of being the cause of this happy commotion; but the pleasure and the honour and the delight belonged equally to them all.

CHAPTER XVII

AN AMERICAN SKETCH

"Here! there's reading for you," said Miss Willsie, throwing upon the family table a little roll of papers. "They tell me there's something of the kind stirring among yourselves. If there's one thing I cannot put up with, it's to see a parcel of young folk setting up to read lessons to the world!"

"Not Agnes!" cried Marian eagerly; "only wait till it comes out. I know so well, Miss Willsie, how you will like her book."

"No such thing," said Miss Willsie indignantly. "I would just like to know—twenty years old, and never out of her mother's charge a week at a time—I would just like any person to tell me what Agnes Atheling can have to say to the like of me!"

"Indeed, nothing at all," said Agnes, blushing and laughing; "but it is different with Mr Endicott. Now nobody must speak a word. Here it is."

"No! let me away first," cried Miss Willsie in terror. She was rather abrupt in her exits and entrances. This time she disappeared instantaneously, shaking her hand at some imaginary culprit, and had closed the gate behind her with a swing, before Agnes was able to begin the series of "Letters from England" which were to immortalise the name of Mr Foggo S. Endicott. The New World biographist began with his voyage, and all the "emotions awakened in his breast" by finding himself at sea; and immediately thereafter followed a special chapter, headed "Killiecrankie Lodge."

"How delightful," wrote the traveller, "so many thousand miles from home, so far away from those who love us, to meet with the sympathy and communion of kindred blood! To this home of the domestic affections I am glad at once to introduce my readers, as a beautiful example of that Old England felicity, which is, I grieve to say, so sadly outbalanced by oppression and tyranny and crime! This beautiful suburban retreat is the home of my respected relatives, Mr F. and his maiden sister Miss Wilhelmina F. Here they live with old books, old furniture, and old pictures around them, with old plate upon their table, old servants in waiting, and an old cat coiled up in comfort upon their cosy hearth! A graceful air of antiquity pervades everything. The inkstand from which I write belonged to a great-grandfather; the footstool under my feet was worked by an old lady of the days of the lovely Queen Mary; and I cannot define the date of the china in that carved cabinet: all this, which would be out of place in one of the splendid palaces of our buzy citizens, is here in perfect harmony with the character of the inmates. It is such a house as naturally belongs to an old country, an old family, and an old and secluded pair.

"My uncle is an epitome of all that is worthy in man. Like most remarkable Scotsmen, he takes snuff; and to perceive his penetration and wise sagacity, one has only to look at the noble head which he carries with a hereditary loftiness. His sister is a noble old lady, and entirely devoted to him. In fact, they are all the world to each other; and the confidence with which the brother confides all his cares and sorrows to the faithful bosom of his sister, is a truly touching sight; while Miss Wilhelmina F., on her part, seldom makes an observation without winding up by a reference to 'my brother.' It is a long time since I have found anywhere so fresh and delightful an object of study as the different characteristics of this united pair. It is beautiful to watch the natural traits unfolding themselves. One has almost as much pleasure in the investigation as one has in studying the developments of childhood; and my admirable relatives are as delightfully unconscious of their own distinguishing qualities as even children could be.

"Their house is a beautiful little suburban villa, far from the noise and din of the great city. Here they spend their beautiful old age in hospitality and beneficence; beggars (for there are always beggars in England) come to the door every morning with patriarchal familiarity, and receive their dole through an opening in the door, like the ancient buttery-hatch; every morning, upon the garden paths crumbs are strewed for the robins and the sparrows, and the birds come hopping fearlessly about the old lady's feet, trusting in her gracious nature. All the borders are filled with wallflowers, the favourite plant of Miss Wilhelmina, and they seemed to me to send up a sweeter fragrance when she watered them with her delicate little engine, or pruned them with her own hand; for everything, animate and inanimate, seems to know that she is good.

"To complete this delightful picture, there is just that shade of solicitude and anxiety wanting to make it perfect. They have a nephew, this excellent couple, over whom they watch with the characteristic jealousy of age watching youth. While my admirable uncle eats his egg at breakfast, he talks of Harry;

while aunt Wilhelmina pours out the tea from her magnificent old silver teapot, she makes apologies and excuses for him. They will make him their heir, I do not doubt, for he is a handsome and prepossessing youth; and however this may be to my injury, I joyfully waive my claim; for the sight of their tender affection and beautiful solicitude is a greater boon to a student of mankind like myself than all their old hereditary hoards or patrimonial acres; and so I say, Good fortune to Harry, and let all my readers say Amen!"

We are afraid to say how difficult Agnes found it to accomplish this reading in peace; but in spite of Marian's laughter and Mrs Atheling's indignant interruptions, Agnes herself was slightly impressed by these fine sentiments and pretty sentences. She laid down the paper with an air of extreme perplexity, and could scarcely be tempted to smile. "Perhaps that is how Mr Endicott sees things," said Agnes; "perhaps he has so fine a mind—perhaps—Now, I am sure, mamma, if you had not known Miss Willsie, you would have thought it very pretty. I know you would."

"Do not speak to me, child," cried Mrs Atheling energetically. "Pretty! why, he is coming here to-night!"

And Marian clapped her hands. "Mamma will be in the next one!" cried Marian; "and he will find out that Agnes is a great author, and that we are all so anxious about Charlie. Oh, I hope he will send us a copy. What fun it would be to read about papa and his newspaper, and what everybody was doing at home here in Bellevue!"

"It would be very impertinent," said Mrs Atheling, reddening with anger; "and if anything of the kind should happen, I will never forgive Mr Foggo. You will take care to speak as little as possible to him, Marian; he is not a safe person. Pretty! Does he think he has a right to come into respectable houses and make his pretty pictures? You must be very much upon your guard, girls. I forbid you to be friendly with such a person as that!"

"But perhaps"—said Agnes.

"Perhaps—nonsense," cried Mamma indignantly; "he must not come in here, that I am resolved. Go and tell Susan we will sit in the best room to-night."

But Agnes meditated the matter anxiously—perhaps, though she did not say it—perhaps to be a great literary personage, it was necessary to "find good in everything," after the newest fashion, like Mr Endicott. Agnes was much puzzled, and somewhat discouraged, on her own account. She did not think it possible she could ever come to such a sublime and elevated view of ordinary things; she felt herself a woeful way behind Mr Endicott, and with a little eagerness looked forward to his visit. Would he justify himself—what would he say?

CHAPTER XVIII

COMPANY

The best room was not by any means so bright, so cheerful, or so kindly as the family parlour, with its family disarrangement, and the amateur paperhanging upon its walls. Before their guests arrived the girls made an effort to improve its appearance. They pulled the last beautiful bunches of the lilac to fill the little glass vases, and placed candles in the ornamental glass candlesticks upon the mantelpiece. But even a double quantity of light did not bring good cheer to this dull and solemn apartment. Had it been winter, indeed, a fire might have made a difference; but it was early summer—one of those balmy nights so sweet out of doors, which give an additional shade of gloom to dark-complexioned parlours, shutting out the moon and the stars, the night air and the dew. Agnes and Marian, fanciful and visionary, kept the door open themselves, and went wandering about the dark garden, where the summer flowers came slowly, and the last primrose was dying pale and sweet under the poplar tree. They went silently and singly, one after the other, through the garden paths, hearing, without observing, the two different footsteps which came to the front door. If they were thinking, neither of them knew or could tell what she was thinking about, and they returned to the house without a word, only knowing how much more pleasant it was to be out here in the musical and breathing darkness, than to be shut closely within the solemn enclosure of the best room.

But there, by the table where Marian had maliciously laid his paper, was the stately appearance of Mr Endicott, holding high his abstracted head, while Harry Oswald, anxious, and yet hesitating, lingered at the door, eagerly on the watch for the light step of which he had so immediate a perception when it came. Harry, who indeed had no great inducement to be much in love with himself, forgot himself altogether as his quick ear listened for the foot of Marian. Mr Endicott, on the contrary, added a loftier shape to his abstraction, by way of attracting and not expressing admiration. Unlucky Harry was in love with Marian; his intellectual cousin only aimed at making Marian in love with him.

And she came in, slightly conscious, we admit, that she was the heroine of the night, half aware of the rising rivalry, half-enlightened as to the different character of these two very different people, and of the one motive which brought them here. So a flitting changeable blush went and came upon the face of Marian. Her eyes, full of the sweet darkness and dew of the night, were dazzled by the lights, and would not look steadily at any one; yet a certain gleam of secret mischief and amusement in her face betrayed itself to Harry Oswald, though not at all to the unsuspicious American. She took her seat very sedately at the table, and busied herself with her fancy-work. Mr Endicott sat opposite, looking at her; and Harry, a moving shadow in the dim room, hovered about, sitting and standing behind her chair.

Besides these young people, Mr Atheling, Mr Foggo, and Mamma, were in the room, conversing among themselves, and taking very little notice of the other visitors. Mamma was making a little frock, upon which she bestowed unusual pains, as it seemed; for no civility of Mr Endicott could gain any answer beyond a monosyllable from the virtuous and indignant mistress of the house. He was playing with his own papers as Agnes and Marian came to the table, affectionately turning them over, and looking at the heading of the "Letter from England" with a loving eye.

"You are interested in literature, I believe?" said Mr Endicott. Agnes, Marian, and Harry, all of them glancing at him in the same moment, could not tell which he addressed; so there was a confused murmur of reply. "Not in the slightest," cried Harry Oswald, behind Marian's chair. "Oh, but Agnes is!" cried Marian; and Agnes herself, with a conscious blush, acknowledged—"Yes, indeed, very much."

"But not, I suppose, very well acquainted with the American press?" said Mr Endicott. "The bigotry of Europeans is marvellous. We read your leading papers in the States, but I have not met half-a-dozen people in England—actually not six individuals—who were in the frequent habit of seeing the Mississippi Gazette."

"We rarely see any newspapers at all," said Agnes, apologetically. "Papa has his paper in the evenings, but except now and then, when there is a review of a book in it—"

"That is the great want of English contemporary literature," interrupted Mr Endicott. "You read the review—good! but you feel that something else is wanted than mere politics—that votes and debates do not supply the wants of the age!"

"If the wants of the age were the wants of young ladies," said Harry Oswald, "what would become of my uncle and Mr Atheling? Leave things in their proper place, Endicott. Agnes and Marian want something different from newspaper literature and leading articles. Don't interfere with the girls."

"These are the slavish and confined ideas of a worn out civilisation," said the man of letters; "in my country we respect the opinions of our women, and give them full scope."

"Respect!—the old humbug!" muttered Harry behind Marian's chair. "Am I disrespectful? I choose to be judged by you."

Marian glanced over her shoulder with saucy kindness. "Don't quarrel," said Marian. No! Poor Harry was so glad of the glance, the smile, and the confidence, that he could have taken Endicott, who was the cause of it, to his very heart.

"The functions of the press," said Mr Endicott, "are unjustly limited in this country, like most other enlightened influences. In these days we have scarcely time to wait for books. It is not with us as it was in old times, when the soul lay fallow for a century, and then blossomed into its glorious epic, or drama, or song! Our audience must perceive the visible march of mind, hour by hour and day by day. We are no longer concerned about mere physical commotions, elections, or debates, or votes of the Senate. In these days we care little for the man's opinions; what we want is an advantageous medium for studying the man."

As she listened to this, Agnes Atheling held her breath, and suspended her work unawares. It sounded very imposing, indeed—to tell the truth, it sounded something like that magnificent conversation in books over which Marian and she had often marvelled. Then this simple girl believed in everybody; she was rather inclined to suppose of Mr Endicott that he was a man of very exalted mind.

"I do not quite know," said Agnes humbly, "whether it is right to tell all about great people in the newspapers, or even to put them in books. Do you think it is, Mr Endicott?"

"I think," said the American, solemnly, "that a public man, and, above all, a literary man, belongs to the world. All the exciting scenes of life come to us only that we may describe and analyse them for the advantage of others. A man of genius has no private life. Of what benefit is the keenness of his emotions if he makes no record of them? In my own career," continued the literary gentleman, "I have been sometimes annoyed by foolish objections to the notice I am in the habit of giving of friends who cross my way. Unenlightened people have complained of me, in vulgar phrase, that I 'put them in the newspapers.' How strange a misconception! for you must perceive at once that it was not with any consideration of them, but simply that my readers might see every scene I passed through, and in reality feel themselves travelling with me!"

"Oh!" Agnes made a faint and very doubtful exclamation; Harry Oswald turned on his heel, and left the room abruptly; while Marian bent very closely over her work, to conceal that she was laughing. Mr Endicott thought it was a natural youthful reverence, and gave her all due credit for her "ingenuous emotions."

"The path of genius necessarily reveals certain obscure individuals," said Mr Endicott; "they cross its light, and the poet has no choice. I present to my audience the scenes through which I travel. I introduce the passengers on the road. Is it for the sake of these passengers? No. It is that my readers may be enabled, under all circumstances, to form a just realisation of me. That is the true vocation of a poet: he ought to be in himself the highest example of everything—joy, delight, suffering, remorse, and ruin—yes, I am bold enough to say, even crime. No man should be able to suppose that he can hide himself in an indescribable region of emotion where the poet cannot follow. Shall murder be permitted to attain an experience beyond the reach of genius? No! Everything must be possessed by the poet's intuitions, for he himself is the great lesson of the world."

"Charlie," said Harry Oswald behind the door, "come in, and punch this fellow's head."

CHAPTER XIX

CONVERSATION

Charlie came in, but not to punch the head of Mr Endicott. The big boy gloomed upon the dignified American, pushed Harry Oswald aside, and brought his two grammars to the table. "I say, what do you want with me?" said Charlie; he was not at all pleased at having been disturbed.

"Nobody wanted you, Charlie,—no one ever wants you, you disagreeable boy," said Marian: "it was all Harry Oswald's fault; he thought we were too pleasant all by ourselves here."

To which complimentary saying Mr Endicott answered by a bow. He quite understood what Miss Marian meant! he was much flattered to have gained her sympathy! So Marian pleased both her admirers for once, for Harry Oswald laughed in secret triumph behind her chair.

"And you are still with Mr Bell, Harry," said Mrs Atheling, suddenly interposing. "I am very glad you like this place—and what a pleasure it must be to all your sisters! I begin to think you are quite settled now."

"I suppose it was time," said Harry the unlucky, colouring a little, but smiling more as he came out from the shadow of Marian's chair, in compliment to Marian's mother; "yes, we get on very well,—we are not overpowered with our practice; so much the better for me."

"But you ought to be more ambitious,—you ought to try to extend your practice," said Mrs Atheling, immediately falling into the tone of an adviser, in addressing one to whom everybody gave good advice.

"I might have some comfort in it, if I was a poet," said Harry; "but to kill people simply in the way of business is too much for me.—Well, uncle, it is no fault of mine. I never did any honour to my doctorship. I am as well content to throw physic to the dogs as any Macbeth in the world."

"Ay, Harry," said Mr Foggo; "but I think it is little credit to a man to avow ill inclinations, unless he has the spirit of a man to make head against them. That's my opinion—but I know you give it little weight."

"A curious study!" said Mr Endicott, reflectively. "I have watched it many times,—the most interesting conflict in the world."

But Harry, who had borne his uncle's reproof with calmness, reddened fiercely at this, and seemed about to resent it. The study of character, though it is so interesting a study, and so much pursued by superior minds, is not, as a general principle, at all liked by the objects of it. Harry Oswald, under the eye of his cousin's curious inspection, had the greatest mind in the world to knock that cousin down.

"And what do you think of our domestic politics, on the other side of the Atlantic?" asked Papa, joining the more general conversation: "a pretty set of fellows manage us in Old England here. I never take up a newspaper but there's a new job in it. If it were only for other countries, they might have a sense of shame!"

"Well, sir," said Mr Endicott, "considering all things—considering the worn-out circumstances of the old country, your oligarchy and your subserviency, I am rather disposed, on the whole, to be in favour of the government of England. So far as a limited intelligence goes, they really appear to me to get on pretty well."

"Humph!" said Mr Atheling. He was quite prepared for a dashing republican denunciation, but this cool patronage stunned the humble politician—he did not comprehend it. "However," he continued, reviving after a little, and rising into triumph, "there is principle among them yet. They cannot tolerate a man who wants the English virtue of keeping his word; no honourable man will keep office with a traitor. Winterbourne's out. There's some hope for the country when one knows that."

"And who is Winterbourne, papa?" asked Agnes, who was near her father.

Mr Atheling was startled. "Who is Lord Winterbourne, child? why, a disgraced minister—everybody knows!"

"You speak as if you were glad," said Agnes, possessed with a perfectly unreasonable pertinacity: "do you know him, papa,—has he done anything to you?"

"I!" cried Mr Atheling, "how should I know him? There! thread your needle, and don't ask ridiculous questions. Lord Winterbourne for himself is of no consequence to me."

From which everybody present understood immediately that this unknown personage was of consequence to Mr Atheling—that Papa certainly knew him, and that he had "done something" to call for so great an amount of virtuous indignation. Even Mr Endicott paused in the little account he proposed to give of Viscount Winterbourne's title and acquirements, and his own acquaintance with the Honourable George Rivers, his lordship's only son. A vision of family feuds and mysteries crossed the active mind of the American: he stopped to make a mental note of this interesting circumstance; for Mr Endicott did not disdain to embellish his "letters" now and then with a fanciful legend, and this was certainly "suggestive" in the highest degree.

"I remember," said Mrs Atheling, suddenly, "when we were first married, we went to visit an old aunt of papa's, who lived quite close to Winterbourne Hall. Do you remember old Aunt Bridget, William? We have not heard anything of her for many a day; she lived in an old house, half made of timber, and ruinous with ivy. I remember it very well; I thought it quite pretty when I was a girl."

"Ruinous! you mean beautiful with ivy, mamma," said Marian.

"No, my dear; ivy is a very troublesome thing," said Mrs Atheling, "and makes a very damp house, I assure you, though it looks pretty. This was just upon the edge of a wood, and on a hill. There was a very fine view from it; all the spires, and domes, and towers looked beautiful with the morning sun upon them. I suppose Aunt Bridget must still be living, William? I wonder why she took offence at us. What a pleasant place that would have been to take the children in summer! It was called the Old Wood Lodge, and there was a larger place near which was the Old Wood House, and the nearest house to that, I believe, was the Hall. It was a very pretty place; I remember it so well."

Agnes and Marian exchanged glances; this description was quite enough to set their young imaginations a-glow;—perhaps, for the sake of her old recollections, Mamma would like this better than the sea-side.

"Should you like to go again, mamma?" said Agnes, in a half whisper. Mamma smiled, and brightened, and shook her head.

"No, my dear, no; you must not think of such a thing—travelling is so very expensive," said Mrs Atheling; but the colour warmed and brightened on her cheek with pleasure at the thought.

"And of course there's another family of children," said Papa, in a somewhat sullen under-tone. "Aunt Bridget, when she dies, will leave the cottage to one of them. They always wanted it. Yes, to be sure,—to him that hath shall be given,—it is the way of the world."

"William, William; you forget what you say!" cried Mrs Atheling, in alarm.

"I mean no harm, Mary," said Papa, "and the words bear that meaning as well as another: it is the way of the world."

"Had I known your interest in the family, I might have brought you some information," interposed Mr Endicott. "I have a letter of introduction to Viscount Winterbourne—and saw a great deal of the Honourable George Rivers when he travelled in the States."

"I have no interest in them—not the slightest," said Mr Atheling, hastily; and Harry Oswald moved away from where he had been standing to resume his place by Marian, a proceeding which instantly distracted the attention of his cousin and rival. The girls were talking to each other of this new imaginary paradise. Harry Oswald could not explain how it was, but he began immediately with all his skill to make a ridiculous picture of the old house, which was half made of timber, and ruinous with ivy: he could not make out why he listened with such a jealous pang to the very name of this Old Wood Lodge.

CHAPTER XX

"Very strange!" said Mr Atheling—he had just laid upon the breakfast-table a letter edged with black, which had startled them all for the moment into anxiety,—"very strange!"

"What is very strange?—who is it, William?" asked Mrs Atheling, anxiously.

"Do you remember how you spoke of her last night?—only last night—my Aunt Bridget, of whom we have not heard for years? I could almost be superstitious about this," said Papa. "Poor old lady! she is gone at last."

Mrs Atheling read the letter eagerly. "And she spoke of us, then?—she was sorry. Who could have persuaded her against us, William?" said the good mother—"and wished you should attend her funeral. You will go?—surely you must go." But as she spoke, Mrs Atheling paused and considered—travelling is not so easy a matter, when people have only two hundred a-year.

"It would do her no pleasure now, Mary," said Mr Atheling, with a momentary sadness. "Poor Aunt Bridget; she was the last of all the old generation; and now it begins to be our turn."

In the mean time, however, it was time for the respectable man of business to be on his way to his office. His wife brushed his hat with gravity, thinking upon his words. The old old woman who was gone, had left no responsibility behind her; but these children!—how could the father and the mother venture to die, and leave these young ones in the unfriendly world!

Charlie had gone to his office an hour ago—other studies, heavier and more discouraging even than the grammars, lay in the big law-books of Mr Foggo's office, to be conquered by this big boy. Throughout the day he had all the miscellaneous occupations which generally fall to the lot of the youngest clerk. Charlie said nothing about it to any one, but went in at these ponderous tomes in the morning. They were frightfully tough reading, and he was not given to literature; he shook his great fist at them, his natural enemies, and went in and conquered. These studies were pure pugilism so far as Charlie was concerned: he knocked down his ponderous opponent, mastered him, stowed away all his wisdom in his own prodigious memory, and replaced him on his shelf with triumph. "Now that old fellow's done for," said Charlie—and next morning the young student "went in" at the next.

Agnes and Marian were partly in this secret, as they had been in the previous one; so these young ladies came down stairs at seven o'clock to make breakfast for Charlie. It was nine now, and the long morning began to merge into the ordinary day; but the girls arrested Mamma on the threshold of her daily business to make eager inquiry about the Aunt Bridget, of whom, the only one among all their relatives, they knew little but the name.

"My dears, this is not a time to ask me," said Mrs Atheling: "there is Susan waiting, and there is the baker and the butterman at the door. Well, then, if you must know, she was just simply an old lady, and your grandpapa's sister; and she was once governess to Miss Rivers, and they gave her the old Lodge when the young lady should have been married. They made her a present of it—at least the old lord did—and she lived there ever after. It had been once in your grandpapa's family. I do not know the rights of the story—you can ask about it some time from your papa; but Aunt Bridget took quite a dislike to us after we were married—I cannot tell you why; and since the time I went to the Old Wood Lodge to pay her a visit, when I was a bride, I have never heard a kind word from her, poor old lady, till to-day. Now, my dears, let me go; do you see the people waiting? I assure you that is all."

And that was all that could be learned about Aunt Bridget, save a few unimportant particulars gleaned from the long conversation concerning her, which the father and the mother, much moralising, fell into that night. These young people had the instinct of curiosity most healthily developed; they listened eagerly to every new particular—heard with emotion that she had once been a beauty, and incontinently wove a string of romances about the name of the aged and humble spinster; and then what a continual centre of fancy and inquiry was that Old Wood Lodge!

A few days passed, and Aunt Bridget began to fade from her temporary prominence in the household firmament. A more immediate interest possessed the mind of the family—the book was coming out! Prelusive little paragraphs in the papers, which these innocent people did not understand to be advertisements, warned the public of a new and original work of fiction by a new author, about to be brought out by Mr Burlington, and which was expected to make a sensation when it came. Even the known and visible advertisements themselves were read with a startling thrill of interest. Hope Hazlewood, a History—everybody concluded it was the most felicitous title in the world.

The book was coming out, and great was the excitement of the household heart. The book came out!—there it lay upon the table in the family parlour, six fair copies in shiny blue cloth, with its name in letters of gold. These Mr Burlington intended should be sent to influential friends: but the young author had no influential friends; so one copy was sent to Killiecrankie Lodge, to the utter amazement of Miss Willsie, and another was carefully despatched to an old friend in the country, who scarcely knew what literature was; then the family made a solemn pause, and waited. What would everybody say?

Saturday came, full of fate. They knew all the names of all those dread and magnificent guides of public opinion, the literary newspapers; and with an awed and trembling heart, the young author waited for their verdict. She was so young, however, and in reality so ignorant of what might be the real issue of this first step into the world, that Agnes had a certain pleasure in her trepidation, and, scarcely knowing what she expected, knew only that it was in the highest degree novel, amusing, and extraordinary that these sublime and lofty people should ever be tempted to notice her at all. It was still only a matter of excitement and curiosity and amusing oddness to them all. If the young adventurer had been a man, this would have been a solemn crisis, full of fate: it was even so to a woman, seeking her own independence; but Agnes Atheling was only a girl in the heart of her family, and, looking out with laughing eyes upon her fortune, smiled at fate.

It is Saturday—yes, Saturday afternoon, slowly darkening towards the twilight. Agnes and Marian at the window are eagerly looking out, Mamma glances over their bright heads with unmistakable impatience, Papa is palpably restless in his easy-chair. Here he comes on flying feet, that big messenger of fortune—crossing the whole breadth of Bellevue in two strides, with ever so many papers in his hands. "Oh, I wonder what they will say!" cries Marian, clasping her pretty fingers. Agnes, too breathless to speak, makes neither guess nor answer—and here he comes!

It is half dark, and scarcely possible to read these momentous papers. The young author presses close to the window with the uncut Athenæum. There is Papa, half-risen from his chair; there is Mamma anxiously contemplating her daughter's face; there is Marian, reading over her shoulder; and Charlie stands with his hat on in the shade, holding fast in his hand the other papers. "One at a time!" says Charlie. He knows what they are, the grim young ogre, but he will not say a word.

And Agnes begins to read aloud—reads a sentence or two, suddenly stops, laughs hurriedly. "Oh, I cannot read that—somebody else take it," cried Agnes, running a rapid eye down the page; her cheeks are tingling, her eyes overflowing, her heart beating so loud that she does not hear her own voice. And now it is Marian who presses close to the window and reads aloud. Well! after all, it is not a very astonishing paragraph; it is extremely condescending, and full of the kindest patronage; recognises many beauties—a great deal of talent; and flatteringly promises the young author that by-and-by she will do very well. The reading is received with delight and disappointment. Mrs Atheling is not quite pleased that the reviewer refuses entire perfection to Hope Hazlewood, but by-and-by even the good mother is reconciled. Who could the critic be?—innocent critic, witting nothing of the tumult of kindly and grateful feelings raised towards him in a moment! Mrs Atheling cannot help setting it down certainly that he must be some unknown friend.

The others come upon a cooled enthusiasm—nobody feels that they have said the first good word. Into the middle of this reading Susan suddenly interposes herself and the candles. What tell-tales these lights are! Papa and Mamma, both of them, look mighty dazzled and unsteady about the eyes, and Agnes's cheeks are burning crimson-deep, and she scarcely likes to look at any one. She is half ashamed in her innocence—half as much ashamed as if they had been love-letters detected and read aloud.

And then after a while they come to a grave pause, and look at each other. "I suppose, mamma, it is sure to succeed now," says Agnes, very timidly, shading her face with her hand, and glancing up under its cover; and Papa, with his voice somewhat shaken, says solemnly, "Children, Agnes's fortune has come to-night."

For it was so out of the way—so uncommon and unexpected a fortune, to their apprehension, that the father and the mother looked on with wonder and amazement, as if at something coming down, without any human interposition, clear out of the hand of Providence, and from the treasures of heaven.

Upon the Monday morning following, Mr Atheling had another letter. It was a time of great events, and the family audience were interested even about this. Papa looked startled and affected, and read it without saying a word; then it was handed to Mamma: but Mrs Atheling, more demonstrative, ran over it with a constant stream of comment and exclamation, and at last read the whole epistle aloud. It ran thus:—

"DEAR SIR,—Being intrusted by your Aunt, Miss Bridget Atheling, with the custody of her will, drawn up about a month before her death, I have now to communicate to you, with much pleasure, the particulars of the same. The will was read by me, upon the day of the funeral, in presence of the Rev. Lionel Rivers, rector of the parish; Dr Marsh, Miss Bridget's medical attendant; and Mrs Hardwicke, her niece. You are of course aware that your aunt's annuity died with her. Her property consisted of a thousand pounds in the Three per Cents, a small cottage in the village of Winterbourne, three acres of land in the hundred of Badgeley, and the Old Wood Lodge.

"Miss Bridget has bequeathed her personal property, all except the two last items, to Mrs Susannah Hardwicke, her niece—the Old Wood Lodge and the piece of land she bequeaths to you, William Atheling, being part, as she says, 'of the original property of the family.' She leaves it to you 'as a token that she had now discovered the falseness of the accusations made to her, twenty years ago, against you, and desires you to keep and to hold it, whatever attempts may be made to dislodge you, and whatever it may cost.' A copy of the will, pursuant to her own directions, will be forwarded to you in a few days.

"As an old acquaintance, I gladly congratulate you upon this legacy; but I am obliged to tell you, as a friend, that the property is not of that value which could have been desired. The land, which is of inferior quality, is let for fifteen shillings an acre, and the house, I am sorry to say, is not in very good condition, is very unlikely to find a tenant, and would cost half as much as it is worth to put it in tolerable repair—besides which, it stands directly in the way of the Hall, and was, as I understand, a gift to Miss Bridget only, with power, on the part of the Winterbourne family, to reclaim after her death. Under these circumstances, I doubt if you will be allowed to retain possession; notwithstanding, I call your attention to the emphatic words of my late respected client, to which you will doubtless give their due weight.—I am, dear sir, faithfully yours,

"FRED. R. LEWIS, Attorney."

"And what shall we do? If we were only able to keep it, William—such a thing for the children!" cried Mrs Atheling, scarcely pausing to take breath. "To think that the Old Wood Lodge should be really ours—how strange it is! But, William, who could possibly have made false accusations against you?"

"Only one man," said Mr Atheling, significantly. The girls listened with interest and astonishment. "Only one man."

"No, no, my dear—no, it could not be—," cried his wife: "you must not think so, William—it is quite impossible. Poor Aunt Bridget! and so she found out the truth at last."

"It is easy to talk," said the head of the house, looking over his letter; "very easy to leave a bequest like this, which can bring nothing but difficulty and trouble. How am I 'to keep and to hold it, at whatever cost?' The old lady must have been crazy to think of such a thing: she had much better have given it to my Lord at once without making any noise about it; for what is the use of bringing a quarrel upon me?"

"But, papa, it is the old family property," said Agnes, eagerly.

"My dear child, you know nothing about it," said Papa. "Do you think I am able to begin a lawsuit on behalf of the old family property? How were we to repair this tumble-down old house, if it had been ours on the securest holding? but to go to law about it, and it ready to crumble over our ears, is rather too much for the credit of the family. No, no; nonsense, children; you must not think of it for a moment; and you, Mary, surely you must see what folly it is."

But Mamma would not see any folly in the matter; her feminine spirit was roused, and her maternal pride. "You may depend upon it, Aunt Bridget had some motive," said Mrs Atheling, with a little excitement, "and real property, William, would be such a great thing for the children. Money might be lost or spent; but property—land and a house. My dear, you ought to consider how important it is for the children's sake."

Mr Atheling shook his head. "You are unreasonable," said the family father, who knew very well that he was pretty sure to yield to them, reason or no—"as unreasonable as you can be. Do you suppose I am a landed proprietor, with that old crazy Lodge, and forty-five shillings a-year? Mary, Mary, you ought to know better. We could not repair it, I tell you, and we could not furnish it; and nobody would rent it from us. We should gain nothing but an enemy, and that is no great advantage for the children. I do not remember that Aunt Bridget was ever remarkable for good sense; and it was no such great thing, after all, to transfer her family quarrel to me."

"Oh, papa, the old family property, and the beautiful old house in the country, where we could go and live in the summer!" said Marian. "Agnes is to be rich—Agnes would be sure to want to go somewhere in the country. We could do all the repairs ourselves—and mamma likes the place. Papa, papa, you will never have the heart to let other people have it. I think I can see the place; we could all go down when Agnes comes to her fortune—and the country would be so good for Bell and Beau."

This, perhaps, was the most irresistible of arguments. The eyes of the father and mother fell simultaneously upon the twin babies. They were healthy imps as ever did credit to a suburban atmosphere—yet somehow both Papa and Mamma fancied that Bell and Beau looked pale to-day.

"It is ten minutes past nine," exclaimed Mr Atheling, solemnly rising from the table. "I have not been so late for years—see what your nonsense has brought me to. Now, Mary, think it over reasonably, and I will hear all that you have to say to-night."

So Mr Atheling hastened to his desk to turn over this all-important matter as he walked and as he laboured. The Old Wood Lodge obliterated to the good man's vision the very folios of his daily companionship—old feelings, old incidents, old resentment and pugnacity, awoke again in his kindly but not altogether patient and self-commanded breast. The delight of being able to leave something—a certain patrimonial inheritance—to his son after him, gradually took possession of his mind and fancy; and the pleasant dignity of a house in the country—the happy power of sending off his wife and his children to the sweet air of his native place—won upon him gradually before he was aware. By slow degrees Mr Atheling brought himself to believe that it would be dishonourable to give up this relic of the family belongings, and make void the will of the dead. The Old Wood Lodge brightened before him into a very bower for his fair girls. The last poor remnant of his yeoman grandfather's little farm became a hereditary and romantic nucleus, which some other Atheling might yet make into a great estate. "There is Charlie—he will not always be a lawyer's clerk, that boy!" said his father to himself, with involuntary pride; and then he muttered under his breath, "and to give it up to him!"

Under this formidable conspiracy of emotions, the excellent Mr Atheling had no chance: old dislike, pungent and prevailing, though no one knew exactly its object or its cause, and present pride and tenderness still more strong and earnest, moved him beyond his power of resistance. There was no occasion for the attack, scientifically planned, which was to have been made upon him in the evening. If they had been meditating at home all day upon this delightful bit of romance in their own family history, and going over, with joy and enthusiasm, every room and closet in Miss Bridget's old house, Papa had been no less busy at the office. The uncertain tenor of a lawsuit had no longer any place in the good man's memory, and the equivocal advantage of the ruinous old house oppressed him no longer. He began to think, by an amiable and agreeable sophistry, self-delusive, that it was his sacred duty to carry out the wishes of the dead.

CHAPTER XXI

Steadily and laboriously these early summer days trudged on with Charlie, bringing no romantic visions nor dreams of brilliant fortune to tempt the imagination of the big boy. How his future looked to him no one knew. Charlie's aspirations—if he had any—dwelt private and secure within his own capacious breast. He was not dazzled by his sudden heirship of the Old Wood Lodge; he was not much disturbed by the growing fame of his sister; those sweet May mornings did not tempt him to the long ramble through the fields, which Agnes and Marian did their best to persuade him to. Charlie was not insensible to the exhilarating morning breeze, the greensward under foot, and the glory of those great thorn-hedges, white with the blossoms of the May—he was by no means a stoic either, as regarded his own ease and leisure, to which inferior considerations this stout youth attached their due importance; but still it remained absolute with Charlie, his own unfailing answer to all temptations—he had "something else to do!"

And his ordinary day's work was not of a very elevating character; he might have kept to that for years without acquiring much knowledge of his profession; and though he still was resolute to occupy no sham position, and determined that neither mother nor sisters should make sacrifices for him, Charlie felt no hesitation in making a brief and forcible statement to Mr Foggo on the subject. Mr Foggo listened with a pleased and gracious ear. "I'm not going to be a copying-clerk all my life," said Charlie. He was not much over seventeen; he was not remarkably well educated; he was a poor man's son, without connection, patronage, or influence. Notwithstanding, the acute old Scotsman looked at Charlie, lifting up the furrows of his brow, and pressing down his formidable upper-lip. The critical old lawyer smiled, but believed him. There was no possibility of questioning that obstinate big boy.

So Mr Foggo (acknowledged to be the most influential of chief clerks, and supposed to be a partner in the firm) made interest on behalf of Charlie, that he might have access, before business hours, to the law library of the house. The firm laughed, and gave permission graciously. The firm joked with its manager upon his credulity: a boy of seventeen coming at seven o'clock to voluntary study—and to take in a Scotsman—old Foggo! The firm grew perfectly jolly over this capital joke. Old Foggo smiled too, grimly, knowing better; and Charlie accordingly began his career.

It was not a very dazzling beginning. At seven o'clock the office was being dusted; in winter, at that hour, the fires were not alight, and extremely cross was the respectable matron who had charge of the same. Charlie stumbled over pails and brushes; dusters descended—unintentionally—upon his devoted head; he was pursued into every corner by his indefatigable enemy, and had to fly before her big broom with his big folio in his arms. But few people have pertinacity enough to maintain a perfectly unprofitable and fruitless warfare. Mrs Laundress, a humble prophetic symbol of that other virago, Fate, gave in to Charlie. He sat triumphant upon his high stool, no longer incommoded by dusters. While the moted sunbeams came dancing in through the dusty office window, throwing stray glances on his thick hair, and on the ponderous page before him, Charlie had a good round with his enemy, and got him down. The big boy plundered the big books with silent satisfaction, arranged his spoil on the secret shelves and pigeon-holes of that big brain of his, all ready and in trim for using; made his own comments on the whole complicated concern, and, with his whole mind bent on what was before him, mastered that, and thought of nothing else. Let nobody suppose he had the delight of a student in these strange and unattractive studies, or regarded with any degree of affectionateness the library of the House. Charlie looked at these volumes standing in dim rows, within their wired case, as Captain Bobadil might have looked at the army whom—one down and another come on—he meant to demolish, man by man.

When he came to a knotty point, more hard than usual, the lad felt a stir of lively pleasure: he scorned a contemptible opponent, this stout young fighter, and gloried in a conquest which proved him, by stress and strain of all his healthful faculties, the better man. If they had been easy, Charlie would scarcely have cared for them. Certainly, mere literature, even were it as attractive as Peter Simple, could never have tempted him to the office at seven o'clock. Charlie stood by himself, like some primitive and original champion, secretly hammering out the armour which he was to wear in the field, and taking delight in the accomplishment of gyve and breastplate and morion, all proved and tested steel. Through the day he went about all his common businesses as sturdily and steadily as if his best ambition was to be a copying-clerk. If any one spoke of ambition, Charlie said "Stuff!" and no one ever heard a word of his own anticipations; but on he went, his foot ringing clear upon the pavement, his obstinate purpose holding as sure as if it were written on a rock. While all the household stirred and fluttered with the new tide of imaginative life which brightened upon it in all these gleams of the future, Charlie held stoutly on, pursuing his own straightforward and unattractive path. With his own kind of sympathy he eked out the pleasure of the family, and no one of them ever felt a lack in him; but nothing yet which had happened to the household in the slightest degree disturbed Charlie from his own bold, distinct, undemonstrative, and self-directed way.

CHAPTER XXII

ANOTHER EVENT

We will not attempt to describe the excitement, astonishment, and confusion produced in the house of the Athelings by the next communication received from Mr Burlington. It came at night, so that every one had the benefit, and its object was to announce the astounding and unexampled news of A Second Edition!

The letter dropped from Agnes's amazed fingers; Papa actually let fall his newspaper; and Charlie, disturbed at his grammar, rolled back the heavy waves of his brow, and laughed to himself. As for Mamma and Marian, each of them read the letter carefully over. There was no mistake about it—Hope Hazelwood was nearly out of print. True, Mr Burlington confessed that this first edition had been a small one, but the good taste of the public demanded a second; and the polite publisher begged to have an interview with Miss Atheling, to know whether she would choose to add or revise anything in the successful book.

Upon this there ensued a consultation. Mrs Atheling was doubtful as to the proprieties of the case; Papa was of opinion that the easiest and simplest plan was, that the girls should call; but Mamma, who was something of a timid nature, and withal a little punctilious, hesitated, and did not quite see which was best. Bellevue, doubtless, was very far out of the way, and the house, though so good a house, was not "like what Mr Burlington must have been accustomed to." The good mother was a long time making up her mind; but at last decided, with some perturbation, on the suggestion of Mr Atheling. "Yes, you can put on your muslin dresses; it is quite warm enough for them, and they always look well; and you must see, Marian, that your collars and sleeves are very nice, and your new bonnets. Yes, my dears, as there are two of you, I think you may call."

The morning came; and by this time it was the end of June, almost midsummer weather. Mrs Atheling herself, with the most anxious care, superintended the dressing of her daughters. They were dressed with the most perfect simplicity; and nobody could have supposed, to see the result, that any such elaborate overlooking had been bestowed upon their toilette. They were dressed well, in so far that their simple habiliments made no pretension above the plain pretty inexpensive reality. They were not intensely fashionable, like Mrs Tavistock's niece, who was a regular Islingtonian "swell" (if that most felicitous of epithets can be applied to anything feminine), and reminded everybody who saw her of work-rooms and dressmakers and plates of the fashions. Agnes and Marian, a hundred times plainer, were just so many times the better dressed. They were not quite skilled in the art of gloves—a difficult branch of costume, grievously embarrassing to those good girls, who had not much above a pair in three months, and were constrained to select thrifty colours; but otherwise Mrs Atheling herself was content with their appearance as they passed along Bellevue, brightening the sunny quiet road with their light figures and their bright eyes. They had a little awe upon them—that little shade of sweet embarrassment and expectation which gives one of its greatest charms to youth. They were talking over what they were to say, and marvelling how Mr Burlington would receive them; their young footsteps chiming as lightly as any music to her tender ear—their young voices sweeter than the singing of the birds, their bright looks more pleasant than the sunshine—it is not to be wondered at if the little street looked somewhat dim and shady to Mrs Atheling when these two young figures had passed out of it, and the mother stood alone at the window, looking at nothing better than the low brick-walls and closed doors of Laurel House and Green View.

And so they went away through the din and tumult of the great London, with their own bright young universe surrounding them, and their own sweet current of thought and emotion running as pure as if they had been passing through the sweetest fields of Arcadia. They had no eyes for impertinent gazers, if such things were in their way. Twenty stout footmen at their back could not have defended them so completely as did their own innocence and security. We confess they did not even shrink, with a proper sentimental horror, from all the din and all the commotion of this noonday Babylon; they liked their rapid glance at the wonderful shop-windows; they brightened more and more as their course lay along the gayest and most cheerful streets. It was pleasant to look at the maze of carriages, pleasant to see the throngs of people, exhilarating to be drawn along in this bright flood-tide and current of the world. But they grew a little nervous as they approached the house of Mr Burlington—a little more irregular in their pace, lingering and hastening as timidity or eagerness got the upper hand—and a great deal more silent, being fully occupied with anticipations of, and preparations for, this momentous interview. What should Agnes—what would Mr Burlington say?

This silence and shyness visibly increased as they came to the very scene and presence of the redoubtable publisher—where Agnes called the small attendant clerk in the outer office "Sir" and deferentially asked for Mr Burlington. When they had waited there for a few minutes, they were shown into a matted parlour containing a writing-table and a coal-scuttle, and three chairs. Mr Burlington would be disengaged in a few minutes, the little clerk informed them, as he solemnly displaced two of the chairs, an intimation that they were to sit down. They sat down accordingly, with the most matter-of-course obedience, and held their breath as they listened for the coming steps of Mr Burlington. But the minutes passed, and Mr Burlington did not come. They began to look round with extreme interest and curiosity, augmented all the more by their awe. There was nothing in the least interesting in this bare little apartment, but their young imaginations could make a great deal out of nothing. At Mr Burlington's door stood a carriage, with a grand powdered coachman on the box, and the most superb of flunkies gracefully lounging before the door. No doubt Mr Burlington was engaged with the owner of all this splendour. Immediately they ran over all the great names they could remember, forgetting for the moment that authors, even of the greatest, are not much given, as a general principle, to gilded coaches and flunkies of renown. Who could it be?

When they were in the very height of their guessing, the door suddenly opened. They both rose with a start; but it was only the clerk, who asked them to follow him to the presence of Mr Burlington. They went noiselessly along the long matted passage after their conductor, who was not much of a Ganymede. At the very end, a door stood open, and there were two figures half visible between them and a big round-headed window, full of somewhat pale and cloudy sky. These two people turned round, as some faint sound of the footsteps of Ganymede struck aside from the matting. "Oh, what a lovely creature!—what a beautiful girl! Now I do hope that is the one!" cried, most audibly, a feminine voice. Marian, knowing by instinct that she was meant, shrank back grievously discomfited. Even Agnes was somewhat dismayed by such a preface to their interview; but Ganymede was a trained creature, and much above the weakness of a smile or hesitation—he pressed on unmoved, and hurried them into the presence and the sanctum of Mr Burlington. They came into the full light of the big window, shy, timid, and graceful, having very little self-possession to boast of, their hearts beating, their colour rising—and for the moment it was scarcely possible to distinguish which was the beautiful sister; for Agnes was very near as pretty as Marian in the glow and agitation of her heart.

CHAPTER XXIII

A NEW FRIEND

The big window very nearly filled up the whole room. The little place had once been the inmost heart of a long suite of apartments when this was a fashionable house—now it was an odd little nook of seclusion, with panelled walls, painted of so light a colour as to look almost white in the great overflow of daylight; and what had looked like a pale array of clouds in the window at a little distance, made itself out now to be various blocks and projections of white-washed wall pressing very close on every side, and leaving only in the upper half-circle a clear bit of real clouds and unmistakable sky. The room had a little table, a very few chairs, and the minutest and most antique of Turkey carpets laid over the matting. The walls were very high; there was not even a familiar coal-scuttle to lessen the solemnity of the publisher's retreat and sanctuary; and Mr Burlington was not alone.

And even the inexperienced eyes of Agnes and Marian were not slow to understand that the lady who stood by Mr Burlington's little table was a genuine fine lady, one of that marvellous and unknown species which flourishes in novels, but never had been visible in such a humble hemisphere as the world of Bellevue. She was young still, but had been younger, and she remained rich in that sweetest of all mere external beauties, the splendid English complexion, that lovely bloom and fairness, which is by no means confined to the flush of youth. She looked beautiful by favour of these natural roses and lilies, but she was not beautiful in reality from any other cause. She was lively, good-natured, and exuberant to an extent which amazed these shy young creatures, brought up under the quiet shadow of propriety, and accustomed to the genteel deportment of Bellevue. They, in their simple girlish dress, in their blushes, diffidence, and hesitation—and she, accustomed to see everything yielding to her pretty caprices, arbitrary, coquettish, irresistible, half a spoiled child and half a woman of the world—they stood together, in the broad white light of that big window, like people born in different planets. They could scarcely form the slightest conception of each other. Nature itself had made difference enough; but how is it possible to estimate the astonishing difference between Mayfair and Bellevue?

"Pray introduce me, Mr Burlington; oh pray introduce me!" cried this pretty vision before Mr Burlington himself had done more than bow to his shy young visitors. "I am delighted to know the author of Hope Hazlewood! charmed to be acquainted with Miss Atheling! My dear child, how is it possible, at your age, to know so much of the world?"

"It is my sister," said Marian very shyly, almost under her breath. Marian was much disturbed by this mistake of identity; it had never occurred to her before that any one could possibly be at a loss for the real Miss Atheling. The younger sister was somewhat indignant at so strange a mistake.

"Now that is right! that is poetic justice! that is a proper distribution of gifts!" said the lady, clasping her hands with a pretty gesture of approval. "If you will not introduce me, I shall be compelled to do it myself, Mr Burlington: Mrs Edgerley. I am charmed to be the first to make your acquaintance; we were all dying to know the author of Hope Hazlewood. What a charming book it is! I say there has been nothing like it since Ellen Fullarton, and dear Theodosia herself entirely agrees with me. You are staying in town? Oh I am delighted! You must let me see a great deal of you, you must indeed; and I shall be charmed to introduce you to Lady Theodosia, whose sweet books every one loves. Pray, Mr Burlington, have you any very great secrets to say to these young ladies, for I want so much to persuade them to come with me?"

"I shall not detain Miss Atheling," said the publisher, with a bow, and the ghost of a smile: "we will bring out the second edition in a week or two; a very pleasant task, I assure you, and one which repays us for our anxiety. Now, how about a preface? I shall be delighted to attend to your wishes."

But Agnes, who had thought so much about him beforehand, had been too much occupied hitherto to do more than glance at Mr Burlington. She scarcely looked up now, when every one was looking at her, but said, very low and with embarrassment, that she did not think she had any wishes—that she left it entirely to Mr Burlington—he must know best.

"Then we shall have no preface?" said Mr Burlington, deferentially.

"No," said Agnes, faltering a little, and glancing up to see if he approved; "for indeed I do not think I have anything to say."

"Oh that is what a preface is made for," cried the pretty Mrs Edgerley. "You dear innocent child, do you never speak except when you have something to say? Delightful! charming! I shall not venture to introduce you to Lady Theodosia; if she but knew, how she would envy me! You must come home with me to luncheon—you positively must; for I am quite sure Mr Burlington has not another word to say."

The two girls drew back a little, and exchanged glances. "Indeed you are very good, but we must go home," said Agnes, not very well aware what she was saying.

"No, you must come with me—you must positively; I should break my heart," said their new acquaintance, with a pretty affectation of caprice and despotism altogether new to the astonished girls. "Oh, I assure you no one resists me. Your mamma will not have a word to say if you tell her it is Mrs Edgerley. Good morning, Mr Burlington; how fortunate I was to call to-day!"

So saying, this lady of magic swept out, rustling through the long matted passages, and carrying her captives, half delighted, half afraid, in her train. They were too shy by far to make a pause and a commotion by resisting; they had nothing of the self-possession of the trained young ladies of society. The natural impulse of doing what they were told was very strong upon them, and before they were half aware, or had time to consider, they were shut into the carriage by the sublime flunky, and drove off into those dazzling and undiscovered regions, as strange to them as Lapland or Siberia, where dwells The World. Agnes was placed by the side of the enchantress; Marian sat shyly opposite, rather more afraid of Mrs Edgerley's admiring glance than she had ever been before of the gaze of strangers. It seemed like witchcraft and sudden magic—half-an-hour ago sitting in the little waiting-room, looking out upon the fairy chariot, and now rolling along in its perfumy and warm enclosure over the aristocratic stones of St James's. The girls were bewildered with their marvellous position, and could not make it out, while into their perplexity stole an occasional thought of what Mamma would say, and how very anxious she would grow if they did not get soon home.

Mrs Edgerley in the meanwhile ran on with a flutter of talk and enthusiasm, pretty gestures, and rapid inquiries, so close and constant that there was little room for answer and none for comment. And then, long before they could be at their ease in the carriage, it drew up, making a magnificent commotion, before a door which opened immediately to admit the mistress of the house. Agnes and Marian followed her humbly as she hastened up-stairs. They were bewildered with the long suite of lofty apartments through which their conductress hurried, scarcely aware, they supposed, that they, not knowing what else to do, followed where she led, till they came at last to a pretty boudoir, furnished, as they both described it unanimously, "like the Arabian Nights!" Here Mrs Edgerley found some letters, the object, as it seemed, of her search, and good-naturedly paused, with her correspondence in her hand, to point out to them the Park, which could be seen from the window, and the books upon the tables. Then she left them, looking at each other doubtfully, and half afraid to remain. "Oh, Agnes, what will mamma say?" whispered Marian. All their innocent lives, until this day, they had never made a visit to any one without the permission or sanction of Mamma.

"We could not help it," said Agnes. That was very true; so with a relieved conscience, but very shyly, they turned over the pretty picture-books, the pretty nicknacks, all the elegant nothings of Mrs Edgerley's pretty bower. Good Mrs Atheling could very seldom be tempted to buy anything that was not useful, and there was scarcely a single article in the whole house at home which was not good for something. This being the case, it is easy to conceive with what perverse youthful delight the girls contemplated the hosts of pretty things around, which were of no use whatever, nor good for anything in the world. It gave them an idea of exuberance, of magnificence, of prodigality, more than the substantial magnitude of the great house or the handsome equipage. Besides, they were alone for the moment, and so much less embarrassed, and the rose-coloured atmosphere charmed them all the more that they were quite unaccustomed to it. Yet they spoke to each other in whispers as they peeped into the sunny Park, all bright and green in the sunshine, and marvelled much what Mamma would say, and how they should get home.

When Mrs Edgerley returned to them, they were stooping over the table together, looking over some of the most splendid of the "illustrated editions" of this age of sumptuous bookmaking. When they saw their patroness they started, and drew a little apart from each other. She came towards them through the great drawing-room, radiant and rustling, and they looked at her with shy admiration. They were by no means sure of their own position, but their new acquaintance certainly was the kindest and most delightful of all sudden friends.

"Do you forgive me for leaving you?" said Mrs Edgerley, holding out both her pretty hands; "but now we must not wait here any longer, but go to luncheon, where we shall be all by ourselves, quite a snug little party; and now, you dear child, come and tell me everything about it. What was it that first made you think of writing that charming book?"

Mrs Edgerley had drawn Agnes's arm within her own, a little to the discomposure of the shy young genius, and, followed closely by Marian, led them down stairs. Agnes made no answer in her confusion. Then they came to a pretty apartment on the lower floor, with a broad window looking out to the Park. The table was near the window; the pretty scene outside belonged to the little group within, as they placed themselves at the table, and the room itself was green and cool and pleasant, not at all splendid, lined with books, and luxurious with easy-chairs. There was a simple vase upon the table, full of roses, but there was no profusion of prettinesses here.

"This is my own study; I bring every one to see it. Is it not a charming little room?" said Mrs Edgerley (it would have contained both the parlours and the two best bedrooms of Number Ten, Bellevue); "but now I am quite dying to hear—really, how did it come into your head to write that delightful book?"

"Indeed I do not know," said Agnes, smiling and blushing. It seemed perfectly natural that the book should have made so mighty a sensation, and yet it was rather embarrassing, after all.

"I think because she could not help it," said Marian shyly, her beautiful face lighting up as she spoke with a sweet suffusion of colour. Their hearts were beginning to open to the kindness of their new friend.

"And you are so pleased and so proud of your sister—I am sure you are—it is positively delightful," said Mrs Edgerley. "Now tell me, were you not quite heartbroken when you finished it—such a delightful interest one feels in one's characters—such an object it is to live for, is it not? The first week after my first work was finished I was triste beyond description. I am sure you must have been quite miserable when you were obliged to come to an end."

The sisters glanced at each other rather doubtfully across the table. Everybody else seemed to have feelings so much more elevated than they—for they both remembered with a pang of shame that Agnes had actually been glad and jubilant when this first great work was done.

"And such a sweet heroine—such a charming character!" said Mrs Edgerley. "Ah, I perceive you have taken your sister for your model, and now I shall always feel sure that she is Hope Hazlewood; but at your age I cannot conceive where you got so much knowledge of the world. Do you go out a great deal? do you see a great many people? But indeed, to tell the truth," said Mrs Edgerley, with a pretty laugh, "I do believe you have no right to see any one yet. You ought to be in the schoolroom, young creatures like you. Are you both out?"

This was an extremely puzzling question, and some answer was necessary this time. The girls again looked at each other, blushing over neck and brow. In their simple honesty they thought themselves bound to make a statement of their true condition—what Miss Willsie would have called "their rank in life."

"We see very few people. In our circumstances people do not speak about coming out," said Agnes, hesitating and doubtful—the young author had no great gift of elegant expression. But in fact Mrs Edgerley did not care in the slightest degree about their "circumstances." She was a hundred times more indifferent on that subject than any genteel and respectable matron in all Bellevue.

"Oh then, that is so much better," said Mrs Edgerley, "for I see you must have been observing character all your life. It is, after all, the most delightful study; but such an eye for individuality! and so young! I declare I shall be quite afraid to make friends with you."

"Indeed, I do not know at all about character," said Agnes hurriedly, as with her pretty little ringing laugh, Mrs Edgerley broke off in a pretty affected trepidation; but their patroness shook her hand at her, and turned away in a graceful little terror.

"I am sure she must be the most dreadful critic, and keep you quite in awe of her," said their new friend, turning to Marian. "But now pray tell me your names. I have such an interest in knowing every one's Christian name; there is so much character in them. I do think that is the real advantage of a title. There is dear Lady Theodosia, for instance: suppose her family had been commoners, and she had been called Miss Piper! Frightful! odious! almost enough to make one do some harm to oneself, or get married. And now tell me what are your names?"

"My sister is Agnes, and I am Marian," said the younger. Now we are obliged to confess that by this time, though Mrs Edgerley answered with the sweetest and most affectionate of smiles and a glance of real admiration, she began to feel the novelty wear off, and flagged a little in her sudden enthusiasm. It was clear to her young visitors that she did not at all attend to the answer, despite the interest with which she had asked the question. A shade of weariness, half involuntary, half of will and purpose, came over her face. She rushed away immediately upon another subject; asked another question with great concern, and was completely indifferent to the answer. The girls were not used to this phenomenon, and did not understand it; but at last, after hesitating and doubting, and consulting each other by glances, Agnes made a shy movement of departure, and said Mamma would be anxious, and they should have to go away.

"The carriage is at the door, I believe," said Mrs Edgerley, with her sweet smile; "for of course you must let me send you home—positively you must, my love. You are a great author, but you are a young lady, and your sister is much too pretty to walk about alone. Delighted to have seen you both! Oh, I shall write to you very soon; do not fear. Everybody wants to make your acquaintance. I shall be besieged for introductions. You are engaged to me for Thursday next week, remember! I never forgive any one who disappoints me. Good-by! Adieu! I am charmed to have met you both."

While this valedictory address was being said, the girls were slowly making progress to the door; then they were ushered out solemnly to the carriage which waited for them. They obeyed their fate in their going as they did in their coming. They could not help themselves; and with mingled fright, agitation, and pleasure, were once more shut up by that superbest of flunkies, but drove off at a slow pace, retarded by the intense bewilderment of the magnificent coachman as to the locality of Bellevue.

CHAPTER XXIV

GOING HOME

Driving slowly along while the coachman ruminated, Agnes and Marian, in awe and astonishment, looked in each other's faces—then they put up their hands simultaneously to their faces, which were a little heated with the extreme confusion, embarrassment, and wonder of the last two hours—lastly, they both fell into a little outburst of low and somewhat tremulous laughter—laughing in a whisper, if that is possible—and laughing, not because they were very merry, but because, in their extreme amazement, no other expression of their sentiments occurred to them. Were they two enchanted princesses? and had they been in fairyland?

"Oh Agnes!" exclaimed Marian under her breath, "what will mamma say?"

"I do not think mamma can be angry," said Agnes, who had gained some courage, "for I am sure we could not help ourselves. What could we do?—but when they see us coming home like this—oh May!"

There was another pause. "I wonder very much what she has written. We have never heard of her," said Marian, "and yet I suppose she must be quite a great author. How respectful Mr Burlington was! I am afraid it will not be good for you, Agnes, that we live so much out of the world—you ought to know people's names at least."

Agnes did not dispute this advantage. "But I don't quite think she can be a great author," said the young genius, looking somewhat puzzled, "though I am sure she was very kind—how kind she was, Marian! And do you think she really wants us to go on Thursday? Oh, I wonder what mamma will say!"

As this was the burden of the whole conversation, constantly recurring, as every new phase of the question was discussed, the conversation itself was not quite adapted for formal record. While it proceeded, the magnificent coachman blundered towards the unknown regions of Islington, much marvelling, in his lofty and elevated intelligence, what sort of people his mistress's new acquaintants could be. They reached Bellevue at last by a grievous roundabout. What a sound and commotion they made in this quiet place, where a doctor's brougham was the most fashionable of equipages, and a pair of horses an unknown glory! The dash of that magnificent drawing-up startled the whole neighbourhood, and the population of Laurel House and Buena Vista flew to their bedroom windows when the big footman made that prodigious assault upon the knocker of Number Ten. Then came the noise of letting down the steps and opening the carriage door; then the girls alighted, almost as timid as Susan, who stood scared and terror-stricken within the door; and then Agnes, in sudden temerity, but with a degree of respectfulness, offered, to the acceptance of the footman, a precious golden half-sovereign, intrusted to her by her mother this morning, in case they should want anything. Poor Mrs Atheling, sitting petrified in her husband's easy-chair, did not know how the coin was being disposed of. They came in—the humble door was closed—they stood again in the close little hall, with its pegs and its painted oil-cloth—what a difference!—while the fairy coach and the magical bay-horses, the solemn coachman and the superb flunky, drove back into the world again with a splendid commotion, which deafened the ears and fluttered the heart of all Bellevue.

"My dears, where have you been? What have you been doing, girls? Was that Mr Burlington's carriage? Have you seen any one? Where have you been?" asked Mrs Atheling, while Agnes cried eagerly, "Mamma, you are not to be angry!" and Marian answered, "Oh, mamma! we have been in fairyland!"

And then they sat down upon the old hair-cloth sofa beside the family table, upon which, its sole ornaments, stood Mrs Atheling's full work-basket, and some old toys of Bell's and Beau's; and thus, sometimes speaking together, sometimes interrupting each other, with numberless corrections on the part of Marian and supplementary remarks from Agnes, they told their astonishing story. They had leisure now to enjoy all they had seen and heard when they were safe in their own house, and reporting it all to Mamma. They described everything, remembered everything, went over every word and gesture of Mrs Edgerley, from her first appearance in Mr Burlington's room until their parting with her; and Marian faithfully recorded all her compliments to Hope Hazlewood, and Agnes her admiration of Marian. It was the prettiest scene in the world to see them both, flushed and animated, breaking in, each upon the other's narrative, contradicting each other, after a fashion; remonstrating "Oh Agnes!" explaining, and adding description to description; while the mother sat before them in her easy-chair, sometimes quietly wiping her eyes, sometimes interfering or commanding, "One at a time, my dears," and all the time thinking to herself that the honours that were paid to "girls like these!" were no such wonder after all. And indeed Mrs Atheling would not be sufficiently amazed at all this grand and wonderful story. She was extremely touched and affected by the kindness of Mrs Edgerley, and dazzled with the prospect of all the great people who were waiting with so much anxiety to make acquaintance with the author of Hope Hazlewood, but she was by no means properly surprised.

"My dears, I foresaw how it would be," said Mrs Atheling with her simple wisdom. "I knew quite well all this must happen, Agnes. I have not read about famous people for nothing, though I never said much about it. To be sure, my dear, I knew people would appreciate you—it is quite natural—it is quite proper, my dear child! I know they will never make you forget what is right, and your duty, let them flatter as they will!"

Mrs Atheling said this with a little effusion, and with wet eyes. Agnes hung her head, blushed very deeply, grew extremely grave for a moment, but concluded by glancing up suddenly again with a little overflow of laughter. In the midst of all, she could not help recollecting how perfectly ridiculous it was to make all this commotion about her. "Me!" said Agnes with a start; "they will find me out directly—they must, mamma. You know I cannot talk or do anything; and indeed everybody that knew me would laugh to think of people seeing anything in me!"

Now this was perfectly true, though the mother and the sister, for the moment, were not quite inclined to sanction it. Agnes was neither brilliant nor remarkable, though she had genius, and was, at twenty and a half, a successful author in her way. As she woke from her first awe and amazement, Agnes began to find out the ludicrous side of her new fame. It was all very well to like the book; there was some reason in that, the young author admitted candidly; but surely those people must expect something very different from the reality, who were about to besiege Mrs Edgerley for introductions to "me!"

However, it was very easy to forget this part of the subject in returning to the dawn of social patronage, and in anticipating the invitation they had received. Mrs Atheling, too, was somewhat disappointed that they had made so little acquaintance with Mr Burlington, and could scarcely even describe him, how he looked or what he said. Mr Burlington had quite gone down in the estimation of the girls. His lady client had entirely eclipsed, overshadowed, and taken the glory out of the publisher. The talk was all of Mrs Edgerley, her beauty, her kindness, her great house, her approaching party. They began already to be agitated about this, remembering with terror the important article of dress, and the simple nature and small variety of their united wardrobe. Before they had been an hour at home, Miss Willsie made an abrupt and sudden visit from Killiecrankie Lodge, to ascertain all about the extraordinary apparition of the carriage, and to find out where the girls had been; and it did not lessen their own excitement to discover the extent of the commotion which they had caused in Bellevue. The only drawback was, that a second telling of the story was not practicable for the instruction and advantage of Papa—for, for the first time in a dozen years, Mr Atheling, all by himself, and solitary, was away from home.

Papa was away from home. That very day on which the charmed light of society first shone upon his girls, Papa, acting under the instructions of a family conference, hurried at railway speed to the important neighbourhood of the Old Wood Lodge. He was to be gone three days, and during that time his household constituents expected an entire settlement of the doubtful and difficult question which concerned their inheritance. Charlie, perhaps, might have some hesitation on the subject, but all the rest of the family believed devoutly in the infallible wisdom and prowess of Papa.

Yet it was rather disappointing that he should be absent at such a crisis as this, when there was so much to tell him. They had to wonder every day what he would think of the adventure of Agnes and Marian, and how contemplate their entrance into the world; and great was the family satisfaction at the day and hour of his return. Fortunately it was evening; the family tea-table was spread with unusual care, and the best china shone and glistened in the sunshine, as Agnes, Marian, and Charlie set out for the railway to meet their father. They went along together very happily, excited by the expectation of all there was to tell, and all there was to hear. The suburban roads were full of leisurely people, gossiping, or meditating like old Isaac at eventide, with a breath of the fields before them, and the big boom of the great city filling all the air behind. The sun slanted over the homely but pleasant scene, making a glorious tissue of the rising smoke, and brightening the dusky branches of the wayside trees. "If we could but live in the country!" said Agnes, pausing, and turning round to trace the long sun-bright line of road, falling off into that imaginary Arcadia, or rather into the horizon, with its verge of sunny and dewy fields. The dew falls upon the daisies even in the vicinity of Islington—let students of natural history bear this significant fact in mind.

"Stuff! the train's in," said Charlie, dragging along his half-reluctant sister, who, quite proud of his bigness and manly stature, had taken his arm. "Charlie, don't make such strides—who do you think can keep up with you?" said Marian. Charlie laughed with the natural triumphant malice of a younger brother; he was perfectly indifferent to the fact that one of them was a genius and the other a beauty; but he liked to claim a certain manly and protective superiority over "the girls."

To the great triumph, however, of these victims of Charlie's obstinate will, the train was not in, and they had to walk about upon the platform for full five minutes, pulling (figuratively) his big red ear, and waiting for the exemplary second-class passenger, who was scrupulous to travel by that golden mean of respectability, and would on no account have put up with a parliamentary train. Happy Papa, it was better than Mrs Edgerley's magnificent pair of bays pawing in superb impatience the plebeian causeway. He caught a glimpse of three eager faces as he looked out of his little window—two pretty figures springing forward, one big one holding back, and remonstrating. "Why, you'll lose him in the crowd—do you hear?" cried Charlie. "What good could you do, a parcel of girls? See! you stand here, and I'll fetch my father out."

Grievously against their will, the girls obeyed. Papa was safely evolved out of the crowd, and went off at once between his daughters, leaving Charlie to follow—which Charlie did accordingly, with Mr Atheling's greatcoat in one hand and travelling-bag in the other. They made quite a little procession as they went home, Marian half dancing as she clasped Papa's arm, and tantalised him with hints of their wondrous tale; Agnes walking very demurely on the other side, with a pretence of rebuking her giddy sister; Charlie trudging with his burden in the rear. By way of assuring him that he was not to know till they got home, Papa was put in possession of all the main facts of their adventure, before they came near enough to see two small faces at the bright open window, shouting with impatience to see him. Happy Papa! it was almost worth being away a year, instead of three days, to get such a welcome home.

"Well, but who is this fine lady—and how were you introduced to her—and what's all this about a carriage?" said Papa. "Here's Bell and Beau, with all their good sense, reduced to be as crazy as the rest of you. What's this about a carriage?"

For Bell and Beau, we are constrained to confess, had made immense ado about the "two geegees" ever since these fabulous and extraordinary animals drew up before the gate with that magnificent din and concussion which shook to its inmost heart the quiet of Bellevue.

"Oh, it is Mrs Edgerley's, papa," said Marian; "such a beautiful pair of bay horses—she sent us home in it—and we met her at Mr Burlington's, and we went to luncheon at her house—and we are going there again on Thursday to a great party. She says everybody wishes to see Agnes; she thinks there never was a book like Hope. She is very pretty, and has the grandest house, and is kinder than anybody I ever saw. You never saw such splendid horses. Oh, mamma, how pleasant it would be to keep a carriage! I wonder if Agnes will ever be as rich as Mrs Edgerley; but then, though she is an author, she is a great lady besides."

"Edgerley!" said Mr Atheling; "do you know, I heard that name at the Old Wood Lodge."

"But, papa, what about the Lodge? you have never told us yet: is it as pretty as you thought it was? Can we go to live there? Is there a garden? I am sure now," said Agnes, blushing with pleasure, "that we will have money enough to go down there—all of us—mamma, and Bell and Beau!"

"I don't deny it's rather a pretty place," said Mr Atheling; "and I thought of Agnes immediately when I looked out from the windows. There is a view for you! Do you remember it, Mary?—the town below, and the wood behind, and the river winding about everywhere. Well, I confess to you it is pretty, and not in such bad order either, considering all things; and nothing said against our title yet, Mr Lewis tells me. Do you know, children, if you were really to go down and take possession, and then my lord made any attempt against us, I should be tempted to stand out against him, cost what it might?"

"Then, papa, we ought to go immediately," said Marian. "To be sure, you should stand out—it belonged to our family; what has anybody else got to do with it? And I tell you, Charlie, you ought to read up all about it, and make quite sure, and let the gentleman know the real law."

"Stuff! I'll mind my own business," said Charlie. Charlie did not choose to have any allusion made to his private studies.

"And there are several people there who remember us, Mary," said Mr Atheling. "My lord is not at home—that is one good thing; but I met a youth at Winterbourne yesterday, who lives at the Hall they say, and is a—a—sort of a son; a fine boy, with a haughty look, more like the old lord a great deal. And what did you say about Edgerley? There's one of the Rivers's married to an Edgerley. I won't have such an acquaintance, if it turns out one of them."

"Why, William?" said Mrs Atheling. "Fathers and daughters are seldom very much like each other. I do not care much about such an acquaintance myself," added the good mother, in a moralising tone. "For though it may be very pleasant for the girls at first, I do not think it is good, as Miss Willsie says, to have friends far out of our own rank of life. My dear, Miss Willsie is very sensible, though she is not always pleasant; and I am sure you never can be very easy or comfortable with people whom you cannot have at your own house; and you know such a great lady as that could not come here."

Agnes and Marian cast simultaneous glances round the room—it was impossible to deny that Mrs Atheling was right.

"But then the Old Wood Lodge, mamma!" cried Agnes, with sudden relief and enthusiasm. "There we could receive any one—anybody could come to see us in the country. If the furniture is not very good, we can improve it a little. For you know, mamma—." Agnes once more blushed with shy delight and satisfaction, but came to a sudden conclusion there, and said no more.

"Yes, my dear, I know," said Mrs Atheling, with a slight sigh, and a careful financial brow; "but when your fortune comes, papa must lay it by for you, Agnes, or invest it. William, what did you say it would be best to do?"

Mr Atheling immediately entered con amore into a consideration of the best means of disposing of this fabulous and unarrived fortune. But the girls looked blank when they heard of interest and percentage; they did not appreciate the benefits of laying by.

"Are we to have no good of it, then, at all?" said Agnes disconsolately.

Mr Atheling's kind heart could not resist an appeal like this. "Yes, Mary, they must have their pleasure," said Papa; "it will not matter much to Agnes's fortune, the little sum that they will spend on the journey, or the new house. No, you must go by all means; I shall fancy it is in mourning for poor old Aunt Bridget, till my girls are there to pull her roses. If I knew you were all there, I should begin to think again that Winterbourne and Badgely Wood were the sweetest places in the world."

"And there any one could come to see us," said Marian, clapping her hands. "Oh, papa, what a good thing for Agnes that Aunt Bridget left you the Old Wood Lodge!"

CHAPTER XXVI

MRS EDGERLY'S THURSDAY

Mr Atheling's visit to the country had, after all, not been so necessary as the family supposed; no one seemed disposed to pounce upon the small bequest of Miss Bridget. The Hall took no notice either of the death or the will which changed the proprietorship of the Old Wood Lodge. It remained intact and unvisited, dilapidated and picturesque, with Miss Bridget's old furniture in its familiar place, and her old maid in possession. The roses began to brush the little parlour window, and thrust their young buds against the panes, from which no one now looked out upon their sweetness. Papa himself, though his heart beat high to think of his own beautiful children blooming in this retired and pleasant place, wept a kindly tear for his old aunt, as he stood in the chamber of her long occupation, and found how empty and mournful was this well-known room. It was a quaint and touching mausoleum, full of relics; and good Mr Atheling felt himself more and more bound to carry out the old lady's wishes as he stood in the vacant room.

And then it would be such a good thing for Agnes! That was the most flattering and pleasant view of the subject possible; and ambitious ideas of making the Old Wood Lodge the prettiest of country cottages, entered the imagination of the house. It was pretty enough for anything, Papa said, looking as he spoke at his beautiful Marian, who was precisely in the same condition; and if some undefined notion of a prince of romance, carrying off from the old cottage the sweetest bride in the world, did flash across the thoughts of the father and mother, who would be hard enough to blame so natural a vision? As for Marian herself, she thought of nothing but Agnes, unless, indeed, it was Mrs Edgerley's party; and there must, indeed, have been quite a moral earthquake in London had all the invitees to this same party been as much disturbed about it as these two sisters. They wondered a hundred times in a day if it was quite right to go without any further invitation—if Mrs Edgerley would write to them—who would be there? and finally, and most momentous of all, if it would be quite proper to go in those simple white dresses, which were, in fact, the only dresses they could wear. Over these girlish robes there was great discussion, and councils manifold; people, however, who have positively no choice, have facilities for making up their minds unknown to more encumbered individuals, and certainly there was no alternative here.

Another of these much discussed questions was likewise very shortly set to rest. Mrs Edgerley did write to Agnes the most affectionate and emphatic of notes—deeply, doubly underscored in every fourth word, adjuring her to "remember that I NEVER forgive any one who forgets my Thursday." Nobody could possibly be more innocent of this unpardonable crime than Agnes and Marian, from whose innocent minds, since they first heard of it, Mrs Edgerley's Thursday had scarcely been absent for an hour at a stretch; but they were mightily gratified with this reminder, and excited beyond measure with the prospect before them. They had also ascertained with much care and research the names of their new acquaintance's works—of which one was called Fashion, one Coquetry, and one The Beau Monde. On the title-page of these famous productions she was called the Honourable Mrs Edgerley—a distinction not known to them before; and the girls read with devotion the three sets of three volumes each, by which their distinguished friend had made herself immortal. These books were not at all like Hope Hazlewood. It was not indeed very easy to define what they were like; they were very fine, full of splendid upholstery and elevated sentiments, diamonds of the finest water, and passions of the loftiest strain. The girls prudently reserved their judgment on the matter. "It is only some people who can write good books," said Marian, in the tone of an indulgent critic; and nobody disputed the self-evident truth.

Meanwhile Mr Foggo continued to pay his usual visit every night, and Miss Willsie, somewhat curious and full of disapprovals, "looked in" through the day. Miss Willsie, who in secret knew Hope Hazlewood nearly by heart, disapproved of everything. If there was one thing she did not like, it was young people setting up their opinion, and especially writing books; and if there was one thing she could not bear, it was to see folk in a middling way of life aiming to be like their betters. Miss Willsie "could not put up with" Mrs Edgerley's presumption in sending the girls home in her carriage; she thought it was just as much as taunting decent folk because they had no carriage of their own. Altogether the mistress of Killiecrankie was out of temper, and would not be pleased—nothing satisfied her; and she groaned in spirit over the vanity of her young protégés.

"Silly things!" said Miss Willsie, as she came in on the eventful morning of Thursday itself, that golden day; "do you really think there's satisfaction in such vanities? Do you think any person finds happiness in the pleasures of this world?"

"Oh, Miss Willsie! if they were not very pleasant, why should people be so frightened for them?" cried Marian, who was carefully trimming, with some of her mother's lace, the aforesaid white dress.

"And then we are not trying to find happiness," said Agnes, looking up from her similar occupation with a radiant face, and a momentary perception of the philosophy of the matter. After all, that made a wonderful difference. Miss Willsie was far too Scotch to remain unimpressed by the logical distinction.

"Well, that's true," acknowledged Miss Willsie; "but you're no to think I approve of such a way of spending your happiness, though ye have got it, ye young prodigals. If there is one thing I cannot endure, it's countenancing the like of you in your nonsense and extravagance; but I'm no for doing things by halves either—Here!"

Saying which, Miss Willsie laid a parcel upon the table and disappeared instantly, opening the door for herself, and closing it after her with the briskest energy. There was not much time lost in examining the parcel; and within it, in a double wrapper, lay two little pairs of satin shoes, the whitest, daintiest, prettiest in the world.

Cinderella's glass slippers! But Cinderella in the story was not half so much disturbed as these two girls. It seemed just the last proof wanting of the interest all the world took in this momentous and eventful evening. Miss Willsie, the general critic and censor, who approved of nothing! If it had not been for a little proper pride in the presence of Susan, who just then entered the parlour, Marian and Agnes would have been disposed for half a minute to celebrate this pleasure, in true feminine fashion, by a very little "cry."

And then came the momentous duties of the toilette. The little white bedchamber looked whiter to-night than it had done all its days before, under the combined lustre of the white dresses, the white ribbons, and the white shoes. They were both so young and both so bright that their colourless and simple costume looked in the prettiest harmony imaginable with their sweet youth—which was all the more fortunate, that they could not help themselves, and had nothing else to choose. One of those useful and nondescript vehicles called "flies" stood at the door. Charlie, with his hat on, half laughing, half ashamed of his office, lingered in the hall, waiting to accompany them. They kissed Bell and Beau (dreadfully late for this one night, and in the highest state of exultation) with solemnity—submitted themselves to a last inspection on the part of Mrs Atheling, and with a little fright and sudden terror were put into the "carriage." Then the carriage drove away through the late summer twilight, rambling into the distance and the darkness. Then at last Mamma ventured to drop into the easy-chair, and rest for a moment from her labours and her anxieties. At this great crisis of the family history, small events looked great events to Mrs Atheling; as if they had been going out upon a momentous enterprise, this good mother paused awhile in the darkness, and blessed them in her heart.

CHAPTER XXVII

THE WORLD

They were bewildered, yet they lost nothing of the scene. The great rooms radiant with light, misty with hangings, gleaming with mirrors—the magnificent staircase up which they passed, they never could tell how, ashamed of the echo of their own names—the beautiful enchantress of a hostess, who bestowed upon each of them that light perfumy kiss of welcome, at the momentary touch of which the girls blushed and trembled—the strange faces everywhere around them—their own confusion, and the shyness which they thought so awkward. Though all these things together united to form a dazzling jumble for the first moment, the incoherence of the vision lasted no longer. With a touch of kindness Mrs Edgerley led them (for of course they were scrupulously early, and punctual to the hour) to her pretty boudoir, where they had been before, and which was not so bright nor like to be so thronged as the larger rooms. Here already a young matron sat in state, with a little circle of worshippers. Mrs Edgerley broke into the midst of them to introduce to the throned lady her young strangers. "They have no one with them—pray let them be beside you," whispered the beautiful hostess to her beautiful guest. The lady bowed, and stared, and assented. When Mrs Edgerley left them, Agnes and Marian looked after her wistfully, the only face they had ever seen before, and stood together in their shy irresolute grace, blushing, discouraged, and afraid. They supposed it was not right to speak to any one whom they had not been introduced to; but no one gave them any inconvenience for the moment in the matter of conversation. They stood for a short time shyly, expecting some notice from their newly-elected chaperone, but she had half-a-dozen flirtations in hand, and no leisure for a charge which was a bore. This, it must be confessed, was somewhat different from Mrs Edgerley's anticipation of being "besieged for introductions" to the author of Hope Hazlewood. The young author looked wistfully into the brightness of the great drawing-room, with some hope of catching the eye of her patroness; but Mrs Edgerley was in the full business of "receiving," and had no eye except for the brilliant stream of arrivals. Marian began to be indignant, and kept her beautiful eyes full upon Agnes, watching her sister with eager sympathy. Never before, in all their serene and quiet lives, had they needed to be proud. For a moment the lip of Agnes curved and quivered—a momentary pang of girlish mortification passed over her face—then they both drew back suddenly to a table covered with books and portfolios, which stood behind them. They did not say a word to each other—they bent down over the prints and pictures with a sudden impulse of self-command and restraint: no one took the slightest notice of them; they stood quite alone in these magnificent rooms, which were slowly filling with strange faces. Agnes was afraid to look up, lest any one should see that there were actual tears under her eyelids. How she fancied she despised herself for such a weakness! But, after all, it was a hard enough lesson for neophytes so young and innocent,—so they stood very silent, bending closely over the picture-books, overcoming as they could their sudden mortification and disappointment. No one disturbed them in their solitary enjoyment of their little table, and for once in their life they did not say a word to each other, but bravely fought out the crisis within themselves, and rose again with all the pride of sensitive and imaginative natures to the emergency. With a sudden impulsive movement Agnes drew a chair to the table, and made Marian sit down upon it. "Now, we will suppose we are at the play," said Agnes, with youthful contempt and defiance, leaning her arm upon the back of the chair, and looking at the people instead of the picture-books. Marian was not so rapid in her change of mood—she sat still, shading her face with her hand, with a flush upon her cheek, and an angry cloud on her beautiful young brow. Yes, Marian was extremely angry. Mortification on her own account did not affect her—but that all these people, who no doubt were only rich people and nobodies—that they should neglect Agnes!—this was more than her sisterly equanimity could bear.

Agnes Atheling was not beautiful. When people looked at her, they never thought of her face, what were its features or its complexion. These were both agreeable enough to make no detraction from the interest of the bright and animated intelligence which was indeed the only beauty belonging to her. She did not know herself with what entire and transparent honesty her eyes and her lips expressed her sentiments; and it never occurred to her that her own looks, as she stood thus, somewhat defiant, and full of an imaginative and heroical pride, looking out upon all those strangers, made the brightest comment possible upon the scene. How her eye brightened with pleasure as it fell on a pleasant face—how her lip laughed when something ridiculous caught her rapid attention—how the soft lines on her forehead drew together when something displeased her delicate fancy—and how a certain natural delight in the graceful grouping and brilliant action of the scene before her lighted up all her face—was quite an unknown fact to Agnes. It was remarkable enough, however, in an assembly of people whose looks were regulated after the most approved principles, and who were generally adepts in the admirable art of expressing nothing. And then there was Marian, very cloudy, looking up under the shadow of her hand like an offended fairy queen. Though Mrs Edgerley was lost in the stream of her arriving guests, and the beautiful young chaperone she had committed them to took no notice whatever of her charge, tired eyes, which were looking out for something to interest them, gradually fixed upon Agnes and Marian. One or two observers asked who they were, but nobody could answer the question. They were quite by themselves, and evidently knew no one; and a little interest began to rise about them, which the girls, making their own silent observations upon everything, and still sometimes with a little wistfulness looking for Mrs Edgerley, had not yet begun to see.

When an old gentleman came to their table, and startled them a little by turning over the picture-books. He was an ancient beau—the daintiest of old gentlemen—with a blue coat and a white waistcoat, and the most delicate of ruffles. His hair—so much as he had—was perfectly white, and his high bald forehead, and even his face, looked like a piece of ivory curiously carved into wrinkles. He was not by any means a handsome old man, yet it was evident enough that this peculiar look and studied dress belonged to a notability, whose coat and cambric, and the great shining diamond upon whose wrinkled ashen-white hand, belonged to his character, and were part of himself. He was an old connoisseur, critic, and fine gentleman, with a collection of old china, old jewels, rare small pictures, and curious books, enough to craze the whole dilettanti world when it came to the prolonged and fabulous sale, which was its certain end. And he was a connoisseur in other things than silver and china. He was somewhat given to patronising young people; and the common judgment gave him credit for great kindness and benignity. But it was not benignity and kindness which drew Mr Agar to the side of Agnes and Marian. Personal amusement was a much more prevailing inducement than benevolence with the dainty old dilettante. They were deceived, of course, as youth is invariably; for despite the pure selfishness of the intention, the effect, as it happened, was kind.

Mr Agar began a conversation by remarking upon the books, and drew forth a shy reply from both; then he managed gradually to change his position, and to survey the assembled company along with them, but with his most benign and patriarchal expression. He was curious to hear in words those comments which Agnes constantly made with her eyes; and he was pleased to observe the beauty of the younger sister—the perfect unconscious grace of all her movements and attitudes. They thought they had found the most gracious of friends, these simple girls; they had not the remotest idea that he was only a connoisseur.

"Then you do not know many of those people?" said Mr Agar, following Agnes's rapid glances. "Ah, old Lady Knightly! is that a friend of yours?"

"No; I was thinking of the old story of 'Thank you for your Diamonds,'" said Agnes, who could not help drawing back a little, and casting down her eyes for the moment, while the sound of her own voice, low as it was, brought a sudden flush to her cheek. "I did not think diamonds had been so pretty; they look as if they were alive."

"Ah, the diamonds!" said the old critic, looking at the unconscious object of Agnes's observation, who was an old lady, wrinkled and gorgeous, with a leaping, twinkling band of light circling her time-shrivelled brow. "Yes, she looks as if she had dressed for a masquerade in the character of Night—eh? Poor old lady, with her lamps of diamonds! Beauty, you perceive, does not need so many tapers to show its whereabouts."

"But there are a great many beautiful people here," said Agnes, "and a great many jewels. I think, sir, it is kind of people to wear them, because all the pleasure is to us who look on."

"You think so? Ah, then beauty itself, I suppose, is pure generosity, and we have all the pleasure of it," said the amused old gentleman; "that is comfortable doctrine, is it not?" And he looked at Marian, who glanced up blushingly, yet with a certain pleasure. He smiled, yet he looked benignant and fatherly; and this was an extremely agreeable view of the matter, and made it much less embarrassing to acknowledge oneself pretty. Marian felt herself indebted to this kind old man.

"And you know no one—not even Mrs Edgerley, I presume?" said the old gentleman. They both interrupted him in haste to correct this, but he only smiled the more, and went on. "Well, I shall be benevolent, and tell you who your neighbours are; but I cannot follow those rapid eyes. Yes, I perceive you have made a good pause for a beginning—that is our pretty hostess's right honourable papa. Poor Winterbourne! he was sadly clumsy about his business. He is one of those unfortunate men who cannot do a wicked thing without doing it coarsely. You perceive, he is stopping to speak to Lady Theodosia—dear Lady Theodosia, who writes those sweet books! Nature intended she should be merry and vulgar, and art has made her very fine, very sentimental, and full of tears. There is an unfortunate youth wandering alone behind everybody's back. That is a miserable new poet, whom Mrs Edgerley has deluded hither under the supposition that he is to be the lion of the evening. Poor fellow! he is looking demoniacal, and studying an epigram. Interested in the poet—eh?"

"Yes, sir," said Agnes, with her usual respect; "but we were thinking of ourselves, who were something the same," she added quickly; for Mr Agar had seen the sudden look which passed between the sisters.

"Something the same! then I am to understand that you are a poet?" said the old gentleman, with his unvarying benignity. "No!—what then? A musician? No; an artist? Come, you puzzle me. I shall begin to suppose you have written a novel if you do not explain."

The animated face of Agnes grew blank in a moment; she drew farther back, and blushed painfully. Marian immediately drew herself up and stood upon the defensive. "Is it anything wrong to write a novel?" said Marian. Mr Agar turned upon her with his benignant smile.

"It is so, then?" said the old gentleman; "and I have not the least doubt it is an extremely clever novel. But hold! who comes here? Ah, an American! Now we must do our best to talk very brilliantly, for friend Jonathan loves the conversation of distinguished circles. Let me find a seat for you, and do not be angry that I am not an enthusiast in literary matters. We have all our hobbies, and that does not happen to be mine."

Agnes sat down passively on the chair he brought for her. The poor girl felt grievously ashamed of herself. After all, what was that poor little book, that she should ground such mighty claims upon it? Who cared for the author of Hope Hazlewood? Mr Agar, though he was so kind, did not even care to inquire what book it was, nor showed the smallest curiosity about its name. Agnes was so much cast down that she scarcely noticed the upright figure approaching towards them, carrying an abstracted head high in the air, and very like to run over smaller people; but Mr Agar stepped aside, and Marian touched her sister's arm. "It is Mr Endicott—look, Agnes!" whispered Marian. Both of them were stirred with sudden pleasure at sight of him; it was a known face in this dazzling wilderness, though it was not a very comely one. Mr Endicott was as much startled as themselves when glancing downward from his lofty altitude, his eye fell upon the beautiful face which had made sunshine even in the shady place of that Yankee young gentleman's self-admiring breast. The sudden discovery brightened his lofty languor for a moment. He hastened to shake hands with them, so impressively that the pretty lady and her cloud of admirers paused in their flutter of satire and compliment to look on.

"This is a pleasure I was not prepared for," said Mr Endicott. "I remember that Mr Atheling had an early acquaintance with Viscount Winterbourne—I presume an old hereditary friendship. I am rejoiced to find that such things are, even in this land of sophistication. This is a brilliant scene!"

"Indeed I do not think papa knows Lord Winterbourne," said Agnes hastily; but her low voice did not reach the ears which had been so far enlightened by Mr Endicott. "Hereditary friendship—old connections of the family; no doubt daughters of some squire in Banburyshire," said their beautiful neighbour, in a half-offended tone, to one of her especial retainers, who showed strong symptoms of desertion, and had already half-a-dozen times asked Marian's name. Unfortunate Mr Endicott! he gained a formidable rival by these ill-advised words.

"I find little to complain of generally in the most distinguished circles of your country," said Mr Endicott. "Your own men of genius may be neglected, but a foreigner of distinction always finds a welcome. This is true wisdom—for by this means we are enabled to carry a good report to the world."

"I say, what nice accounts these French fellows give of us!" burst in suddenly a very young man, who stood under the shadow of Mr Endicott. The youth who hazarded this brilliant remark did not address anybody in particular, and was somewhat overpowered by the unexpected honour of an answer from Mr Agar.

"Trench journalists, and newspaper writers of any country, are of course the very best judges of manners and morals," said the old gentleman, with a smile; "the other three estates are more than usually fallible; the fourth is the nearest approach to perfection which we can find in man."

"Sir," said Mr Endicott, "in my country we can do without Queen, Lords, and Commons; but we cannot do without the Press—that is, the exponent of every man's mind and character, the legitimate vehicle of instructive experiences. The Press, sir, is Progress—the only effective agency ever invented for the perfection of the human race."

"Oh, I am sure I quite agree with you. I am quite in love with the newspapers; they do make one so delightfully out of humour," said Mrs Edgerley, suddenly making her appearance; "and really, you know, when they speak of society, it is quite charming—so absurd! Sir Langham Portland—Miss Atheling. I have been so longing to come to you. Oh, and you must know Mr Agar. Mr Agar, I want to introduce you to my charming young friend, the author of Hope Hazlewood; is it not wonderful? I was sure you, who are so fond of people of genius, would be pleased to know her. And there is dear Lady Theodosia, but she is so surrounded. You must come to the Willows—you must indeed; I positively insist upon it. For what can one do in an evening? and so many of my friends want to know you. We go down in a fortnight. I shall certainly calculate upon you. Oh, I never take a refusal; it was so kind of you to come to-night."

Before she had ceased speaking, Mrs Edgerley was at the other end of the room, conversing with some one else, by her pretty gestures. Sir Langham Portland drew himself up like a guardsman, as he was, on the other side of Marian, and made original remarks about the picture-books, somewhat to the amusement, but more to the dismay of the young beauty, unaccustomed to such distinguished attentions. Mr Agar occupied himself with Agnes; he told her all about the Willows, Mrs Edgerley's pretty house at Richmond, which was always amusing, said the old gentleman. He was very pleasantly amused himself with Agnes's bright respondent face, which, however, this wicked old critic was fully better pleased with while its mortification and disappointment lasted. Mr Endicott remained standing in front of the group, watching the splendid guardsman with a misanthropic eye. This, however, was not very amusing; and the enlightened American gracefully took from his pocket the daintiest of pocket-books, fragrant with Russia leather and clasped with gold. From this delicate enclosure Mr Endicott selected with care a letter and a card, and, armed with these formidable implements, turned round upon the unconscious old gentleman. When Mr Agar caught a glimpse of this impending assault, his momentary look of dismay would have delighted himself, could he have seen it. "I have the honour of bearing a letter of introduction," said Mr Endicott, closing upon the unfortunate connoisseur, and thrusting before his eyes the weapons of offence—the moral bowie-knife and revolver, which were the weapons of this young gentleman's warfare. Mr Agar looked his assailant in the face, but did not put forth his hand.

"At my own house," said the ancient beau, with a gracious smile: "who could be stoic enough to do justice to the most distinguished of strangers, under such irresistible distractions as I find here?"

Poor Mr Endicott! He did not venture to be offended, but he was extinguished notwithstanding, and could not make head against his double disappointment; for there stood the guardsman speaking through his mustache of Books of Beauty, and holding his place like the most faithful of sentinels by Marian Atheling's side.

CHAPTER XXVIII

A FOE

"I shall have to relinquish my charge of you," said the young chaperone, for the first time addressing Agnes. Agnes started immediately, and rose.

"It is time for us to go," she said with eager shyness, "but I did not like. May we follow you? If it would not trouble you, it would be a great kindness, for we know no one here."

"Why did you come, then?" said the lady. Agnes's ideas of politeness were sorely tried to-night.

"Indeed," said the young author, with a sudden blush and courage, "I cannot tell why, unless because Mrs Edgerley asked us; but I am sure it was very foolish, and we will know better another time."

"Yes, it is always tiresome, unless one knows everybody," said the pretty young matron, slowly rising, and accepting with a careless grace the arm which somebody offered her. The girls rose hastily to follow. Mr Agar had left them some time before, and even the magnificent guardsman had been drawn away from his sentryship. With a little tremor, looking at nobody, and following very close in the steps of their leader, they glided along through the brilliant groups of the great drawing-room. But, alas! they were not fated to reach the door in unobserved safety. Mr Endicott, though he was improving his opportunities, though he had already fired another letter of introduction at somebody else's head, and listened to his heart's content to various snatches of that most brilliant and wise conversation going on everywhere around him, had still kept up a distant and lofty observation of the lady of his love. He hastened forward to them now, as with beating hearts they pursued their way, keeping steadily behind their careless young guide. "You are going?" said Mr Endicott, making a solemn statement of the fact. "It is early; let me see you to your carriage."

But they were glad to keep close to him a minute afterwards, while they waited for that same carriage, the Islingtonian fly, with Charlie in it, which was slow to recognise its own name when called. Charlie rolled himself out as the vehicle drew up, and came to the door like a man to receive his sisters. A gentleman stood by watching the whole scene with a little amusement—the shy girls, the big brother, the officious American. This was a man of singularly pale complexion, very black hair, and a face over which the skin seemed to be strained so tight that his features were almost ghastly. He was old, but he did not look like his age; and it was impossible to suppose that he ever could have looked young. His smile was not at all a pleasant smile. Though it came upon his face by his own will, he seemed to have no power of putting it off again; and it grew into a faint spasmodic sneer, offensive and repellent. Charlie looked him in the face with a sudden impulse of pugnacity—he looked at Charlie with this bloodless and immovable smile. The lad positively lingered, though his fly "stopped the way," to bestow another glance upon this remarkable personage, and their eyes met in a full and mutual stare. Whether either person, the old man or the youth, were moved by a thrill of presentiment, we are not able to say; but there was little fear hereafter of any want of mutual recognition. Despite the world of social distinction, age, and power which lay between them, Charlie Atheling looked at Lord Winterbourne, and Lord Winterbourne looked at Charlie. It was their first point of contact; neither of them could read the fierce mutual conflict, the ruin, despair, and disgrace which lay in the future, in that first look of impulsive hostility; but as the great man entered his carriage, and the boy plunged into the fly, their thoughts for the moment were full of each other—so full that neither could understand the sudden distinct recognition of this first touch of fate.

"No; mamma was quite right," said Agnes; "we cannot be great friends nor very happy with people so different from ourselves."

And the girls sighed. They were pleased, yet they were disappointed. It was impossible to deny that the reality was as far different from the imagination as anything could be; and really nobody had been in the smallest degree concerned about the author of Hope Hazlewood. Even Marian was compelled to acknowledge that.

"But then," cried this eager young apologist, "they were not literary people; they were not good judges; they were common people, like what you might see anywhere, though they might be great ladies and fine gentlemen; it was easy to see we were not very great, and they did not understand you."

"Hush," said Agnes quickly; "they were rather kind, I think—especially Mr Agar; but they did not care at all for us: and why should they, after all?"

"So it was a failure," said Charlie. "I say, who was that man—that fellow at the door?"

"Oh, Charlie, you dreadful boy! that was Lord Winterbourne," cried Marian. "Mr Agar told us who he was."

"Who's Mr Agar?" asked Charlie. "And so that's him—that's the man that will take the Old Wood Lodge! I wish he would. I knew I owed him something. I'd like to see him try!"

"And Mrs Edgerley is his daughter," said Agnes. "Is it not strange? And I suppose we shall all be neighbours in the country. But Mr Endicott said quite loud, so that everybody could hear, that papa was a friend of Lord Winterbourne's. I do not like people to slight us; but I don't like to deceive them either. There was that gentleman—that Sir Langham. I suppose he thought we were great people, Marian, like the rest of the people there."

In the darkness Marian pouted, frowned, and laughed within herself. "I don't think it matters much what Sir Langham thought," said Marian; for already the young beauty began to feel her "greatness," and smiled at her own power.

CHAPTER XXIX

FAMILY SENTIMENTS

When the fly jumbled into Bellevue, the lighted window, which always illuminated the little street, shone brighter than ever in the profound darkness of this late night, when all the respectable inhabitants for more than an hour had been asleep. Papa and Mamma, somewhat drowsily, yet with a capacity for immediate waking-up only to be felt under these circumstances, had unanimously determined to sit up for the girls; and the window remained bright, and the inmates wakeful, for a full hour after the rumbling "fly," raising all the dormant echoes of the neighbourhood, had rolled off to its nightly shelter. The father and the mother listened with the most perfect patience to the detail of everything, excited in spite of themselves by their children's companionship with "the great," yet considerably resenting, and much disappointed by the failure of those grand visions, in which all night the parental imagination had pictured to itself an admiring assembly hanging upon the looks of those innocent and simple girls. Mr and Mrs Atheling on this occasion were somewhat disposed, we confess, to make out a case of jealousy and malice against the fashionable guests of Mrs Edgerley. It was always the way, Papa said. They always tried to keep everybody down, and treated aspirants superciliously; and in the climax of his indignation, under his breath, he added something about those "spurns which patient merit of the unworthy takes." Mrs Atheling did not quote Shakespeare, but she was quite as much convinced that it was their "rank in life" which had prevented Agnes and Marian from taking a sovereign place in the gay assembly they had just left. The girls themselves gave no distinct judgment on the subject; but now that the first edge of her mortification had worn off, Agnes began to have great doubts upon this matter. "We had no claim upon them—not the least," said Agnes; "they never saw us before; we were perfect strangers; why should they trouble themselves about us, simply because I had written a book?"

"Do not speak nonsense, my dear—do not tell me," said Mrs Atheling, with agitation: "they had only to use their own eyes and see—as if they often had such an opportunity! My dear, I know better; you need not speak to me!"

"And everybody has read your book, Agnes—and no doubt there are scores of people who would give anything to know you," said Papa with dignity. "The author of Hope Hazlewood is a different person from Agnes Atheling. No, no—it is not that they don't know your proper place; but they keep everybody down as long as they can. Now, mind, one day you will turn the tables upon them; I am very sure of that."

Agnes said no more, but went up to her little white room completely unconvinced upon the subject. Miss Willsie saw the tell-tale light in this little high window in the middle of the night—when it was nearly daylight, the old lady said—throwing a friendly gleam upon the two young controversialists as they debated this difficult question. Agnes, of course, with all the heat of youth and innovation, took the extreme side of the question. "It is easy enough to write—any one can write," said the young author, triumphant in her argument, yet in truth somewhat mortified by her triumph. "But even if it was not, there are greater things in this world than books, and almost all other books are greater than novels; and I do think it was the most foolish thing in the world to suppose that clever people like these—for they were all clever people—would take any notice of me."

To which arguments, all and several, Marian returned only a direct, unhesitating, and broad negative. It was not easy to write, and there were not greater things than books, and it was not at all foolish to expect a hundred times more than ever their hopes had expected. "It is very wrong of you to say so, Agnes," said Marian. "Papa is quite right; it will all be as different as possible by-and-by; and if you have nothing more sensible to say than that, I shall go to sleep."

Saying which, Marian turned round upon her pillow, virtuously resisted all further temptations, and closed her beautiful eyes upon the faint grey dawn which began to steal in between the white curtains. They thought their minds were far too full to go to sleep. Innocent imaginations! five minutes after, they were in the very sweetest enchanted country of the true fairyland of dreams.

While Charlie, in his sleep in the next room, laboriously struggled all night with a bloodless apparition, which smiled at him from an open doorway—fiercely fought and struggled against it—mastered it—got it down, but only to begin once more the tantalising combat. When he rose in the morning, early as usual, the youth set his teeth at the recollection, and with an attempt to give a reason for this instinctive enmity, fiercely hoped that Lord Winterbourne would try to take from his father his little inheritance. Charlie, who was by no means of a metaphysical turn, did not trouble himself at all to inquire into the grounds of his own unusual pugnacity. He "knew he owed him something," and though my Lord Winterbourne was a viscount and an ex-minister, and Charlie only a poor man's son and a copying-clerk, he fronted the great man's image with indomitable confidence, and had no more doubt of his own prowess than of his entire goodwill in the matter. He did not think very much more of his opponent in this case than he did of the big folios in the office, and had as entire confidence in his own ability to bring the enemy down.

But it was something of a restless night to Papa and Mamma. They too talked in their darkened chamber, too proper and too economical to waste candlelight upon subjects so unprofitable, of old events and people half forgotten;—how the first patroness of Agnes should be the daughter of the man between whom and themselves there existed some unexplained connection of old friendship or old enmity, or both;—how circumstances beyond their guidance conspired to throw them once more in the way of persons and plans which they had heard nothing of for more than twenty years. These things were very strange and troublous events to Mr Atheling and his wife. The past, which nearer grief and closer pleasure—all their family life, full as that was of joy and sorrow—had thrown so far away and out of remembrance, came suddenly back before them in all the clearness of youthful recollection. Old feelings returned strong and fresh into their minds. They went back, and took up the thread of this history, whatever it might be, where they had dropped it twenty years ago; and with a thrill of deeper interest, wondered and inquired how this influence would affect their children. To themselves now little could happen; their old friend or their old enemy could do neither harm nor benefit to their accomplished lives—but the children!—the children, every one so young, so hopeful, and so well endowed; all so strangely brought into sudden contact, at a double point, with this one sole individual, who had power to disturb the rest of the father and the mother. They relapsed into silence suddenly, and were quieted by the thought.

"It is not our doing—it is not our seeking," said Mr Atheling at length. "If the play wants a last act, Mary, it will not be your planning nor mine; and as for the children, they are in the hands of God."

So in the grey imperfect dawn which lightened on the faces of the sleeping girls, whose sweet youthful rest was far too deep to be broken even by the growing light, these elder people closed their eyes, not to sleep, but to pray. If evil were about to come—if danger were lurking in the air around them—they had this only defence against it. It was not the simple faith of youth which dictated these prayers; it was a deeper and a closer urgency, which cried aloud and would not cease, but yet was solemn with the remembrance of times when God's pleasure was not to grant them their petitions. The young ones slept in peace, but with fights and triumphs manifold in their young dreams. The father and the mother held a vigil for them, holding up holy hands for their defence and safety; and so the morning came at last, brightly, to hearts which feared no evil, or when they feared, put their apprehensions at once into the hand of God.

CHAPTER XXX

AGNES'S FORTUNE

The morning, like a good fairy, came kindly to these good people, increasing in the remembrance of the girls the impression of pleasure, and lessening that of disappointment. They came, after all, to be very well satisfied with their reception at Mrs Edgerley's. And now her second and most important invitation remained to be discussed—the Willows—the pretty house at Richmond, with the river running sweetly under the shadow of its trees; the company, which was sure to include, as Mr Agar said, some people worth knowing, and which that ancient connoisseur himself did not refuse to join. Agnes and Marian looked with eager eyes on the troubled brow of Mamma; a beautiful vision of the lawn and the river, flowers and sunshine, the sweet silence of "the country," and the unfamiliar music of running water and rustling trees, possessed the young imaginations for the time to the total disregard of all sublunary considerations. They did not think for a moment of Lord Winterbourne's daughter, and the strange chance which could make them inmates of her house; for Lord Winterbourne himself was not a person of any importance in the estimation of the girls. But more than that, they did not even think of their wardrobe, important as that consideration was; they did not recollect how entirely unprovided they were for such a visit, nor how the family finances, strait and unelastic, could not possibly stretch to so new and great an expenditure. But all these things, which brought no cloud upon Agnes and Marian, conspired to embarrass the brow of the family mother. She thought at the same moment of Lord Winterbourne and of the brown merinos; of this strange acquaintanceship, mysterious and full of fate as it seemed; and of the little black silk cloaks which were out of fashion, and the bonnets with the faded ribbons. It was hard to deny the girls so great a pleasure; but how could it be done?

And for a day or two following the household remained in great uncertainty upon this point, and held every evening, on the engrossing subject of ways and means, a committee of the whole house. This, however, we are grieved to say, was somewhat of an unprofitable proceeding; for the best advice which Papa could give on so important a subject was, that the girls must of course have everything proper if they went. "If they went!—that is exactly the question," said the provoked and impatient ruler of all. "But are they to go? and how are we to get everything proper for them?" To these difficult questions Mr Atheling attempted no answer. He was a wise man, and knew his own department, and prudently declined any interference in the legitimate domain of the other head of the house.

Mrs Atheling was by no means addicted to disclosing the private matters of her own family life, yet she carried this important question through the faded wallflowers to crave the counsel of Miss Willsie. Miss Willsie was not at all pleased to have such a matter submitted to her. Her supreme satisfaction would have lain in criticising, finding fault, and helping on. Now reduced to the painful alternative of giving an opinion, the old lady pronounced a vague one in general terms, to the effect that if there was one thing she hated, it was to see poor folk striving for the company of them that were in a different rank in life; but whenever this speech was made, and her conscience cleared, Miss Willsie began to inquire zealously what "the silly things had," and what they wanted, and set about a mental turning over of her own wardrobe, where were a great many things which she had worn in her own young days, and which were "none the worse," as she said—but they were not altogether adapted for the locality of the Willows. Miss Willsie turned them over not only in her own mind, but in her own parlour, where her next visitor found her as busy with her needle and her shears as any cottar matron ever was, and anxiously bent on the same endeavour to "make auld things look amaist as weel's the new." It cost Miss Willsie an immense deal of trouble, but it was not half so successful a business as the repairs of that immortal Saturday Night.

But the natural course of events, which had cleared their path for them many times before, came in once more to make matters easy. Mr Burlington, of whom nothing had been heard since the day of that eventful visit to his place—Mr Burlington, who since then had brought out a second edition of Hope Hazlewood, announced himself ready to "make a proposal" for the book. Now, there had been many and great speculations in the house on this subject of "Agnes's fortune." They were as good at the magnificent arithmetic of fancy as Major Pendennis was, and we will not say that, like him, they had not leaped to their thousands a-year. They had all, however, been rather prudent in committing themselves to a sum—nobody would guess positively what it was to be—but some indefinite and fabulous amount, a real fortune, floated in the minds of all: to the father and mother a substantial provision for Agnes, to the girls an inexhaustible fund of pleasure, comfort, and charity. The proposal came—it was not a fabulous and magnificent fortune, for the author of Hope Hazlewood was only Agnes Atheling, and not Arthur Pendennis. For the first moment, we are compelled to confess, they looked at each other with blank faces, entirely cast down and disappointed: it was not an inexhaustible fairy treasure—it was only a hundred and fifty pounds.

Yes, most tender-hearted reader! these were not the golden days of Sir Walter, nor was this young author a literary Joan of Arc. She got her fortune in a homely fashion like other people—at first was grievously disappointed about it—formed pugnacious resolutions, and listened to all the evil stories of the publishing ghouls with satisfaction and indignant faith. But by-and-by this angry mood softened down; by-and-by the real glory of such an unrealisable heap of money began to break upon the girls. A hundred and fifty pounds, and nothing to do with it—no arrears to pay—nothing to make up—can any one suppose a position of more perfect felicity? They came to see it bit by bit dawning upon them in gradual splendour—content blossomed into satisfaction, satisfaction unfolded into delight. And then to think of laying by such a small sum would be foolish, as the girls reasoned; so its very insignificance increased the pleasure. It was not a dull treasure, laid up in a bank, or "invested," as Papa had solemnly proposed to invest "Agnes's fortune;" it was a delightful little living stream of abundance, already in imagination overflowing and brightening everything. It would buy Mamma the most magnificent of brocades, and Bell and Beau such frocks as never were seen before out of fairyland. It would take them all to the Old Wood Lodge, or even to the seaside; it would light up with books and pictures, and pretty things, the respectable family face of Number Ten, Bellevue. There was no possibility of exhausting the capacities of this marvellous sum of money, which, had it been three or four times as much, as the girls discovered, could not have been half as good for present purposes. The delight of spending money was altogether new to them: they threw themselves into it with the most gleeful abandonment (in imagination), and threw away their fortune royally, and with genuine enjoyment in the process; and very few millionaires have ever found as much pleasure in the calculation of their treasures as Agnes and Marian Atheling, deciding over and over again how they were to spend it, found in this hundred and fifty pounds.

In the mean time, however, Papa carried it off to the office, and locked it up there for security—for they all felt that it would not be right to trust to the commonplace defences of Bellevue with such a prodigious sum of money in the house.

CHAPTER XXXI

EXTRAVAGANCE

It was a July day, brilliant and dazzling; the deep-blue summer sky arched over these quiet houses, a very heaven of sunshine and calm; the very leaves were golden in the flood of light, and grateful shadows fell from the close walls, and a pleasant summer fragrance came from within the little enclosures of Bellevue. Nothing was stirring in the silent little suburban street—the very sounds came slow and soft through the luxurious noonday air, into which now and then blew the little capricious breath of a cool breeze, like some invisible fairy fan making a current in the golden atmosphere. Safe under the shelter of green blinds and opened windows, the feminine population reposed in summer indolence, mistresses too languid to scold, and maids to be improved by the same. In the day, the other half of mankind, all mercantile and devoted to business, deserted Bellevue and perhaps were not less drowsy in their several offices, where dust had to answer all the purpose of those trim venetian defences, than their wives and daughters were at home.

But before the door of Number Ten stood a vehicle—let no one scorn its unquestioned respectability,—it was The Fly. The fly was drawn by an old white horse, of that bony and angular development peculiar to this rank of professional eminence. This illustrious animal gave character and distinction at once to the equipage. The smartest and newest brougham in existence, with such a steed attached to it, must at once have taken rank, in the estimation of all beholders, as a true and unmistakable Fly. The coachman was in character; he had a long white livery-coat, and a hat very shiny, and bearing traces of various indentations. As he sat upon his box in the sunshine, he nodded in harmony with the languid branches of the lilac-bushes. Though he was not averse to a job, he marvelled much how anybody who could stay at home went abroad under this burning sun, or troubled themselves with occupations. So too thought the old white horse, switching his old white tail in vain pursuit of the summer flies which troubled him; and so even thought Hannah, Miss Willsie's pretty maid, as she looked out from the gate of Killiecrankie Lodge, shading her eyes with her hand, marvelling, half in envy, half in pity, how any one could think even of "pleasuring" on such a day.

With far different sentiments from these languid and indolent observers, the Athelings prepared for their unusual expedition. Firmly compressed into Mrs Atheling's purse were five ten-pound notes, crisp and new, and the girls, with a slight tremor of terror enhancing their delight, had secretly vowed that Mamma should not be permitted to bring anything in the shape of money home. They were going to spend fifty pounds. That was their special mission—and when you consider that very rarely before had they helped at the spending of more than fifty shillings, you may fancy the excitement and delight of this family enterprise. They had calculated beforehand what everything was to cost—they had left a margin for possibilities—they had all their different items written down on a very long piece of paper, and now the young ladies were dancing Bell and Beau through the garden, and waiting for Mamma.

For the twin babies were to form part of this most happy party. Bell and Beau were to have an ecstatic drive in that most delightful of carriages which the two big children and the two little ones at present stood regarding with the sincerest admiration. If Agnes had any doubt at all about the fly, it was a momentary fear lest somebody should suppose it to be their own carriage—a contingency not at all probable. In every other view of the question, the fly was scarcely second even to Mrs Edgerley's sublime and stately equipage; and it is quite impossible to describe the rapture with which this magnificent vehicle was contemplated by Bell and Beau.

At last Mamma came down stairs in somewhat of a flutter, and by no means satisfied that she was doing right in thus giving in to the girls. Mrs Atheling still, in spite of all their persuasions, could not help thinking it something very near a sin to spend wilfully, and at one doing, so extraordinary a sum as fifty pounds—"a quarter's income!" she said solemnly. But Papa was very nearly as foolish on the subject as Agnes and Marian, and the good mother could not make head against them all. She was alarmed at this first outbreak of "awful" extravagance, but she could not quite refuse to be pleased either with the pleasant piece of business, with the delight of the girls, and the rapture of the babies, nor to feel the glory in her own person of "shopping" on so grand a scale—

"My sister and my sister's child, Myself and children three."

The fly was not quite so closely packed as the chaise of Mrs Gilpin, yet it was very nearly as full as that renowned conveyance. They managed to get in "five precious souls," and the white horse languidly set out upon his journey, and the coachman, only half awake, still nodded on his box. Where they went to, we will not betray their confidence by telling. It was an erratic course, and included all manner of shops and purchases. Before they had got nearly to the end of their list, they were quite fatigued with their labours, and found it rather cumbrous, after all, to choose the shops they wanted from the "carriage" windows, a splendid but inconvenient necessity. Then Bell and Beau grew very tired, wanted to go home, and were scarcely to be solaced even with cakes innumerable. Perfect and unmixed delights are not to be found under the sun; and though the fly went back to Bellevue laden with parcels beyond the power of arithmetic; though the girls had accomplished their wicked will, and the purse of Mrs Atheling had shrunk into the ghost of its former size, yet the accomplished errand was not half so delightful as were those exuberant and happy intentions, which could now be talked over no more. They all grew somewhat silent, as they drove home—"vanity of vanities—" Mrs Atheling and her daughters were in a highly reflective state of mind, and rather given to moralising; while extremely wearied, sleepy, and uncomfortable were poor little Bell and Beau.

But at last they reached home—at last the pleasant sight of Susan, and the fragrance of the tea, which, as it was now pretty late in the afternoon, Susan had prepared to refresh them, restored their flagging spirits. They began to open out their parcels, and fight their battles over again. They examined once more, outside and inside, the pretty little watches which Papa had insisted on as the first of all their purchases. Papa thought a watch was a most important matter—the money spent in such a valuable piece of property was invested; and Mrs Atheling herself, as she took her cup of tea, looked at these new acquisitions with extreme pride, good pleasure, and a sense of importance. They had put their bonnets on the sofa—the table overflowed with rolls of silk and pieces of ribbon half unfolded; Bell and Beau, upon the hearth-rug, played with the newest noisiest toys which could be found for them; and even Susan, when she came to ask if her mistress would take another cup, secretly confessed within herself that there never was such a littered and untidy room.

When there suddenly came a dash and roll of rapid wheels, ringing into all the echoes. Suddenly, with a gleam and bound, a splendid apparition crossed the window, and two magnificent bay-horses drove up before the little gate. Her very watch, new and well-beloved, almost fell from the fingers of Agnes. They looked at each other with blank faces—they listened in horror to the charge of artillery immediately discharged upon their door—nobody had self-possession to apprehend Susan on the way, and exhort her to remember the best room. And Susan, greatly fluttered, forgot the sole use of this sacred apartment. They all stood dismayed, deeply sensible of the tea upon the table, and the extraordinary confusion of the room, when suddenly into the midst of them, radiant and splendid, floated Mrs Edgerley—Mayfair come to visit Bellevue.

CHAPTER XXXII

A GREAT VISITOR

Mayfair came in, radiant, blooming, splendid, with a rustle of silks, a flutter of feathers, an air of fragrance, like a fairy creature not to be molested by the ruder touches of fortune or the world. Bellevue stood up to receive her in the person of Mrs Atheling, attired in a black silk gown which had seen service, and hastily setting down a cup of tea from her hand. The girls stood between the two, an intermediate world, anxious and yet afraid to interpret between them; for Marian's beautiful hair had fallen down upon her white neck, and Agnes's collar had been pulled awry, and her pretty muslin dress sadly crushed and broken by the violent hands of Bell and Beau. The very floor on which Mrs Edgerley's pretty foot pressed the much-worn carpet, was strewed with little frocks for those unruly little people. The sofa was occupied by three bonnets, and Mamma's new dress hung over the back of the easy-chair. You may laugh at this account of it, but Mamma, and Marian, and Agnes were a great deal more disposed to cry at the reality. To think that, of all days in the world, this great lady should have chosen to come to-day!

"Now, pray don't let me disturb anything. Oh, I am so delighted to find you quite at home! It is quite kind of you to let me come in," cried Mrs Edgerley—"and indeed you need not introduce me. When one has read Hope Hazlewood, one knows your mamma. Oh, that charming, delightful book! Now, confess you are quite proud of her. I am sure you must be."

"She is a very good girl," said Mrs Atheling doubtfully, flattered, but not entirely pleased—"and we are very deeply obliged to Mrs Edgerley for the kindness she has shown to our girls."

"Oh, I have been quite delighted," said Mayfair; "but pray don't speak in the third person. How charmingly fragrant your tea is!—may I have some? How delightful it must be to be able to keep rational hours. What lovely children! What beautiful darlings! Are they really yours?"

"My youngest babies," said Bellevue, somewhat stiffly, yet a little moved by the question. "We have just come in, and were fatigued. Agnes, my dear!"

But Agnes was already gone, seizing the opportunity to amend her collar, while Marian put away the bonnets, and cleared the parcels from the feet of Mrs Edgerley. With this pretty figure half-bending before her, and the other graceful cup-bearer offering her the homely refreshment she had asked for, Mrs Edgerley, though quite aware of it, did not think half so much as Mrs Atheling did about their "rank in life." The great lady was not at all nervous on this subject, but was most pleasantly and meritoriously conscious, as she took her cup of tea from the hand of Agnes, that by so doing she set them all "at their ease."

"And pray, do tell me now," said Mrs Edgerley, "how you manage in this quarter, so far from everything? It is quite delightful, half as good as a desolate island—such a pretty, quiet place! You must come to the Willows—I have quite made up my mind and settled it: indeed, you must come—so many people are dying to know you. And I must have your mamma know," said the pretty flutterer, turning round to Mrs Atheling with that air of irresistible caprice and fascinating despotism which was the most amazing thing in the world to the family mother, "that no one ever resists me: I am always obeyed, I assure you. Oh, you must come; I consider it quite a settled thing. Town gets so tiresome just at this time—don't you think so? I always long for the Willows—for it is really the sweetest place, and in the country one cares so much more for one's home."

"You are very kind," said Mrs Atheling, not knowing what other answer to make, and innocently supposing that her visitor had paused for a reply.

"Oh, I assure you, nothing of the kind—perfectly selfish, on the contrary," said Mrs Edgerley, with a sweet smile. "I shall be so charmed with the society of my young friends. I quite forgot to ask if you were musical. We have the greatest little genius in the world at the Willows. Such a voice!—it is a shame to hide such a gift in a drawing-room. She is—a sort of connection—of papa's family. I say it is very good of him to acknowledge her even so far, for people seldom like to remember their follies; but of course the poor child has no position, and I have even been blamed for having her in my house. She is quite a genius—wonderful: she ought to be a singer—it is quite her duty—but such a shy foolish young creature, and not to be persuaded. What charming tea! I am quite refreshed, I assure you. Oh, pray, do not disturb anything. I am so pleased you have let me come when you were quite at home. Now, Tuesday, remember! We shall have a delightful little party. I know you will quite enjoy it. Good-by, little darlings. On Tuesday, my love; you must on no account forget the day."

"But I am afraid they will only be a trouble—and they are not used to society," said Mrs Atheling, rising hastily before her visitor should have quite flown away; "they have never been away from home. Excuse me—I am afraid—"

"Oh, I assure you, nobody ever resists me," cried Mrs Edgerley, interrupting this speech; "I never hear such a naughty word as No. It is not possible—you cannot conceive how it would affect me; I should break my heart! It is quite decided—oh, positively it is—Tuesday—I shall so look forward to it! And a charming little party we shall be—not too many, and so congenial! I shall quite long for the day."

Saying which, Mrs Edgerley took her departure, keeping up her stream of talk while they all attended her to the door, and suffering no interruption. Mrs Atheling was by no means accustomed to so dashing and sudden an assault. She began slowly to bring up her reasons for declining the invitation as the carriage rolled away, carrying with it her tacit consent. She was quite at a loss to believe that this visit was real, as she returned into the encumbered parlour—such haste, patronage, and absoluteness were entirely out of Mrs Atheling's way.

"I have no doubt she is very kind," said the good mother, puzzled and much doubting; "but I am not at all sure that I approve of her—indeed, I think I would much rather you did not go."

"But she will expect us, mamma," said Agnes.

That was unquestionable. Mrs Atheling sat very silent all the remainder of the day, pondering much upon this rapid and sudden visitation, and blaming herself greatly for her want of readiness. And then the "poor child" who had no position, and whose duty it was to be a singer, was she a proper person to breathe the same air as Agnes and Marian? Bellevue was straiter in its ideas than Mayfair. The mother reflected with great self-reproach and painful doubts; for the girls were so pleased with the prospect, and it was so hard to deny them the expected pleasure. Mrs Atheling at last resigned herself with a sigh. "If you must go, I expect you to take great care whom you associate with," said Mrs Atheling, very pointedly; and she sent off their new purchases up-stairs, and gave her whole attention, with a certain energy and impatience, to the clearing of the room. This had not been by any means a satisfactory day.

CHAPTER XXXIII

GOING FROM HOME

"My dear children," said Mrs Atheling solemnly, "you have never been from home before."

Suddenly arrested by the solemnity of this preamble, the girls paused—they were just going up-stairs to their own room on the last evening before setting out for the Willows. Marian's pretty arms were full of a collection of pretty things, white as the great apron with which Susan had girded her. Agnes carried her blotting-book, two or three other favourite volumes, and a candle. They stood in their pretty sisterly conjunction, almost leaning upon each other, waiting with youthful reverence for the address which Mamma was about to deliver. It was true they were leaving home for the first time, and true also that the visit was one of unusual importance. They prepared to listen with great gravity and a little awe.

"My dears, I have no reason to distrust your good sense," said Mrs Atheling, "nor indeed to be afraid of you in any way—but to be in a strange house is very different from being at home. Strangers will not have the same indulgence as we have had for all your fancies—you must not expect it; and people may see that you are of a different rank in life, and perhaps may presume upon you. You must be very careful. You must not copy Mrs Edgerley, or any other lady, but observe what they do, and rule yourselves by it; and take great care what acquaintances you form; for even in such a house as that," said Mamma, with emphasis and dignity, suddenly remembering the "connection of the family" of whom Mrs Edgerley had spoken, "there may be some who are not fit companions for you."

"Yes, mamma," said Agnes. Marian looked down into the apronful of lace and muslin, and answered nothing. A variable blush and as variable a smile testified to a little consciousness on the part of the younger sister. Agnes for once was the more matter-of-fact of the two.

"At your time of life," continued the anxious mother, "a single day may have as much effect as many years. Indeed, Marian, my love, it is nothing to smile about. You must be very careful; and, Agnes, you are the eldest—you must watch over your sister. Oh, take care!—you do not know how much harm might be done in a single day."

"Take care of what, mamma?" said Marian, glancing up quickly, with that beautiful faint blush, and a saucy gleam in her eye. What do you suppose she saw as her beautiful eyes turned from her mother with a momentary imaginative look into the vacant space? Not the big head of Charlie, bending over the grammars, but the magnificent stature of Sir Langham Portland, drawn up in sentry fashion by her side; and at the recollection Marian's pretty lip could not refuse to smile.

"Hush, my dear!—you may easily know what I mean," said Mrs Atheling uneasily. "You must try not to be awkward or timid; but you must not forget how great a difference there is between Mrs Edgerley's friends and you."

"Nonsense, Mary," cried her husband, energetically. "No such thing, girls. Don't be afraid to let them know who you are, or who you belong to. But as for inferiority, if you yield to such a notion, you are no girls of mine! One of the Riverses! A pretty thing! You, at least, can tell any one who asks the question that your father is an honest man."

"But I suppose, papa, no one is likely to have any doubt upon the subject," said Agnes, with a little spirit. "It will be time enough to publish that when some one questions it; and that, I am sure, was not what mamma meant."

"No, my love, of course not," said Mamma, who was somewhat agitated. "What I meant is, that you are going to people whom we used to know—I mean, whom we know nothing of. They are great people—a great deal richer and higher in station than we are; and it is possible Papa may be brought into contact with them about the Old Wood Lodge; and you are young and inexperienced, and don't know the dangers you may be subjected to;—and, my dear children, what I have to say to you is, just to remember your duty, and read your Bibles, and take care!"

"Mamma! we are only going to Richmond—we are not going away from you," cried Marian in dismay.

"My dears," said Mrs Atheling, putting her handkerchief to her eyes, "I am an old woman—I know more than you do. You cannot tell where you are going; you are going into the world."

No one spoke for the moment. The young travellers themselves looked at their mother with concern and a little solemnity. Who could tell? All the young universe of romance lay at their very feet. They might be going to their fate.

"And henceforward I know," said the good mother, rising into homely and unconscious dignity, "our life will no longer be your boundary, nor our plans all your guidance. My darlings, it is not any fault of yours; you are both as obedient as when you were babies; it is Providence, and comes to every one. You are going away from me, and both your lives may be determined before you come back again. You, Marian! it is not your fault, my love; but, oh! take care."

Under the pressure of this solemn and mysterious caution, the girls at length went up-stairs. Very gravely they entered the little white room, which was somewhat disturbed out of its usual propriety, and in respectful silence Marian began to arrange her burden. She sat down upon the white bed, with her great white apron full of snowy muslin and dainty morsels of lace, stooping her beautiful head over them, with her long bright hair falling down at one side like a golden framework to her sweet cheek. Agnes stood before her holding the candle. Both were perfectly grave, quite silent, separating the sleeves and kerchiefs and collars as if it were the most solemn work in the world.

At length suddenly Marian looked up. In an instant smiles irrestrainable threaded all the soft lines of those young faces. A momentary electric touch sent them both from perfect solemnity into saucy and conscious but subdued laughter. "Agnes! what do you suppose mamma could mean?" asked Marian; and Agnes said "Hush!" and softly closed the door, lest Mamma should hear the low and restrained overflow of those sudden sympathetic smiles. Once more the apparition of the magnificent Sir Langham gleamed somewhere in a bright corner of Marian's shining eye. These incautious girls, like all their happy kind, could not be persuaded to regard with any degree of terror or solemnity the fate that came in such a shape as this.

CHAPTER XXXIV

EVERYBODY'S FANCIES

But the young adventurers had sufficient time to speculate upon their "fate," and to make up their minds whether this journey of theirs was really a fortnight's visit to Richmond, or a solemn expedition into the world, as they drove along the pleasant summer roads on their way to the Willows. They had leisure enough, but they had not inclination; they were somewhat excited, but not at all solemnised. They thought of the unknown paradise to which they were going—of their beautiful patroness and her guests; but they never paused to inquire, as they bowled pleasantly along under the elms and chestnuts, anything at all about their fate.

"How grave every one looked," said Marian. "What are all the people afraid of? for I am sure Miss Willsie wanted us to go, though she was so cross; and poor Harry Oswald, how he looked last night!"

At this recollection Marian smiled. To tell the truth, she was at present only amused by the gradual perception dawning upon her of the unfortunate circumstances of these young gentlemen. She might never have found it out had she known only Harry Oswald; but Sir Langham Portland threw light upon the subject which Marian had scarcely guessed at before. Do you think she was grateful on that account to the handsome Guardsman? Marian's sweet face brightened all over with amused half-blushing smiles. It was impossible to tell.

"But, Marian," said Agnes, "I want to be particular about one thing. We must not deceive any one. Nobody must suppose we are great ladies. If anything should happen of any importance, we must be sure to tell who we are."

"That you are the author of Hope Hazlewood," said Marian, somewhat provokingly. "Oh! Mrs Edgerley will tell everybody that; and as for me, I am only your sister—nobody will mind me."

So they drove on under the green leaves, which grew less and less dusty as they left London in the distance, through the broad white line of road, now and then passing by orchards rich with fruit—by suburban gardens and pretty villakins of better fashion than their own; now and then catching silvery gleams of the river quivering among its low green banks, like a new-bended bow. They knew as little where they were going as what was to befall them there, and were as unapprehensive in the one case as in the other. At home the mother went about her daily business, pondering with a mother's anxiety upon all the little embarrassments and distresses which might surround them among strangers, and seeing in her motherly imagination a host of pleasant perils, half alarming, half complimentary, a crowd of admirers and adorers collected round her girls. At Messrs Cash and Ledger's, Papa brooded over his desk, thinking somewhat darkly of those innocent investigators whom he had sent forth into an old world of former connections, unfortified against the ancient grudge, if such existed, and unacquainted with the ancient story. Would anything come of this acquaintanceship? Would anything come of the new position which placed them once more directly in the way of Lord Winterbourne? Papa shook his head slowly over his daybook, as ignorant as the rest of us what might have to be written upon the fair blank of the very next page—who could tell?

Charlie meanwhile, at Mr Foggo's office, buckled on his harness this important morning with a double share of resolution. As his brow rolled down with all its furrows in a frown of defiance at the "old fellow" whom he took down from the wired bookcase, it was not the old fellow, but Lord Winterbourne, against whom Charlie bit his thumb. In the depths of his heart he wished again that this natural enemy might "only try!" to usurp possession of the Old Wood Lodge. A certain excitement possessed him regarding the visit of his sisters. Once more the youth, in his hostile imagination, beheld the pale face at the door, the bloodless and spasmodic smile. "I knew I owed him something," muttered once more the instinctive enmity; and Charlie was curious and excited to come once more in contact with this mysterious personage who had raised so active and sudden an interest in his secret thoughts.

But the two immediate actors in this social drama—the family doves of inquiry, who might bring back angry thorns instead of olive branches—the innocent sweet pioneers of the incipient strife, went on untroubled in their youthful pleasure, looking at the river and the sunshine, dreaming the fairy dreams of youth. What new life they verged and bordered—what great consequences might grow and blossom from the seedtime of to-day—how their soft white hands, heedless and unconscious, might touch the trembling strings of fate—no one of all these anxious questions ever entered the charmed enclosure of this homely carriage, where they leant back into their several corners, and sung to themselves, in unthinking sympathy with the roll and hum of the leisurely wheels, conveying them on and on to their new friends and their future life. They were content to leave all questions of the kind to a more suitable season—and so, singing, smiling, whispering (though no one was near to interrupt them), went on, on their charmed way, with their youth and their light hearts, to Armida and her enchanted garden—to the world, with its syrens and its lions—forecasting no difficulties, seeing no evil. They had no day-book to brood over like Papa. To-morrow's magnificent blank of possibility was always before them, dazzling and glorious—they went forward into it with the freshest smile and the sweetest confidence. Of all the evils and perils of this wicked world, which they had heard so much of, they knew none which they, in their happy safety, were called upon to fear.

VOLUME II

CHAPTER I

THE WILLOWS

The Willows was a large low house, with no architectural pretensions, but bright as villa could be upon the sunniest side of the Thames. The lawn sloped to the river and ended in a deep fringe and border of willows, sweeping into the water; while half-way across the stream lay a little fairy island, half enveloped in the same silvery foliage, but with bowers and depths of leaves within, through which some stray sunbeam was always gleaming. The flower-beds on the lawn were in a flush with roses; the crystal roof of a large conservatory glistened in the sun. Flowers and sunshine, fragrance and stillness, the dew on the grass, and the morning light upon the river—no marvel that to eyes so young and inexperienced, this Richmond villa looked like a paradise on earth.

It was early morning—very early, when nobody seemed awake but themselves in the great house; and Agnes and Marian came down stairs softly, and, half afraid of doing wrong, stole out upon the lawn. The sun had just begun to gather those blobs of dew from the roses, but all over the grass lay jewels, bedded deep in the close-shorn sod, and shining in the early light. An occasional puff of wind came crisp across the river, and turned to the sun the silvery side of all those drooping willow-leaves, and the willows themselves swayed and sighed towards the water, and the water came up upon them now and then with a playful plunge and flow. The two girls said nothing to each other as they wandered along the foot of the slope, looking over to the island, where already the sun had penetrated to his nest of trees. All this simple beauty, which was not remarkable to the fashionable guests of Mrs Edgerley, went to the very heart of these simple children of Bellevue. It moved them to involuntary delight—joy which could give no reason, for they thought there had never been such a beautiful summer morning, or such a scene.

And by-and-by they began to talk of last night—last night, their first night at the Willows, their first entrance into the home life of "the great." They had no moral maxims at their finger-ends, touching the vanity of riches, nor had the private opinion entertained by Papa and Mamma, that "the country" paid for the folly of "the aristocracy," and that the science of Government was a mere piece of craft for the benefit of "the privileged classes," done any harm at all to the unpolitical imaginations of Agnes and Marian. They were scarcely at their ease yet, and were a great deal more timid than was comfortable; yet they took very naturally to this fairy life, and found an unfailing fund of wonder and admiration in it. They admired everything indeed, had a certain awe and veneration for everybody, and could not sufficiently admire the apparent accomplishments and real grace of their new associates.

"Agnes!—I wonder if there is anything I could learn?" said Marian, rather timidly; "everybody here can do something; it is very different from doing a little of everything, like Miss Tavistock at Bellevue—and we used to think her accomplished!—but do you think there is anything I could learn?"

"And me!" said Agnes, somewhat disconsolately.

"You? no, indeed, you do not need it," said Marian, with a little pride. "You can do what none of them can do;—but they can talk about everything these people, and every one of them can do something. There is that Sir Langham—you would think he was only a young gentleman—but Mrs Edgerley says he makes beautiful sketches. We did not understand people like these when we were at home."

"What do you think of Sir Langham, May?" asked Agnes seriously.

"Think of him? oh, he is very pleasant," said Marian, with a smile and a slight blush: "but never mind Sir Langham; do you think there is anything I could learn?"

"I do not know," said Agnes; "perhaps you could sing. I think you might sing, if you would only take courage and try."

"Sing! oh no, no!"; said Marian; "no one could venture to sing after the young lady—did you hear her name, Agnes?—who sang last night. She did not speak to any one, she was more by herself than we were. I wonder who she could be."

"Mrs Edgerley called her Rachel," said Agnes. "I did not hear any other name. I think it must be the same that Mrs Edgerley told mamma about; you remember she said—"

"I am here," said a low voice suddenly, close beside them. The girls started back, exceedingly confused and ashamed. They had not perceived a sort of little bower, woven among the willows, from which now hastily appeared the third person who spoke. She was a little older than Agnes, very slight and girlish in her person—very dark of complexion, with a magnificent mass of black hair, and large liquid dark eyes. Nothing else about her was remarkable; her features were small and delicate, her cheeks colourless, her very lips pale; but her eyes, which were not of a slumbrous lustre, but full of light, rapid, earnest, and irregular, lighted up her dark pallid face with singular power and attractiveness. She turned upon them quickly as they stood distressed and irresolute before her.

"I did not mean to interrupt you," said this new-comer; "but you were about to speak of me, and I thought it only honest to give you notice that I was here."

"Thank you," said Agnes with humility. "We are strangers, and did not know—we scarcely know any one here; and we thought you were nearly about our own age, and perhaps would help us—" Here Agnes stopped short; she was not skilled in making overtures of friendship.

"No, indeed no," cried their new acquaintance, hurriedly. "I never make friends. I could be of no use. I am only a dependent, scarcely so good as that. I am nothing here."

"And neither are we," said Agnes, following shyly the step which this strange girl took away from them. "We never were in a house like this before. We do not belong to great people. Mrs Edgerley asked us to come, because we met her at Mr Burlington's, and she has been very kind, but we know no one. Pray, do not go away."

The thoughtful eyes brightened into a sudden gleam. "We are called Atheling," said Marian, interposing in her turn. "My sister is Agnes, and I am Marian—and you Miss—"

"My name is Rachel," said their new friend, with a sudden and violent blush, making all her face crimson. "I have no other—call me so, and I will like it. You think I am of your age; but I am not like you—you do not know half so much as I know."

"No—that is very likely," said Agnes, somewhat puzzled; "but I think you do not mean education," said the young author immediately, seeing Marian somewhat disposed to resent on her behalf this broad assertion. "You mean distress and sorrow. But we have had a great deal of grief at home. We have lost dear little children, one after another. We are not ignorant of grief."

Rachel looked at them with strange observation, wonder, and uncertainty. "But you are ignorant of me—and I am ignorant of you," she said slowly, pausing between her words. "I suppose you mean just what you say, do you? and I am not much used to that. Do you know what I am here for?—only to sing and amuse the people—and you still want to make friends with me!"

"Mrs Edgerley said you were to be a singer, but you did not like it," said Marian; "and I think you are very right."

"Did she say so?—and what more?" said Rachel, smiling faintly. "I want to hear now, though I did not when I heard your voices first."

"She said you were a connection of the family," said Agnes.

The blood rushed again to the young stranger's brow. "Ah! I understand," she said; "she implied—yes. I know how she would do. And you will still be friends with me?"

At that moment it suddenly flashed upon the recollection of both the girls that Mamma had disapproved of this prospective acquaintance. They both blushed with instant consciousness, and neither of them spoke. In an instant Rachel became frozen into a haughtiness far exceeding anything within the power of Mrs Edgerley. Little and slight as she was, her girlish frame rose to the dignity of a young queen. Before Agnes could say a word, she had left them with a slight and lofty bow. Without haste, but with singular rapidity, she crossed the dewy lawn, and went into the house, acknowledging, with a stately inclination of her head, some one who passed her. The girls were so entirely absorbed, watching her progress, that they did not perceive who this other person was.

CHAPTER II

AN EMBARRASSING COMPANION

"Strange creature!" said Sir Langham Portland, who had joined the girls almost before they were aware; "Odd girl! If Lucifer had a sister, I should know where to find her; but a perfect siren so far as music is concerned. Did you hear her sing last night—that thing of Beethoven's—what is the name of it? Do you like Beethoven, though? She, I suppose, worships him."

"We know very little about music," said Marian. She thought it proper to make known the fact, but blushed in spite of herself, and was much ashamed of her own ignorance. Marian was quite distressed and impatient to find herself so much behind every one else.

"Oh!" said Sir Langham—which meant that the handsome guardsman was a good deal flattered by the blush, and did not care at all for the want of information—in fact, he was cogitating within himself, being no great master of the art of conversation, what to speak of next.

"I am afraid Miss—Rachel was not pleased," said Agnes; "we disturbed her here. I am afraid she will think we were rude."

"Eh!" said Sir Langham, with a look of astonishment. "Oh, don't trouble yourself—she's accustomed to that. Pretty place this. Suppose a fellow on the island over there, what a capital sketch he could make;—with two figures instead of three, the effect would be perfect!"

"We were two figures before you came," said Marian, turning half away, and with a smile.

"Ah! quite a different suggestion," said Sir Langham. "Your two figures were all white and angelical—maiden meditation—mine would be—Elysium. Happy sketcher! happier hero!—and you could not suppose a more appropriate scene."

But Agnes and Marian were much too shy and timid to answer this as they might have answered Harry Oswald under the same circumstances. Agnes half interrupted him, being somewhat in haste to change the conversation. "You are an artist yourself?" said Agnes.

"No," said Sir Langham; "not at all,—no more than everybody else is. I have no doubt you know a hundred people better at it than I."

"I do not think, counting every one," said Marian, "that we know a hundred, or the half of a hundred, people altogether; and none of them make sketches. Mrs Edgerley said yours were quite remarkable."

"A great many things are quite remarkable with Mrs Edgerley," said Sir Langham through his mustache. "But what an amazing circle yours must be! One must do something with one's spare time. That old fellow is the hardest rascal to kill of any I know—don't you find him so?"

"No—not when we are at home," said Marian.

"Ah! in the country, I suppose; and you are Lady Bountifuls, and attend to all the village," said Sir Langham. He had quite made up his mind that these young girls, who were not fashionable nor remarkable in any way, save for the wonderful beauty of the youngest, were daughters of some squire in Banburyshire, whom it was Lord Winterbourne's interest to do a service to.

"No, indeed, we have not any village—we are not Lady Bountifuls; but we do a great many things at home," said Marian. Something restrained them both, however, from their heroic purpose of declaring at once their "rank in life;" they shrank, with natural delicacy, from saying anything about themselves to this interrogator, and were by no means clear that it would be right to tell Sir Langham Portland that they lived in Bellevue.

"May we go through the conservatory, I wonder?" said Agnes;—the elder sister, remembering the parting charge of her mother, began to be somewhat uneasy about their handsome companion—he might possibly fall in love with Marian—that was not so very dreadful a hypothesis,—for Agnes was human, and did not object to see the natural enemies of womankind taken captive, subjugated, or even entirely slain. But Marian might fall in love with him! That was an appalling thought; two distinct lines of anxiety began to appear in Agnes's forehead; and the imagination of the young genius instantly called before her the most touching and pathetic picture, of a secret love and a broken heart.

"Marian, we may go into the conservatory," repeated Agnes; and she took her sister's hand and led her to where the Scotch gardener was opening the windows of that fairy palace. Sir Langham still gave them his attendance, following Marian as she passed through the ranks of flowers, and echoing her delight. Sir Langham was rather relieved to find them at last in enthusiasm about something. This familiar and well-known feature of young ladyhood set him much more at his ease.

And the gardener, with benign generosity, gathered some flowers for his young visitors. They thanked him with such thoroughly grateful thanks, and were so respectful of his superior knowledge, that this worthy functionary brightened under their influence. Sir Langham followed surprised and amused. He thought Marian's simple ignorance of all those delicate splendid exotic flowers, as pretty as he would have thought her acquaintance with them had she been better instructed; and when one of her flowers fell from her hand, lifted it up with the air of a paladin, and placed it in his breast. Marian, though she had turned aside, saw him do it by some mysterious perception—not of the eye—and blushed with a secret tremor, half of pleasure, half of amusement. Agnes regarded it a great deal more seriously. Agnes immediately discovered that it was time to go in. She was quite indifferent, we are grieved to say, to the fate of Sir Langham, and thought nothing of disturbing the peace of that susceptible young gentleman; but her protection and guardianship of Marian was a much more serious affair. Their windows were in the end of the house, and commanded no view—so Mrs Edgerley, with a hundred regrets, was grieved to tell them—but these windows looked over an orchard and a clump of chestnuts, where birds sang and dew fell, and the girls were perfectly contented with the prospect; they had three rooms—a dressing-room, and two pretty bedchambers—into all of which the morning sun threw a sidelong glance as he passed; and they had been extremely delighted with their pretty apartments last night.

"Well!" said Agnes, as they arranged their flowers and put them in water, "everything is very pretty, May, but I almost wish we were at home."

"Why?" said Marian; but the beautiful sister had so much perception of the case, that she did not look up, nor show any particular surprise.

"Why?—because—because people don't understand what we are, nor who we belong to, nor how different— Marian, you know quite well what is the cause!"

"But suppose people don't want to know?" said Marian, who was provokingly calm and at her ease; "we cannot go about telling everybody—no one cares. Suppose we were to tell Sir Langham, Agnes? He would think we meant that he has to come to Bellevue; and I am sure you would not like to see him there!"

This was a very conclusive argument, but Agnes had made up her mind to be annoyed.

"And there was Rachel," said Agnes, "I wonder why just at that moment we should have thought of mamma—and now I am sure she will not speak to us again."

"Mamma did not think it quite proper," said Marian doubtfully;—"I am sure I cannot tell why—but we were very near making up friendship without thinking; perhaps it is better as it is."

"It is never proper to hurt any one's feelings—and she is lonely and neglected and by herself," said Agnes. "Mamma cannot be displeased when I tell her; and I will try all I can to-day to meet with Rachel again. I think Rachel would think better of our house than of the Willows. Though it is a beautiful place, it is not kindly; it never could look like home."

"Oh, nonsense! if we had it to ourselves, and they were all here!" cried Marian. That indeed was a paradisaical conception. Agnes's uneasy mood could not stand against such an idea, and she arranged her hair with renewed spirits, having quite given up for the moment all desire for going home.

CHAPTER III

SOCIETY

But Rachel did not join the party either in their drives, their walks, or their conversations. She was not to be seen during the whole day, either out of doors or in, and did not even make her appearance at the dinner-table; and Agnes could not so much as hear any allusion made to her except once, when Mrs Edgerley promised a new arrival, "some really good music," and launched forth in praise of an extraordinary little genius, whom nothing could excuse for concealing her gift from the world. But if Rachel did not appear, Sir Langham did, following Marian with his eyes when he could not follow in person, and hovering about the young beauty like a man bewitched. The homage of such a cavalier was not to be despised; in spite of herself, the smile and the blush brightened upon the sweet face of Marian—she was pleased—she was amused—she was grateful to Sir Langham—and besides had a certain mischievous pleasure in her power over him, and loved to exercise the sway of despotism. Marian new little about coquetry, though she had read with attention Mrs Edgerley's novel on the subject; but, notwithstanding, had "a way" of her own, and some little practice in tantalising poor Harry Oswald, who was by no means so superb a plaything as the handsome guardsman. The excitement and novelty of her position—the attentions paid to her—the pretty things around her—even her own dress, which never before had been so handsome, brightened, with a variable and sweet illumination, the beauty which needed no aggravating circumstance. Poor Sir Langham gave himself up helpless and unresisting, and already, in his honest but somewhat slow imagination, made formal declarations to the supposititious Banburyshire Squire.

Agnes meanwhile sat by Marian's side, rather silent, eagerly watching for the appearance of Rachel—for now it was evening, and the really good music could not be long deferred, if it was to come to-night. Agnes was not neglected, though she had no Sir Langham to watch her movements. Mrs Edgerley herself came to the young genius now and then to introduce some one who was "dying to know the author of Hope Hazlewood;" and half disconcerted, half amused, Agnes began to feel herself entering upon the enjoyment of her reputation. No one could possibly suppose anything more different from the fanciful and delicate fame which charms the young poetic mind with imaginary glories, than these drawing-room compliments and protestations of interest and delight, to which, at first with a deep blush and overpowering embarrassment, and by-and-by with an uneasy consciousness of something ridiculous, the young author sat still and listened. The two sisters kept always close together, and had not courage enough to move from the corner in which they had first established themselves. Agnes, for the moment, had become the reigning whim in the brain of Mrs Edgerley. She came to her side now and then to whisper a few words of caressing encouragement, or to point out to her somebody of note; and when she left her young guest, Mrs Edgerley flew at once to the aforesaid somebody to call his or her attention to the pair of sisters, one of whom had such genius, and the other such beauty. Marian, occupied with her own concerns, took all this very quietly. Agnes grew annoyed, uneasy, displeased; she did not remember that she had once been mortified at the neglect of her pretty hostess, nor that Mrs Edgerley's admiration was as evanescent as her neglect. She began to think everybody was laughing at her claims to distinction, and that she amused the people, sitting here uneasily receiving compliments, immovable in her chair—and she was extremely grateful to Mr Agar, her former acquaintance, when he came, looking amused and paying no compliments, to talk to her, and to screen her from observation. Mr Agar had been watching her uneasiness, her embarrassment, her self-annoyance. He was quite pleased with the "study;" it pleased him as much as a Watteau, or a cabinet of old china; and what could connoisseur say more?

"You must confide your annoyance to me. I am your oldest acquaintance," said Mr Agar. "What has happened? Has your pretty sister been naughty—eh? or are all the people so much delighted with your book?"

"Yes," said Agnes, holding down her head a little, with a momentary shame that her two troubles should have been so easily found out.

"And why should they not be delighted?" said the ancient beau. "You would have liked me a great deal better had I been the same, when I first saw you; do you not like it now?"

"No," said Agnes.

"Yes; no. Your eyes do not talk in monosyllables," said the old gentleman, "eh? What has poor Sir Langham done to merit that flash of dissatisfaction? and I wonder what is the meaning of all these anxious glances towards the door?"

"I was looking for—for the young lady they call Rachel," said Agnes. "Do you know who she is, sir?—can you tell me? I am afraid she thought we were rude this morning, when we met her; and I wish very much to see her to-night."

"Ah! I know nothing of the young lady, but a good deal of the voice," said Mr Agar; "a fine soprano,—a good deal of expression, and plenty of fire. Yes, she needs nothing but cultivation to make a great success."

"I think, sir," said Agnes, suddenly breaking in upon this speech, "if you would speak to Mrs Edgerley for her, perhaps they would not teaze her about being a singer. She hates it. I know she does; and it would be very good of you to help her, for she has no friends."

Mr Agar looked at the young pleader with a smile of surprised amusement. "And why should I interfere on her behalf? and why should she not be a singer? and how do you suppose I could persuade myself to do such an injury to Art?"

"She dislikes it very much," said Agnes. "She is a woman—a girl—a delicate mind; it would be very cruel to bring her before the world; and indeed I am sure if you would speak to Mrs Edgerley—"

"My dear young lady," cried Mr Agar, with a momentary shrug of his eyebrows, and look of comic distress, "you entirely mistake my rôle. I am not a knight-errant for the rescue of distressed princesses. I am a humble servant of the beautiful; and a young lady's tremors are really not cause enough to induce me to resign a fine soprano. No. I bow before my fair enslavers," said the ancient Corydon, with a reverential obeisance, which belonged, like his words, to another century; "but my true and only mistress is Art."

Agnes was silenced in a moment; but whether by this declaration, or by the entrance of Rachel, who suddenly appeared, gliding in at a side-door, could not be determined. Rachel came in, so quickly, and with such a gliding motion, that anybody less intently on the watch could not have discovered the moment of her appearance. She was soon at the piano, and heard immediately; but she came there in a miraculous manner to all the other observers, as if she had dropped from heaven.

And while the connoisseur stood apart to listen undisturbed, and Mrs Edgerley's guests were suddenly stayed in their flutter of talk and mutual criticism by the "really good music" which their hostess had promised them, Agnes sat listening, moved and anxious,—not to the song, but to the singer. She thought the music—pathetic, complaining, and resentful—instead of being a renowned chef-d'œuvre of a famous composer, was the natural outcry of this lonely girl. She thought she could hear the solitary heart, the neglected life, making its appeal indignant and sorrowful to some higher ear than all these careless listeners. She bent unconsciously towards the singer, forgetting all her mother's rules of manners, and, leaning forward, supported her rapt and earnest face with her hand. Mrs Edgerley paused to point out to some one the sweet enthusiasm, the delightful impressionable nature of her charming young friend; but to tell the truth, Agnes was not thinking at all of the music. It seemed to her a strange impassioned monologue,—a thing of which she was the sole hearer,—an irrepressible burst of confidence, addressed to the only one here present who cared to receive the same.

When it was over she raised herself almost painfully from her listening posture; she did not join in any of the warm expressions of delight which burst from her neighbours; and with extreme impatience Agnes listened to the cool criticism of Mr Agar, who was delivering his opinion very near her. Her heart ached as she saw the musician turn haughtily aside, and heard her say, "I am here when you want me again;" and Rachel withdrew to a sofa in a corner, and, shading her delicate small face entirely with her hand, took up a book and read, or pretended to read. Agnes looked on with eager interest, while several people, one after another, approached the singer to offer her some of the usual compliments, and retreated immediately, disconcerted by their reception. Leaning back in her corner, with her book held obstinately before her, and the small pale hand shading the delicate face, it was impossible to intrude upon Rachel. Agnes sat watching her, quite absorbed and sad—thinking in her own quick creative mind, many a proud thought for Rachel—and fancying she could read in that unvarying and statue-like attitude a world of tumultuous feelings. She was so much occupied that she took no notice of Sir Langham; and even Marian, though she appealed to her twenty times, did not get more than a single word in reply.

"Is she not the most wonderful little genius?" cried Mrs Edgerley, making one of her sudden descents upon Agnes. "I tell everybody she is next to you—quite next to you in talent. I expect she will make quite a furor next season when she makes her début."

"But she dislikes it so much," said Agnes.

"What, music? Oh, you mean coming out: poor child, she does not know what is for her own advantage," said Mrs Edgerley. "My love, in her circumstances, people have no right to consult their feelings; and a successful singer may live quite a fairy life. Music is so entrancing—these sort of people make fortunes immediately, and then, of course, she could retire, and be as private as she pleased. Oh, yes, I am sure she will be delighted to gratify you, Mr Agar: she will sing again."

It scarcely required a word from Mrs Edgerley—scarcely a sign. Rachel seemed to know by intuition when she was wanted, and, putting down her book, went to the piano again;—perhaps Agnes was not so attentive this time, for she felt herself suddenly roused a few minutes after by a sudden tremor in the magnificent voice—a sudden shake and tremble, having the same effect upon the singing which a start would have upon the frame. Agnes looked round eagerly to see the cause—there was no cause apparent—and no change whatever in the company, save for the pale spasmodic face of Lord Winterbourne, newly arrived, and saluting his daughter at the door.

Was it this? Agnes could not wait to inquire, for immediately the music rose and swelled into such a magnificent burst and overflow that every one held his breath. To the excited ear of Agnes, it sounded like a glorious challenge and defiance, irrestrainable and involuntary; and ere the listeners had ceased to wonder, the music was over, and the singer gone.

"A sudden effect—our young performer is not without dramatic talent," said Mr Agar. Agnes said nothing; but she searched in the corner of the sofa with her eyes, watched the side-door, and stole sidelong looks at Lord Winterbourne. He never seemed at his ease, this uncomfortable nobleman; he had a discomfited look to-night, like a man defeated, and Agnes could not help thinking of Charlie, with his sudden enmity, and the old acquaintance of her father, and all the chances connected with Aunt Bridget's bequest; for the time, in her momentary impulse of dislike and repulsion, she thought her noble neighbour, ex-minister and peer of the realm as he was, was not a match for the big boy.

"Agnes, somebody says Lord Winterbourne is her father—Rachel's father—and she cannot bear him. Was that what Mrs Edgerley meant?" whispered Marian in her ear with a look of sorrow. "Did you hear her voice tremble—did you see how she went away? They say she is his daughter—oh, Agnes, can it be true?"

But Agnes did not know, and could not answer: if it was true, then it was very certain that Rachel must be right; and that there were depths and mysteries and miseries of life, of which, in spite of all their innocent acquaintance with sorrow, these simple girls had scarcely heard, and never knew.

CHAPTER IV

MAKING FRIENDS

The next morning, and the next again, Agnes and Marian vainly sought the little bower of willows looking for Rachel. Once they saw her escape hastily out of the shrubbery as they returned from their search, and knew by that means that she wished to avoid them; but though they heard her sing every night, they made no advance in their friendship, for that was the only time in which Rachel was visible, and then she defied all intrusion upon her haughty solitude. Mr Agar himself wisely kept aloof from the young singer. The old gentleman did not choose to subject himself to the chance of a repulse.

But if Rachel avoided them, Sir Langham certainly did not. This enterprising youth, having discovered their first early walk, took care to be in the way when they repeated it, and on the fourth morning, without saying anything to each other, the sisters unanimously decided to remain within the safe shelter of their own apartments. From a corner of their window they could see Sir Langham in vexation and impatience traversing the slope of the lawn, and pulling off the long ashy willow-leaves to toss them into the river. Marian laughed to herself without giving a reason, and Agnes was very glad they had remained in the house; but the elder sister, reasoning with elaborate wisdom, made up her mind to ask no further questions about Sir Langham, how Marian liked him, or what she thought of his attentions. Agnes thought too many inquiries might "put something into her head."

Proceeding upon this astute line of policy, Agnes took no notice whatever of all the assiduities of the handsome guardsman, not even his good-natured and brotherly attentions to herself. They were only to remain a fortnight at the Willows—very little harm, surely, could be done in that time, and they had but a slender chance of meeting again. So the elder sister, in spite of her charge of Marian, quieted her conscience and her fears—and in the mean time the two girls, with thorough and cordial simplicity, took pleasure in their holiday, finding everybody kind to them, and excusing with natural humbleness any chance symptom of neglect.

They had been a week at the Willows, and every day had used every means in their power to see Rachel again, when one morning, suddenly, without plot or premeditation, Agnes encountered her in a long passage which ran from the hall to the morning-room of Mrs Edgerley. There was a long window at the end of this passage, against which the small rapid figure, clothed in a dark close-fitting dress, without the smallest relief of ornament, stood out strangely, outlined and surrounded by the light. Agnes had some flowers in her hand, the gift of her acquaintance the gardener. She fancied that Rachel glanced at them wistfully, and she was eager of the opportunity. "They are newly gathered—will you take some?" said Agnes, holding out her hands to her. The young stranger paused, and looked for an instant distrustfully at her and the flowers. Agnes hoped nothing better than to be dismissed with a haughty word of thanks; but while Rachel lingered, the door of the morning-room was opened, and an approaching footstep struck upon the tiled floor. The young singer did not look behind her, did not pause to see who it was, but recognising the step, as it seemed, with a sudden start and tremor, suddenly laid her hand on Agnes's arm, and drew her hurriedly in within a door which she flung open. As soon as they were in, Rachel closed the door with haste and force, and stood close by it with evident agitation and excitement. "I beg your pardon—but hush, do not speak till he is past," she said in a whisper. Agnes, much discomposed and troubled, went to the window, as people generally do in embarrassment, and looked out vacantly for a moment upon the kitchen-garden and the servants' "offices," the only prospect visible from it. She could not help sharing a little the excitement of her companion, as she thought upon her own singular position here, and listened with an involuntary thrill to the slow step of the unknown person from whom they had fled, pacing along the long cool corridor to pass this door.

But he did not pass the door; he made a moment's pause at it, and then entered, coming full upon Rachel as she stood, agitated and defiant, close upon the threshold. Agnes scarcely looked round, yet she could see it was Lord Winterbourne.

"Good morning, Rachel. I trust you get on well here," said the new-comer in a soft and stealthy tone: "is this your sitting-room? Ah, bare enough, I see. Your are in splendid voice, I am glad to hear; some one is coming to-night, I understand, whose good opinion is important. You must take care to do yourself full justice. Are you well, child?"

He had approached close to her, and bestowed a cold kiss upon the brow which burned under his touch. "Perfectly well," said Rachel, drawing back with a voice unusually harsh and clear. Her agitation and excitement had for the moment driven all the music from her tones.

"And your brother is quite well, and all going on in the usual way at Winterbourne," continued the stranger. "I expect to have the house very full in a few weeks, and you must arrange with the housekeeper where to bestow yourselves. You, of course, I shall want frequently. As for Louis, I suppose he does nothing but fish and mope as usual. I have no desire to see more than I can help of him."

"There is no fear; his desire is as strong as yours," cried Rachel suddenly, her face varying from the most violent flush to a sudden passionate paleness. Lord Winterbourne answered by his cold smile of ridicule.

"I know his amiable temper," he said. "Now, remember what I have said about to-night. Do yourself justice. It will be for your advantage. Good-by. Remember me to Louis."

The door opened again, and he was gone. Rachel closed it almost violently, and threw herself upon a chair. "We owe him no duty—none. I will not believe it," cried Rachel. "No—no—no—I do not belong to him! Louis is not his!"

All this time, in the greatest distress and embarrassment, Agnes stood by the window, grieved to be an unwilling listener, and reluctant to remind Rachel of her presence by going away. But Rachel had not forgotten that she was there. With a sudden effort this strange solitary girl composed herself and came up to Agnes. "Do you know Lord Winterbourne?" she said quickly; "have you heard of him before you came here?"

"I think— but, indeed, I may be mistaken," said Agnes timidly; "I think papa once knew him long ago."

"And did he think him a good man?" said Rachel.

This was a very embarrassing question. Agnes turned away, retreated uneasily, blushed, and hesitated. "He never speaks of him; I cannot tell," said Agnes.

"Do you know," said Rachel, eagerly, "they say he is my father—Louis's father; but we do not believe it, neither I nor he."

To this singular statement Agnes made no answer, save by a look of surprise and inquiry; the frightful uncertainty of such a position as this was beyond the innocent comprehension of Agnes Atheling. She looked with a blank and painful surprise into her young companion's face.

"And I will not sing to-night; I will not, because he bade me!" said Rachel. "Is it my fault that I can sing? but I am to be punished for it; they make me come to amuse them; and they want me to be a public singer. I should not care," cried the poor girl suddenly, in a violent burst of tears, passing from her passion and excitement to her natural character—"I would not mind it for myself, if it were not for Louis. I would do anything they bade me myself; I do not care, nothing matters to me; but Louis—Louis! he thinks it is disgrace, and it would break his heart!"

"Is that your brother?" said Agnes, bending over her, and endeavouring to soothe her excitement. Rachel made no immediate answer.

"He has disgrace enough already, poor boy," said Rachel. "We are nobody's children; or we are Lord Winterbourne's; and he who might be a king's son—and he has not even a name! Yes, he is my brother, my poor Louis: we are twins; and we have nobody but each other in the whole world."

"If he is as old as you," said Agnes, who was only accustomed to the usages of humble houses, and knew nothing of the traditions of a noble race, "you should not stay at Winterbourne: a man can always work—you ought not to stay."

"Do you think so?" cried Rachel eagerly. "Louis says so always, and I beg and plead with him. When he was only eighteen he ran away: he went and enlisted for a soldier—a common man—and was away a year, and then they bought him off, and promised to get him a commission; and I made him promise to me—perhaps it was selfish, for I could not live when he was gone—I made him promise not to go away again. And there he is at Winterbourne. I know you never saw any one like him; and now all these heartless people are going there, and Lord Winterbourne is afraid of him, and never will have him seen, and the whole time I will be sick to the very heart lest he should go away."

"But I think he ought to go away," said Agnes gravely.

Her new friend looked up in her face with an earnest and trembling scrutiny. This poor girl had a great deal more passion and vehemence in her character than had ever been called for in Agnes, but, an uninstructed and ill-trained child, knew nothing of the primitive independence, and had never been taught to think of right and wrong.

"We have a little house there," said Agnes, with a sudden thought. "Do you know the Old Wood Lodge? Papa's old aunt left it to him, and they say it is very near the Hall."

At the name Rachel started suddenly, rose up at once with one of her quick inconsiderate movements, and, throwing her arms round Agnes, kissed her cheek. "I knew I ought to know you," said Rachel, "and yet I did not think of the name. Dear old Miss Bridget, she loved Louis. I am sure she loved him; and we know every room in the house, and every leaf on the trees. If you come there, we will see you every day."

"We are coming there—and my mother," said Agnes. "I know you will be pleased to see mamma," said the good girl, her face brightening, and her eyes filling in spite of herself; "every one thinks she is like their own mother—and when you come to us you will think you are at home."

"We never had any mother," said Rachel, sadly; "we never had any home; we do not know what it is. Look, this is my home here."

Agnes looked round the large bare apartment, in which the only article of furniture worth notice was an old piano, and which looked only upon the little square of kitchen-garden and the servants' rooms. It was somewhat larger than both the parlours in Bellevue, and for a best room would have rejoiced Mrs Atheling's ambitious heart; but Agnes was already a little wiser than she had been in Islington, and it chilled her heart to compare this lonely and dreary apartment with all the surrounding luxuries, which Rachel saw and did not share.

"Come up with me and see Marian," said Agnes, putting her arm through her companion's; "you are not to avoid us now any more; we are all to be friends after to-day."

And Rachel, who did not know what friendship was, yielded, thinking of Louis. Had she been wrong throughout in keeping him, by her entreaties, so long at Winterbourne? A vision of a home, all to themselves, burst once in a great delight upon the mind of Rachel. If Louis would only consent to it! With such a motive before her as that, the poor girl fancied she "would not mind" being a singer after all.

CHAPTER V

CONFIDENTIAL

When the first ice was broken, Rachel became perfectly confidential with her new friends—perfectly confidential—far more so than they, accustomed to the domestic privateness of humble English life, could understand. This poor girl had no restraint upon her for family pride or family honour; no compensation in family sympathy; and her listeners, who had very little skill in the study of character, though one of them had written a novel, were extremely puzzled with a kind of doubleness, perfectly innocent and unconscious, which made Rachel's thoughts and words at different moments like the words and the thoughts of two different people. At one time she was herself, humble, timid, and content to do anything which any authority bade her do; but in a moment she remembered Louis; and the change was instantaneous—she became proud, stately, obdurate, even defiant. She was no longer herself, but the shadow and representative of her brother; and in this view Rachel resisted and defied every influence, anchoring her own wavering will upon Louis, and refusing, with unreasonable and unreasoning obstinacy, all injunctions and all persuasions coming from those to whom her brother was opposed. She seemed, indeed, to have neither plan nor thought for herself: Louis was her inspiration. She seemed to have been born for no other purpose but to follow, to love, and to serve this brother, who to her was all the world. As she sat on the pretty chintz sofa in that sunny little dressing-room where Agnes and Marian passed the morning, running rapidly over the environs of the Old Wood Lodge, and telling them about their future neighbours, they were amazed and amused to find the total absence of personal opinion, and almost of personal liking, in their new acquaintance. She had but one standard, to which she referred everything, and that was Louis. They saw the very landscape, not as it was, but as it appeared to this wonderful brother. They became acquainted with the village and its inhabitants through the medium of Louis's favourites and Louis's aversions. They were young enough and simple enough themselves to be perfectly ready to invest any unknown ideal person with all the gifts of fancy; and Louis immediately leaped forth from the unknown world, a presence and an authority to them both.

"The Rector lives in the Old Wood House," said Rachel, for the first time pausing, and looking somewhat confused in her rapid summary. "I am sure I do not know what to think—but Louis does not like him. I suppose you will not like him; and yet,"—here a little faint colour came upon the young speaker's pale face—"sometimes I have fancied he would have been a friend if we had let him; and he is quite sure to like you."

Saying this, she turned a somewhat wistful look upon Agnes—blushing more perceptibly, but with no sunshine or brightness in her blush. "Yes," said Rachel slowly, "he will like you—he will do for you; and you," she added, turning with sudden eagerness to Marian, "you are for Louis—remember! You are not to think of any one else till you see Louis. You never saw any one like him; he is like a prince to look at, and I know he is a great genius. Your sister shall have the Rector, and Louis shall be for you."

All this Rachel said hurriedly, but with the most perfect gravity, even with a tinge of sadness—grieved, as they could perceive, that her brother did not like the Rector, but making no resistance against a doom so unquestionable as the dislike of Louis: but her timid heart was somehow touched upon the subject; she became thoughtful, and lingered over it with a kind of melancholy pleasure. "Perhaps Louis might come to like him if he was connected with you," said Rachel meditatively; and the faint colour wavered and flickered on her face, and at last passed away with a low but very audible sigh.

"But they are all Riverses," she continued, in her usual rapid way. "The Rector of Winterbourne is always a Rivers—it is the family living; and if Lord Winterbourne's son should die, I suppose Mr Lionel would be the heir. His sister lives with him, quite an old lady: and then there is another Miss Rivers, who lives far off, at Abingford all the way. Did you ever hear of Miss Anastasia? But she does not call herself Miss— only the Honourable Anastasia Rivers. Old Miss Bridget was once her governess. Lord Winterbourne will never permit her to see us; but I almost think Louis would like to be friends with her, only he will not take the trouble. They are not at all friends with her at Winterbourne."

"Is she a relation?" said Agnes. The girls by this time were so much interested in the family story that they did not notice this admirable reason for the inclination of Louis towards this old lady unknown.

"She is the old lord's only child," said Rachel. "The old lord was Lord Winterbourne's brother, and he died abroad, and no one knew anything about him for a long time before he died. We want very much to hear about him; indeed, I ought not to tell you—but Louis thinks perhaps he knew something about us. Louis will not believe we are Lord Winterbourne's children; and though we are poor disgraced children any way, and though he hates the very name of Rivers, I think he would almost rather we belonged to the old lord; for he says," added Rachel with great seriousness, "that one cannot hate one's father, if he is dead."

The girls drew back a little, half in horror; but though she spoke in this rebellious fashion, there was no consciousness of wrong in Rachel's innocent and quiet face.

"And we have so many troubles," burst forth the poor girl suddenly. "And I sometimes sit and cry all day, and pray to God to be dead. And when anybody is kind to me," she continued, some sudden remembrance moving her to an outburst of tears, and raising the colour once more upon her colourless cheek, "I am so weak and so foolish, and would do anything they tell me. I do not care, I am sure, what I do—it does not matter to me; but Louis—no, certainly, I will not sing to-night."

"I wish very much," said Agnes, with an earnestness and courage which somewhat startled Marian—"I wish very much you could come home with us to our little house in Bellevue."

"Yes," said Marian doubtfully; but the younger sister, though she shared the generous impulse, could not help a secret glance at Agnes—an emphatic reminder of Mamma.

"No, I must make no friends," said Rachel, rising under the inspiration of Louis's will and injunctions. "It is very kind of you, but I must not do it. Oh, but remember you are to come to Winterbourne, and I will try to bring Louis to see you; and I am sure you know a great deal better, and could talk to him different from me. Do you know," she continued solemnly, "they never have given me any education at all, except to sing? I have never been taught anything, nor indeed Louis either, which is much worse than me—only he is a great genius, and can teach himself. The Rector wanted to help him; that is why I am always sure, if Louis would let him, he would be a friend."

And again a faint half-distinguishable blush came upon Rachel's face. No, it meant nothing, though Agnes and Marian canvassed and interpreted after their own fashion this delicate suffusion; it only meant that the timid gentle heart might have been touched had there been room for more than Louis; but Louis was supreme, and filled up all.

CHAPTER VI

THREE FRIENDS

That night, faithful to her purpose, Rachel did not appear in the drawing-room. How far her firmness would have supported her, had she been left to herself, it is impossible to tell; but she was not left to herself. "Mrs Edgerley came, saying just the same things as Lord Winterbourne," said Rachel, "and I knew I should be firm. Louis cannot endure Mrs Edgerley." She said this with the most entire unconsciousness that she revealed the whole motive and strength of her resistance in the words. Rachel, indeed, was perfectly unaware of the entire subjection in which she kept even her thoughts and her affections to her brother; but she could not help a little anxiety and a little nervousness as to whether "Louis would like" her new acquaintances. She herself brightened wonderfully under the influence of these companions—expanded out of her dull and irritable solitude, and with girlish eagerness forecast their fortunes, seizing at once, in idea, upon Marian as the destined bride of Louis, and with a voluntary self-sacrifice making over, with a sigh and a secret thrill of pride, the only person who had ever wakened any interest in her own most sisterly bosom, to Agnes. She pleased herself greatly with these visions, and built them on a foundation still more brittle than that of Alnaschar—for it was possible that all her pleasant dreams might be thrown into the dust in a moment, if—dreadful possibility!—"Louis did not like" these first friends of poor Rachel's youth.

And when she brightened under this genial influence, and softened out of the haughtiness and solitary state which, indeed, was quite foreign to her character, Rachel became a very attractive little person. Even the sudden change in her sentiments and bearing when she returned to her old feeling of representing Louis, added a charm. Her large eyes troubled and melting, her pale small features which were very fine and regular, though so far from striking, her noble little head and small pretty figure, attracted in the highest degree the admiration of her new friends. Marian, who rather suspected that she herself was rather pretty, could not sufficiently admire the grace and refinement of Rachel; and

Agnes, though candidly admitting that there was "scarcely any one" so beautiful as Marian, notwithstanding bestowed a very equal share of her regard upon the attractions of their companion. And the trio fell immediately into all the warmth of girlish friendship. The Athelings went to visit Rachel in her great bare study, and Rachel came to visit them in their pretty little dressing-room; and whether in that sun-bright gay enclosure, or within the sombre and undecorated walls of the room which looked out on the kitchen-garden, a painter would have been puzzled to choose which was the better scene. They were so pretty a group anywhere—so animated—so full of eager life and intelligence—so much disposed to communicate everything that occurred to them, that Rachel's room brightened under the charm of their presence as she herself had done. And this new acquaintanceship made a somewhat singular revolution in the drawing-room—where the young musician, after her singing, was instantly joined by her two friends. She was extremely reserved and shy of every one else, and even of them occasionally, under the eyes of Mrs Edgerley; but she was no longer the little tragical princess who buried herself in the book and the corner, and neither heard nor saw anything going around her. And the fact that they had some one whose position was even more doubtful and uneasy than their own, to give heart and courage to, animated Agnes and Marian, as nothing else could have done. They recovered their natural spirits, and were no longer overawed by the great people surrounding them; they had so much care for Rachel that they forgot to be self-conscious, or to trouble themselves with inquiries touching their own manners and deportment, and what other people thought of the same; and on the whole, though their simplicity was not quite so amusing as at first, "other people" began to have a kindness for the fresh young faces, always so honest, cloudless, and sincere.

But Agnes's "reputation" had died away, and left very little trace behind it. Mrs Edgerley had found other lions, and at the present moment held in delusion an unfortunate young poet, who was much more like to be harmed by the momentary idolatry than Agnes. The people who had been dying to know the author of Hope Hazlewood, had all found out that the shy young genius did not talk in character— had no gift of conversation, and, indeed, did nothing at all to keep up her fame; and if Agnes chanced to feel a momentary mortification at the prompt desertion of all her admirers, she wisely kept the pang to herself, and said nothing about it. They were not neglected—for the accomplished authoress of Coquetry and the Beau Monde had some kindness at her heart after all, and had always a smile to spare for her young guests when they came in her way; they were permitted to roam freely about the gardens and the conservatory; they were by no means hindered in their acquaintance with Rachel, whom Mrs Edgerley was really much disposed to bring out and patronise; and one of them, the genius or the beauty, as best suited her other companions, was not unfrequently honoured with a place in Mrs Edgerley's barouche—a pretty shy lay figure in that rustling, radiant, perfumy bouquet of fine ladies, who talked over her head about things and people perfectly unknown to the silent auditor, and impressed her with a vague idea that this elegant and easy gossip was brilliant "conversation," though it did not quite sound, after all, like that grand unattainable conversation to be found in books. After this fashion, liking their novel life wonderfully well, and already making a home of that sunny little dressing-room, they drew gradually towards the end of their fortnight. As yet nothing at all marvellous had happened to them, and even Agnes seemed to have forgotten the absolute necessity of letting everybody know that they "did not belong to great people," but instead of a rural Hall, or Grange of renown, lived only in Number Ten, Bellevue.

CHAPTER VII

A TERRIBLE EVENT

For Agnes, we are grieved to confess, had fallen into all the sudden fervour of a most warm and enthusiastic girlish friendship. She forgot to watch over her sister, though Mrs Atheling's letters did not fail to remind her of her duty; she forgot to ward off the constant regards of Sir Langham. She began to be perfectly indifferent and careless of the superb sentinel who mounted guard upon Marian every night. For the time, Agnes was entirely occupied with Rachel, and with the new world so full of a charmed unknown life, which seemed to open upon them all in this Old Wood Lodge; she spent hours dreaming of some discovery which might change the position of the unfortunate brother and sister; she took up with warmth and earnestness their dislike to Lord Winterbourne. If it sometimes occurred to her what a frightful sentiment this was on the part of children to their father, she corrected herself suddenly, and declared in her own mind, with heart and energy, that he could not be their father—that there was no resemblance between them. But this, it must be confessed, was a puzzling subject, and offered continual ground for speculation; for princes and princesses, stolen away in their childhood, were extremely fictitious personages, even to an imagination which had written a novel; and Agnes could not help a thrill of apprehension when she thought of Louis and Marian, of the little romance which Rachel had made up between them, and how her own honourable father and mother would look upon this unhappy scion of a noble house—this poor boy who had no name.

This future, so full of strange and exciting possibilities, attracted with an irresistible power the imaginative mind of Agnes. She went through it chapter by chapter—through earnest dialogues, overpowering emotions, many a varying and exciting scene. The Old Wood Lodge, the Old Wood House, the Hall, the Rector, the old Miss Rivers, the unknown hero, Louis—these made a little private world of persons and places to the vivid imagination of the young dreamer. They floated down even upon Mrs Edgerley's drawing-room, extinguishing its gay lights, its pretty faces, and its hum of conversation; but with still more effect filled all her mind and meditations, as she rested, half reclining, upon the pretty chintz sofa in the pretty dressing-room, in the sweet summer noon with which this sweet repose was so harmonious and suitable. The window was open, and the soft wind blowing in fluttered all the leaves of that book upon the little table, which the sunshine, entering too, brightened into a dazzling whiteness with all its rims and threads of gold. A fragrant breath came up from the garden, a hum of soft sound from all the drowsy world out of doors. Agnes, in the corner of the sofa, laying back her head among its pretty cushions, with the smile of fancy on her lips, and the meditative inward light shining in her eyes, playing her foot idly on the carpet, playing her fingers idly among a little knot of flowers which lay at her side, and which, in this sweet indolence, she had not yet taken the trouble to arrange in the little vase— was as complete a picture of maiden meditation—of those charmed fancies, sweet and fearless, which belong to her age and kind, as painter or poet could desire to see.

When Marian suddenly broke in upon the retirement of her sister, disturbed, fluttered, a little afraid, but with no appearance of painfulness, though there was a certain distress in her excitement. Marian's eyes were downcast, abashed, and dewy, her colour unusually bright, her lips apart, her heart beating high. She came into the little quiet room with a sudden burst, as if she had fled from some one; but when she came within the door, paused as suddenly, put up her hands to her face, blushed an overpowering blush, and dropped at once with the shyest, prettiest movement in the world, into a low chair which stood behind the door. Agnes, waking slowly out of her own bright mist of fancy, saw all this with a faint wonder—noticing scarcely anything more than that Marian surely grew prettier every day, and indeed had never looked so beautiful all her life.

"May! you look quite—" lovely, Agnes was about to say; but she paused in consideration of her sister's feelings, and said "frightened" instead.

"Oh, no wonder! Agnes, something has happened," said Marian. She began to look even more frightened as she spoke; yet the pretty saucy lip moved a little into something that resembled suppressed and silent laughter. In spite, however, of this one evidence of a secret mixture of amusement, Marian was extremely grave and visibly afraid.

"What has happened? Is it about Rachel?" asked Agnes, instantly referring Marian's agitation to the subject of her own thoughts.

"About Rachel! you are always thinking about Rachel," said Marian, with a momentary sparkle of indignation. "It is something a great deal more important; it is—oh, Agnes! Sir Langham has been speaking to me—"

Agnes raised herself immediately with a start of eagerness and surprise, accusing herself. She had forgotten all about this close and pressing danger—she had neglected her guardianship—she looked with an appalled and pitying look upon her beautiful sister. In Agnes's eyes, it was perfectly visible already that here was an end of Marian's happiness—that she had bestowed her heart upon Sir Langham, and that accordingly this heart had nothing to do but to break.

"What did he say?" asked Agnes solemnly.

"He said— oh, I am sure you know very well what he was sure to say," cried Marian, holding down her head, and tying knots in her little handkerchief; "he said—he liked me—and wanted to know if I would consent. But it does not matter what he said," said Marian, sinking her voice very low, and redoubling the knots upon the cambric; "it is not my fault, indeed, Agnes. I did not think he would have done it; I thought it was all like Harry Oswald; and you never said a word. What was I to do?"

"What did you say?" asked Agnes again, with breathless anxiety, feeling the reproach, but making no answer to it.

"I said nothing: it was in Mrs Edgerley's morning-room, and she came in almost before he was done speaking; and I was so very glad, and ran away. What could I do?" said again the beautiful culprit, becoming a little more at her ease; but during all this time she never lifted her eyes to her sister's face.

"What will you say, then? Marian, you make me very anxious; do not trifle with me," said Agnes.

"It is you who are trifling," retorted the young offender; "for you know if you had told the people at once, as you said you would—but I don't mean to be foolish either," said Marian, rising suddenly, and throwing herself half into her sister's arms; "and now, Agnes, you must go and tell him—indeed you must—and say that we never intended to deceive anybody, and meant no harm."

"I must tell him!" said Agnes, with momentary dismay; and then the elder sister put her arm round the beautiful head which leaned on her shoulder, in a caressing and sympathetic tenderness. "Yes, May," said Agnes sadly, "I will do anything you wish—I will say whatever you wish. We ought not to have come here, where you were sure to meet with all these perils. Marian! for my mother's sake you must try to keep up your heart when we get home."

The answer Marian made to this solemn appeal was to raise her eyes, full of wondering and mischievous brightness, and to draw herself immediately from Agnes's embrace with a low laugh of excitement. "Keep up my heart! What do you mean?" said Marian; but she immediately hastened to her own particular sleeping-room, and, lost within its mazy muslin curtains, waited for no explanation. Agnes, disturbed and grave, and much overpowered by her own responsibility, did not know what to think. Present appearances were not much in favour of the breaking of Marian's heart.

CHAPTER VIII

AN EXPLANATION

"But what am I to say?"

To this most difficult question Agnes could not find any satisfactory answer. Marian, though so nearly concerned in it, gave her no assistance whatever. Marian went wandering about the three little rooms, flitting from one to another with unmistakable restlessness, humming inconsistent snatches of song, sometimes a little disposed to cry, sometimes moved to smiles, extremely variable, and full of a sweet and pleasant agitation. Agnes followed her fairy movements with grave eyes, extremely watchful and anxious—was she grieved?—was she pleased? was she really in love?

But Marian made no sign. She would not intrust her sister with any message from herself. She was almost disposed to be out of temper when Agnes questioned her. "You know very well what must be said," said Marian; "you have only to tell him who we are—and I suppose that will be quite enough for Sir Langham. Do you not think so, Agnes?"

"I think it all depends upon how he feels—and how you feel," said the anxious sister; but Marian turned away with a smile and made no reply. To tell the truth, she could not at all have explained her own sentiments. She was very considerably flattered by the homage of the handsome guardsman, and fluttered no less by the magnificent and marvellous idea of being a ladyship. There was nothing very much on her part to prevent this beautiful Marian Atheling from becoming as pretty a Lady Portland, and by-and-by, as affectionate a one, as even the delighted imagination of Sir Langham could conceive. But Marian was still entirely fancy free—not at all disinclined to be persuaded into love with Sir Langham, but at present completely innocent of any serious emotions—pleased, excited, in the sweetest flutter of girlish expectation, amusement, and triumph—but nothing more.

And from that corner of the window from which they could gain a sidelong glance at the lawn and partial view of the shrubbery, Sir Langham was now to be descried wandering about as restlessly as Marian, pulling off stray twigs and handfuls of leaves in the most ruthless fashion, and scattering them on his path. Marian drew Agnes suddenly and silently to the window, and pointed out the impatient figure loitering about among the trees. Agnes looked at him with dismay. "Am I to go now—to go out and seek him?—is it proper?" said Agnes, somewhat horrified at the thought. Marian took up the open book from the table, and drew the low chair into the sunshine. "In the evening everybody will be there," said Marian, as she began to read, or to pretend to read. Agnes paused for a moment in the most painful doubt and perplexity. "I suppose, indeed, it had better be done at once," she said to herself, taking up her bonnet with very unenviable feelings. Poor Agnes! her heart beat louder and louder, as she tied the strings with trembling fingers, and prepared to go. There was Marian bending down over the book on her knees, sitting in the sunshine with the full summer light burning upon her hair, and one cheek flushed with the pressure of her supporting hand. She glanced up eagerly, but she said nothing; and Agnes, very pale and extremely doubtful, went upon her strange errand. It was the most perplexing and uncomfortable business in the world—and was it proper? But she reassured herself a little as she went down stairs—if any one should see her going out to seek Sir Langham! "I will tell Mrs Edgerley the reason," thought Agnes—she supposed at least no one could have any difficulty in understanding that.

So she hastened along the garden paths, very shyly, looking quite pale, and with a palpitating heart. Sir Langham knew nothing of her approach till he turned round suddenly on hearing the shy hesitating rapid step behind. He thought it was Marian for a moment, and made one eager step forward; then he paused, half expecting, half indignant. Agnes, breathless and hurried, gave him no time to address her—she burst into her little speech with all the eager temerity of fear.

"If you please, Sir Langham, I have something to say to you," said Agnes. "You must have been deceived in us—you do not know who we are. We do not belong to great people—we have never before been in a house like Mrs Edgerley's. I came to tell you at once, for we did not think it honest that you should not know."

"Know—know what?" cried Sir Langham. Never guardsman before was filled with such illimitable amaze.

Agnes had recovered her self-possession to some extent. "I mean, sir," she said earnestly, her face flushing as she spoke, "that we wish you to know who we belong to, and that we are not of your rank, nor like the people here. My father is in the City, and we live at Islington, in Bellevue. We are able to live as we desire to live," said Agnes with a little natural pride, standing very erect, and blushing more deeply than ever, "but we are what people at the Willows would call poor."

Her amazed companion stood gazing at her with a blank face of wonder. "Eh?" said Sir Langham. He could not for his life make it out.

"I suppose you do not understand me," said Agnes, who began now to be more at her ease than Sir Langham was, "but what I have said is quite true. My father is an honourable man, whom we have all a right to be proud of, but he has only—only a very little income every year. I meant to have told every one at first, for we did not want to deceive—but there was no opportunity, and whenever Marian told me, we made up our minds that you ought to know. I mean," said Agnes proudly, with a strange momentary impression that she was taller than Sir Langham, who stood before her biting the head of his cane, with a look of the blankest discomfiture—"I mean that we forget altogether what you said to my sister, and understand that you have been deceived."

She was somewhat premature, however, in her contempt. Sir Langham, overpowered with the most complete amazement, had yet, at all events, no desire whatever that Marian should forget what he had said to her. "Stop," said the guardsman, with his voice somewhat husky; "do you mean that your father is not a friend of Lord Winterbourne's? He is a squire in Banburyshire—I know all about it—or how could you be here?"

"He is not a squire in Banburyshire; he is in an office in the City—and they asked us here because I had written a book," said Agnes, with a little sadness and great humility. "My father is not a friend of Lord Winterbourne's; but yet I think he knew him long ago."

At these last words Sir Langham brightened a little. "Miss Atheling, I don't want to believe you," said the honest guardsman; "I'll ask Lord Winterbourne."

"Lord Winterbourne knows nothing of us," said Agnes, with an involuntary shudder of dislike; "and now I have told you, Sir Langham, and there is nothing more to say."

As she turned to leave him, the dismayed lover awoke out of his blank astonishment. "Nothing more—not a word—not a message; what did she say?" cried Sir Langham, reddening to his hair, and casting a wistful look at the house where Marian was. He followed her sister with an appealing gesture, yet paused in the midst of it. The unfortunate guardsman had never been in circumstances so utterly perplexing; he could not, would not, give up his love—and yet!

"Marian said nothing—nothing more than I have been obliged to say," said Agnes. She turned away now, and left him with a proud and rapid step, inspired with injured pride and involuntary resentment. Agnes did not quite know what she had expected of Sir Langham, but it surely was something different from this.

CHAPTER IX

AN EXPERIMENT

But there was a wonderful difference between this high-minded and impetuous girl, as she crossed the lawn with a hasty foot, which almost scorned to sink into its velvet softness, and the disturbed and bewildered individual who remained behind her in the bowery path where this interview had taken place. Sir Langham Portland had no very bigoted regard for birth, and no avaricious love of money. He was a very good fellow after his kind, as Sir Langhams go, and would not have done a dishonourable thing, with full knowledge of it, for the three kingdoms; but Sir Langham was a guardsman, a man of fashion, a man of the world; he was not so blinded by passion as to be quite oblivious of what befalls a man who marries a pretty face; he was not wealthy enough or great enough to indulge such a whim with impunity, and the beauty which was enough to elevate a Banburyshire Hall, was not sufficient to gild over the unmentionable enormity of a house in Islington and a father in the City. Fathers in the City who are made of gold may be sufficiently tolerable, but a City papa who was poor, and had "only a very small income every year," as Agnes said, was an unimaginable monster, scarcely realisable to the brilliant intellect of Sir Langham. This unfortunate young gentleman wandered about Mrs Edgerley's bit of shrubbery, tearing off leaves and twigs on every side of him, musing much in his perturbed and cloudy understanding, and totally unable to make it out. Let nobody suppose he had given up Marian; that would have made a settlement of the question. But Sir Langham was not disposed to give up his beauty, and not disposed to make a mésalliance; and between the terror of losing her and the terror of everybody's sneer and compassion if he gained her, the unhappy lover vibrated painfully, quite unable to come to any decision, or make up his mighty mind one way or the other. He stripped off the leaves of the helpless bushes, but it did him no service; he twisted his mustache, but there was no enlightenment to be gained from that interesting appendage; he collected all his dazzled wits to the consideration of what sort of creature a man might be who was in an office in the City. Finally, a very brilliant and original idea struck upon the heavy intelligence of Sir Langham. He turned briskly out of the byways of the shrubbery, and said to himself with animation, "I'll go and see!"

When Agnes entered again the little dressing-room where her beautiful sister still bent over her book, Marian glanced up at her inquiringly, and finding no information elicited by that, waited a little, then rose, and came shyly to her side. "I only want to know," said Marian, "not because I care; but what did he say?"

"He was surprised," said Agnes proudly, turning her head away; and Agnes would say nothing more, though Marian lingered by her, and tried various hints and measures of persuasion. Agnes was extremely stately, and, as Marian said, "just a little cross," all day. It was rather too bad to be cross, if she was so, to the innocent mischief-maker, who might be the principal sufferer. But Agnes had made up her mind to suffer no talk about Sir Langham; she had quite given him up, and judged him with the most uncompromising harshness. "Yes!" cried Agnes (to herself), with lofty and poetic indignation, "this I suppose is what these fashionable people call love!"

She was wrong, as might have been expected; for that poor honest Sir Langham, galloping through the dusty roads in the blazing heat of an August afternoon, was quite as genuine in this proof of his affection as many a knight of romance. It was quite a serious matter to this poor young man of fashion, before whose tantalised and tortured imagination some small imp of an attendant Cupid perpetually held up the sweetest fancy-portrait of that sweetest of fair faces. This visionary tormentor tugged at his very heart-strings as the white summer dust rose up in a cloud, marking his progress along the whole long line of the Richmond road. He was not going to slay the dragon, the enemy of his princess—that would have been easy work. He was, unfortunate Sir Langham! bound on a despairing enterprise to find out the house which was not a hall in Banburyshire, to make acquaintance, if possible, with the papa who was in the City, and to see "if it would do."

He knew as little, in reality, about the life which Agnes and Marian lived at home, and about their father's house and all its homely economics and quiet happiness, as if he had been a New Zealand chief instead of a guardsman—and galloped along as gravely as if he were going to a funeral, with, all the way, that wicked little imp of a Cupidon tugging at his heart.

Mrs Atheling was alone with her two babies, sighing a little, and full of weariness for the return of the girls; but Susan, better instructed this time, ushered the magnificent visitor into the best room. He stood gazing upon it in blank amazement; upon the haircloth sofa, and the folded leaf of the big old mahogany table in the corner; and the coloured glass candlesticks and flower-vases on the mantel-shelf. Mrs Atheling, who was a little fluttered, and the rosy boy, who clung to her skirts, and, spite of her audible entreaties in the passage, would not suffer her to enter without him, rather increased the consternation of Sir Langham. She was comely; she had a soft voice; a manner quite unpretending and simple, as good in its natural quietness as the highest breeding; yet Sir Langham, at sight of her, heaved from the depths of his capacious bosom a mighty sigh. It would not do; that little wretch of a Cupid, what a wrench it gave him as he tried to cast it out! If it had been a disorderly house or a slatternly mother, Sir Langham might have taken some faint comfort from the thought of rescuing his beautiful Marian from a family unworthy of her; but even to his hazy understanding it became instantly perceptible that this was a home not to be parted with, and a mother much beloved. Marian, a prince might have been glad to marry; but Sir Langham could not screw his fortitude to the pitch of marrying all that little, tidy, well-ordered house in Bellevue.

So he made a great bungle of his visit, and invented a story about being in town on business, and calling to carry the Miss Athelings' messages for home; and made the best he could of so bad a business by a very expeditious retreat. Anything that he did say was about Agnes; and the mother, though a little puzzled and startled by the visit, was content to set it down to the popularity of her young genius. "I suppose he wanted to see what kind of people she belonged to," said Mrs Atheling, with a smile of satisfaction, as she looked round her best room, and drew back with her into the other parlour the rosy little rogues who held on by her gown. She was perfectly correct in her supposition; but, alas! how far astray in the issue of the same.

Sir Langham went to his club—went to the opera—could not rest anywhere, and floundered about like a man bewitched. It would not do—it would not do; but the merciless little Cupid hung on by his heart-strings, and would not be off for all the biddings of the guardsman. He did not return to Richmond; he was heartily ashamed of himself—heartily sick of all the so-called pleasures with which he tried to cheat his disappointment. But Sir Langham had a certain kind of good sense though he was in love, so he applied himself to forgetting "the whole business," and made up his mind finally that it would not do.

The sisters at the Willows, when they found that Sir Langham did not appear that night, and that no one knew anything of him, made their own conclusions on the subject, but did not say a word even to each other. Agnes sat apart silently indignant, and full of a sublime disdain. Marian, with, a deeper colour than usual on her cheek, was, on the contrary, a great deal more animated than was her wont, and attracted everybody's admiration. Had anybody cared to think of the matter, it would have been the elder sister, and not the younger, whom the common imagination could have supposed to have lost a lover; but they went to rest very early that night, and spent no pleasant hour in the pleasant gossip which never failed between them. Sir Langham was not to be spoken of; and Agnes lay awake, wondering what Marian's feelings were, long after Marian, forgetting all about her momentary pique and anger, was fast and sweet asleep.

CHAPTER X

GOING HOME

And now it had come to an end—all the novelty, the splendour, and the excitement of this first visit—and Agnes and Marian were about to go home. They were very much pleased, and yet a little disappointed—glad and eager to return to their mother, yet feeling it would have been something of a compliment to be asked to remain.

Rachel, who was a great deal more vehement and demonstrative than either of them, threw herself into their arms with violent tears. "I have been so happy since ever I knew you," said Rachel—"so happy, I scarcely thought it right when I was not with Louis—and I think I could almost like to be your servant, and go home with you. I could do anything for you."

"Hush!" said Agnes.

"No; it is quite true," cried poor Rachel—"quite true. I should like to be your servant, and live with your mother. Oh! I ought to say," she continued, raising herself with a little start and thrill of terror, "that if we were in a different position, and could meet people like equals, I should be so glad—so very glad to be friends."

"But how odd Rachel would think it to live in Bellevue," said Marian, coming to the rescue with a little happy ridicule, which did better than gravity, "and to see no one, even in the street, but the milkman and the greengrocer's boy! for Rachel only thinks of the Willows and Winterbourne; she does not know in the least how things look in Bellevue."

Rachel was beguiled into a laugh—a very unusual indulgence. "When you say that, I think it is a very little cottage like one of the cottages in the village; but you know that is all wrong. Oh, when do you think you will go to Winterbourne?"

"We will write and tell you," said Agnes, "all about it, and how many are going; for I do not suppose Charlie will come, after all; and you will write to us—how often? Every other day?"

Rachel turned very red, then very pale, and looked at them with considerable dismay. "Write!" she said, with a falter in her voice; "I—I never thought of that—I never wrote to any one; I daresay I should do it very badly. Oh no; I shall be sure to find out whenever you come to the Old Wood Lodge."

"But we shall hear nothing of you," said Agnes. "Why should you not write to us? I am sure you do to your brother at home."

"I do not," said Rachel, once more drawing herself up, and with flashing eyes. "No one can write letters to us, who have no name."

She was not to be moved from this point; she repeated the same words again and again, though with a very wistful and yielding look in her face. All for Louis! Her companions were obliged to give up the question, after all.

So there was another weeping, sobbing, vehement embrace, and Rachel disappeared without a word into the big bare room down stairs—disappeared to fall again, without a struggle, into her former forlorn life—to yield on her own account, and to struggle with fierce haughtiness for the credit of Louis—leaving the two sisters very thoughtful and compassionate, and full of a sudden eager generous impulse to run away with and take her home.

"Home—to mamma! It would be like heaven to Rachel," said Agnes, in a little enthusiasm, with tears in her eyes.

"Ay, but it would not be like the Willows," said the most practical Marian; and they both looked out with a smile and a sigh upon the beautiful sunshiny lawn, the river in an ecstasy of light and brightness, the little island with all its ruffled willow-leaves, and bethought themselves, finding some amusement in the contrast, of Laurel House, and Myrtle Cottage, and the close secluded walls of Bellevue.

Mrs Atheling had sent the Fly for her daughters—the old Islingtonian fly, with the old white horse, and the coachman with his shiny hat. This vehicle, which had once been a chariot of the gods, looked somewhat shabby as it stood in the broad sunshine before the door of the Willows, accustomed to the fairy coach of Mrs Edgerley. They laughed to themselves very quietly when they caught their first glimpse of it, yet in a momentary weakness were half ashamed; for even Agnes's honest determination to let everybody know their true "rank in life" was not troubled by any fear lest this respectable vehicle should be taken for their own carriage now.

"Going, my love?" cried Mrs Edgerley; "the fatal hour—has it really come so soon?—You leave us all desolée, of course; how shall we exist to-day? And it was so good of you to come. Remember! we shall be dying till we have a new tale from the author of Hope Hazlewood. I long to see it. I know it will be charming, or it could not be yours.—And, my love, you look quite lovely—such roses! I think you quite the most exquisite little creature in the world. Remember me to your excellent mamma. Is your carriage waiting? Ah, I am miserable to part with you. Farewell—that dreadful word—farewell!"

Again that light perfumy touch waved over one blushing cheek and then another. Mrs Edgerley continued to wave her hand and make them pretty signals till they reached the door, whither they hastened as quickly and as quietly as possible, not desiring any escort; but few were the privileged people in Mrs Edgerley's morning-room, and no one cared to do the girls so much honour. Outside the house their friend the gardener waited with two bouquets, so rare and beautiful that the timid recipients of the same, making him their humble thanks, scarcely knew how to express sufficient gratitude. Some one was arriving as they departed—some one who, making the discovery of their presence, stalked towards them, almost stumbling over Agnes, who happened to be nearest to him. "Going away?" said a dismayed voice at a considerable altitude. Mr Endicott's thin head positively vibrated with mortification; he stretched it towards Marian, who stood before him smiling over her flowers, and fixed a look of solemn reproach upon her. "I am aware that beauty and youth flee often from the presence of one who looks upon life with a studious eye. This disappointment is not without its object. You are going away?"

"Yes," said Marian, laughing, but with a little charitable compassion for her own particular victim, "and you are just arriving? It is very odd—you should have come yesterday."

"Permit me," said Mr Endicott moodily;—"no; I am satisfied. This experience is well—I am glad to know it. To us, Miss Atheling," said the solemn Yankee, as he gave his valuable assistance to Agnes—"to us this play and sport of fortune is but the proper training. Our business is not to enjoy; we bear these disappointments for the world."

He put them into their humble carriage, and bowed at them solemnly. Poor Mr Endicott! He did not blush, but grew green as he stood looking after the slow equipage ere he turned to the disenchanted Willows. Though he was about to visit people of distinction, the American young gentleman, being in love, did not care to enter upon this new scene of observation and note-making at this moment; so he turned into the road, and walked on in the white cloud of dust raised by the wheels of the fly. The dust itself had a sentiment in it, and belonged to Marian; and Mr Endicott began the painful manufacture of a sonnet, expressing this "experience," on the very spot.

"But you ought not to laugh at him, Marian, even though other people do," said Agnes, with superior virtue.

"Why not?" said the saucy beauty; "I laughed at Sir Langham—and I am sure he deserved it," she added in an under-tone.

"Marian," said Agnes, "I think—you have named him yourself, or I should not have done it—we had better not say anything about Sir Langham to mamma."

"I do not care at all who names him," said Marian, pouting; but she made no answer to the serious proposition: so it became tacitly agreed between them that nothing was to be said of the superb runaway lover when they got home.

CHAPTER XI

HOME

And now they were at home—the Fly dismissed, the trunks unfastened, and Agnes and Marian sitting with Mamma in the old parlour, as if they had never been away. Yes, they had been away—both of them had come in with a little start and exclamation to this familiar room, which somehow had shrunk out of its proper proportions, and looked strangely dull, dwarfed, and sombre. It was very strange; they had lived here for years, and knew every corner of every chair and every table—and they had only been gone a fortnight—yet what a difference in the well-known room!

"Somebody has been doing something to the house," said Marian involuntarily; and Agnes paused in echoing the sentiment, as she caught a glimpse of a rising cloud on her mother's comely brow.

"Indeed, children, I am grieved to see how soon you have learned to despise your home," said Mrs Atheling; and the good mother reddened, and contracted her forehead. She had watched them with a little jealousy from their first entrance, and they, to tell the truth, had been visibly struck with the smallness and the dulness of the family rooms.

"Despise!" cried Marian, kneeling down, and leaning her beautiful head and her clasped arms upon her mother's knee. "Despise!" said Agnes, putting her arm over Mrs Atheling's shoulder from behind her chair; "oh, mamma, you ought to know better!—we who have learned that there are people in the world who have neither a mother nor a home!"

"Well, then, what is the matter?" said Mrs Atheling; and she began to smooth the beautiful falling hair, which came straying over her old black silk lap, like Danae's shower of gold.

"Nothing at all—only the room is a little smaller, and the carpet a little older than it used to be," said Agnes; "but, mamma, because we notice that, you do not think surely that we are less glad to be at home."

"Well, my dears," said Mrs Atheling, still a little piqued; "your great friend, when he called the other day, did not seem to think there was anything amiss about the house."

"Our great friend!" The girls looked at each other with dismay—who could it be?

"His card is on the mantelpiece," said Mrs Atheling. "He had not very much to say, but he seemed a pleasant young man—Sir Something—Sir Langham; but, indeed, my dear, though, of course, I was pleased to see him, I am not at all sure how far such acquaintances are proper for you."

"He was scarcely my acquaintance, mamma," said Agnes, sorrowfully looking down from behind her mother's chair upon Marian, who had hid her face in Mrs Atheling's lap, and made no sign.

"For our rank in life is so different," pursued the prudent mother; "and even though I might have some natural ambition for you, I do not think, Agnes, that it would really be wishing you well to wish that you should form connections so far out of the sphere of your own family as that."

"Mamma, it was not me," said Agnes again, softly and under her breath.

"It was no one!" cried Marian, rising up hastily, and suddenly seizing and clipping into an ornamental cross Sir Langham's card, which was upon the mantelpiece. "See, Agnes, it will do to wind silk upon; and nobody cares the least in the world for Sir Langham. Mamma, he used to be like Harry Oswald—that is all—and we were very glad when he went away from the Willows, both Agnes and I."

At this statement, made as it was with a blush and a little confusion, Mrs Atheling herself reddened slightly, and instantly left the subject. It was easy enough to warn her children of the evils of a possible connection with people of superior condition; but when such a thing fluttered really and visibly upon the verge of her horizon, Mrs Atheling was struck dumb. To see her pretty Marian a lady—a baronet's wife—the bride of that superb Sir Langham—it was not in the nature of mortal mother to hear without emotion of such an extraordinary possibility. The ambitious imagination kindled at once in the heart of Mrs Atheling: she held her peace.

And the girls, to tell the truth, were very considerably excited about this visit of Sir Langham's. What did it mean? After a little time they strayed into the best room, and stood together looking at it with feelings by no means satisfactory. The family parlour was the family parlour, and, in spite of all that it lacked, possessed something of home and kindness which was not to be found in all the luxurious apartments of the Willows. But, alas! there was nothing but meagre gentility, blank good order, and unloveliness, in this sacred and reserved apartment, where Bell and Beau never threw the charm of their childhood, nor Mrs Atheling dispersed the kindly clippings of her work-basket. The girls consulted each other with dismayed looks—even Rachel, if she came, could not stand against the chill of this grim parlour. Marian pulled the poor haircloth sofa into another position, and altered with impatience the stiff mahogany chairs. They scarcely liked to say to each other how entirely changed was their ideal, or how they shrank from the melancholy state of the best room. "Sir Langham was here, Agnes," said Marian; and within her own mind the young beauty almost added, "No wonder he ran away!"

"It is home—it is our own house," said Agnes, getting up for the occasion a little pride.

Marian shrugged her pretty shoulders. "But Susan had better bring any one who calls into the other room."

Yes, the other room, when they returned to it, had brightened again marvellously. Mrs Atheling had put on her new gown, and had a pink ribbon in her cap. As she sat by the window with her work-basket, she was pleasanter to look at than a dozen pictures; and the sweetest Raphael in the world was not so sweet as these two little lovely fairies playing upon the faded old rug at the feet of Mamma. Not all the luxuries and all the prettinesses of Mrs Edgerley's drawingrooms, not even the river lying in the sunshine, and the ruffled silvery willows drooping round their little island, were a fit balance to this dearest little group, the mother and the children, who made beautiful beyond all telling the sombre face of home.

CHAPTER XII

A NEW ERA

It came to be rather an exciting business to Agnes and Marian making their report of what had happened at the Willows—for it was difficult to distract Mamma's attention from Sir Langham, and Papa was almost angrily interested in everything which touched upon Lord Winterbourne. Rachel, of course, was a very prominent figure in their picture; but Mrs Atheling was still extremely doubtful, and questioned much whether it was proper to permit such an acquaintance to her daughters. She was very particular in her inquiries concerning this poor girl—much approved of Rachel's consciousness of her own equivocal position—thought it "a very proper feeling," and received evidence with some solemnity as to her "manners" and "principles." The girls described their friend according to the best of their ability; but as neither of them had any great insight into character, we will not pretend to say that their audience were greatly enlightened,—and extremely doubtful was the mind of Mrs Atheling. "My dear, I might be very sorry for her, but it would not be proper for me to forget you in my sympathy for her," said Mamma, gravely and with dignity. Like so many tender-hearted mothers, Mrs Atheling took great credit to herself for an imaginary severity, and made up her mind that she was proof to the assaults of pity—she who at the bottom was the most credulous of all, when she came to hear a story of distress.

And Papa, who had been moved at once to forbid their acquaintance with children of Lord Winterbourne's, changed his mind, and became very much interested when he heard of Rachel's horror of the supposed relationship. When they came to this part of the story, Mrs Atheling was scandalised, but Papa was full of pity. He said "Poor child!" softly, and with emotion; while Charlie pricked his big ear to listen, though no one was favoured with the sentiments on this subject of the big boy.

"And about the Rector and the old lady who lives at Abingford—papa, why did you never tell us about these people?" said Marian; "for I am sure you must know very well who Aunt Bridget's neighbours were in the Old Wood Lodge."

"I know nothing about the Riverses," said Papa hastily—and Mr Atheling himself, sober-minded man though he was, grew red with an angry glow—"there was a time when I hated the name," he added in an impetuous and rapid undertone, and then he looked up as though he was perfectly aware of the restraining look of caution which his wife immediately turned upon him.

"Such neighbours as are proper for us you will find out when we get there," said Mrs Atheling quietly. "Papa has not been at Winterbourne for twenty years, and we have had too many things to think of since then to remember people whom we scarcely knew."

"Then, I suppose, since papa hated the name once, and Rachel hates it now, they must be a very wicked family," said Marian; "but I hope the Rector is not very bad, for Agnes's sake."

This little piece of malice called for instant explanation, and Marian was very peremptorily checked by father and mother. "A girl may say a foolish thing to other girls," said Mamma, "and I am afraid this Rachel, poor thing, must have been very badly brought up; but you ought to know better than to repeat a piece of nonsense like that."

"When are we to go, mamma?" said Agnes, coming in to cover the blush, half of shame and half of displeasure, with which Marian submitted to this reproof; "it is August now, and soon it will be autumn instead of summer: we shall be going out of town when all the fashionable people go—but I would rather it was May."

"It cannot be May this year," said Mrs Atheling, involuntarily brightening; "but papa is to take a holiday—three weeks; my dears, I do not think I have been so pleased at anything since Bell and Beau."

Since Bell and Beau! what an era that was! And this, too, was a new beginning, perhaps more momentous, though not such a sweet and great revulsion, out of the darkness into the light. Mamma's manner of dating her joys cast them all back into thought and quietness; and Agnes's heart beat high with a secret and mercenary pleasure, exulting like a miser over her hundred and fifty pounds. At this moment, and at many another moment when the young author had clean forgotten Hope Hazlewood, the thought came upon her with positive delight of the little hoard in Papa's hands, safely laid up in the office, one whole hundred pounds' worth of family good and gladness still; for she had not the same elevated regard for art as her sister's American admirer—she was not, by any means, in her own estimation, or in anybody else's, a representative woman; and Agnes, who began already to think rather meanly of Hope Hazlewood, and press on with the impatience of genius towards a higher excellence, had the greatest satisfaction possible in the earnings of her gentle craft—was it an ignoble delight?

The next morning the two girls, with prudence and caution, began an attack upon the Chancellor of the Exchequer touching the best room. At first Mrs Atheling was entirely horrified at their extravagant ideas. The best room!—what could be desired that was not already attained in that most respectable apartment? but the young rebels held their ground. Mamma put down her work upon her knee, and listened to them quietly. It was not a good sign—she made no interruption as they spoke of mirrors and curtains, carpets and ottomans, couches and easy-chairs: she heard them all to the end with unexampled patience—she only said, "My dears, when you are done I will tell you what I have to say."

What she did say was conclusive upon the subject, though it was met by many remonstrances. "We are going to the Old Wood Lodge," said Mrs Atheling, "and I promise you you shall go into Oxford when we are there, and get some things to make old Aunt Bridget's parlour look a little more like yourselves: but even a hundred pounds, though it is quite a little fortune, will not last for ever—and to furnish two rooms! My dears, you do not know any better; but, of course, it is quite ridiculous, and cannot be done."

Thus ended at present their plan for making a little drawing-room out of the best room; for Mamma's judgment, though it was decisive, was reasonable, and they could make no stand against it. They did all they could do under the circumstances; for the first time, and with compunction, they secretly instructed Susan against the long-standing general order of the head of the house. Strangers were no longer to be ushered into the sacred stranger's apartment; but before Susan had any chance of obeying these schismatical orders, Agnes and Marian themselves were falling into their old familiarity with the old walls and the sombre furniture, and were no longer disposed to criticise, especially as all their minds and all their endeavours were at present set upon the family holiday—the conjoint household visit to the country—the glorious prospect of taking possession of the Old Wood Lodge.

In Bellevue, Charlie alone was to be left behind—Charlie, who had not been long enough in Mr Foggo's office to ask for a holiday, and who did not want one very much, if truth must be told; for neither early hours nor late hours told upon the iron constitution of the big boy. When they pitied him who must stay behind, the young gentleman said, "Stuff! Susan, I suppose, can make my coffee as well as any of you," said Charlie; but nobody was offended that he limited the advantages of their society to coffee-making; and even Mrs Atheling, in spite of her motherly anxieties, left her house and her son with comfortable confidence. Harm might happen to the house, Susan being in it, who was by no means so careful as she ought to be of her fire and her candle; but nobody feared any harm to the heir and hope of the house.

CHAPTER XIII

THE OLD WOOD LODGE

And it was late in August, a sultry day, oppressive and thundery, when this little family of travellers made their first entry into the Old Wood Lodge.

It stood upon the verge of a wood, and the side of a hill, looking down into what was not so much a valley as a low amphitheatre, watered by a maze of rivers, and centred in a famous and wonderful old town. The trees behind the little house had burning spots of autumn colour here and there among the masses of green—colour which scarcely bore its due weight and distinction in the tremulous pale atmosphere which waited for the storm; and the leaves cowered and shivered together, and one terrified bird flew wildly in among them, seeking refuge. Under the shadow of three trees stood the low house of two stories, half stone and half timber, with one quaint projecting window in the roof, and a luxuriant little garden round it. But it was impossible to pause, as the new proprietors intended to have done, to note all the external features of their little inheritance. They hurried in, eager to be under shelter before the thunder; and as Mrs Atheling, somewhat timid of it, hurried over the threshold, the first big drops fell heavily among the late roses which covered the front of the house. They were all awed by the coming storm; and they were not acquainted any of them with the louder crash and fiercer blaze of a thunderstorm in the country. They came hastily into Miss Bridget's little parlour, scarcely seeing what like it was, as the ominous still darkness gathered in the sky, and sat down, very silently, in corners, all except Mr Atheling, whose duty it was to be courageous, and who was neither so timid as his wife, nor so sensitive as his daughters. Then came the storm in earnest—wild lightning rending the black sky in sheets and streams of flames—fearful cannonades of thunder, nature's grand forces besieging some rebellious city in the skies. Then gleams of light shone wild and ghastly in all the pallid rivers, and lighted up with an eerie illumination the spires and pinnacles of the picturesque old town; and the succeeding darkness pressed down like a positive weight upon the Old Wood Lodge and its new inmates, who scarcely perceived yet the old furniture of the old sitting-room, or the trim old maid of Miss Bridget Atheling curtsying at the door.

"A strange welcome!" said Papa, hastily retreating from the window, where he had just been met and half blinded by a sudden flash; and Mamma gathered her babies under her wings, and called to the girls to come closer to her, in that one safe corner which was neither near the window, the fireplace, nor the door.

Yes, it was a strange welcome—and the mind of Agnes, imaginative and rapid, threw an eager glance into the future out of that corner of safety and darkness. A thunderstorm, a convulsion of nature! was there any fitness in this beginning? They were as innocent a household as ever came into a countryside; but who could tell what should happen to them there?

Some one else seemed to share the natural thought. "I wonder, mamma, if this is all for us," whispered Marian, half frightened, half jesting. "Are we to make a great revolution in Winterbourne? It looks like it, to see this storm."

But Mrs Atheling, who thought it profane to show any levity during a thunderstorm, checked her pretty daughter with a peremptory "Hush, child!" and drew her babies closer into her arms. Mrs Atheling's thoughts had no leisure to stray to Winterbourne; save for Charlie—and it was not to be supposed that this same thunder threatened Bellevue—all her anxieties were here.

But as the din out of doors calmed down, and even as the girls became accustomed to it, and were able to share in Papa's calculations as to the gradual retreat of the thunder as it rolled farther and farther away, they began to find out and notice the room within which they had crowded. It had only one window, and was somewhat dark, the small panes being over-hung and half obscured by a wild forest of clematis, and sundry stray branches, still bristling with buds, of that pale monthly rose with evergreen leaves, which covered half the front of the house. The fireplace had a rather fantastic grate of clear steel, with bright brass ornaments, so clear and so resplendent as it only could be made by the labour of years, and was filled, instead of a fire, with soft green moss, daintily ornamented with the yellow everlasting flowers. Hannah did not know that these were immortelles, and consecrated to the memory of the dead. It was only her rural and old-maidenly fashion of decoration, for the same little rustling posies, dry and unfading, were in the little flower-glasses on the high mantel-shelf, before the little old dark-complexioned mirror, with little black-and-white transparencies set in the slender gilding of its frame, which reflected nothing but a slope of the roof, and one dark portrait hanging as high up as itself upon the opposite wall. It put the room oddly out of proportion, this mirror, attracting the eye to its high strip of light, and deluding the unwary to many a stumble; and Agnes already sat fixedly looking at it, and at the dark and wrinkled portrait reflected from the other wall.

Before the fireplace, where there was no fire, stood a large old-fashioned easy-chair, with no one in it. Are you very sure there is no one in it?—for Papa himself has a certain awe of that strangely-placed seat, which seems to have stood before that same fireplace for many a year. In the twilight, Agnes, if you were alone—you, who of all the family are most inclined to a little visionary superstition, you would find it very hard to keep from trembling, or to persuade yourself that Miss Bridget was not there, where she had spent half a lifetime, sitting in that heavy old easy-chair.

The carpet was a faded but rich and soft old Turkey carpet, the furniture was slender and spider-legged, made of old bright mahogany, as black and as polished as ebony. There was an old cabinet in one corner, with brass rings and ornaments; and in another an old musical instrument, of which the girls were not learned enough to know the precise species, though it belonged to the genus piano. The one small square table in the middle of the room was covered with a table-cover, richly embroidered, but the silk was faded, and the bits of gold were black and dull; and there were other little tables, round and square, with spiral legs and a tripod of feet, one holding a china jar, one a big book, and one a case of stuffed birds. On the whole, the room had somewhat the look of a rather refined and very prim old lady. The things in it were all of a delicate kind and antique fashion. It was not in the slightest degree like these fair and fresh young girls, but on the whole it was a place of which people like those, with a wholesome love of ancestry, had very good occasion to be proud.

And at the door stood Hannah, in a black gown and great white apron, smoothing down the same with her hands, and bobbing a kindly curtsy. Hannah's eyes were running over with delight and anxiety to get at Bell and Beau. She passed over all the rest of the family to yearn over the little ones. "Eh, bless us!"

cried Hannah, as, the thunder over, Mrs Atheling began to bestir herself—"children in the house!" It was something almost too ecstatic for her elderly imagination. She volunteered to carry them both up-stairs with the most eager attention. "I ain't so much used to childer," said Hannah, "but, bless ye, ma'am, I love 'um all the same;" and with an instinctive knowledge of this love, Beau condescended to grasp Hannah's spotless white apron, and Bell to mount into her arms. Then the whole family procession went up-stairs to look at the bedrooms—the voices of the girls and the sweet chorus of the babies making the strangest echoes in the lonely house. Hannah acknowledged afterwards, that, half with grief for Miss Bridget, and half for joy of this new life beginning, it would have been a great relief to her to sit down upon the attic stairs and have "a good cry."

CHAPTER XIV

WITHIN AND WITHOUT

The upper floor of the Old Wood Lodge consisted of three rooms; one as large as the parlour down stairs, one smaller, and one, looking to the back, very small indeed. The little one was a lumber-room, and quite unfurnished; the other two were in perfect accordance with the sitting-room. The best bedroom contained a bed of state, with very slender fluted pillars of the same black ebony-like wood, lifting on high a solemn canopy of that ponderous substance called moreen, and still to be found in country inns and seaside lodgings—the colour dark green, with a binding of faded violet. Hangings of the same darkened the low broad lattice window, and chairs of the same were ranged like ghosts along the wall. It was rather a funereal apartment, and the eager investigators were somewhat relieved to find an old-fashioned "tent," with hangings of old chintz, gay with gigantic flowers, in the next room. But the windows!—the broad plain lying low down at their feet, twinkling to the first faint sun-ray which ventured out after the storm—the cluster of spires and towers over which the light brightened and strengthened, striking bold upon the heavy dome which gave a ponderous central point to the landscape, and splintering into a million rays from the pinnacles of Magdalen and St Mary's noble spire, all wet and gleaming with the thunder rain. What a scene it was!—how the passing light kindled all the wan waters, and singled out, for a momentary illumination, one after another of the lesser landmarks of that world unknown. These gazers were not skilled to distinguish between Gothic sham and Gothic real, nor knew much of the distinguishing differences of noble and ignoble architecture. After all, at this distance, it did not much matter—for one by one, as the sunshine found them out, they rose up from the gleaming mist, picturesque and various, like the fairy towers and distant splendours of a morning dream.

"I told you it was pretty, Agnes," said Mr Atheling, who felt himself the exhibitor of the whole scene, and looked on with delight at the success of his private view. Papa, who was to the manner born, felt himself applauded in the admiration of his daughters, and carried Beau upon his shoulder down the creaking narrow staircase, with a certain pride and exultation, calling the reluctant girls to follow him. For lo! upon Miss Bridget's centre table was laid out "such a tea!" as Hannah in all her remembrance had never produced before. Fresh home-made cakes, fresh little pats of butter from the nearest farm—cream! and to crown all, a great china dish full of the last of the strawberries, blushing behind their fresh wet leaves. Hannah, when she had lingered as long as her punctilious good-breeding would permit, and long enough to be very wrathful with Mrs Atheling for intercepting a shower of strawberries from the plates of Bell and Beau, retired to her kitchen slowly, and drawing a chair before the fire, though the evening still was sultry, threw her white apron over her head, and had her deferred and relieving "cry." "Bless you, I'll love 'um all," said Hannah, with a succession of sobs, addressing either herself or some unseen familiar, with whom she was in the habit of holding long conversations. "But it ain't Miss Bridget—that's the truth!"

The ground was wet, the trees were damp, everything had been deluged with the shower of the thunderstorm, and Mrs Atheling did not at all think it prudent that her daughters should go out, though she yielded to them. They went first through the fertile garden, where Marian thought "everything" grew—but were obliged to pause in their researches and somewhat ignorant guesses what everything was, by the unknown charm of that sweet rural atmosphere "after the rain." Though it was very near sunset, the birds were all a-twitter in the neighbouring trees, and everywhere around them rose such a breath of fragrance—open-air fragrance, fresh and cool and sweet, as different from the incense of Mrs Edgerley's conservatory as it was from anything in Bellevue. Running waters trickled somewhere out of sight—it was only the "running of the paths after rain;" and yonder, like a queen, sitting low in a sweet humility, was the silent town, with all its crowning towers. The sunshine, which still lingered on Hannah's projecting window in the roof, had left Oxford half an hour ago—and down over the black dome, the heaven-y-piercing spire and lofty cupola, came soft and grey the shadow of the night.

But behind them, through a thick network of foliage, there were gleams and sparkles of gold, touching tenderly some favourite leaves with a green like the green of spring, and throwing the rest into a shadowy blackness against the half-smothered light. Marian ran into the house to call Hannah, begging her to guide them up into the wood. Agnes, less curious, stood with her hand upon the gate, looking down over this wonderful valley, and wondering if she had not seen it some time in a dream.

"Bless you, miss, if it was to the world's end!" cried Hannah; "but it ain't fit for walking, no more nor a desert; the roads is woeful by Badgeley; look you here!—nought in this wide world but mud and clay."

Marian looked in dismay at the muddy road. "It will not be dry for a week," said the disappointed beauty; "but, Hannah, come here, now that I have got you out, and tell us what every place is—Agnes, here's Hannah—and, if you please, which is the village, and which is the Hall, and where is the Old Wood House?"

"Do you see them white chimneys—and smokes?" said Hannah; "they're a-cooking their dinner just, though tea-time's past—that's the Rector's. But, bless your heart, you ain't likely to see the Hall from here. There's all the park and all the trees atween us and my lord's."

"Do the people like him, Hannah?" asked Agnes abruptly, thinking of her friend.

Hannah paused with a look of alarm. "The people—don't mind nothink about him," said Hannah slowly. "Bless us, miss, you gave me such a turn!"

Agnes looked curiously in the old woman's face, to see what the occasion of this "turn" might be. Marian, paying no such attention, leaned over the low mossy gate, looking in the direction of the Old Wood House. They were quite disposed to enjoy the freedom of the "country," and were neither shawled nor bonneted, though the fresh dewy air began to feel the chill of night. Marian leaned out over the gate, with her little hand thrust up under her hair, looking into the distance with her beautiful smiling eyes. The road which passed this gate was a grassy and almost terraced path, used by very few people, and disappearing abruptly in an angle just after it had passed the Lodge. Suddenly emerging from this angle, with a step which fell noiselessly on the wet grass, meeting the startled gaze of Marian in an instantaneous and ghostlike appearance, came forth what she could see only as, against the light, the figure of a man hastening towards the high-road. He also seemed to start as he perceived the young unknown figures in the garden, but his course was too rapid to permit any interchange of curiosity. Marian did not think he looked at her at all as she withdrew hastily from the gate, and he certainly did not pause an instant in his rapid walk; but as he passed he lifted his hat—a singular gesture of courtesy, addressed to no one, like the salutation of a young king—and disappeared in another moment as suddenly as he came. Agnes, attracted by her sister's low unconscious exclamation, saw him as well as Marian—and saw him as little—for neither knew anything at all of his appearance, save so far as a vague idea of height, rapidity—and the noble small head, for an instant uncovered, impressed their imagination. Both paused with a breathless impulse of respect, and a slight apprehensiveness, till they were sure he must be out of hearing, and then both turned to Hannah, standing in the shadow and the twilight, and growing gradually indistinct all but her white apron, with one unanimous exclamation, "Who is that?"

Hannah smoothed down her apron once more, and made another bob of a curtsy, apparently intended for the stranger. "Miss," said Hannah, gravely, "that's Mr Louis—bless his heart!"

Then the old woman turned and went in, leaving the girls by themselves in the garden. They were a little timid of the great calm and silence; they almost fancied they were "by themselves,"—not in the garden only, but in this whole apparent noiseless world.

CHAPTER XV

THE PARLOUR

And with an excitement which they could not control, the two girls hastened in to the Old Lodge, and to Miss Bridget's dim parlour, where the two candles shed their faint summer-evening light over Mr Atheling reading an old newspaper, and Mamma reclining in the great old easy-chair. The abstracted mirror, as loftily withdrawn from common life as Mr Endicott, refused to give any reflection of these good people sitting far below in their middle-aged and respectable quietness, but owned a momentary vision of Agnes and Marian, as they came in with a little haste and eagerness at the half-open door.

But, after all, to be very much excited, to hasten in to tell one's father and mother, with the heart beating faster than usual against one's breast, and to have one's story calmly received with an "Indeed, my dear!" is rather damping to youthful enthusiasm; and really, to tell the truth, there was nothing at all extraordinary in the fact of Louis passing by a door so near the great house which was his own distasteful home. It was not at all a marvellous circumstance; and as for his salutation, though that was remarkable, and caught their imagination, Marian whispered that she had no doubt it was Louis's "way."

They began, accordingly, to look at the slender row of books in one small open shelf above the little cabinet. The books were in old rich bindings, and were of a kind of reading quite unknown to Agnes and Marian. There were two (odd) volumes of the Spectator, Rasselas, the Poems of Shenstone, the Sermons of Blair; besides these, a French copy of Thomas-à-Kempis, the Holy Living and Dying of Jeremy Taylor, and one of the quaint little books of Sir Thomas Browne. Thrust in hastily beside these ancient and well-attired volumes were two which looked surreptitious, and which were consequently examined with the greatest eagerness. One turned out, somewhat disappointingly, to be a volume of Italian exercises, an old, old school-book, inscribed, in a small, pretty, but somewhat faltering feminine handwriting—handwriting of the last century—with the name of Anastasia Rivers, with a B. A. beneath, which doubtless stood for Bridget Atheling, though it seemed to imply, with a kindly sort of blundering comicality sad enough now, that Anastasia Rivers, though she was no great hand at her exercises, had taken a degree. The other volume was of more immediate interest. It was one of those good and exemplary novels, ameliorated Pamelas, which virtuous old ladies were wont to put into the hands of virtuous young ones, and which was calculated to "instruct as well as to amuse" the unfortunate mind of youth. Marian seized upon this Fatherless Fanny with an instant appropriation, and in ten minutes was deep in its endless perplexities. Agnes, who would have been very glad of the novel, languidly took down the Spectator instead. Yes, we are obliged to confess—languidly; for, with an excited mind upon a lovely summer night, with all the stars shining without, and only two pale candles within, and Mamma visibly dropping to sleep in the easy-chair—who, we demand, would not prefer, even to Steele and Addison, the mazy mysteries of the Minerva Press?

And Agnes did not get on with her reading; she saw visibly before her eyes Marian skimming with an eager interest the pages of her novel. She heard Papa rustling his newspaper, watched the faint flicker of the candles, and was aware of the very gentle nod by which Mamma gave evidence of the condition of her thoughts. Agnes's imagination, never averse to wandering, strayed off into speculations concerning the old lady and her old pupil, and all the life, unknown and unrecorded, which had happed within these quiet walls. Altogether it was somewhat hard to understand the connection between the Athelings and the Riverses—whether some secret of family history lay involved in it, or if it was only the familiar bond formed a generation ago between teacher and child. And this Louis!—his sudden appearance and disappearance—his princely recognition as of new subjects. Agnes made nothing whatever of her Spectator—her mind was possessed and restless—and by-and-by, curious, impatient, and a little excited, she left the room with an idea of hastening up-stairs to the chamber window, and looking out upon the night. But the door of the kitchen stood invitingly open, and Hannah, who had been waiting, slightly expectant of some visit, was to be seen within, rising up hastily with old-fashioned respect and a little wistfulness. Agnes, though she was a young lady of literary tastes, and liked to look out upon moon and stars with the vague sentiment of youth, had, notwithstanding, a wholesome relish for gossip, and was more pleased with talk of other people than we are disposed to confess; so she had small hesitation in changing her course and joining Hannah—that homely Hannah bobbing her odd little curtsy, and smoothing down her bright white apron, in the full glow of the kitchen-fire.

The kitchen was indeed the only really bright room in the Old Wood Lodge, having one strip of carpet only on its white and sanded floor, a large deal table, white and spotless, and wooden chairs hard and clear as Hannah's own toil-worn but most kindly hands. There was an old-fashioned settle by the chimney corner, a small bit of looking-glass hanging up by the window, and gleams of ruddy copper, and homely covers of white metal, polished as bright as silver, ornamenting the walls. Hannah wiped a chair which needed no wiping, and set it directly in front of the fire for "Miss," but would not on any account be so "unmannerly" as to sit down herself in the young lady's presence. Agnes wisely contented herself with leaning on the chair, and smiled with a little embarrassment at Hannah's courtesy; it was not at all disagreeable, but it was somewhat different from Susan at home.

"I've been looking at 'um, miss," said Hannah, "sleeping like angels; there ain't no difference that I can see; they look, as nigh as can be, both of an age."

"They are twins," said Agnes, finding out, with a smile, that Hannah's thoughts were taken up, not about Louis and Rachel, but Bell and Beau.

At this information Hannah brightened into positive delight. "Childer's ne'er been in this house," said Hannah, "till this day; and twins is a double blessing. There ain't no more, miss? But bless us all, the time between them darlins and you!"

"We have one brother, besides—and a great many little brothers and sisters in heaven," said Agnes, growing very grave, as they all did when they spoke of the dead.

Hannah drew closer with a sympathetic curiosity. "If that ain't a heart-break, there's none in this world," said Hannah. "Bless their dear hearts, it's best for them. Was it a fever then, miss, or a catching sickness? Dear, dear, it's all one, when they're gone, what it was."

"Hannah, you must never speak of it to mamma," said Agnes; "we used to be so sad—so sad! till God sent Bell and Beau. Do you know Miss Rachel at the Hall? her brother and she are twins too."

"Yes, miss," said Hannah, with a slight curtsy, and becoming at once very laconic.

"And we know her," said Agnes, a little confused by the old woman's sudden quietness. "I suppose that was her brother who passed to-night."

"Ay, poor lad!" Hannah's heart seemed once more a little moved. "They say miss is to be a play-actress, and I can't abide her for giving in to it; but Mr Louis, bless him! he ought to be a king."

"You like him, then?" asked Agnes eagerly.

"Ay, poor boy!" Hannah went away hastily to the table, where, in a china basin, in their cool crisp green, lay the homely salads of the garden, about to be arranged for supper. A tray covered with a snow-white cloth, and a small pile of eggs, waited in hospitable preparation for the same meal. Hannah, who had been so long in possession, felt like a humble mistress of the house, exercising the utmost bounties of her hospitality towards her new guests. "Least said's best about them, dear," said Hannah, growing more familiar as she grew a little excited—"but, Lord bless us, it's enough to craze a poor body to see the likes of him, with such a spirit, kept out o' his rights."

"What are his rights, Hannah?" cried Agnes, with new and anxious interest: this threw quite a new light upon the subject.

Hannah turned round a little perplexed. "Tell the truth, I dun know no more nor a baby," said Hannah; "but Miss Bridget, she was well acquaint in all the ways of them, and she ever upheld, when his name was named, that my lord kep' him out of his rights."

"And what did he say?" asked Agnes.

"Nay, child," said the old woman, "it ain't no business of mine to tell tales; and Miss Bridget had more sense nor all the men of larning I ever heard tell of. She knew better than to put wickedness into his mind. He's a handsome lad and a kind, is Mr Louis; but I wouldn't be my lord, no, not for all Banburyshire, if I'd done that boy a wrong."

"Then, do you think Lord Winterbourne has not done him a wrong?" said Agnes, thoroughly bewildered.

Hannah turned round upon her suddenly, with a handful of herbs and a knife in her other hand. "Miss, he's an unlawful child!" said Hannah, with the most melodramatic effectiveness. Agnes involuntarily drew back a step, and felt the blood rush to her face. When she had delivered herself of this startling whisper, Hannah returned to her homely occupation, talking in an under-tone all the while.

"Ay, poor lad, there's none can mend that," said Hannah; "he's kep' out of his rights, and never a man can help him. If it ain't enough to put him wild, I dun know."

"And are you quite sure of that? Does everybody think him a son of Lord Winterbourne's?" said Agnes.

"Well, miss, my lord's not like to own to it—to shame hisself," said Hannah; "but they're none so full of charity at the Hall as to bother with other folkses children. My lord's kep' him since they were babies, and sent the lawyer hisself to fetch him when Mr Louis ran away. Bless you, no; there ain't no doubt about it. Whose son else could he be?"

"But if that was true, he would have no rights. And what did Miss Bridget mean by rights?" asked Agnes, in a very low tone, blushing, and half ashamed to speak of such a subject at all.

Hannah, however, who did not share in all the opinions of respectability, but had a leaning rather, in the servant view of the question, to the pariah of the great old house, took up somewhat sharply this unguarded opinion. "Miss," said Hannah, "you'll not tell me that there ain't no rights belonging Mr Louis. The queen on the throne would be glad of the likes of him for a prince and an heir; and Miss Bridget was well acquaint in all the ways of the Riverses, and was as fine to hear as a printed book: for the matter of that," added Hannah, solemnly, "Miss Taesie, though she would not go through the park-gates to save her life, had a leaning to Mr Louis too."

"And who is Miss Taesie?" said Agnes.

"Miss," said Hannah, in a very grave and reproving tone, "you're little acquaint with our ways; it ain't my business to go into stories—you ask your papa."

"So I will, Hannah; but who is Miss Taesie?" asked Agnes again, with a smile.

Hannah answered only by placing her salad on the tray, and carrying it solemnly to the parlour. Amused and interested, Agnes stood by the kitchen fireside thinking over what she had heard, and smiling as she mused; for Miss Taesie, no doubt, was the Honourable Anastasia Rivers, beneath whose name, in the old exercise-book, stood that odd B. A.

CHAPTER XVI

WINTERBOURNE

The next day the family walked forth in a body, to make acquaintance with the "new neighbourhood." There was Papa and Mamma first of all, Mrs Atheling extremely well dressed, and in all the cheerful excitement of an unaccustomed holiday; and then came Agnes and Marian, pleased and curious—and, wild with delight, little Bell and Beau. Hannah, who was very near as much delighted as the children, stood at the door looking after them as they turned the angle of the grassy path. When they were quite out of sight, Hannah returned to her kitchen with a brisk step, to compound the most delicious of possible puddings for their early dinner. It was worth while now to exercise those half-forgotten gifts of cookery which had been lost upon Miss Bridget; and when everything was ready, Hannah, instead of her black ribbon, put new white bows in her cap. At sight of the young people, and, above all, the children, and in the strange delightful bustle of "a full house," hard-featured Hannah, kind and homely, renewed her youth.

The father and mother sent their children on before them, and made progress slowly, recalling and remembering everything. As for Agnes and Marian, they hastened forward with irregular and fluctuating curiosity—loitering one moment, and running another, but, after their different fashion, taking note of all they saw. And between the vanguard and the rearguard a most unsteady main body, fluttering over the grass like two butterflies, as they ran back and forward from Agnes and Marian to Papa and Mamma "with flichterin' noise and glee," came Bell and Beau. These small people, with handfuls of buttercups and clovertops always running through their rosy little fingers, were to be traced along their devious and uncertain path by the droppings of these humble posies, and were in a state of perfect and unalloyed ecstasy. The little family procession came past the Old Wood House, which was a large white square building, a great deal loftier, larger, and more pretending than their own; in fact, a great house in comparison with their cottage. Round two sides of it appeared the prettiest of trim gardens—a little world of velvet lawn, clipped yews, and glowing flower-beds. The windows were entirely obscured with close Venetian blinds, partially excused by the sunshine, but turning a most jealous and inscrutable blankness to the eyes of the new inhabitants; and close behind the house clustered the trees of the park. As they passed, looking earnestly at the house, some one came out—a very young man, unmistakably clerical, with a stiff white band under his monkish chin, a waistcoat which was very High Church, and the blandest of habitual smiles. He looked at the strangers urbanely, with a half intention of addressing them. The girls were not learned in Church politics, yet they recognised the priestly appearance of the smiling young clergyman; and Agnes, for her part, contemplated him with a secret disappointment and dismay. Mr Rivers himself was said to be High Church. Could this be Mr Rivers? He passed, however, and left them to guess vainly; and Papa and Mamma, whose slow and steady pace threatened every now and then to outstrip these irregular, rapid young footsteps, came up and pressed them onward. "How strange!" Marian exclaimed involuntarily: "if that is he, I am disappointed; but how funny to meet them both!"

And then Marian blushed, and laughed aloud, half ashamed to be detected in this evident allusion to Rachel's castles in the air. Her laugh attracted the attention of a countrywoman who just then came out to the door of a little wayside cottage. She made them a little bob of a curtsy, like Hannah's, and asked if they wanted to see the church, "'cause I don't think the gentlemen would mind," said the clerk's wife, the privileged bearer of the ecclesiastical keys; and Mr Atheling, hearing the question, answered over the heads of his daughters, "Yes, certainly they would go." So they all went after her dutifully over the stile, and along a field-path by a rustling growth of wheat, spotted with red poppies, for which Bell and Beau sighed and cried in vain, and came at last to a pretty small church, of the architectural style and period of which this benighted family were most entirely ignorant. Mr Atheling, indeed, had a vague idea that it was "Gothic," but would not have liked to commit himself even to that general principle—for the days of religious architecture and church restorations were all since Mr Atheling's time.

They went in accordingly under a low round-arched doorway, solemn and ponderous, entirely unconscious of the "tressured ornament" which antiquaries came far to see; and, looking with a certain awe at the heavy and solemn arches of the little old Saxon church, were rather more personally attracted, we are pained to confess, by a group of gentlemen within the sacred verge of the chancel, discussing something with solemnity and earnestness, as if it were a question of life and death. Foremost in this group, but occupying, as it seemed, rather an explanatory and apologetic place, and listening with evident anxiety to the deliverance of the others, was a young man of commanding appearance, extremely tall, with a little of the look of ascetic abstraction which belongs to the loftier members of the very high High Church. As the Athelings approached rather timidly under the escort of their humble guide, this gentleman eyed them, with a mixture of observation and haughtiness, as they might have been eyed by the proprietor of the domain. Then he recognised Mr Atheling with such a recognition as the same reigning lord and master might bestow upon an intruder who was only mistaken and not presumptuous. The father of the family rose to the occasion, his colour increased; he drew himself up, and made a formal but really dignified bow to the young clergyman. The little group of advisers did not pause a minute in their discussion; and odd words, which they were not in the habit of hearing, fell upon the ears of Agnes and Marian. "Bad in an archaic point of view—extremely bad; and I never can forgive errors of detail; the best examples are so accessible," said one gentleman. "I do not agree with you. I remember an instance at Amiens," interrupted another. "Amiens, my dear sir!—exactly what I mean to say," cried the first speaker; "behind the date of Winterbourne a couple of hundred years—late work—a debased style. In a church of this period everything ought to be severe."

And accordingly there were severe Apostles in the painted windows—those slender lancet "lights" which at this moment dazzled the eyes of Agnes and Marian; and the new saints in the new little niches were, so far as austerity went, a great deal more correct and true to their "period" than even the old saints, without noses, and sorely worn with weather and irreverence, who were as genuine early English as the stout old walls. But Marian Atheling had no comprehension of this kind of severity. She shrank away from the altar in its religious gloom—the altar with its tall candlesticks, and its cloth, which was stiff with embroidery—marvelling in her innocent imagination over some vague terror of punishments and penances in a church where "everything ought to be severe." Marian took care to be on the other side of her father and mother, as they passed again the academic group discussing the newly restored sedilia, which was not quite true in point of "detail," and drew a long breath of relief when she was safely outside these dangerous walls. "The Rector! that was the Rector. Oh Agnes!" cried Marian, as Papa announced the dreadful intelligence; and the younger sister, horror-stricken, and with great pity, looked sympathetically in Agnes's face. Agnes herself was moved to look back at the tall central figure, using for a dais the elevation of that chancel. She smiled, but she was a little startled—and the girls went on to the village, and to glance through the trees at the great park surrounding the Hall, with not nearly so much conversation as at the beginning of their enterprise. But it was with a sigh instead of a laugh that Marian repeated, when they went home to dinner and Hannah's magnificent pudding—"So, Agnes, we have seen them both."

CHAPTER XVII

THE CLERGY

Several weeks after this passed very quietly over the Old Wood Lodge and its new inhabitants. They saw "Mr Louis," always a rapid and sudden apparition, pass now and then before their windows, and sometimes received again that slight passing courtesy which nobody could return, as it was addressed to nobody, and only disclosed a certain careless yet courteous knowledge on the part of the young prince that they were there; and they saw the Rector on the quiet country Sabbath-days in his ancient little church, with its old heavy arches, and its new and dainty restorations, "intoning" after the loftiest fashion, and preaching strange little sermons of subdued yet often vehement and impatient eloquence—addresses which came from a caged and fiery spirit, and had no business there. The Winterbourne villagers gaped at his Reverence as he flung his thunderbolts over their heads, and his Reverence came down now and then from a wild uncertain voyage heavenward, down, down, with a sudden dreary plunge, to look at all the blank rustical faces, slumberous or wondering, and chafe himself with fiery attempts to come down to their level, and do his duty to his rural flock. With a certain vague understanding of some great strife and tumult in this dissatisfied and troubled spirit, Agnes Atheling followed him in the sudden outbursts of his natural oratory, and in the painful curb and drawing-up by which he seemed to awake and come to himself. Though she was no student of character, this young genius could not restrain a throb of sympathy for the imprisoned and uncertain intellect beating its wings before her very eyes. Intellect of the very highest order was, without question, errant in that humble pulpit—errant, eager, disquieted—an eagle flying at the sun. The simpler soul of genius vaguely comprehended it, and rose with half-respectful, half-compassionating sympathy, to mark the conflict. The family mother was not half satisfied with these preachings, and greatly lamented that the only church within their reach should be so painfully "high," and so decidedly objectionable. Mrs Atheling's soul was grieved within her at the tall candlesticks, and even the "severe" Apostles in the windows were somewhat appalling to this excellent Protestant. She listened with a certain dignified disapproval to the sermons, not much remarking their special features, but contenting herself with a general censure. Marian too, who did not pretend to be intellectual, wondered a little like the other people, and though she could not resist the excitement of this unusual eloquence, gazed blankly at the preacher after it was over, not at all sure if it was right, and marvelling what he could mean. Agnes alone, who could by no means have told you what he meant—who did not even understand, and certainly could not have explained in words her own interest in the irregular prelection—vaguely followed him nevertheless with an intuitive and unexplainable comprehension. They had never exchanged words, and the lofty and self-absorbed Rector knew nothing of the tenants of the Old Wood Lodge; yet he began to look towards the corner whence that intelligent and watching face flashed upon his maze of vehement and uncertain thought. He began to look, as a relief, for the upward glance of those awed yet pitying eyes, which followed him, yet somehow, in their simplicity, were always before him, steadfastly shining in the calm and deep assurance of a higher world than his. It was not by any means, at this moment, a young man and a young woman looking at each other with the mutual sympathy and mutual difference of nature; it was Genius, sweet, human, and universal, tender in the dews of youth—and Intellect, nervous, fiery, impatient, straining like a Hercules after the Divine gift, which came to the other sleeping, as God gives it to His beloved.

The Curate of Winterbourne was the most admirable foil to his reverend principal. This young and fervent churchman would gladly have sat in the lower seat of the restored sedilia, stone-cold and cushionless, at any risk of rheumatism, had not his reverence the Rector put a decided interdict upon so extreme an example of rigid Anglicanism. As it was, his bland and satisfied youthful face in the reading-desk made the strangest contrast in the world to that dark, impetuous, and troubled countenance, lowering in handsome gloom from the pulpit. The common people, who held the Rector in awe, took comfort in the presence of the Curate, who knew all the names of all the children, and was rather pleased than troubled when they made so bold as to speak to him about a place for Sally, or a 'prenticeship for John. His own proper place in the world had fallen happily to this urbane and satisfied young gentleman. He was a parish priest born and intended, and accordingly there was not a better parish priest in all Banburyshire than the Reverend Eustace Mead. While the Rector only played and fretted over these pretty toys of revived Anglicanism, with which he was not able to occupy his rapid and impetuous intellect, they sufficed to make a pleasant reserve of interest in the life of the Curate, who was by no means an impersonation of intellect, though he had an acute and practical little mind of his own, much more at his command than the mind of Mr Rivers was at his. And the Curate preached devout little sermons, which the rustical people did not gape at; while the Rector, out of all question, and to the perception of everybody, was, in the most emphatic sense of the words, the wrong man in the wrong place.

So far as time had yet gone, the only intercourse with their neighbours held by the Athelings was at church, and their nearest neighbours were those clerical people who occupied the Old Wood House. Mr Rivers was said to have a sister living with him, but she was "a great invalid," and never visible; and on no occasion, since his new parishioners arrived, had the close Venetian blinds been raised, or the house opened its eyes. There it stood in the sunshine, in that most verdant of trim old gardens, which no one ever walked in, nor, according to appearances, ever saw, with its three rows of closed windows, blankly green, secluded and forbidding, which no one within ever seemed tempted to open to the sweetest of morning breezes, or the fragrant coolness of the night. Agnes, taking the privilege of her craft, was much disposed to suspect some wonderful secret or mystery in this monkish and ascetic habitation; but it was not difficult to guess the secret of the Rector, and there was not a morsel of mystery in the bland countenance of smiling Mr Mead.

By this time Mrs Atheling and her children were alone. Papa had exhausted his holiday, and with a mixture of pleasure and unwillingness returned to his office duties; and Mamma, though she had so much enjoyment of the country, which was "so good for the children," began to sigh a little for her other household, to marvel much how Susan used her supremacy, and to be seized with great compunctions now and then as to the cruelty "of leaving your father and Charlie by themselves so long." The only thing which really reconciled the good wife to this desertion, was the fact that Charlie himself, without any solicitation, and in fact rather against his will, was to have a week's holiday at Michaelmas, and of course looked forward in his turn to the Old Wood Lodge. Mrs Atheling had made up her mind to return with her son, and was at present in a state of considerable doubt and perplexity touching Agnes and Marian, Bell and Beau. The roses on the cheeks of the little people had blossomed so sweetly since they came to the country, Mrs Atheling almost thought she could trust her darlings to Hannah, and that "another month would do them no harm."

CHAPTER XVIII

A NEW FRIEND

September had begun, but my lord and his expected guests had not yet arrived at the Hall. Much talk and great preparations were reported in the village, and came in little rivulets of intelligence, through Hannah and the humble merchants at the place, to the Old Wood Lodge; but Agnes and Marian, who had not contrived to write to her, knew nothing whatever of Rachel, and vainly peeped in at the great gates of the park, early and late, for the small rapid figure which had made so great an impression upon their youthful fancy. Then came the question, should they speak to Louis, who was to be seen sometimes with a gun and a gamekeeper, deep in the gorse and ferns of Badgeley Wood. Hannah said this act of rebellious freedom had been met by a threat on the part of my lord to "have him up" for poaching, which threat only quickened the haughty boy in his love of sport. "You may say what you like, children, but it is very wrong and very sinful," said Mrs Atheling, shaking her head with serious disapproval, "and especially if he brings in some poor gamekeeper, and risks his children's bread;" and Mamma was scarcely to be satisfied with Hannah's voluble and eager disclaimer—Mr Louis would put no man in peril. This excellent mother held her prejudices almost as firmly as her principles, and compassionately added that it was no wonder—poor boy, considering—for she could not understand how Louis could be virtuous and illegitimate, and stood out with a repugnance, scarcely to be overcome, against any friendship between her own children and these unfortunate orphans at the Hall.

One of these bright afternoons, the girls were in the garden discussing eagerly this difficult question; for it would be very sad to bring Rachel to the house, full of kind and warm expectations, and find her met by the averted looks of Mamma. Her two daughters, however, though they were grieved, did not find it at all in their way to criticise the opinions of their mother; they concerted little loving attacks against them, but thought of nothing more.

And these two found great occupation in the garden, where Bell and Beau played all the day long, and which Mrs Atheling commanded as she sat by the parlour window with her work-basket. This afternoon the family group was fated to interruption. One of the vehicles ascending the high-road, which was not far from the house, drew up suddenly at sight of these young figures in old Miss Bridget's garden. Even at this distance a rather rough and very peremptory voice was audible ordering the groom, and then a singular-looking personage appeared on the grassy path. This was a very tall woman, dressed in an old-fashioned brown cloth pelisse and tippet, with an odd bonnet on her head which seemed an original design, contrived for mere comfort, and owning no fashion at all. She was not young certainly, but she was not so old either, as the archæological "detail" of her costume might have warranted a stranger in supposing. Fifty at the very utmost, perhaps only forty-five, with a fresh cheek, a bright eye, and all the demeanour of a country gentleman, this lady advanced upon the curious and timid girls. That her errand was with them was sufficiently apparent from the moment they saw her, and they stood together very conscious, under the steady gaze of their approaching visitor, continuing to occupy themselves a little with the children, yet scarcely able to turn from this unknown friend. She came along steadily, without a pause, holding still in her hand the small riding-whip which had been the sceptre of her sway over the two stout grey ponies waiting in the high-road—came along steadily to the door, pushed open the gate, entered upon them without either compliment or salutation, and only, when she was close upon the girls, paused for an instant to make the brusque and sudden inquiry, "Well, young people, who are you?"

They did not answer for the moment, being surprised in no small degree by such a question; upon which the stranger repeated it rather more peremptorily. "We are called Atheling," said Agnes, with a mixture of pride and amusement. The lady laid her hand heavily upon the girl's shoulder, and turned her half round to the light. "What relation?" said this singular inquisitor; but while she spoke, there became evident a little moistening and relaxation of her heavy grey eyelid, as if it was with a certain emotion she recalled the old owner of the old lodge, whom she did not name.

"My father was Miss Bridget's nephew; she left the house to him," said Agnes; and Marian too drew near in wondering regard and sympathy, as two big drops, like the thunder-rain, fell suddenly and quietly over this old lady's cheeks.

"So! you are Will Atheling's daughters," said their visitor, a little more roughly than before, as if from some shame of her emotion; "and that is your mother at the window. Where's Hannah? for I suppose you don't know me."

"No," said Agnes, feeling rather guilty; it seemed very evident that this lady was a person universally known.

"Will Atheling married—married—whom did he marry?" said the visitor, making her way to the house, and followed by the girls. "Eh! don't you know, children, what was your mother's name? Franklin? yes, to be sure, I remember her a timid pretty sort of creature; ah! just like Will."

By this time they were at the door of the parlour, which she opened with an unhesitating hand. Mrs Atheling, who had seen her from the window, was evidently prepared to receive the stranger, and stood up to greet her with a little colour rising on her cheek, and, as the girls were astonished to perceive, water in her eyes.

This abrupt and big intruder into the family room showed more courtesy to the mother than she had done to the girls; she made a sudden curtsy, which expression of respect seemed to fill up all the requirements of politeness in her eyes, and addressed Mrs Atheling at once, without any prelude. "Do you remember me?"

"I think so—Miss Rivers?" said Mrs Atheling with considerable nervousness.

"Just so—Anastasia Rivers—once not any older than yourself. So—so—and here are you and all your children in my old professor's room."

"We have made no change in it; everything is left as it was," said Mrs Atheling.

"The more's the pity," answered the abrupt and unscrupulous caller. "Why, it's not like them—not a bit; as well dress them in her old gowns, dear old soul! Ay well, it was a long life—no excuse for grieving; but at the last, you see, at the last, it's come to its end."

"We did not see her," said Mrs Atheling, with an implied apology for "want of feeling," "for more than twenty years. Some one, for some reason, we cannot tell what, prejudiced her mind against William and me."

"Some one!" said Miss Rivers, with an emphatic toss of her head. "You don't know of course who it was. I do: do you wish me to tell you?"

Mrs Atheling made no answer. She looked down with some confusion, and began to trifle with the work which all this time had lain idly on her knee.

"If there's any ill turn he can do you now," said Miss Rivers pointedly, "he will not miss the chance, take my word for it; and in case he tries it, let me know. Will Atheling and I are old friends, and I like the look of the children. Good girls, are they? And is this all your family?"

"All I have alive but one boy," said Mrs Atheling.

"Ah!" said her visitor, looking up quickly. "Lost some?—never mind, child, you'll find them again; and here am I, in earth and heaven a dry tree!"

After a moment's pause she began to speak again, in an entirely different tone. "These young ones must come to see me," said their new friend—"I like the look of them. You are very pretty, my dear, you are quite as good as a picture; but I like your sister just as well as you. Come here, child. Have you had a good education? Are you clever? Nonsense! Why do you blush? People can't have brains without knowing of it. Are you clever, I say?"

"I don't think so," said Agnes, unable to restrain a smile; "but mamma does, and so does Marian." Here she came to an abrupt conclusion, blushing at herself. Miss Rivers rose up from her seat, and stood before her, looking down into the shy eyes of the young genius with all the penetrating steadiness of her own.

"I like an honest girl," said the Honourable Anastasia, patting Agnes's shoulder rather heavily with her strong hand. "Marian—is she called Marian? That's not an Atheling name. Why didn't you call her Bride?"

"She is named for me," said Mrs Atheling with some dignity. And then she added, faltering, "We had a Bridget too; but—"

"Never mind," said Miss Rivers, lifting her hand quickly—"never mind, you'll find them again. She's very pretty—prettier than any one I know about Banburyshire; but for heaven's sake, child, mind what you're about, and don't let any one put nonsense in your head. Your mother could tell you what comes of such folly, and so could I. By the by, children, you are much of an age. Do you know anything of those poor children at the Hall?"

"We know Rachel," said Agnes eagerly. "We met her at Richmond, and were very fond of her; and I suppose she is coming here."

"Rachel!" said Miss Rivers, with a little contempt. "I mean the boy. Has Will Atheling seen the boy?"

"My husband met him once when he came here first," said Mrs Atheling; "and he fancied—fancied—imagined—he was like—"

"My father!" The words were uttered with an earnestness and energy which brought a deep colour over those unyouthful cheeks. "Yes, to be sure—every one says the same. I'd give half my fortune to know the true story of that boy!"

"Rachel says," interposed Agnes, eagerly taking advantage of anything which could be of service to her friend, "that Louis will not believe that they belong to Lord Winterbourne."

The eyes of the Honourable Anastasia flashed positive lightning; then a shadow came over her face. "That's nothing," she said abruptly. "No one who could help it would be content to belong to him. Now, I'll send some day for the children: send them over to see me, will you? Ah, where's Hannah—does she suit you? She was very good to her, dear old soul!"

"And she is very good to the children," said Mrs Atheling, as she followed her visitor punctiliously to the door. When they reached it, Miss Rivers turned suddenly round upon her—

"You are not rich, are you? Don't be offended; but, if you are able, change all this. I'm glad to see you in the house; but this, you know, this is like her gowns and her turbans—make a change."

Here Hannah appeared from her kitchen, curtsying deeply to Miss Taesie, who held a conversation with her at the gate; and finally went away, with her steady step and her riding-whip, having first plucked one of the late pale roses from the wall. Mrs Atheling came in with a degree of agitation not at all usual to the family mother. "The first time I ever saw her," said Mrs Atheling, "when I was a young girl newly married, and she a proud young beauty just on the eve of the same. I remember her, in her hat and her riding-habit, pulling a rose from Aunt Bridget's porch—and there it is again."

"Ma'am," said Hannah, coming in to spread the table, "Miss Taesie never comes here, late or early, but she gathers a rose."

CHAPTER XIX

GOSSIP

"But, mamma, if she was just on the eve of the same, why is she only Miss Rivers now?" asked Marian, very curious on this subject of betrothments and marriages.

"It is a very long story, my dear," said Mrs Atheling. As a general principle, Mamma was not understood to have any special aversion to long stories, but she certainly showed no inclination whatever to enter into this.

"So much the better if you will tell it, mamma," said Agnes; and they came close to her, with their pretty bits of needlework, and their looks of interest; it was not in the heart of woman to refuse.

"Well, my dears," said Mrs Atheling, with a little reluctance, "somehow we seem to be brought into the very midst of it again, though we have scarcely heard their names for twenty years. This lady, though she is almost as old as he is, is niece to Lord Winterbourne. The old lord was only his stepbrother, and a great deal older than he—and Miss Anastasia was the only child of the old lord. You may suppose how disappointed he was, with all his great estates entailed, and the title—and nothing but a daughter; and everybody said, when the old lady died, that he would marry again."

"Did he marry again?" said Marian, as Mamma came to a sudden and unexpected pause.

"No, my dear; for then trouble came," said Mrs Atheling. "Miss Anastasia was a beautiful young lady, always very proud, and very wise and sensible, but a great beauty for all that; and she was to be married to a young gentleman, a baronet and a very great man, out of Warwickshire. The present lord was then the Honourable Reginald Rivers, and dreadful wild. Somehow, I cannot tell how it was, he and Sir Frederick quarrelled, and then they fought; and after his wound that fine young gentleman fell into a wasting and a consumption, and died at twenty-five; and that is the reason why Miss Anastasia has never been married, and I am afraid, though it is so very wrong to say so, hates Lord Winterbourne."

"Oh, mamma! I am sure I should, if I had been like her!" cried Marian, almost moved to tears.

"No, my darling, not to hate him," said Mrs Atheling, shaking her head, "or you would forget all you have been taught since you were a child."

"I do not understand him, mamma," said Agnes: "does everybody hate him—has he done wrong to every one?"

Mrs Atheling sighed. "My dears, if I tell you, you must forget it again, and never mention it to any one. Papa had a pretty young sister, little Bride, as they all called her, the sweetest girl I ever saw. Mr Reginald come courting her a long time, but at last she found out—oh girls! oh, children!—that what he meant was not true love, but something that it would be a shame and a sin so much as to name; and it broke her dear heart, and she died. Her grave is at Winterbourne; that was what papa and I went to see the first day."

"Mamma," cried Agnes, starting up in great excitement and agitation, "why did you suffer us to know any one belonging to such a man?"

"Well, my dear," said Mrs Atheling, a little discomposed by this appeal. "I thought it was for the best. Coming here, we were sure to be thrown into their way—and perhaps he may have repented. And then Mrs Edgerley was very kind to you, and I did not think it right, for the father's sake, to judge harshly of the child."

Marian, who had covered her face with her hands, looked up now with abashed and glistening eyes. "Is that why papa dislikes him so?" said Marian, very low, and still sheltering with her raised hands her dismayed and blushing face.

Mrs Atheling hesitated a moment. "Yes," she said doubtfully, after a pause of consideration—"yes; that and other things."

But the inquiry of the girls could not elicit from Mamma what were the other things which were sufficient to share with this as motives of Mr Atheling's dislike. They were inexpressibly shocked and troubled by the story, as people are who, contemplating evil at a visionary distance, and having only a visionary belief in it, suddenly find a visible gulf yawning at their own feet; and Agnes could not help thinking, with horror and disgust, of being in the same room with this man of guilt, and of that polluting kiss of his, from which Rachel shrank as from the touch of pestilence. "Such a man ought to be marked and singled out," cried Agnes, with unreasoning youthful eloquence: "no one should dare to bring him into the same atmosphere with pure-minded people; everybody ought to be warned of who and what he was."

"Nay; God has not done so," said Mrs Atheling with a sigh. "He has offended God more than he ever could offend man, but God bears with him. I often say so to your father when we speak of the past. Ought we, who are so sinful ourselves, to have less patience than God?"

After this the girls were very silent, saying nothing, and much absorbed with their own thoughts. Marian, who perhaps for the moment found a certain analogy between her father's pretty sister and herself, was wrapt in breathless horror of the whole catastrophe. Her mind glanced back upon Sir Langham—her fancy started forward into the future; but though the young beauty for the moment was greatly appalled and startled, she could not believe in the possibility of anything at all like this "happening to me!" Agnes, for her part, took quite a different view of the matter. The first suggestion of her eager fancy was, what could be done for Louis and Rachel, to deliver them from the presence and control of such a man? Innocently and instinctively her thoughts turned upon her own gift, and the certain modest amount of power it gave her. Louis might get a situation like Charlie, and be helped until he was able for the full weight of his own life; and Rachel, another sister, could come home to Bellevue. So Agnes, who at this present moment was writing in little bits, much interrupted and broken in upon, her second story, rose into a delightful anticipatory triumph, not of its fame or success, though these things did glance laughingly across her innocent imagination, but of its mere ignoble coined recompense, and of all the great things for these two poor orphans which might be done in Bellevue.

And while the mother and the daughters sat at work in the shady little parlour, where the sunshine did not enter, but where a sidelong reflection of one waving bough of clematis, dusty with blossom, waved across the little sloping mirror, high on the wall, Hannah sat outside the open door, watching with visible delight, and sometimes joining for an instant with awkward kindliness, the sports of Bell and Beau. They rolled about on the soft grass, ran about on the garden paths, tumbled over each other and over everything in their way, but, with the happy immunity of children in the country, "took no harm." Hannah had some work in her great white apron, but did not so much as look at it. She had no eye for a rare passenger upon the grassy byway, and scarcely heard the salutation of the Rector's man. All Hannah's soul and thoughts were wrapt up in the "blessed babies," who made her old life blossom and rejoice; and it was without any intervention of their generally punctilious attendant that a light and rapid step came gliding over the threshold of the Lodge, and a quiet little knock sounded lightly on the parlour door. "May I come in, please?" said a voice which seemed to Agnes to be speaking out of her dream; and Mrs Atheling had not time to buckle on her armour of objection when the door opened, and the same little light rapid figure came bounding into the arms of her daughters. Once there, it was not very difficult to reach to the good mother's kindly heart.

CHAPTER XX

RACHEL

"Yes, I only came to-day," said Rachel, who kept her eyes wistfully upon Mrs Atheling, though she spoke to Agnes. "They made me go to town after you left, and then kept me so long at the Willows. Next season they say I am to come out, and somebody has offered me an engagement; but indeed, indeed," cried Rachel, suddenly firing with one of her outbursts of unexpected energy, "I never will!"

The girls scarcely knew what answer to make in presence of their mother. They had not been trained to have independent friendships, and now waited anxiously, turning silent looks of appeal upon Mamma. Mamma all at once had become exceedingly industrious, and neither looked up nor spoke.

"But then you might live in London, perhaps, instead of here; and I should be very glad if you were near us," said Agnes, with a good deal of timidity. Agnes, indeed, was not thinking what she said—her whole attention wandered to her mother.

"I do not mind for myself," said Rachel, with a deep sigh. "I do not think I should care if there were a hundred people to hear me sing, instead of a dozen, for I know very well not one of them would care anything for me; but I have to remember Louis. I cannot disgrace Louis. It is bad enough for him as it is, without adding any more."

Again there was a pause. Rachel's poor little palpitating heart beat very loud and very high. "I thought I should be welcome when I came here," she said, freezing half into her unnatural haughtiness, and half with an unconscious and pitiful tone of appeal; "but I never intruded upon any one—never! and if you do not wish me to be here, I can go away."

She turned to go away as she spoke, her little figure rising and swelling with great subdued emotion; but Mrs Atheling immediately rose and stretched out her hand to detain her. "Do not go away, my dear; the girls are very fond of you," said Mrs Atheling; and it cost this good mother, with her ideas of propriety, a very considerable struggle with herself to say these simple words.

Rachel stood before her a moment irresolute and uncertain, not appearing even to hear what Agnes and Marian, assured by this encouragement, hastened to say. The contest was violent while it lasted between Louis's sister, who was his representative, and the natural little humble child Rachel, who had no pride, and only wanted the kindly succour of love; but at last nature won the day. She seized upon Mrs Atheling's hand hastily and kissed it, with a pretty appealing gesture. "They do everything you tell them," cried Rachel suddenly. "I never had any mother—never even when we were babies. Oh, will you tell me sometimes what I ought to do?"

It was said afterwards in the family that at this appeal Mamma, fairly vanquished and overcome, "almost cried;" and certain it was that Rachel immediately took possession of the stool beside her, and remained there not only during this visit, but on every after occasion when she came. She brightened immediately into all her old anxious communicativeness, concealing nothing, but pouring out her whole heart.

"Louis told me he had seen you in the garden," said Rachel, with a low laugh of pleasure; "but when I asked which it was, he said he knew nothing of Agnes and Marian, but only he had seen a vision looking over the old gate. I never know what Louis means when he speaks nonsense," said Rachel, with an unusual brightness; "and I am so glad. I never heard him speak so much nonsense since we came to the Hall."

"And are you left in the Hall all by yourselves, two young creatures?" asked Mrs Atheling, with curiosity. "It must be very melancholy for you."

"Not to be alone!" cried Rachel. "But very soon my lord is coming, with a great household of people; and then—I almost faint when I think upon it. What shall I do?"

"But, Rachel, Mrs Edgerley is very kind to you," said Agnes.

Rachel answered after her usual fashion: "I do not care at all for myself—it is nothing to me; but Louis—oh, Louis!—if he is ever seen, the people stare at him as they would at a horse or a hound; and Lord Winterbourne tries to have an opportunity to speak and order him away, and when he shoots, he says he will put him in prison. And then Louis knows when they send for me, and sometimes stands under the window and hears me singing, and is white with rage to hear; and then he says he cannot bear it, and must go away, and then I go down upon my knees to him. I know how it will happen—everything, everything! It makes him mad to have to bear it. Oh, I wish I knew anything that I could do!"

"Mamma," said Agnes earnestly, "Rachel used to tell us all this at the Willows. Do you not think he ought to go away?"

Mrs Atheling shook her head in perplexity; and instead of answering, asked a question, "Does he not think it his duty, my dear, to obey your—your father?" said Mamma doubtfully.

"But he is not our father—oh no, no, indeed he is not! I should know he was not, even without Louis," cried Rachel, unaware what a violent affirmation this was. "Louis says we could not have any father who would not be a disgrace to us, being as we are—and Louis must be right; but even though he might be a bad man, he could not be like Lord Winterbourne. He takes pleasure in humiliating us—he never cared for us all our life."

There was something very touching in this entire identification of these two solitary existences which still were but one life; and Rachel was not Rachel till she came to the very last words. Before that, with the strange and constantly varying doubleness of her sisterly character, she had been once again the representative of Louis. One thing struck them all as they looked at her small features, fired with this sudden inspiration of Louis's pride and spirit. About as different as possible—at the extreme antipodes of unresemblance—were their two visitors of this day,—this small little fairy, nervous, timid, and doubtful, fatherless, homeless, and without so much as a name, and that assured and commanding old lady, owning no superior, and as secure of her own position and authority as any reigning monarch. Yes, they were about as dissimilar as two human creatures could be; yet the lookers-on were startled to recognise that subtle link of likeness, seldom a likeness of features, which people call family resemblance. Could it have come through this man, who was so repugnant to them both?

"They are all coming down on Monday next week," said Rachel, "so we have just three days all to ourselves; and I thought, perhaps—perhaps, if you please to let me, I might bring Louis to-night?"

"Surely, my dear," said Mrs Atheling.

"Oh, thank you!—thank you very much!" cried Rachel, once more bestowing an eager yet shy caress upon that motherly hand. "Louis is not like me at all," added the anxious sister, afraid lest he should suffer by any preconceived notion of resemblance. "He is a man; and old Miss Bridget used to call him a noble brave boy, like what you read of in books. I do not know," said Rachel, "I never read of any one, even in a book, like Louis. I think he ought to be a king."

"But, indeed, Rachel," said Agnes, "I am quite sure you are wrong. Ask mamma. You ought to let him go away."

"Do you think so?" said Rachel wistfully, looking up in Mrs Atheling's face.

But Mrs Atheling, though under any other circumstances she would of course have insisted upon the absolute propriety of a young man "making his own way," paused, much perplexed, and answered nothing for the moment. "My dears," she said at last, very doubtfully, "I do not know at all what to say. You should have some one who could advise you better; and it depends on the young gentleman's inclinations, and a great many things beside that I am not able to judge of; for, indeed, though it may only be my old-fashioned notions, I do not like to hear of young people going against the advice of their friends."

CHAPTER XXI

THE YOUNG PRINCE

It may be supposed that, after all they had heard of him, the Athelings prepared themselves with a little excitement for the visit of Louis. Even Mrs Atheling, who disapproved of him, could not prevent herself from wandering astray in long speculations about the old lord—and it seemed less improper to wonder and inquire concerning a boy, whom the Honourable Anastasia herself inquired after and wondered at. As for the girls, Louis had come to be an ideal hero to both of them. The adored and wonderful brother of Rachel—though Rachel was only a girl, and scarcely so wise as themselves—the admiration of Miss Bridget, and the anxiety of Miss Anastasia, though these were only a couple of old ladies, united in a half deification of the lordly young stranger, whose own appearance and manner were enough to have awakened a certain romantic interest in their simple young hearts. They were extremely concerned to-night about their homely tea-table—that everything should look its best and brightest; and even contrived, unknown to Hannah, to filch and convert into a temporary cake-basket that small rich old silver salver, which had been wont to stand upon one of Miss Bridget's little tables for cards. Then they robbed the garden for a sufficient bouquet of flowers; and then Agnes, half against her sister's will, wove in one of those pale roses to Marian's beautiful hair. Marian, though she made a laughing protest against this, and pretended to be totally indifferent to the important question, which dress she should wear? clearly recognised herself as the heroine of the evening. She knew very well, if no one else did, what was the vision which Louis had seen at the old gate, and came down to Miss Bridget's prim old parlour in her pretty light muslin dress with the rose in her hair, looking, in her little flutter and palpitation, as sweet a "vision of delight" as ever appeared to the eyes of man.

And Louis came—came—condescended to take tea—stayed some two hours or so, and then took his departure, hurriedly promising to come back for his sister. This much-anticipated hero—could it be possible that his going away was the greatest relief to them all, and that no one of the little party felt at all comfortable or at ease till he was gone? It was most strange and deplorable, yet it was most true beyond the possibility of question; for Louis, with all a young man's sensitive pride stung into bitterness by his position, haughtily repelled the interest and kindness of all these women. He was angry at Rachel—poor little anxious timid Rachel, who almost looked happy when they crossed this kindly threshold—for supposing these friends of hers, who were all women, could be companions for him; he was angry at himself for his anger; he was in the haughtiest and darkest frame of his naturally impetuous temper, rather disposed to receive as an insult any overture of friendship, and fiercely to plume himself upon his separated and orphaned state. They were all entirely discomfited and taken aback by their stately visitor, whom they had been disposed to receive with the warmest cordiality, and treat as one whom it was in their power to be kind to. Though his sister did so much violence to her natural feelings that she might hold her ground as his representative, Louis did not by any means acknowledge her deputyship. In entire opposition to her earnest and anxious frankness, Louis closed himself up with a jealous and repellant reserve; said nothing he could help saying, and speaking, when he did speak, with a cold and indifferent dignity; did not so much as refer to the Hall or Lord Winterbourne, and checked Rachel, when she was about to do so, with an almost imperceptible gesture, peremptory and full of displeasure. Poor Rachel, constantly referring to him with her eyes, and feeling the ground entirely taken from beneath her feet, sat pale and anxious, full of apprehension and dismay. Marian, who was not accustomed to see her own pretty self treated with such absolute unconcern, took down Fatherless Fanny from the bookshelf, and played with it, half reading, half "pretending," at one of the little tables. Agnes, after many vain attempts to draw Rachel's unmanageable brother into conversation, gave it up at last, and sat still by Rachel's side in embarrassed silence. Mamma betook herself steadily to her work-basket. The conversation fell away into mere questions addressed to Louis, and answers in monosyllables, so that it was an extreme relief to every member of the little party when this impracticable visitor rose at last, bowed to them all, and hastened away.

Rachel sat perfectly silent till the sound of his steps had died upon the road; then she burst out in a vehement apologetic outcry. "Oh, don't be angry with him—don't, please," said Rachel; "he thinks I have been trying to persuade you to be kind to him, and he cannot bear that even from me; and indeed, indeed you may believe me, it is quite true! I never saw him, except once or twice, in such a humour before."

"My dear," said Mrs Atheling, with that dignified tone which Mamma could assume when it was necessary, to the utter discomfiture of her opponent—"my dear, we are very glad to see your brother, but of course it can be nothing whatever to us the kind of humour he is in; that is quite his own concern."

Poor Rachel now, having no other resource, cried. She was only herself in this uncomfortable moment. She could no longer remember Louis's pride or Louis's dignity; for a moment the poor little subject heart felt a pang of resentment against the object of its idolatry, such as little Rachel had sometimes felt when Louis was "naughty," and she, his unfortunate little shadow, innocently shared in his punishment; but now, as at every former time, the personal trouble of the patient little sister yielded to the dread that Louis "was not understood." "You will know him better some time," she said, drying her sorrowful appealing eyes. So far as appearances went at this moment, it did not seem quite desirable to know him better, and nobody said a word in return.

After this the three girls went out together to the garden, still lying sweet in the calm of the long summer twilight, under a young moon and some early stars. They did not speak a great deal. They were all considerably absorbed with thoughts of this same hero, who, after all, had not taken an effective method of keeping their interest alive.

And Marian did not know how or whence it was that this doubtful and uncertain paladin came to her side in the pleasant darkness, but was startled by his voice in her ear as she leaned once more over the low garden-gate. "It was here I saw you first," said Louis, and Marian's heart leaped in her breast, half with the suddenness of the words, half with—something else. Louis, who had been so haughty and ungracious all the evening—Louis, Rachel's idol, everybody's superior—yet he spoke low in the startled ear of Marian, as if that first seeing had been an era in his life.

"Come with us," said Louis, as Rachel at sight of him hastened to get her bonnet—"come along this enchanted road a dozen steps into fairyland, and back again. I forget everything, even myself, on such a night."

And they went, scarcely answering, yet more satisfied with this brief reference to their knowledge of him, than if the king had forsaken his nature, and become as confidential as Rachel. They went their dozen steps on what was merely the terraced pathway, soft, dark, and grassy, to Agnes and Rachel, who went first in anxious conversation, but which the other two, coming silently behind, had probably a different idea of. Marian at least could not help cogitating these same adjectives, with a faint inquiry within herself, what it was which could make this an enchanted road or fairyland.

CHAPTER XXII

A BEGINNING

The next morning, while the mother and daughters were still in the full fervour of discussion about this same remarkable Louis, he himself was seen for the first time in the early daylight passing the window, with that singular rapidity of step which he possessed in common with his sister. They ceased their argument after seeing him—why, no one could have told; but quite unresolved as the question was, and though Mamma's first judgment, unsoftened by that twilight walk, was still decidedly unfavourable to Louis, they all dropped the subject tacitly and at once. Then Mamma went about various domestic occupations; then Agnes dropped into the chair which stood before that writing-book upon the table, and, with an attention much broken and distracted, gradually fell away into her own ideal world; and then Marian, leading Bell and Beau with meditative hands, glided forth softly to the garden, with downcast face and drooping eyes, full of thought. The children ran away from her at once when their little feet touched the grass, but Marian went straying along the paths, absorbed in her meditation, her pretty arms hanging by her side, her pretty head bent, her light fair figure gliding softly in shadow over the low mossy paling and the close-clipped hedge within. She was thinking only what it was most natural she should think, about the stranger of last night; yet now and then into the stream of her musing dropped, with the strangest disturbance and commotion, these few quiet words spoken in her ear,—"It was here I saw you first." How many times, then, had Louis seen her? and why did he recollect so well that first occasion? and what did he mean?

While she was busy with these fancies, all at once, Marian could not tell how, as suddenly as he appeared last night, Louis was here again—here, within the garden of the Old Wood Lodge, walking by Marian's side, a second long shadow upon the close-clipped hedge and the mossy paling, rousing her to a guilty consciousness that she had been thinking of him, which brought blush after blush in a flutter of "sweet shamefacednesse" to her cheek, and weighed down still more heavily the shy and dreamy lids of these beautiful eyes.

The most unaccountable thing in the world! but Marian, who had received with perfect coolness the homage of Sir Langham, and whose conscience smote her with no compunctions for the slaying of the gifted American, had strangely lost her self-possession to-day. She only replied in the sedatest and gravest manner possible to the questions of her companion—looked anxiously at the parlour window for an opportunity of calling Agnes, and with the greatest embarrassment longed for the presence of some one to end this tête-à-tête. Louis, on the contrary, exerted himself for her amusement, and was as different from the Louis of last night as it was possible to conceive.

"Ay, there it is," said Louis, who had just asked her what she knew of Oxford—"there it is, the seat of learning, thrusting up all its pinnacles to the sun; but I think, if the world were wise, this glitter and shining might point to the dark, dark ignorance outside of it, even more than to the little glow within."

Now this was not much in Marian's way—but her young squire, who would have submitted himself willingly to her guidance had she given any, was not yet acquainted at all with the ways of Marian.

She said, simply looking at the big dome sullenly throwing off the sunbeams, and at the glancing arrowheads, of more impressible and delicate kind, "I think it is very pretty, with all those different spires and towers; but do you mean it is the poor people who are so very ignorant? It seems as though people could scarcely help learning who live there."

"Yes, the poor people—I mean all of us," said Louis slowly, and with a certain painful emphasis. "A great many of the villagers, it is true, have never been to school; but I do not count a man ignorant who knows what he has to do, and how to do it, though he never reads a book, nor has pen in hand all his life. I save my pity for a more unfortunate ignorance than that."

"But that is very bad," said Marian decidedly, "because there is more to do than just to work, and we ought to know about—about a great many things. Agnes knows better than I."

This was said very abruptly, and meant that Agnes knew better what Marian meant to say than she herself did. The youth at her side, however, showed no inclination for any interpreter. He seemed, indeed, to be rather pleased than otherwise with this breaking off.

"When I was away, I was in strange enough quarters, and learnt something about knowledge," said Louis, "though not much knowledge itself—heaven help me! I suppose I was not worthy of that."

"And did you really run away?" asked Marian, growing bolder with this quickening of personal interest.

"I really ran away," said the young man, a hot flush passing for an instant over his brow; and then he smiled—a kind of daring desperate smile, which seemed to say "what I have done once I can do again."

"And what did you do?" said Marian, continuing her inquiries: she forgot her shyness in following up this story, which she knew and did not know.

"What all the village lads do who get into scrapes and break the hearts of the old women," said Louis, with a somewhat bitter jesting. "I listed for a soldier—but there was not even an old woman to break her heart for me."

"Oh, there was Rachel!" cried Marian eagerly.

"Yes, indeed, there was Rachel, my good little sister," answered the young man; "but her kind heart would have mended again had they let me alone. It would have been better for us both."

He said this with a painful compression of his lip, which a certain wistful sympathy in the mind of Marian taught her to recognise as the sign of tumult and contention in this turbulent spirit. She hastened with a womanly instinct to direct him to the external circumstances again.

"And you were really a soldier—a—not an officer—only a common man." Marian shrunk visibly from this, which was an actual and possible degradation, feared as the last downfall for the "wild sons" of the respectable families in the neighbourhood of Bellevue.

"Yes, I belong to a class which has no privileges; there was not a drummer in the regiment but was of better birth than I," exclaimed Louis. "Ah, that is folly—I did very well. In Napoleon's army, had I belonged to that day!—but in my time there was neither a general nor a war."

"Surely," said Marian, who began to be anxious about this unfortunate young man's "principles," "you would not wish for a war?"

"Should you think it very wrong?" said Louis with a smile.

"Yes," answered the young Mentor with immediate decision; for this conversation befell in those times, not so very long ago, when everybody declared that such convulsions were over, and that it was impossible, in the face of civilisation, steamboats, and the electric telegraph, to entertain the faintest idea of a war.

They had reached this point in their talk, gradually growing more at ease and familiar with each other, when it suddenly chanced that Mamma, passing from her own sleeping-room to that of the girls, paused a moment to look out at the small middle window in the passage between them, and looking down, was amazed to see this haughty and misanthropic Louis passing quietly along the trim pathway of the garden, keeping his place steadily by Marian's side. Mrs Atheling was not a mercenary mother, neither was she one much given to alarm for her daughters, lest they should make bad marriages or fall into unfortunate love; but Mrs Atheling, who was scrupulously proper, did not like to see her pretty Marian in such friendly companionship with "a young man in such an equivocal position," even though he was the brother of her friend. "We may be kind to them," said Mamma to herself, "but we are not to go any further; and, indeed, it would be very sad if he should come to more grief about Marian, poor young man;—how pretty she is!"

Yes, it was full time Mrs Atheling should hasten down stairs, and, in the most accidental manner in the world, step out into the garden. Marian, unfortunate child! with her young roses startled on her sweet young cheeks by this faint presaging breath of a new existence, had never been so pretty all her life.

CHAPTER XXIII

THE YOUNG PEOPLE

What Louis did or said, or how he made interest for himself in the tender heart of Mamma, no one very well knows; yet a certain fact it was, that from henceforward Mrs Atheling, like Miss Anastasia, became somewhat contemptuous of Rachel in the interest of Louis, and pursued eager and long investigations in her own mind—investigations most fruitless, yet most persevering—touching the old lord and the unknown conclusion of his life. All that was commonly known of the last years of the last Lord Winterbourne was, that he had died abroad. Under the pressure of family calamity he had gone to Italy, and there, people said, had wandered about for several years, leading a desultory and unsettled life, entirely out of the knowledge of any of his friends; and when the present bearer of the title came home, bearing the intelligence of his elder brother's death, the most entire oblivion closed down upon the foreign grave of the old lord. Back into this darkness Mrs Atheling, who knew no more than common report, made vain efforts to strain her kindly eyes, but always returned with a sigh of despair. "No!" said Mamma, "he might be proud, but he was virtuous and honourable. I never heard a word said against the old lord. Louis is like him, but it must only be a chance resemblance. No! Mr Reginald was always a wild bad man. Poor things! they must be his children; for my lord, I am sure, never betrayed or deceived any creature all his life."

But still she mused and dreamed concerning Louis; he seemed to exercise a positive fascination over all these elder people; and Mrs Atheling, more than she had ever desired a friendly gossip with Miss Willsie, longed to meet once more with the Honourable Anastasia, to talk over her conjectures and guesses respecting "the boy."

In the mean time, Louis himself, relieved from that chaperonship and anxious introduction by his sister, which the haughty young man could not endure, made daily increase of his acquaintance with the strangers. He began to form part of their daily circle, expected and calculated upon; and somehow the family life seemed to flow in a stronger and fuller current with the addition of this vigorous element, the young man, who oddly enough seemed to belong to them rather more than if he had been their brother. He took the three girls, who were now so much like three sisters, on long and wearying excursions through the wood and over the hill. He did not mind tiring them out, nor was he extremely fastidious about the roads by which he led them; for, generous at heart as he was, the young man had the unconscious wilfulness of one who all his life had known no better guidance than his own will. Sometimes, in those long walks of theirs, the young Athelings were startled by some singular characteristic of their squire, bringing to light in him, by a sudden chance, things of which these gentle-hearted girls had never dreamed. Once they discovered, lying deep among the great fern-leaves, all brown and rusty with seed, the bright plumage of some dead game, for the reception of which a village boy was making a bag of his pinafore. "Carry it openly," said Louis, at whose voice the lad started; "and if any one asks you where it came from, send them to me." This was his custom, which all the village knew and profited by; he would not permit himself to be restrained from the sport, but he scorned to lift the slain bird, which might be supposed to be Lord Winterbourne's, and left it to be picked up by the chance foragers of the hamlet. At the first perception of this, the girls, we are obliged to confess, were greatly shocked—tears even came to Marian's eyes. She said it was cruel, in a little outbreak of terror, pity, and indignation. "Cruel—no!" said Louis: "did my gun give a sharper wound than one of the score of fashionable guns that will be waking all the echoes in a day or two?" But Marian only glanced up at him hurriedly with her shy eyes, and said, with a half smile, "Perhaps though the wound was no sharper, the poor bird might have liked another week of life."

And the young man looked up into the warm blue sky over-head, all crossed and trellised with green leaves, and looked around into the deep September foliage, flaming here and there in a yellow leaf, a point of fire among the green. "I think it very doubtful," he said, sinking his voice, though every one heard him among the noonday hush of the trees, "if I ever can be so happy again. Do you not suppose it would be something worth living for, instead of a week or a year of sadder chances, to be shot upon the wing now?"

Marian did not say a word, but shrank away among the bushes, clinging to Rachel's arm, with a shy instinctive motion. "Choose for yourself," said Agnes; "but do not decide so coolly upon the likings of the poor bird. I am sure, had he been consulted, he would rather have taken his chance of the guns next week than lain so quiet under the fern-leaves now."

Whereupon the blush of youth for his own super-elevated and unreal sentiment came over Louis's face. Agnes, by some amusing process common to young girls who are elder sisters, and whom nobody is in love with, had made herself out to be older than Louis, and was rather disposed now and then to interfere for the regulation of this youth's improper sentiments, and to give him good advice.

And Lord Winterbourne arrived: they discovered the fact immediately by the entire commotion and disturbance of everything about the village, by the noise of wheels, and the flight of servants, to be descried instantly in the startled neighbourhood. Then they began to see visions of sportsmen, and flutters of fine ladies; and even without these visible and evident signs, it would have been easy enough to read the information of the arrivals in the clouded and lowering brow of Louis, and in poor little Rachel's distress, anxiety, and agitation. She, poor child, could no longer join their little kindly party in the evening; and when her brother came without her, he burst into violent outbreaks of rage, indignation, and despair, dreadful to see. Neither mother nor daughters knew how to soothe him; for it was even more terrible in their fancy than in his experience to be the Pariah and child of degradation in this great house. Moved by the intolerable burden of this his time of trial, Louis at last threw himself upon the confidence of his new friends, confided his uncertain and conflicting plans to them, relieved himself of his passionate resentment, and accepted their sympathy. Every day he came goaded half to madness, vowing his determination to bear it no longer; but every day, as he sat in the old easy-chair, with his handsome head half-buried in his hands, a solace, sweet and indescribable, stole into Louis's heart; he was inspired to go at the very same moment that he was impelled to stay, by that same vision which he had first seen in the summer twilight at the old garden-gate.

CHAPTER XXIV

A MEETING

This state of things continued for nearly a fortnight after the arrival of Lord Winterbourne and his party at the Hall. They saw Mrs Edgerley passing through the village, and in church; but she either did not see them, or did not think it necessary to take any notice of the girls. Knowing better now the early connection between their own family and Lord Winterbourne's, they were almost glad of this—almost; yet certainly it would have been pleasanter to decline her friendly advances, than to find her, their former patroness, quietly dropping acquaintance with them.

The grassy terraced road which led from Winterbourne village to the highway, and which was fenced on one side by the low wall which surrounded the stables and outhouses of the Rector, and by the hedge and paling of the Old Wood Lodge, but on the other side was free and open to the fields, which sloped down from it to the low willow-dropped banks of one of those pale rivers, was not a road adapted either for vehicles or horses. The Rivers family, however, holding themselves monarchs of all they surveyed, stood upon no punctilio in respect to the pathway of the villagers, and the family temper, alike in this one particular, brought about a collision important enough to all parties concerned, and especially to the Athelings; for one of those days, when a riding-party from the Hall cantered along the path with a breezy waving and commotion of veils and feathers and riding-habits, and a pleasant murmur of sound, voices a little louder than usual under cover of the September gale mixed only with the jingle of the harness—for the horses' hoofs struck no sound but that of a dull tread from the turf of the way—it pleased Miss Anastasia, at the very hour and moment of their approach, to drive her two grey ponies to the door of the Old Wood Lodge. Of course, it was the simplest "accident" in the world, this unpremeditated "chance" meeting. There was no intention nor foresight whatever in the matter. When she saw them coming, Miss Anastasia "growled" under her breath, and marvelled indignantly how they could dream of coming in such a body over the grassed road of the villagers, cutting it to pieces with their horses' hoofs. She never paused to consider how the wheels of her own substantial vehicle ploughed the road; and for her part, the leader of the fair equestrians brightened with an instant hope of amusement. "Here is cousin Anastasia, the most learned old lady in Banburyshire. Delightful! Now, my love, you shall see the lion of the county," cried Mrs Edgerley to one of her young companions, not thinking nor caring whether her voice reached her kinswoman or not. Lord Winterbourne, who was with his daughter, drew back to the rear of the group instinctively. Whatever was said of Lord Winterbourne, his worst enemy could not say that he was brave to meet the comments of those whom he had harmed or wronged.

Miss Anastasia stepped from her carriage in the most deliberate manner possible, nodded to Marian and Agnes, who were in the garden—and to whose defence, seeing so many strangers, hastily appeared their mother—and stood patting and talking to her ponies, in her brown cloth pelisse and tippet, and with that oddest of comfortable bonnets upon her head.

"Cousin Anastasia, I vow! You dear creature, where have you been all these ages? Would any one believe it? Ah, how delightful to live always in the country; what a penalty we pay for town and its pleasures! Could any one suppose that my charming cousin was actually older than me?"

And the fashionable beauty, though she did begin to be faded, threw up her delicate hands with their prettiest gesture, as she pointed to the stately old lady before her, in her antique dress, and with unconcealed furrows in her face. Once, perhaps, not even that beautiful complexion of Mrs Edgerley was sweeter than that of Anastasia Rivers; but her beauty had gone from her long ago—a thing which she cared not to retain. She looked up with her kind imperious face, upon which were undeniable marks of years and age. She perceived with a most evident and undisguised contempt the titter with which this comparison was greeted. "Go on your way, Louisa," said Miss Rivers; "you were pretty once, whatever people say of you now. Don't be a fool, child; and I advise you not to meddle with me."

"Delightful! is she not charming?" cried the fine lady, appealing to her companion; "so fresh, and natural, and eccentric—such an acquisition in the Hall! Anastasia, dear, do forget your old quarrel. It was not poor papa's fault that you were born a woman, though I cannot help confessing it was a great mistake, certainly; but, only for once, you who are such a dear, kind, benevolent creature, come to see me."

"Go on, Louisa, I advise you," said the Honourable Anastasia with extreme self-control. "Poor child, I have no quarrel with you, at all events. You did not choose your father—there, pass on. I leave the Hall to those who choose it; the Old Wood Lodge has more attraction for me."

"And I protest," cried Mrs Edgerley, "it is my sweet young friend, the author of —: my dearest child, what is the name of your book? I have such a memory. Quite the sweetest story of the season; and I am dying to hear of another. Are you writing again? Oh, pray say you are. I should be heartbroken to think of waiting very long for it. You must come to the Hall. There are some people coming who are dying to know you, and I positively cannot be disappointed: no one ever disobeys me! Come here and let me kiss, you pretty creature. Is she not the sweetest little beauty in the world? and her sister has so much genius; it is quite delightful! So you know my cousin Anastasia; isn't she charming? Now, good morning, coz.—good morning, dear—and be sure you come to the Hall."

Miss Anastasia stood aside, watching grimly this unexpected demonstration of friendship, and keenly criticising Agnes, who coloured high with youthful dignity and resentment, and Marian, who drew back abashed, with a painful blush, and a grieved and anxious consciousness that Louis, unseen but seeing, was a spectator of this salutation, and somehow would be quite as like to resent Mrs Edgerley's careless compliment to herself, "as if I had been his sister." With a steady observation the old lady kept her eyes upon her young acquaintances till the horsemen and horsewomen of Mrs Edgerley's train had passed. Then she drew herself up to the utmost pitch of her extreme height, and, without raising her eyes, made a profound curtsy to the last of the train—he on his part lifted his hat, and bent to his saddle-bow. This was how Lord Winterbourne and his brother's daughter recognised each other. Perhaps the wandering eyes in his bloodless face glanced a moment, shifting and uncertain as they were, upon the remarkable figure of Miss Rivers, but they certainly paused to take in, with one fixed yet comprehensive glance, the mother and the daughters, the children playing in the garden—the open door of the house—even it was possible he saw Louis, though Louis had been behind, at the end of the little green, out of sight, trying to train a wild honeysuckle round an extempore bower. Lord Winterbourne scarcely paused, and did not offer the slightest apology for his stare, but they felt, all of them, that he had marked the house, and laid them under the visionary curse of his evil eye. When he had passed, Miss Rivers put them in before her, with an imperative gesture. "Let me know what's brewing," said the Honourable Anastasia, as she reposed herself on the little new sofa in the old parlour. "There's mischief in his eye."

CHAPTER XXV

THE BREWING OF THE STORM

The visit of Miss Rivers was the most complimentary attention which she could show to her new friends, for her visits were few, and paid only to a very limited number of people, and these all of her own rank and class. She was extremely curious as to their acquaintance with Mrs Edgerley, and demanded to know every circumstance from its beginning until now; and this peremptory old lady was roused to quite an eager and animated interest in the poor little book of which, Agnes could not forget, Mrs Edgerley did not remember so much as the name. The Honourable Anastasia declared abruptly that she never read novels, yet demanded to have Hope Hazlewood placed without an instant's delay in her pony-carriage. "Do it at once, my dear: a thing which is done at the moment cannot be forgotten," said Miss Rivers. "You write books, eh? Well, I asked you if you were clever; why did you not tell me at once?"

"I did not think you would care; it was not worth while," said Agnes with some confusion, and feeling considerably alarmed by the idea of this formidable old lady's criticism. Miss Rivers only answered by hurrying her out with the book, lest it might possibly be forgotten. When the girls were gone, she turned to Mrs Atheling. "What can he do to you," said Miss Anastasia, abruptly, "eh? What's Will Atheling doing? Can he harm Will?"

"No," said Mamma, somewhat excited by the prospect of an enemy, yet confident in the perfect credit and honour of the family father, whose good name and humble degree of prosperity no enemy could overthrow. "William has been where he is now for twenty years."

"So, so," said Miss Rivers—"and the boy? Take care of these girls; it might be in his devilish way to harm them; and I tell you, when you come to know of it, send me word. So she writes books, this girl of yours? She is no better than a child. Do you mean to say you are not proud?"

Mrs Atheling answered as mothers answer when such questions are put to them, half with a confession, half with a partly-conscious sophism, about Agnes being "a good girl, and a great comfort to her papa and me."

The girls, when they had executed their commission, looked doubtingly for Louis, but found him gone as they expected. While they were still lingering where he had been, Miss Rivers came to the door again, going away, and when she had said good-by to Mamma, the old lady turned back again without a word, and very gravely gathered one of the roses. She did it with a singular formality and solemness as if it was a religious observance rather than a matter of private liking; and securing it somewhere out of sight in the fastenings of her brown pelisse, waved her hand to them, saying in her peremptory voice, quite loud enough to be heard at a considerable distance, that she was to send for them in a day or two. Then she took her seat in the little carriage, and turned her grey ponies, no very easy matter, towards the high-road. Her easy and complete mastery over them was an admiration to the girls. "Bless you, miss, she'd follow the hounds as bold as any squire," said Hannah; "but there's a deal o' difference in Miss Taesie since the time she broke her heart."

Such an era was like to be rather memorable. The girls thought so, somewhat solemnly, as they went to their work beside their mother. They seemed to be coming to graver times themselves, gliding on in an irresistible noiseless fashion upon their stream of fate.

Louis came again as usual in the evening. He had heard Mrs Edgerley, and did resent her careless freedom, as Marian secretly knew he would; which fact she who was most concerned, ascertained by his entire and pointed silence upon the subject, and his vehement and passionate contempt, notwithstanding, for Mrs Edgerley.

"I suppose you are safe enough," he said, speaking to the elder sister. "You will not break your heart because she has forgotten the name of your book—but, heaven help them, there are hearts which do! There are unfortunate fools in this crazy world mad enough to be elated and to be thrown into misery by a butterfly of a fine lady, who makes reputations. You think them quite contemptible, do you? but there are such."

"I suppose they must be people who have no friends and no home—or to whom it is of more importance than it is to me," said Agnes; "for I am only a woman, and nothing could make me miserable out of this Old Lodge, or Bellevue."

"Ah—that is now," said Louis quickly, and he glanced with an instinctive reference at Marian, whose pallid roses and fluctuating mood already began to testify to some anxiety out of the boundary of these charmed walls. "The very sight of your security might possibly be hard enough upon us who have no home—no home! nothing at all under heaven."

"Except such trifles as strength and youth and a stout heart, a sister very fond of you, and some—some friends—and heaven itself, after all, at the end. Oh, Louis!" said Agnes, who on this, as on other occasions, was much disposed to be this "boy's" elder sister, and advised him "for his good."

He did not say anything. When he looked up at all from his bending attitude leaning over the table, it was to glance with fiery devouring eyes at Marian—poor little sweet Marian, already pale with anxiety for him. Then he broke out suddenly—"That poor little sister who is very fond of me—do you know what she is doing at this moment—singing to them!—like the captives at Babylon, making mirth for the spoilers. And my friends— heaven! you heard what that woman ventured to say to-day."

"My dear," said Mrs Atheling, who confessed to treating Louis as a "son of her own," "think of heaven all the day long, and so much the better for you—but I cannot have you using in this way such a name."

This simple little reproof did more for Louis than a hundred philosophies. He laughed low, and with emotion took Mrs Atheling's hand for a moment between his own—said "thank you, mother," with a momentary smile of delight and good pleasure. Then his face suddenly flushed with a dark and violent colour; he cast an apprehensive yet haughty glance at Mrs Atheling, and drew his hand away. The stain in his blood was a ghost by the side of Louis, and scarcely left him for an instant night nor day.

When he left them, they went to the door with him as they had been wont to do, the mother holding a shawl over her cap, the girls with their fair heads uncovered to the moon. They stood all together at the gate speaking cheerfully, and sending kind messages to Rachel as they bade him good-night—and none of the little group noticed a figure suddenly coming out of the darkness and gliding along past the paling of the garden. "What, boy, you here?" cried a voice suddenly behind Louis, which made him start aside, and they all shrank back a little to recognise in the moonlight the marble-white face of Lord Winterbourne.

"What do you mean, sir, wandering about the country at this hour?" said the stranger—"what conspiracy goes on here, eh?—what are you doing with a parcel of women? Home to your den, you skulking young vagabond—what are you doing here?"

Marian, the least courageous of the three, moved by a sudden impulse, which was not courage but terror, laid her hand quickly upon Louis's arm. The young man, who had turned his face defiant and furious towards the intruder, turned in an instant, grasping at the little timid hand as a man in danger might grasp at a shield invulnerable, "You perceive, my lord, I am beyond the reach either of your insults or your patronage here," said the youth, whose blood was dancing in his veins, and who at that moment cared less than the merest stranger, who had never heard his name, for Lord Winterbourne.

"Come, my lad, if you are imposing upon these poor people—I must set you right," said the man who was called Louis's father. "Do you know what he is, my good woman, that you harbour this idle young rascal in despite of my known wishes? Home, you young vagabond, home! This boy is—"

"My lord, my lord," interposed Mrs Atheling, in sudden agitation, "if any disgrace belongs to him, it is yours and not his that you should publish it. Go away, sir, from my door, where you once did harm enough, and don't try to injure the poor boy—perhaps we know who he is better than you."

What put this bold and rash speech into the temperate lips of Mamma, no one could ever tell; the effect of it, however, was electric. Lord Winterbourne fell back suddenly, stared at her with his strained eyes in the moonlight, and swore a muttered and inaudible oath. "Home, you hound!" he repeated in a mechanical tone, and then, waving his hand with a threatening and unintelligible gesture, turned to go away. "So long as the door is yours, my friend, I will take care to make no intrusion upon it," he said significantly before he disappeared; and then the shadow departed out of the moonlight, the stealthy step died on the grass, and they stood alone again with beating hearts. Mamma took Marian's hand from Louis, but not unkindly, and with an affectionate earnestness bade him go away. He hesitated long, but at length consented, partly for her entreaty, partly for the sake of Rachel. Under other circumstances this provocation would have maddened Louis; but he wrung Agnes's hand with an excited gaiety as he lingered at the door watching a shadow on the window whither Marian had gone with her mother. "I had best not meet him on the road," said Louis: "there is the Curate—for once, for your sake, and the sake of what has happened, I will be gracious and take his company; but to tell the truth, I do not care for anything which can befall me to-night."

CHAPTER XXVI

A CRISIS

Marian, whom her mother tenderly put to sleep that night, as if she had been a child, yet who lay awake in the long cold hours before the dawn in a vague and indescribable emotion, her heart stirring within her like something which did not belong to her—a new and strange existence—slept late the next morning, exhausted and worn out with all this sudden and stormy influx of unknown feelings. Mamma, who, on the contrary, was very early astir, came into the bed-chamber of her daughters at quite an unusual hour, and, thankfully perceiving Marian's profound youthful slumber, stood gazing at the beautiful sleeper with tears in her eyes. Paler than usual, with a shadow under her closed eyelids, and still a little dew upon the long lashes—with one hand laid in childish fashion under her cheek, and the other lying, with its pearly rose-tipped fingers, upon the white coverlid, Marian, but for the moved and human agitation which evidently had worn itself into repose, might have looked like the enchanted beauty of the tale—but indeed she was rather more like a child who had wept itself to sleep. Her sister, stealing softly from her side, left her sleeping, and they put the door ajar that they might hear when she stirred before they went, with hushed steps and speaking in a whisper, down stairs.

Mrs Atheling was disturbed more than she would tell; what she did say, as Agnes and she sat over their silent breakfast-table, was an expedient which herself had visibly no faith in. "My dear, we must try to prevent him saying anything," said Mrs Atheling, with her anxious brow: it was not necessary to name names, for neither of them could forget the scene of last night.

Then by-and-by Mamma spoke again. "I almost fancy we should go home; she might forget it if she were away. Agnes, my love, you must persuade him not to say anything; he pays great attention to what you say."

"But, mamma—Marian?" said Agnes.

"Oh, Agnes, Agnes, my dear beautiful child," said Mrs Atheling, with a sudden access of emotion, "it was only friendship, sympathy—her kind heart; she will think no more of it, if nothing occurs to put it into her head."

Agnes did not say anything, though she was extremely doubtful on this subject; but then it was quite evident that Mamma had no faith in her own prognostications, and regarded this first inroad into the family with a mixture of excitement, dread, and agitation which it was not comfortable to see.

After their pretended breakfast, mother and daughter once more stole up-stairs. They had not been in the room a moment, when Marian woke—woke—started with fright and astonishment to see Agnes dressed, and her mother standing beside her; and beginning to recollect, suddenly blushed, and turning away her face, burning with that violent suffusion of colour, exclaimed, "I could not help it—I could not help it; would you stand by and see them drive him mad? Oh mamma, mamma!"

"My darling, no one thinks of blaming you," said Mrs Atheling, who trembled a good deal, and looked very anxious. "We were all very sorry for him, poor fellow; and you only did what you should have done, like a brave little friend—what I should have done myself, had I been next to him," said Mamma, with great gravity and earnestness, but decidedly overdoing her part.

This did not seem quite a satisfactory speech to Marian. She turned away again petulantly, dried her eyes, and with a sidelong glance at Agnes, asked, "Why did you not wake me?—it looks quite late. I am not ill, am I? I am sure I do not understand it—why did you let me sleep?"

"Hush, darling! because you were tired and late last night," said Mamma.

Now this sympathy and tenderness seemed rather alarming than soothing to Marian. Her colour varied rapidly, her breath came quick, tears gathered to her eyes. "Has anything happened while I have been sleeping?" she asked hastily, and in a very low tone.

"No, no, my love, nothing at all," said Mamma tenderly, "only we thought you must be tired."

"Both you and Agnes were as late as me,—why were not you tired?" said Marian, still with a little jealous fear. "Please, mamma, go away; I want to get dressed and come down stairs."

They left her to dress accordingly, but still with some anxiety and apprehension, and Mamma waited for Marian in her own room, while Agnes went down to the parlour—just in time, for as she took her seat, Louis, flushed and impatient, burst in at the door.

Louis made a most hasty salutation, and was a great deal too eager and hurried to be very well bred. He looked round the room with sudden anxiety and disappointment. "Where is she?—I must see Marian," cried Louis. "What! you do not mean to say she is ill, after last night?"

"Not ill, but in her own room," said Agnes, somewhat confused by the question.

"I will wait as long as you please, if I must wait," said Louis impatiently; "but, Agnes! why should you be against me? Of course, I forget myself; do you grudge that I should? I forget everything except last night; let me see Marian. I promise you I will not distress her, and if she bids me, I will go away."

"No, it is not that," said Agnes with hesitation; "but, Louis, nothing happened last night—pray do not think of it. Well, then," she said earnestly, as his hasty gesture denied what she said, "mamma begs you, Louis, not to say anything to-day."

He turned round upon her with a blank but haughty look. "I understand—my disgrace must not come here," he said; "but she did not mind it; she, the purest lily upon earth! Ah! so that was a dream, was it? And her mother—her mother says I am to go away?"

"No, indeed—no," said Agnes, almost crying. "No, Louis, you know better; do not misunderstand us. She is so young, so gentle, and tender. Mamma only asked, for all our sakes, if you would consent not to say anything now."

To this softened form of entreaty the eager young man paid not the slightest attention. He began to use the most unblushing cajolery to win over poor Agnes. It did not seem to be Louis; so entirely changed was his demeanour. It was only an extremely eager and persevering specimen of the genus "lover," without any personal individuality at all.

"What! not say anything? Could anybody ask such a sacrifice?" cried this wilful and impetuous youth. "It might, as you say, be nothing at all, though it seems life—existence, to me. Not know whether that hand is mine or another's—that hand which saved me, perhaps from murder?—for he is an old man, though he is a fiend incarnate, and I might have killed him where he stood."

"Louis! Louis!" cried Agnes, gazing at him in terror and excitement. He grew suddenly calm as he caught her eye.

"It is quite true," he said with a grave and solemn calmness. "This man, who has cursed my life, and made it miserable—this man, who dared insult me before her and you—do you think I could have been a man, and still have borne that intolerable crown of wrong?"

As he spoke, he began to pace the little parlour with impatient steps and a clouded brow. Mrs Atheling, who had heard his voice, but had restrained her anxious curiosity as long as possible, now came down quietly, unable to keep back longer. Louis sprang to her side, took her hand, led her about the room, pleading, reasoning, persuading. Mamma, whose good heart from the first moment had been an entire and perfect traitor, was no match at all for Louis. She gave in to him unresistingly before half his entreaties were over; she did not make even half so good a stand as Agnes, who secretly was in the young lover's interest too. But when they had just come to the conclusion that he should be permitted to see Marian, Marian herself, whom no one expected, suddenly entered the room. The young beauty's pretty brow was lowering more than any one before had ever seen it lower; a petulant contraction was about her red lips, and a certain angry dignity, as of an offended child, in her bearing. "Surely something very strange has happened this morning," said Marian, with a little heat; "even mamma looks as if she knew some wonderful secret. I suppose every one is to hear of it but me."

At this speech the dismayed conspirators against Marian's peace fell back and separated. The other impetuous principal in the matter hastened at once to the angry Titania, who only bowed, and did not even look at him. The truth was, that Marian, much abashed at thought of her own sudden impulse, was never in a mood less propitious; she felt as if she herself had not done quite right—as if somehow she had betrayed a secret of her own, and, now found out and detected, was obliged to use the readiest means to cover it up again; and, besides, the hasty little spirit, which had both pride and temper of its own, could not at all endure the idea of having been petted and excused this morning, as if "something had happened" last night. Now that it was perfectly evident nothing had happened—now that Louis stood before her safe, handsome, and eager, Marian concluded that it was time for her to stand upon her defence.

CHAPTER XXVII

CLOUDS

The end of it all was, of course—though Louis had an amount of trouble in the matter which that impetuous young gentleman had not counted upon—that Marian yielded to his protestations, and came forth full of the sweetest agitation, tears, and blushes, to be taken to the kind breast of the mother who was scarcely less agitated, and to be regarded with a certain momentary awe, amusement, and sympathy by Agnes, whose visionary youthful reverence for this unknown magician was just tempered by the equally youthful imp of mischief which plays tricks upon the same. But Mrs Atheling's brow grew sadder and sadder with anxiety, as she looked at the young man who now claimed to call her mother. What he was to do—how Marian could bear all the chances and changes of the necessarily long probation before them—what influence Lord Winterbourne might have upon the fortunes of his supposed son—what Papa himself would say to this sudden betrothal, and how he could reconcile himself to receive a child, and a disgraced child of his old enemy, into his own honourable house,—these considerations fluttered the heart and disturbed the peace of the anxious mother, who already began to blame herself heavily, yet did not see, after all, what else she could have done. A son of shame, and of Lord Winterbourne!—a young man hitherto dependent, with no training, no profession, no fortune, of no use in the world. And her prettiest Marian!—the sweet face which won homage everywhere, and which every other face involuntarily smiled to see. Darker and darker grew the cloud upon the brow of Mrs Atheling; she went in, out of sight of these two happy young dreamers, with a sick heart. For the first time in her life she was dismayed at the thought of writing to her husband, and sat idly in a chair drawn back from her window, wearying herself out with most vain and unprofitable speculations as to things which might have been done to avert this fate.

No very long time elapsed, however, before Mrs Atheling found something else to occupy her thoughts. Hannah came in to the parlour, solemnly announcing a man at the door who desired to see her. With a natural presentiment, very naturally arising from the excited state of her own mind, Mrs Atheling rose, and hastened to the door. The man was an attorney's clerk, threadbare and respectable, who gave into her hand an open paper, and after it a letter. The paper, which she glanced over with hasty alarm, was a formal notice to quit, on pain of ejection, from the house called the Old Wood Lodge, the property of Reginald, Lord Winterbourne. "The property of Lord Winterbourne!—it is our—it is my husband's property. What does this mean?" cried Mrs Atheling.

"I know nothing of the business, but Mr Lewis's letter will explain it," said the messenger, who was civil but not respectful; and the anxious mistress of the house hastened in with great apprehension and perplexity to open the letter and see what this explanation was. It was not a very satisfactory one. With a friendly spirit, yet with a most cautious and lawyer-like regard to the interest of his immediate client, Mr Lewis, the same person who had been intrusted with the will of old Miss Bridget, and who was Lord Winterbourne's solicitor, announced the intention of his principal to "resume possession" of Miss Bridget's little house. "You will remember," wrote the lawyer, "that I did not fail to point out to you at the time the insecure nature of the tenure by which this little property was held. Granted, as I believe it was, as a gift simply for the lifetime of Miss Bridget Atheling, she had, in fact, no right to bequeath it to any one, and so much of her will as relates to this is null and void. I am informed that there are documents in existence proving this fact beyond the possibility of dispute, and that any resistance would be entirely vain. As a friend, I should advise you not to attempt it; the property is actually of very small value, and though I speak against the interest of my profession, I think it right to warn you against entering upon an expensive lawsuit with a man like Lord Winterbourne, to whom money is no consideration. For the sake of your family, I appeal to you whether it would not be better, though at a sacrifice of feeling, to give up without resistance the old house, which is of very little value to any one, if it were not for my lord's whim of having no small proprietors in his neighbourhood. I should be sorry that he was made acquainted with this communication. I write to you merely from private feelings, as an old friend."

Mrs Atheling rose from her seat hastily, holding the papers in her hand. "Resist him!" she exclaimed—
"yes, certainly, to the very last;" but at that moment there came in at the half-open door a sound of
childish riot, exuberant and unrestrained, which arrested the mother's words, and subdued her like a
spell. Bell and Beau, rather neglected and thrown into the shade for the first time in their lives, were
indemnifying themselves in the kitchen, where they reigned over Hannah with the most absolute and
unhesitating mastery. Mamma fell back again into her seat, silent, pale, and with pain and terror in her
face. Was this the first beginning of the blight of the Evil Eye?

And then she remained thinking over it sadly and in silence; sometimes, disposed to blame herself for
her rashness—sometimes with a natural rising of indignation, disposed to repeat again her first outcry,
and resist this piece of oppression—sometimes starting with the sudden fright of an anxious and timid
mother, and almost persuaded at once, without further parley, to flee to her own safe home, and give
up, without a word, the new inheritance. But she was not learned in the ways of the world, in law, or
necessary ceremonial. Resist was a mere vague word to her, meaning she knew not what, and no step
occurred to her in the matter but the general necessity for "consulting a lawyer," which was of itself an
uncomfortable peril. As she argued with herself, indeed, Mrs Atheling grew quite hopeless, and gave up
the whole matter. She had known, through many changes, the success of this bad man, and in her
simple mind had no confidence in the abstract power of the law to maintain the cause, however just, of
William Atheling, who would have hard ado to pay a lawyer's fees, against Lord Winterbourne.

Then she called in her daughters, whom Louis then only, and with much reluctance, consented to leave,
and held a long and agitated counsel with them. The girls were completely dismayed by the news, and
mightily impressed by that new and extraordinary "experience" of a real enemy, which captivated
Agnes's wandering imagination almost as much as it oppressed her heart. As for Marian, she sat looking
at them blankly, turning from Mamma to Agnes, and from Agnes to Mamma, with a vague perception
that this was somehow because of Louis, and a very heavy heartbreaking depression in her agitated
thoughts. Marian, though she was not very imaginative, had caught a tinge of the universal romance at
this crisis of her young life, and, cast down with the instant omen of misfortune, saw clouds and storms
immediately rising through that golden future, of which Louis's prophecies had been so pleasant to
hear.

And there could be no doubt that this suddenly formed engagement, hasty, imprudent, and ill-advised
as it was, added a painful complication to the whole business. If it was known—and who could conceal
from the gossip of the village the constant visits of Louis, or his undisguised devotion?—then it would
set forth evidently in public opposition the supposed father and son. "But Lord Winterbourne is not his
father!" cried Marian suddenly, with tears and vehemence. Mrs Atheling shook her head, and said that
people supposed so at least, and this would be a visible sign of war.

But no one in the family counsel could advise anything in this troubled moment. Charlie was coming—
that was a great relief and comfort. "If Charlie knows anything, it should be the law," said Mrs Atheling,
with a sudden joy in the thought that Charlie had been full six months at it, and ought to be very well
informed indeed upon the subject. And then Agnes brought her blotting-book, and the good mother sat
down to write the most uncomfortable letter she had ever written to her husband in all these two-and-
twenty years. There was Marian's betrothal, first of all, which was so very unlike to please him—he who
did not even know Louis, and could form no idea of his personal gifts and compensations—and then
there was the news of this summons, and of the active and powerful enemy suddenly started up against
them. Mrs Atheling took a very long time composing the letter, but sighed heavily to think how soon
Papa would read it, to the destruction of all his pleasant fancies about his little home in the country, and

his happy children. Charlie was coming—they had all a certain faith in Charlie, boy though he was; it was the only comfort in the whole prospect to the anxious eyes of Mamma.

CHAPTER XXVIII

THE REV. LIONEL RIVERS

The next day, somewhat to the consternation of this disturbed and troubled family, they were honoured by a most unlooked-for and solemn visit from the Rector. The Rector, in stature, form, and features, considerably resembled Miss Anastasia, and was, as she herself confessed, an undeniable Rivers, bearing all the family features and not a little of the family temper. He seemed rather puzzled himself to give a satisfactory reason for his call—saying solemnly that he thought it right for the priest of the parish to be acquainted with all his parishioners—words which did not come with half so much unction or natural propriety from his curved and disdainful lip, as they would have done from the bland voice of Mr Mead. Then he asked some ordinary questions how they liked the neighbourhood, addressing himself to Mamma, though his very grave and somewhat haughty looks were principally directed to Agnes. Mrs Atheling, in spite of her dislike of the supreme altitude of his churchmanship, had a natural respect for the clergyman, who seemed the natural referee and adviser of people in trouble; and though he was a Rivers, and the next heir after Lord Winterbourne's only son, it by no means followed on that account that the Rector entertained any affectionate leaning towards Lord Winterbourne.

"I knew your old relative very well," said the Rector; "she was a woman of resolute will and decided opinions, though her firmness, I am afraid, was in the cause of error rather than of truth. I believe she always entertained a certain regard for me, connected as she was with the family, though I felt it my duty to warn her against her pernicious principles before her death."

"Her pernicious principles! Was poor Aunt Bridget an unbeliever?" cried Agnes, with an involuntary interest, and yet an equally involuntary and natural spirit of opposition to this stately young man.

"The word is a wide one. No—not an unbeliever, nor even a disbeliever, so far as I am aware," said the churchman, "but, even more dangerous than a positive error of doctrine, holding these fatal delusions concerning private opinion, which have been the bane of the Church."

There was a little pause after this, the unaccustomed audience being somewhat startled, yet quite unprepared for controversy, and standing beside in a little natural awe of the Rector, who ought to know so much better than they did. Agnes alone felt a stirring of unusual pugnacity—for once in her life she almost forgot her natural diffidence, and would have liked nothing better than to throw down her woman's glove to the rampant churchman, and make a rash and vehement onslaught upon him, after the use and wont of feminine controversy.

"My own conviction is," said the Rector with a little solemnity, yet with a dissatisfied and fiery gleam in his eager dark eyes, "that there is no medium between the infallible authority of the Church and the wildest turmoil of heresy. This one rock a man may plant his foot upon—all beyond is a boundless and infinite chaos. Therefore I count it less perilous to be ill-informed or indifferent concerning some portions of the creed, than to be shaken in the vital point of the Church's authority—the only flood-gate that can be closed against the boiling tide of error, which, but for this safeguard, would overpower us all."

Having made this statement, which somehow he enunciated as if it were a solemn duty, Mr Rivers left the subject abruptly, and returned to common things.

"You are acquainted, I understand," he said, with haste and a little emotion, "with my unfortunate young relatives at the Hall?"

The question was so abrupt and unlooked for, that all the three, even Mamma, who was not very much given to blushing, coloured violently. "Louis and Rachel? Yes; we know them very well," said Mrs Atheling, with as much composure as she could summon to meet the emergency—which certainly was not enough to prevent the young clergyman from discovering a rather unusual degree of interest in the good mother's answer. He looked surprised, and turned a hurried glance upon the girls, who were equally confused under his scrutiny. It was impossible to say which was the culprit, if culprit there was. Mr Rivers, who was tall enough at first, visibly grew a little taller, and became still more stately in his demeanour than before.

"I am not given to gossip," he said, with a faint smile, "yet I had heard that they were much here, and had given their confidence to your family. I have not been so favoured myself," he added, with a slight curl of disdain upon his handsome lip. "The youth I know nothing of, except that he has invariably repelled any friendship I could have shown him; but I feel a great interest in the young lady. Had my sister been in better health, we might have offered her an asylum, but that is impossible in our present circumstances. You are doubtless better acquainted with their prospects and intentions than I am. In case of the event which people begin to talk about, what does Lord Winterbourne intend they should do?"

"We have not heard of any event—what is it?" cried Mrs Atheling, very anxiously.

"I have no better information than common report," said the Rector; "yet it is likely enough—and I see no reason to doubt; it is said that Lord Winterbourne is likely to marry again."

They all breathed more freely after this; and poor little Marian, who had been gazing at Mr Rivers with a blanched face and wide-open eyes, in terror of some calamity, drooped forward upon the table by which she was sitting, and hid her face in her hands with sudden relief. Was that all?

"I was afraid you were about to tell us of some misfortune," said Mrs Atheling.

"It is no misfortune, of course; nor do I suppose they are like to be very jealous of a new claimant upon Lord Winterbourne's affections," said the Rector; "but it seems unlikely, under their peculiar and most unhappy circumstances, that they can remain at the Hall."

"Oh, mamma!" exclaimed Marian, in a half whisper, "he will be so very, very glad to go away!"

"What I mean," resumed Mr Rivers, who by no means lost this, though he took no immediate notice of it—"what I wish is, that you would kindly undertake to let them know my very sincere wish to be of service to them. I cannot at all approve of the demeanour of the young man—yet there may be excuses for him. If I can assist them in any legitimate way, I beg you to assure them my best endeavours are at their service."

"Thank you, sir, thank you—thank you!" cried Mrs Atheling, faltering, and much moved. "God knows they have need of friends!"

"I suppose so," said the Rector; "it does not often happen—friends are woeful delusions in most cases—and indeed I have little hope of any man who does not stand alone."

"Yet you offer service," said Agnes, unable quite to control her inclination to dispute his dogmatisms; "is not your opinion a contradiction to your kindness?"

"I hold no opinions," said the Rector haughtily, with, for the instant, a superb absurdity almost equal to Mr Endicott: he perceived it himself, however, immediately, reddened, flashed his fiery eyes with a half defiance upon his young questioner, and made an incomprehensible explanation.

"I am as little fortified against self-contradiction as my fellows," said Mr Rivers, "but I eschew vague opinions; they are dangerous for all men, and doubly dangerous in a clergyman. I may be wrong in matters of feeling; opinions I have nothing to do with—they are not in my way."

Again there followed a pause, for no one present was at all acquainted with sentiments like these.

"I am not sure whether we will continue long here," said Mrs Atheling, with a slight hesitation, half afraid of him, yet feeling, in spite of herself, that she could consult no one so suitably as the Rector. "Lord Winterbourne is trying to put us away; he says the house was only given to old Miss Bridget for her life!"

"Ah! but that is false, is it not?" said the Rector without any ceremony.

Mrs Atheling brightened at once. "We think so," she said, encouraged by the perfectly cool tone of this remark, which proved a false statement on the part of my lord no wonder at all to his reverend relative; "but, indeed, the lawyer advises us not to contest the matter, since Lord Winterbourne does not care for expense, and we are not rich. I do not know what my husband will say; but I am sure I will have a great grudge at the law if we are forced, against justice, to leave the Old Wood Lodge."

"Papa says it was once the property of the family, long, long before Aunt Bridget got it from Lord Winterbourne," said Agnes, with a little eagerness. This shadow of ancestry was rather agreeable to the imagination of Agnes.

"And have you done anything—are you doing anything?" said the Hector. "I should be glad to send my own man of business to you; certainly you ought not to give up your property without at least a legal opinion upon the matter."

"We expect my son to-morrow," said Mrs Atheling, with a little pride. "My son, though he is very young, has a great deal of judgment; and then he has been—brought up to the law."

The Rector bowed gravely as he rose. "In that case, I can only offer my good wishes," said the churchman, "and trust that we may long continue neighbours in spite of Lord Winterbourne. My sister would have been delighted to call upon you, had she been able, but she is quite a confirmed invalid. I am very glad to have made your acquaintance. Good morning, madam; good morning, Miss Atheling. I am extremely glad to have met with you."

The smallest shade of emphasis in the world invested with a different character than usual these clergymanly and parochial words: for the double expression of satisfaction was addressed to Agnes; it was to her pointedly that his stately but reverential bow bore reference. He had come to see the family; but he was glad to know Agnes, the intelligent listener who followed his sermons—the eager bright young eyes which flashed warfare and defiance on his solemn deliverances—and, unawares to herself, saw through the pretences of his disturbed and troubled spirit. Lionel Rivers was not very sensitively alive to the beautiful: he saw little to attract his eye, much less his heart, in that pretty drooping Marian, who was to every other observer the sweetest little downcast princess who ever gained the magic succours of a fairy tale. The Rector scarcely turned a passing glance upon her, as she sat in her tender beauty by the table, leaning her beautiful head upon her hands. But with a different kind of observation from that of Mr Agar, he read the bright and constant comment on what he said himself, and what others said, that ran and sparkled in the face of Agnes. She who never had any lovers, had attracted one at least to watch her looks and her movements with a jealous eye. He was not "in love,"—not the smallest hairbreadth in the world. In his present mood, he would gladly have seen her form an order of sisters, benevolent votaresses of St Frideswide, or of some unknown goddess of the medieval world, build an antique house in the "pointed" style, and live a female bishop ruling over the inferior parish, and being ruled over by the clergy. Such a colleague the Rector fancied would be highly "useful," and he had never seen any one whom he could elect to the office with so much satisfaction as Agnes Atheling. How far she would have felt herself complimented by this idea was entirely a different question, and one of which the Rector never thought.

CHAPTER XXIX

CHARLIE

The next day was the day of Charlie's arrival. His mother and sisters looked for him with anxiety, pleasure, and a little nervousness—much concerned about Papa's opinion, and not at all indifferent to Charlie's own. Rachel, who for two days past had been in a state of perfectly flighty and overpowering happiness, joined the Athelings this evening, at the risk of being "wanted" by Mrs Edgerley, and falling under her displeasure, with a perfectly innocent and unconscious disregard of any possible wish on the part of her friends to be alone with their new-come brother. Rachel could form no idea whatever of that half-wished-for, half-dreaded judgment of Papa, the anticipation of which so greatly subdued Marian, and made Mrs Atheling herself so grave and pale. Louis, with a clearer perception of the family crisis, kept away, though, as his sister wisely judged, at no great distance, chewing the cud of desperate and bitter fancy, almost half-repenting, for the moment, of the rash attachment which had put himself and all his disadvantages upon the judicial examination of a father and a brother. The idea of this family committee sitting upon him, investigating and commenting upon his miserable story, galled to the utmost the young man's fiery spirit. He had no real idea whatever of that good and affectionate father, who was to Marian the first of men,—and had not the faintest conception of the big boy. So it was only an abstract father and brother—the most disagreeable of the species—at whom Louis chafed in his irritable imagination. He too had come already out of the first hurried flush of delight and triumph, to consider the step he had taken. Strangely into the joy and pride of the young lover's dream came bitter and heavy spectres of self-reproach and foreboding—he, who had ventured to bind to himself the heart of a sensitive and tender girl—he, who had already thrown a shadow over her young life, filled her with premature anxieties, and communicated to these young eyes, instead of their fearless natural brightness, a wistful forecasting gaze into an adverse world—he, who had not even a name to share with his bride! On this memorable evening, Louis paced about by himself, crushing down the rusted fern as he strode through the wood in painful self-communion. The wind was high among the trees, and grew wild and fitful as the night advanced, bringing down showers of leaves into all the hollows, and raving with the most desolate sound in nature among the high tops of the Scotch firs, which stood grouped by themselves, a reserved and austere brotherhood, on one side of Badgeley Wood. Out of this leafy wilderness, the evening lay quiet enough upon the open fields, the wan gleams of water, and the deserted highway; but the clouds opened in a clear rift of wistful, windy, colourless sky, just over Oxford, catching with its pale half-light the mingled pinnacles and towers. Louis was too much engrossed either to see or to hear the eerie sights and sounds of the night, yet they had their influence upon him unawares.

In the mean time, and at the same moment, in the quiet country gloaming, which was odd, but by no means melancholy to him, Charlie trudged sturdily up the high-road, carrying his own little bag, and thinking his own thoughts. And down the same road, one talking a good deal, one very little, and one not at all, the three girls went to meet him, three light and graceful figures, in dim autumnal dresses—for now the evenings became somewhat cold—fit figures for this sweet half-light, which looked pleasant here, though it was so pale and ghostly in the wood. The first was Rachel, who, greatly exhilarated by her unusual freedom, and by all that had happened during these few days past, almost led the little party, protesting she was sure to know Charlie, and very near giddy in her unthinking and girlish delight. The second was Agnes, who was very thoughtful and somewhat grave, yet still could answer her companion; the third, a step behind, coming along very slow and downcast, with her veil over her drooping face, and a shadow upon her palpitating little heart, was Marian, in whose gentle mind was something very like a heavy and despondent shadow of the tumult which distracted her betrothed. Yet not that either—for there was no tumult, but only a pensive and oppressive sadness, under which the young sufferer remained very still, not caring to say a word. "What would papa say?" that was the only audible voice in Marian Atheling's heart.

"There now, I am sure it is him—there he is," cried Rachel; and it was Charlie, beyond dispute, shouldering his carpet-bag. The greeting was kindly enough, but it was not at all sentimental, which somewhat disappointed Rachel, at whom Charlie gazed with visible curiosity. When they turned with him, leading him home, Marian fell still farther back, and drooped more than ever. Perhaps the big boy was moved with a momentary sympathy—more likely it was simple mischief. "So," said Charlie in her ear, "the Yankee's cut out."

Marian started a little, looked at him eagerly, and put her hand with an appealing gesture on his arm. "Oh, Charlie, what did papa say?" asked Marian, with her heart in her eyes.

Charlie wavered for a moment between his boyish love of torture and a certain dormant tenderness at the bottom of his full man's heart, which this great event happening to Marian had touched into life all at once. The kinder sentiment prevailed after a moment's pause of wicked intention. "My father was not angry, May," said the lad; and he drew his shrinking sister's pretty hand through his own arm roughly but kindly, pleased to feel his own boyish strength a support to her. Marian was so young too—very little beyond the rapid vicissitudes of a child. She bounded forward on Charlie's arm at the words, drooping no longer, but triumphant and at ease in a moment, hurrying him up the ascending high-road at a pace which did not at all suit Charlie, and outstripping the entire party in her sudden flight to her mother with the good news. That Papa should not be angry was all that Marian desired or hoped.

At the door, in the darkness, the hasty girl ran into Mamma's arms. "My father is not angry," she exclaimed, out of breath, faithfully repeating Charlie's words; and then Marian, once more the most serviceable of domestic managers, hastened to light the candles on the tea-table, to draw the chairs around this kindly board, to warn Hannah of the approach of the heir of the house. Hannah came out into the hall to stand behind Mrs Atheling, and drop a respectful curtsy to the young gentleman. The punctilious old family attendant would have been inconsolable had she missed this opportunity of "showing her manners," and was extremely grateful to Miss Marian, who did not forget her, though she had so many things to think of of her own.

The addition of Rachel slightly embarrassed the family party, and it had the most marvellous effect upon Charlie, who had never before known any female society except that of his sisters. Charlie was full three years younger than the young stranger—distance enough to justify her in treating him as a boy, and him in conceiving the greatest admiration for her. Charlie, of all things in the world, grew actually shy in the company of his sisters' friend. He became afraid of committing himself, and at last began partly to believe his mother's often-repeated strictures on his "manners." He did unquestionably look so big, so brusque, so clumsy, beside this pretty little fairy Rachel, and his own graceful sisters. Charlie hitched up his great shoulders, retreated under the shadow of all those cloudy furrows on his brow, and had actually nothing to say. And Mrs Atheling, occupied with her husband's long and anxious letter, forbore to question him; and the girls, anxious as they still were, did not venture to say anything before Rachel. They were not at all at their ease, and somewhat dull as they sat in the dim parlour, inventing conversation, and trying not to show their visitor that she was in the way. But she found it out at last, with a little uneasy start and blush, and hastened to get her bonnet and say good-night. No one seemed to fear that it would be difficult to find Rachel's escort, who was found accordingly the moment they appeared in the garden, starting, as he did the first time of their meeting, from the darkness of the angle at the end of the hedge. Marian ran forward to him, giving Charlie's message as it came all rosy and hopeful through the alembic of her own comforted imagination. "Papa is quite pleased," said Marian, with her smiles and her blushes. She did not perceive the suppressed vexation of Louis's brow as he tried to brighten at her news. For Marian could not have understood how this haughty and undisciplined young spirit could scarcely manage to bow itself to the approbation and judgment even of Papa.

CHAPTER XXX

A CONSULTATION

"And now, Charlie, my dear boy, I quite calculate on your knowing about it, since you have been so long at the law," said Mrs Atheling: "your father is so much taken up about other matters, that he really says very little about this. What are we to do?"

Charlie, whose mobile brow was shifting up and shifting down with all the marks of violent cogitation, bit his thumb at this, and took time before he answered it. "The first thing to be done," said Charlie, with a little dogmatism, "is to see what evidence can be had—that's what we have got to do. Has nobody found any papers of the old lady's?—she was sure to have a lot—all your old women have."

"No one even thought of looking," said Agnes, suddenly glancing up at the old cabinet with all its brass rings—while Marian, restored to all her gay spirits, promptly took her brother to task for his contempt of old women. "You ought to see Miss Anastasia—she is a great deal bigger than you," cried Marian, pulling a shaggy lock of Charlie's black hair.

"Stuff!—who's Miss Anastasia?" was the reply.

"And that reminds me," said Mrs Atheling, "that we ought to have let her know. Do you remember what she said, Agnes?—she was quite sure my lord was thinking of something—and we were to let her know."

"What about, mother?—and who's Miss Anastasia?" asked Charlie once more: he had to repeat his question several times before any answer came.

"Who is Miss Anastasia? My dear, I forgot you were a stranger. She is—well, really I cannot pretend to describe Miss Rivers," said Mrs Atheling, with a little nervousness. "I have always had a great respect for her, and so has your father. She is a very remarkable person, Charlie. I never have known any one like her all my life."

"But who is she, mother? Is she any good?" repeated the impatient youth.

Mrs Atheling looked at her son with a certain horror.

"She is one of the most remarkable persons in the county," said Mrs Atheling, with all the local spirit of a Banburyshire woman, born and bred—"she is a great scholar, and a lady of fortune, and the only child of the old lord. How strange the ways of Providence are, children!—what a difference it might have made in everything had Miss Anastasia been born a man instead of a woman." "Indeed," confessed Mamma, breaking off in an under-tone, "I do really believe it would have been more suitable, even for herself."

"I suppose we're to come at it at last," said Charlie despairingly: "she's a daughter of the tother lord— now, I want to know what she's got to do with us."

"My dear," said Mrs Atheling eagerly, and with evident pleasure, "I wrote to your father, I am sure, all about it. She has called upon us twice in the most friendly way, and has quite taken a liking for the girls."

"And she was old Aunt Bridget's pupil, and her great friend; and it was on account of her that the old lord gave Aunt Bridget this house," added Agnes, finding out, though not very cleverly, what Charlie's questions meant.

"And she hates Lord Winterbourne," said Marian in an expressive appendix, with a distinct emphasis of sympathy and approval on the words.

"Now I call that satisfaction," said Charlie,—"that's something like the thing. So I suppose she must have had to do with the whole business, and knows all about it—eh? Why didn't you tell me so at once?— why, she's the first person to see, of course. I had better seek her out to-morrow morning—first thing."

"You!" Mamma looked with motherly anxiety, mixed with disapproval. It was so impossible, even with the aid of all partialities, to make out Charlie to be handsome. And Miss Anastasia came of a handsome race, and had a prejudice in favour of good looks. Then, though his large loose limbs began to be a little more firmly knitted and less unmanageable, and though he was now drawing near eighteen, he was still only a boy. "My dear," said Mrs Atheling, "she is a very particular old lady, and takes dislikes sometimes, and very proud besides, and might not desire to be intruded on; and I think, after all, as you do not know her, and they do, I think it would be much better if the girls were to go."

"The girls!" exclaimed Charlie with a boy's contempt—"a great deal they know about the business! You listen to me, mother. I've been reading up hard for six months, and I know something about the evidence that does for a court of law—women don't—it's not in reason; for I'd like to see the woman that could stand old Foggo's office, pegging in at these old fellows for precedent, and all that stuff. You don't suppose I mind what your old lady thinks of me—and I know what I want, which is the main thing, after all. You tell me where she lives—that's all I want to know—and see if I don't make something of it before another day."

"Where she lives?—it is six miles off, Charlie: you don't know the way—and, indeed, you don't know her either, my poor boy."

"Don't you trouble about that—that's my business, mother," said Charlie; "and a man can't lose his way in the country unless he tries—a long road, and a fingerpost at every crossing. When a man wants to lose himself, he had better go to the City—there's no fear in your plain country roads. You set me on the right way—you know all the places hereabout—and just for this once, mother, trust me, and let me manage it my own way."

"I always did trust you, Charlie," said Mrs Atheling evasively; but she did not half like her son's enterprise, and greatly objected to put Miss Anastasia's friendship in jeopardy by such an intrusion as this.

However, the young gentleman now declared himself tired, and was conducted up-stairs in state, by his mother and sisters—first to Mrs Atheling's own room to inspect it, and kiss, half reluctantly, half with genuine fondness, the little slumbering cherub faces of Bell and Beau. Then he had a glimpse of the snowy decorations of that young-womanly and pretty apartment of his sisters, and was finally ushered into the little back-room, his own den, from which the lumber had been cleared on purpose for his reception. They left him then to his repose, and dreams, if the couch of this young gentleman was ever visited by such fairy visitants, and retired again themselves to that dim parlour, to read over in conclave Papa's letter, and hold a final consultation as to what everybody should do.

Papa's letter was very long, very anxious, and very affectionate, and had cost Papa all the leisure of two long evenings, and all his unoccupied hours for two days at the office. He blamed his wife a little, but it was very quietly,—he was grieved for the premature step the young people had taken, but did not say a great deal about his grief,—and he was extremely concerned, and evidently did not express half of his concern, about his pretty Marian, for whom he permitted himself to say he had expected a very different fate. There was not much said of personal repugnance to Louis, and little comment upon his parentage, but they could see well enough that Papa felt the matter very deeply, and that it needed all his affection for themselves, and all his charity for the stranger, to reconcile him to it. But they were both very young, he said, and must do nothing precipitate—which sentence Papa made very emphatic by a very black and double underscoring, and which Mrs Atheling, but fortunately not Marian, understood to mean that it was a possibility almost to be hoped for, that this might turn out one of those boy-and-girl engagements made to be broken, and never come to anything after all.

It was consolatory certainly, and set their minds at rest, but it was not a very cheering letter, and by no means justified Marian's joyful announcement that "papa was quite pleased." And so much was the good father taken up with his child's fortune, that it was only in a postscript he took any notice of Lord Winterbourne's summons and their precarious holding of the Old Wood Lodge. "We will resist, of course," said Papa. He did not know a great deal more about how to resist than they did, so he wisely left the question to Charlie, and to "another day."

And now came the question, what everybody was to do? which gradually narrowed into much smaller limits, and became wholly concerned with what Charlie was to do, and whether he should visit Miss Anastasia. He had made up his mind to it with no lack of decision. What could his mother and his sisters say, save make a virtue of necessity, and yield their assent?

CHAPTER XXXI

CHARLIE'S MISSION

Early on the next morning, accordingly, Charlie set out for Abingford. It was with difficulty he escaped a general superintendence of his toilette, and prevailed upon his mother to content herself with brushing his coat, and putting into something like arrangement the stray locks of his hair; but at last, tolerably satisfied with his appearance, and giving him many anxious instructions as to his demeanour towards Miss Anastasia, Mrs Atheling suffered him to depart upon his important errand. The road was the plainest of country roads, through the wood and over the hill, with scarcely a turn to distract the regard of the traveller. A late September morning, sunny and sweet, with yellow leaves sometimes dropping down upon the wind, and all the autumn foliage in a flush of many colours under the cool blue, and floating clouds of a somewhat dullish yet kindly sky. The deep underground of ferns, where they were not brown, were feathering away into a rich yellow, which relieved and brought out all the more strongly the harsh dark green of these vigorous fronds, rusted with seed; and piles of firewood stood here and there, tied up in big fagots, provision for the approaching winter. The birds sang gaily, still stirring among the trees; and now and then into the still air, and far-off rural hum, came the sharp report of a gun, or the ringing bark of a dog. Charlie pushed upon his way, wasting little time in observation, yet observing for all that, with the novel pleasure of a town-bred lad, and owning a certain exhilaration in his face, and in his breast, as he sped along the country road, with its hedges and strips of herbage; that straight, clear, even road, with its milestones and fingerposts, and one market-cart coming along in leisurely rural fashion, half a mile off upon the far-seen way. The walk to Abingford was a long walk even for Charlie, and it was nearly an hour and a half from the time of his leaving home, when he began to perceive glimpses through the leaves of a little maze of water, two or three streams, splitting into fantastic islands the houses and roofs before him, and came in sight of an old gateway, with two windows and a high peaked roof over it, which strode across the way. Charlie, who was entirely unacquainted with such peculiarities of architecture, made a pause of half-contemptuous boyish observation, looking up at the windows, and supposing it must be rather odd to live over an archway. Then he bethought him of asking a loitering country lad to direct him to the Priory, which was done in the briefest manner possible, by pointing round the side of the gate to a large door which almost seemed to form part of it. "There it be," said Charlie's informant, and Charlie immediately made his assault upon the big door.

Miss Rivers was at home. He was shown into a large dim room full of books, with open windows, and green blinds let down to the floor, through which the visitor could only catch an uncertain glimpse of waving branches, and a lawn which sloped to the pale little river: the room was hung with portraits, which there was not light enough to see, and gave back a dull glimmer from the glass of its great bookcases. There was a large writing-table before the fireplace, and a great easy-chair placed by it. This was where Miss Anastasia transacted business; but Charlie had not much time, if he had inclination, for a particular survey of the apartment, for he could hear a quick and decided step descending a stair, as it seemed, and crossing over the hall. "Charles Atheling—who's Charles Atheling?" said a peremptory voice outside. "I know no one of the name."

With the words on her lips Miss Anastasia entered the room. She wore a loose morning-dress, belted round her waist with a buckled girdle, and a big tippet of the same; and her cap, which was not intended to be pretty, but only to be comfortable, came down close over her ears, snow white, and of the finest cambric, but looking very homely and familiar indeed to the puzzled eyes of Charlie. Not her homely cap, however, nor her odd dress, could make Miss Anastasia less imperative or formidable. "Well sir," she said, coming in upon him without very much ceremony, "which of the Athelings do you belong to, and what do you want with me?"

"I belong to the Old Wood Lodge," said Charlie, almost as briefly, "and I want to ask what you know about it, and how it came into Aunt Bridget's hands."

"What I know about it? Of course I know everything about it," said Miss Anastasia. "So you're young Atheling, are you? You're not at all like your pretty sisters; not clever either, so far as I can see, eh? What are you good for, boy?"

Charlie did not say "stuff!" aloud, but it was only by a strong effort of self-control. He was not at all disposed to give any answer to the question. "What has to be done in the mean time is to save my father's property," said Charlie, with a boyish flush of offence.

"Save it, boy! who's threatening your father's property? What! do you mean to tell me already that he's fallen foul of Will Atheling?" said the old lady, drawing her big easy-chair to her big writing-table, and motioning Charlie to draw near. "Eh? why don't you speak? tell me the whole at once."

"Lord Winterbourne has sent us notice to leave," said Charlie; "he says the Old Wood Lodge was only Aunt Bridget's for life, and is his now. I have set the girls to look up the old lady's papers; we ourselves know nothing about it, and I concluded the first thing to be done was to come and ask you."

"Good," said Miss Anastasia; "you were perfectly right. Of course it is a lie."

This was said perfectly in a matter-of-course fashion, without the least idea, apparently, on the part of the old lady, that there was anything astonishing in the lie which came from Lord Winterbourne.

"I know everything about it," she continued; "my father made over the little house to my dear old professor, when we supposed she would have occasion to leave me: that turned out a vain separation, thanks to him again;" and here Miss Rivers grew white for an instant, and pressed her lips together. "Please Heaven, my boy, he'll not be successful this time. No. I know everything about it; we'll foil my lord in this."

"But there must have been a deed," said Charlie; "do you know where the papers are?"

"Papers! I tell you I am acquainted with every circumstance—I myself. You can call me as a witness," said the old lady. "No, I can't tell you where the papers are. What's about them? eh? Do you mean to say they are of more consequence than me?"

"There are sure to be documents on the other side," said Charlie; "the original deed would settle the question, without needing even a trial: without it Lord Winterbourne has the better chance. Personal testimony is not equal to documents in a case like this."

"Young Atheling," said Miss Rivers, drawing herself up to her full height, "do you think a jury of this county would weigh his word against mine?"

Charlie was considerably embarrassed. "I suppose not," he said, somewhat abruptly; "but this is not a thing of words. Lord Winterbourne will never appear at all; but if he has any papers to produce proving his case, the matter will be settled at once; and unless we have counterbalancing evidence of the same kind, we'd better give it up before it comes that length."

He said this half impatient, half despairing. Miss Rivers evidently took up this view of the question with dissatisfaction; but as he persevered in it, came gradually to turn her thoughts to other means of assisting him. "But I know of no papers," she said, with disappointment; "my father's solicitor, to be sure, he is the man to apply to. I shall make a point of seeing him to-morrow; and what papers I have I will look over. By the by, now I remember it, the Old Wood Lodge belonged to her grandfather or great-grandfather, dear old soul, and came to us by some mortgage or forfeit. It was given back—restored, not bestowed upon her. For her life!—I should like to find out now what he means by such a lie!"

Charlie, who could throw no light upon this subject, rose to go, somewhat disappointed, though not at all discouraged. The old lady stopped him on his way, carried him off to another room, and administered, half against Charlie's will, a glass of wine. "Now, young Atheling, you can go," said Miss Anastasia. "I'll remember both you and your business. What are they bringing you up to? eh?"

"I'm in a solicitor's office," said Charlie.

"Just so—quite right," said Miss Anastasia. "Let me see you baffle him, and I'll be your first client. Now go away to your pretty sisters, and tell your mother not to alarm herself. I'll come to the Lodge in a day or two; and if there's documents to be had, you shall have them. Under any circumstances," continued the old lady, dismissing him with a certain stateliness, "you can call me."

But though she was a great lady, and the most remarkable person in the county, Charlie did not appreciate this permission half so much as he would have appreciated some bit of wordy parchment. He walked back again, much less sure of his case than when he set out with the hope of finding all he wanted at Abingford.

CHAPTER XXXII

SEARCH

When Charlie reached home again, very tired, and in a somewhat moody frame of mind, he found the room littered with various old boxes undergoing examination, and Agnes seated before the cabinet, with a lapful of letters, and her face bright with interest and excitement, looking them over. At the present moment, she held something of a very perplexing nature in her hand, which the trained eye of Charlie caught instantly, with a flash of triumph. Agnes herself was somewhat excited about it, and Marian stood behind her, looking over her shoulder, and vainly trying to decipher the ancient writing. "It's something, mamma," cried Agnes. "I am sure, if Charlie saw it, he would think it something; but I cannot make out what it is. Here is somebody's seal and somebody's signature, and there, I am sure, that is Atheling; and a date, 'xiij. of May, M.D.LXXII.' What does that mean, Marian? M. a thousand, D. five hundred; there it is! I am sure it is an old deed—a real something ancestral—1572!"

"Give it to me," said Charlie, stretching his hand for it over her shoulder. No one had heard him come in.

"Oh, Charlie, what did Miss Anastasia say?" cried Marian; and Agnes immediately turned round away from the cabinet, and Mamma laid down her work. Charlie, however, took full time to examine the yellow old document they had found, though he did not acknowledge that it posed him scarcely less than themselves, before he spoke.

"She said she'd look up her papers, and speak to the old gentleman's solicitor. I don't see that she's much good to us," said Charlie. "She says I might call her as a witness, but what's the good of a witness against documents? This has nothing to do with Aunt Bridget, Agnes—have you found nothing more than this? Why, you know there must have been a deed of some kind. The old lady could not have been so foolish as to throw away her title. Property without title-deeds is not worth a straw; and the man that drew up her will is my lord's solicitor! I say, he must be what the Yankees call a smart man, this Lord Winterbourne."

"I am afraid he has no principle, my dear," said Mrs Atheling with a sigh.

"And a very bad man—everybody hates him," said Marian under her breath.

She spoke so low that she did not receive that reproving look of Mamma which was wont to check such exclamations. Marian, though she had a will of her own, and was never like to fall into a mere shadow and reflection of her lover, as his poor little sister did, had unconsciously imbibed Louis's sentiments. She did not know what it was to hate, this innocent girl. Had she seen Lord Winterbourne thrown from his horse, or overturned out of his carriage, these ferocious sentiments would have melted in an instant into help and pity; but in the abstract view of the matter, Marian pronounced with emotion the great man's sentence, "Everybody hates Lord Winterbourne."

"That is what the old lady said," exclaimed Charlie; "she asked me who I thought would believe him against her? But that's not the question. I don't want to pit one man against another. My father's worth twenty of Lord Winterbourne! But that's no matter. The law cares nothing at all for his principles. What title has he got, and what title have you?—that's what the law's got to say. Now, I'll either have something to put in against him or I'll not plead. It's no use taking a step in the matter without proof."

"And won't that do, Charlie?" asked Mrs Atheling, looking wistfully at the piece of parchment, signed and sealed, which was in Charlie's hands.

"That! why, it's two hundred and fifty years old!" said Charlie. "I don't see what it refers to yet, but it's very clear it can't be to Miss Bridget. No, mother, that won't do."

"Then, my dear," said Mrs Atheling, "I am very sorry to think of it; but, after all, we have not been very long here, and we might have laid out more money, and formed more attachments to the place, if we had gone on much longer; and I think I shall be very glad to get back to Bellevue. Marian, my love, don't cry; this need not make any difference with anything; but I think it is far better just to make up our minds to it, and give up the Old Wood Lodge."

"Mother! do you think I mean that?" cried Charlie; "we must find the papers, that's what we must do. My father's as good an Englishman as the first lord in the kingdom; I'd not give in to the king unless he was in the right."

"And not even then, unless you could not help it," said Agnes, laughing; "but I am not half done yet; there is still a great quantity of letters—and I should not be at all surprised if this romantic old cabinet, like an old bureau in a novel, had a secret drawer."

Animated by this idea, Marian ran to the antique little piece of furniture, pressing every projection with her pretty fingers, and examining into every creak. But there was no secret drawer—a fact which became all the more apparent when a drawer was discovered, which once had closed with a spring. The spring was broken, and the once-secret place was open, desolate, and empty. Miss Bridget, good old lady, had no secrets, or at least she had not made any provision for them here.

Agnes went on with her examination the whole afternoon, drawn aside and deluded to pursue the history of old Aunt Bridget's life through scores of yellow old letters, under the pretence that something might be found in some of them to throw light upon this matter; for a great many letters of Miss Bridget's own—careful "studies" for the production itself—were tied up among the others; and it would have been amusing, if it had not been sad, to sit on this little eminence of time, looking over that strange faithful self-record of the little weaknesses, the ladylike pretences, the grand Johnsonian diction of the old lady who was dead. Poor old lady! Agnes became quite abashed and ashamed of herself when she felt a smile stealing over her lip. It seemed something like profanity to ransack the old cabinet, and smile at it. In its way, this, as truly as the grass-mound, in Winterbourne churchyard, was Aunt Bridget's grave.

But still nothing could be found. Charlie occupied himself during the remainder of the day in giving a necessary notice to Mr Lewis the solicitor, that they had made up their minds to resist Lord Winterbourne's claim; and when the evening closed in, and the candles were lighted, Louis made his first public appearance since the arrival of the stranger, somewhat cloudy, and full of all his old haughtiness. This cloud vanished in an instant at the first glance. Whatever Charlie's qualities were, criticism was not one of them; it was clear that though his "No" might be formidable enough of itself, Charlie had not been a member of any solemn committee, sitting upon the pretensions of Louis. He gave no particular regard to Louis even now, but sat poring over the old deed, deciphering it with the most patient laboriousness, with his head very close over the paper, and a pair of spectacles assisting his eyes. The spectacles were lent by Mamma, who kept them, not secretly, but with a little reserve, in her work-basket, for special occasions when she had some very fine stitching to do, or was busy with delicate needlework by candle-light; and nothing could have been more oddly inappropriate to the face of Charlie, with all the furrows of his brow rolled down over his eyebrows, and his indomitable upper-lip pressed hard upon its fellow, than these same spectacles. Then they made him short-sighted, and were only of use when he leaned closely over the paper—Charlie did not mind, though his shoulders ached and his eyes filled with water. He was making it out!

And Agnes, for her part, sat absorbed with her lapful of old letters, reading them all over with passing smiles and gravities, growing into acquaintance with ever so many extinct affairs,—old stories long ago come to the one conclusion which unites all men. Though she felt herself virtuously reading for a purpose, she had forgotten all about the purpose long ago, and was only wandering on and on by a strange attraction, as if through a city of the dead. But it was quite impossible to think of the dead among these yellow old papers—the littlest trivial things of life were so quite living in them, in these unconscious natural inferences and implications. And Louis and Marian, sometimes speaking and often silent, were going through their own present romance and story; and Mamma, in her sympathetic middle age, with her work-basket, was tenderly overlooking all. In the little dim country parlour, lighted with the two candles, what a strange epitome there was of a whole world and a universal life.

CHAPTER XXXIII

DOUBTS AND FEARS

Louis had not been told till this day of the peril which threatened the little inheritance of the Athelings. When he did hear of it, the young man gnashed his teeth with that impotent rage which is agony, desperate under the oppression which makes even wise men mad. He scorned to say a word of any further indignities put upon himself; but Rachel told of them with tears and outcries almost hysterical— how my lord had challenged him with bitter taunts to put on his livery and earn the bread he ate—how he had been expelled from his room which he had always occupied, and had an apartment now among the rooms of the servants—and how Lord Winterbourne threatened to advertise him publicly as a vagabond and runaway if he ventured beyond the bounds of the village, or tried to thrust himself into any society. Poor little Rachel, when she came in the morning faint and heart-broken to tell her story, could scarcely speak for tears, and was only with great difficulty soothed to a moderate degree of calm. But still she shrank with the strangest repugnance from going away. It scarcely could be attachment to the home of her youth, for it had always been an unhappy shelter—nor could it be love for any of the family; the little timid spirit feared she knew not what terrors in the world with which she had so little acquaintance. Lord Winterbourne to her was not a mere English peer, of influence only in a certain place and sphere, but an omnipotent oppressor, from whose power it would be impossible to escape, and whose vigilance could not be eluded. If she tried to smile at the happy devices of Agnes and Marian, how to establish herself in their own room at Bellevue, and lodge Louis close at hand, it was a very wan and sickly smile. She confessed it was dreadful to think that he should remain, exposed to all these insults; but she shrank with fear and trembling from the idea of Louis going away.

The next evening, just before the sun set, the whole youthful party—for Rachel, by a rare chance, was not to be "wanted" to-night—strayed along the grassy road in a body towards the church. Agnes and Marian were both with Louis, who had been persuaded at last to speak of his own persecutions, while Rachel came behind with Charlie, kindly pointing out for him the far-off towers of Oxford, the two rivers wandering in a maze, and all the features of the scene which Charlie did not know, and amused, sad as she was, in her conscious seniority and womanhood, at the shyness of the lad. Charlie actually began to be touched with a wandering breath of sentiment, had been seen within the last two days reading a poetry book, and was really in a very odd and suspicious "way."

"No," said Louis, upon whom his betrothed and her sister were hanging eagerly, comforting and persuading—"no; I am not in a worse position. It stings me at the moment, I confess; but I am filled with contempt for the man who insults me, and his words lose their power. I could almost be seduced to stay when he begins to struggle with me after this downright fashion; but you are perfectly right for all that, and within a few days I must go away."

"A few days? O Louis!" cried Marian, clinging to his arm.

"Yes; I have a good mind to say to-morrow, to enhance my own value," said Louis. "I am tempted—ay, both to go and stay—for sake of the clinging of these little hands. Never mind, our mother will come home all the sooner; and what do you suppose I will do?"

"I think indeed, Louis, you should speak to the Rector," said Agnes, with a little anxiety. "O no; it is very cruel of you, and you are quite wrong; he did not mean to be very kind in that mocking way—he meant what he said—he wanted to do you service; and so he would, and vindicate you when you were gone, if you only would cease to be so very grand for two minutes, and let him know."

"Am I so very grand?" said Louis, with a momentary pique. "I have nothing to do with your rectors—I know what he meant, whatever he might say."

"It is a great deal more than he does himself, I am sure of that," said Agnes with a puzzled air. "He means what he says, but he does not always know what he means; and neither do I."

Marian tried a trembling little laugh at her sister's perplexity, but they were rather too much moved for laughing, and it did not do.

"Now, I will tell you what my plan is," said Louis. "I do not know what he thinks of me, nor do I expect to find his opinion very favourable; but as that is all I can look for anywhere, it will be the better probation for me," he added, with a rising colour and an air of haughtiness. "I will not enlist, Marian. I have no longer any dreams of the marshal's baton in the soldier's knapsack. I give up rank and renown to those who can strive for them. You must be content with such honour as a man can have in his own person, Marian. When I leave you, I will go at once to your father."

"Oh, Louis, will you? I am so glad, so proud!" and again the little hands pressed his arm, and Marian looked up to him with her radiant face. He had not felt before how perfectly magnanimous and noble his resolution was.

"I think it will be very right," said Agnes, who was not so enthusiastic; "and my father will be pleased to see you, Louis, though you doubt him as you doubt all men. But look, who is this coming here?"

They were scarcely coming here, seeing they were standing still under the porch of the church, a pair of very tall figures, very nearly equal in altitude, though much unlike each other. One of them was the Rector, who stood with a solemn bored look at the door of his church, which he had just closed, listening, without any answer save now and then a grave and ceremonious bow, to the other "individual," who was talking very fluently, and sufficiently loud to be heard by others than the Rector. "Oh, Agnes!" cried Marian, and "Hush, May!" answered her sister; they both recognised the stranger at a glance.

"Yes, this is the pride of the old country," said the voice; "here, sir, we can still perceive upon the sands of time the footprints of our Saxon ancestors. I say ours, for my youthful and aspiring nation boasts as the brightest star in her banner the Anglo-Saxon blood. We preserve the free institutions—the hatred of superstition, the freedom of private judgment and public opinion, the great inheritance developed out of the past; but Old England, sir, a land which I venerate, yet pity, keeps safe in her own bosom the external traces full of instruction, the silent poetry of Time—that only poetry which she can refuse to share with us."

To this suitable and appropriate speech, congenial as it must have been to his feelings, the Rector made no answer, save that most deferential and solemn bow, and was proceeding with a certain conscientious haughtiness to show his visitor some other part of the building, when his eye was attracted by the approaching group. He turned to them immediately with an air of sudden relief.

So did Mr Endicott, to whom, to do him justice, not all the old churches in Banburyshire, nor all the opportunities of speechmaking, nor even half-a-dozen rectors who were within two steps of a peerage, could have presented such powerful attractions as did that beautiful blushing face of Marian Atheling, drooping and falling back under the shadow of Louis. The Yankee hastened forward with his best greeting.

"When I remember our last meeting," said Mr Endicott, bending his thin head forward with the most unusual deference, that tantalising vision of what might have been, "I think myself fortunate indeed to have found you so near your home. I have been visiting your renowned city—one of those twins of learning, whose antiquity is its charm. In my country our antiquities stretch back into the eternities; but we know nothing of the fourteenth or the fifteenth century in our young soil. My friend the Rector has been showing me his church."

Mr Endicott's friend the Rector stared at him with a haughty amazement, but came forward without saying anything to the new-comers; then he seemed to pause a moment, doubtful how to address Louis—a doubt which the young man solved for him instantly by taking off his hat with an exaggerated and solemn politeness. They bowed to each other loftily, these two haughty young men, as two duellists might have saluted each other over their weapons. Then Louis turned his fair companion gently, and, without saying anything, led her back again on the road they had just traversed. Agnes followed silently, and feeling very awkward, with the Rector and Mr Endicott on either hand. The Rector did not say a word. Agnes only answered in shy monosyllables. The gifted American had it all his own way.

"I understand Viscount Winterbourne and Mrs Edgerley are at Winterbourne Hall," said Mrs Endicott. "She is a charming person; the union of a woman of fashion and a woman of literature is one so rarely seen in this land."

"Yes," said Agnes, who knew nothing else to say.

"For myself," said Mr Endicott solemnly, "I rejoice to find the poetic gift alike in the palace of the peer and the cottage of the peasant, bringing home to all hearts the experiences of life; in the sumptuous apartments of the Hall with Mrs Edgerley, or in the humble parlour of the worthy and respectable middle class—Miss Atheling, with you."

"Oh!" cried Agnes, starting under this sudden blow, and parrying it with all the skill she could find. "Do you like Oxford, Mr Endicott? Have you seen much of the country about here?"

But it was too late. Mr Endicott caught a shy backward glance of Marian, and, smothering a mortal jealousy of Louis, eagerly thrust himself forward to answer it—and the Rector had caught his unfortunate words. The Rector drew himself up to a still more lofty height, if that was possible, and walked on by Agnes's side in a solemn and stately silence—poor Agnes, who would have revived a little in his presence but for that arrow of Mr Endicott's, not knowing whether to address him, or whether her best policy was to be silent. She went on by his side, holding down her head, looking very small, very slight, very young, beside that dignified and stately personage. At last he himself condescended to speak.

"Am I to understand, Miss Atheling," said the Rector, very much in the same tone as he might have asked poor little Billy Morrell at school, "Are you the boy who robbed John Parker's orchard?"—"Am I to understand, as I should be disposed to conclude from what this person says, that, like my fashionable cousin at the Hall, you have written novels?—or is it only the hyperbole of that individual's ordinary speech?"

"No," said Agnes, very guilty, a convicted culprit, yet making bold to confess her guilt. "I am very sorry he said it, but it is true; only I have written just one novel. Do you think it wrong?"

"I think a woman's intellect ought to be receptive without endeavouring to produce," said the Rector, in a slightly acerbated tone. "Intelligence is the noblest gift of a woman; originality is neither to be wished nor looked for."

"I do not suppose I am very guilty of that either," said Agnes, brightening again with that odd touch of pugnacity, as she listened once more to this haughty tone of dogmatism from the man who held no opinions. "If you object only to originality, I do not think you need be angry with me."

She was half inclined to play with the lion, but the lion was in a very ill humour, and would see no sport in the matter. To tell the truth, the Rector was very much fretted by this unlooked-for intelligence. He felt as if it were done on purpose, and meant as a personal offence to him, though really, after all, for a superior sister of St Frideswide, this unfortunate gift of literature was rather a recommendation than otherwise, as one might have thought.

So the Rev. Lionel Rivers stalked on beside Agnes past his own door, following Louis, Marian, and Mr Endicott to the very gate of the Old Wood Lodge. Then he took off his hat to them all, wished them a ceremonious good-night, and went home extremely wrathful, and in a most unpriestly state of mind. He could not endure to think that the common outer world had gained such a hold upon that predestined Superior of the sisters of St Frideswide.

CHAPTER XXXIV

SOME PROGRESS

After a long and most laborious investigation of the old parchment, Charlie at last triumphantly made it out to be an old conveyance, to a remote ancestor, of this very little house, and sundry property adjoining, on which the Athelings had now no claim. More than two hundred and fifty years ago!—the girls were as much pleased with it as if it had been an estate, and even Charlie owned a thrill of gratification. They felt themselves quite long-descended and patrician people, in right of the ancestor who had held "the family property" in 1572.

But it was difficult to see what use this could be of in opposition to the claim of Lord Winterbourne. Half the estates in the country at least had changed hands during these two hundred and fifty years; and though it certainly proved beyond dispute that the Old Wood Lodge had once been the property of the Athelings, it threw no light whatever on the title of Miss Bridget. Mrs Atheling looked round upon the old walls with much increase of respect; she wondered if they really could be so old as that; and was quite reverential of her little house, being totally unacquainted with the periods of domestic architecture, and knowing nothing whatever of archaic "detail."

Miss Anastasia, however, remembered her promise. Only two or three days after Charlie's visit to her, the two grey ponies made their appearance once more at the gate of the Old Wood Lodge. She was not exactly triumphant, but had a look of satisfaction on her face, and evidently felt she had gained something. She entered upon her business without a moment's delay.

"Young Atheling, I have brought you all that Mr Temple can furnish me with," said Miss Anastasia—"his memorandum taken from my father's instructions. He tells me there was a deed distinct and formal, and offers to bear his witness of it, as I have offered mine."

Charlie took eagerly out of her hand the paper she offered to him. "It is a copy out of his book," said Miss Anastasia. It was headed thus: "Mem.—To convey to Miss Bridget Atheling, her heirs and assigns, the cottage called the Old Wood Lodge, with a certain piece of land adjoining, to be described—partly as a proof of Lord Winterbourne's gratitude for services, partly as restoring property acquired by his father—to be executed at once."

The date was five-and-twenty years ago; and perhaps nothing but justice to her dead friend and to her living ones could have fortified Miss Anastasia to return upon that time. She sat still, looking at Charlie while he read it, with her cheek a little blanched and her eye brighter than usual. He laid it down with a look of impatience, yet satisfaction. "Some one," said Charlie, "either for one side or for the other side, must have this deed."

"Your boy is hard to please," said Miss Rivers. "I have offered to appear myself, and so does Mr Temple. What, boy, not content!"

"It is the next best," said Charlie; "but still not so good as the deed; and the deed must exist somewhere; nobody would destroy such a thing. Where is it likely to be?"

"Young Atheling," said Miss Anastasia, half amused, half with displeasure, "when I want to collect evidence, you shall do it for me. Has he had a good education?—eh?"

"To you I am afraid he will seem a very poor scholar," said Mrs Atheling, with a little awe of Miss Anastasia's learning; "but we did what we could for him; and he has always been a very industrious boy, and has studied a good deal himself."

To this aside conversation Charlie paid not the smallest attention, but ruminated over the lawyer's memorandum, making faces at it, and bending all the powers of his mind to the consideration—where to find this deed! "If it's not here, nor in her lawyer's, nor with this old lady, he's got it," pronounced Charlie; but this was entirely a private process, and he did not say a word aloud.

"I've read her book," said Miss Rivers, with a glance aside at Agnes; "it's a very clever book: I approve of it, though I never read novels: in my day, girls did no such things—all the better for them now. Yes, my child, don't be afraid. I'll not call you unfeminine—in my opinion, it's about the prettiest kind of fancy-work a young woman can do."

Under this applause Agnes smiled and brightened; it was a great deal more agreeable than all the pretty sayings of all the people who were dying to know the author of Hope Hazlewood, in the brief day of her reputation at the Willows.

"And as for the pretty one," said Miss Anastasia, "she, I suppose, contents herself with lovers—eh? What is the meaning of this? I suppose the child's heart is in it. The worse for her—the worse for her!"

For Marian had blushed deeply, and then become very pale; her heart was touched indeed, and she was very despondent. All the other events of the time were swallowed up to Marian by one great shadow—Louis was going away!

Whereupon Mrs Atheling, unconsciously eager to attract the interest of Miss Anastasia, who very likely would be kind to the young people, sent Marian up-stairs upon a hastily-invented errand, and took the old lady aside to tell her what had happened. Miss Rivers was a good deal surprised—a little affected. "So—so—so," she said slowly, "these reckless young creatures—how ready they are to plunge into all the griefs of life! And what does Will Atheling say to this nameless boy?"

"I cannot say my husband is entirely pleased," said Mrs Atheling, with a little hesitation; "but he is a very fine young man; and to see our children happy is the great thing we care for, both William and me."

"How do you know it will make her happy?" asked Miss Anastasia somewhat sharply. "The child flushes and pales again, pretty creature as she is, like a woman come into her troubles. A great deal safer to write novels! But what is done can't be undone; and I am glad to hear of it on account of the boy."

Then Miss Anastasia made a pause, thinking over the matter. "I have found some traces of my father's wanderings," she said again, with a little emotion: "if the old man was tempted to sin in his old days, though it would be a shame to hear of, I should still be glad to make sure; and if by any chance," continued the old lady, reddening with the maidenly and delicate feeling of which her fifty years could not deprive her—"if by any chance these unfortunate children should turn out to be nearly related to me, I will of course think it my duty to provide for them as if they were lawful children of my father's house."

It cost her a little effort to say this—and Mrs Atheling, not venturing to make any comment, looked on with respectful sympathy. It was very well for Miss Anastasia to say, but how far Louis would tolerate a provision made for him was quite a different question. The silence was broken again by the old lady herself.

"This bold boy of yours has set me to look over all my old papers," said Miss Anastasia, with a twinkle of satisfaction and amusement in her eye, as she looked over at Charlie, still making faces at the lawyer's note. "Now that I have begun for her sake, dear old soul, I continue for my own, and for curiosity: I would give a great deal to find out the story of these children. Young Atheling, if I some time want your services, will you give them to me?"

Charlie looked up with a boyish flush of pleasure. "As soon as this business is settled," said Charlie. Miss Anastasia, whom his mother feared to look at lest she should be offended, smiled approvingly; patted the shoulder of Agnes as she passed her, left "her love for the other poor child," and went away. Mrs Atheling looked after her with a not unnatural degree of complacency. "Now, I think it very likely indeed that she will either leave them something, or try what she can do for Louis," said Mamma; she did not think how impossible it would be to do anything for Louis, until Louis graciously accepted the service; nor indeed, that the only thing the young man could do under his circumstances was to trust to his own exertions solely, and seek service from none.

CHAPTER XXXV

A GREAT DISCOVERY

The visit of Miss Rivers was an early one, some time before their mid-day dinner; and the day went on quietly after its usual fashion, and fell into the stillness of a sunny afternoon, which looked like a reminiscence of midsummer among these early October days. Mrs Atheling sat in her big chair, knitting, with a little drowsiness, a little stocking—though this was a branch of art in which Hannah was found to excel, and had begged her mistress to leave to her. Agnes sat at the table with her blotting-book, busy with her special business; Charlie was writing out a careful copy of the old deed. The door was open, and Bell and Beau, under the happy charge of Rachel, ran back and forwards, out and in, from the parlour to the garden, not omitting now and then a visit to the kitchen, where Hannah, covered all over with her white bib and apron, was making cakes for tea. Their merry childish voices and prattling feet gave no disturbance to the busy people in the parlour; neither did the light fairy step of Rachel, nor even the songs she sang to them in her wonderful voice—they were all so well accustomed to its music now. Marian and Louis, who did not like to lose sight of each other in these last days, were out wandering about the fields, or in the wood, thinking of little in the world except each other, and that great uncertain future which Louis penetrated with his fiery glances, and of which Marian wept and smiled to hear. Mamma sitting at the window, between the pauses of her knitting and the breaks of her gentle drowsiness, looked out for them with a little tender anxiety. Marian, the only one of her children who was "in trouble," was nearest of all at that moment to her mother's heart.

When suddenly a violent sound of wheels from the high-road broke in upon the stillness, then a loud voice calling to horses, and then a dull plunge and heavy roll. Mrs Atheling lifted her startled eyes, drowsy no longer, to see what was the matter, just in time to behold, what shook the little house like the shock of a small earthquake, Miss Anastasia's two grey horses, trembling with unusual exertion, draw up with a bound and commotion at the little gate.

And before the good mother could rise to her feet, wondering what could be the cause of this second visit, Miss Rivers herself sprang out of the carriage, and came into the house like a wind, almost stumbling over Rachel, and nearly upsetting Bell and Beau. She did not say a word to either mother or daughter, she only came to the threshold of the parlour, waved her hand imperiously, and cried, "Young Atheling, I want you!"

Charlie was not given to rapid movements, but there was no misunderstanding the extreme emotion of this old lady. The big boy got up at once and followed her, for she went out again immediately. Then Mrs Atheling, sitting at the window in amaze, saw her son and Miss Anastasia stand together in the garden, conversing with great earnestness. She showed him a book, which Charlie at first did not seem to understand, to the great impatience of his companion. Mrs Atheling drew back troubled, and in the most utter astonishment—what could it mean?

"Young Atheling," said Miss Anastasia abruptly, "I want you to give up this business of your father's immediately, and set off to Italy on mine. I have made a discovery of the most terrible importance: though you are only a boy I can trust you. Do you hear me?—it is to bring to his inheritance my father's son!"

Charlie looked up in her face astonished, and without comprehension. "My father's business is of importance to us," he said, with a momentary sullenness.

"So it is; my own man of business shall undertake it; but I want an agent, secret and sure, who is not like to be suspected," said Miss Anastasia. "Young Atheling, look here!"

Charlie looked, but not with enthusiasm. The book she handed him was an old diary of the most commonplace description, each page divided with red lines into compartments for three days, with printed headings for Monday, Tuesday, Wednesday, and so on, and columns for money. The wind fluttered the leaves, so that the only entry visible to Charlie was one relating to some purchase, which he read aloud, bewildered and wondering. Miss Anastasia, who was extremely moved and excited, looked furious, and as if she was almost tempted to administer personal chastisement to the blunderer. She turned over the fluttered leaves with an impetuous gesture. "Look here," she said, pointing to the words with her imperative finger, and reading them aloud in a low, restrained, but most emphatic voice. The entry was in the same hand, duly dated under the red line—"Twins—one boy—and Giulietta safe. Thank God. My sweet young wife."

"Now go—fly!" cried Miss Anastasia, "find out their birthday, and then come to me for money and directions. I will make your fortune, boy; you shall be the richest pettifogger in Christendom. Do you hear me, young Atheling—do you hear me! He is the true Lord Winterbourne—he is my father's lawful son!"

To say that Charlie was not stunned by this sudden suggestion, or that there was no answer of young and generous enthusiasm, as well as of professional eagerness in his mind, to the address of Miss Rivers, would have been to do him less than justice. "Is it Italy?—I don't know a word of Italian," cried Charlie. "Never mind, I'll go to-morrow. I can learn it on the way."

The old lady grasped the boy's rough hand, and stepped again into her carriage. "Let it be to-morrow," she said, speaking very low; "tell your mother, but no one else, and do not, for any consideration, let it come to the ears of Louis—Louis, my father's boy!—But I will not see him, Charlie; fly, boy, as if you had wings!—till you come home. I will meet you to-morrow at Mr Temple's office—you know where that is—at twelve o'clock. Be ready to go immediately, and tell your mother to mention it to no creature till I see her again."

Saying which, Miss Rivers turned her ponies, Charlie hurried into the house, and his mother sat gazing out of the window, with the most blank and utter astonishment. Miss Anastasia had not a glance to spare for the watcher, and took no time to pull her rose from the porch. She drove home again at full speed, solacing her impatience with the haste of her progress, and repeating, under her breath, again and again, the same words. "One boy—and Giulietta safe. My sweet young wife!"

VOLUME III

CHAPTER I

AN OLD STORY

"Now, mother," said Charlie, "I'm in real earnest. My father would tell me himself if he were here. I want to understand the whole concern."

Mrs Atheling and her son were in Charlie's little room, with its one small lattice-window, overshadowed and embowered in leaves—its plain uncurtained bed, its small table, and solitary chair. Upon this chair, with a palpitating heart, sat Mrs Atheling, and before her stood the resolute boy.

And she began immediately, yet with visible faltering and hesitation, to tell him the story she had told the girls of the early connection between the present Lord Winterbourne and the Atheling family. But Charlie's mind was excited and preoccupied. He listened, almost with impatience, to the sad little romance of his father's young sister, of whom he had never heard before. It did not move him at all as it had moved Agnes and Marian. Broken hearts and disappointed loves were very far out of Charlie's way; something entirely different occupied his own imagination. He broke forth with a little effusion of impatience when the story came to an end. "And is this all? Do you mean to say this is the whole, mother? And my father had never anything to do with him but through a girl!"

"You are very unfeeling, Charlie," said Mrs Atheling, who wiped her eyes with real emotion, yet with a little policy too, and to gain time. "She was a dear innocent girl, and your father was very fond of her—reason enough to give him a dislike, if it were not sinful, to the very name of Lord Winterbourne."

"I had better go on with my packing, then," said Charlie. "So, that was all? I suppose any scamp in existence might do the same. Do you really mean to tell me, mother, that there was nothing but this?"

Mrs Atheling faltered still more under the steady observation of her son. "Charlie," said his mother, with agitation, "your father never would mention it to anyone. I may be doing very wrong. If he only were here himself to decide! But if I tell you, you must give me your word never so much as to hint at it again."

Charlie did not give the necessary pledge, but Mrs Atheling made no pause. She did not even give him time to speak, however he might have been inclined, but hastened on in her own disclosure with agitation and excitement. "You have heard Papa tell of the young gentleman—he whom you all used to be so curious about—whom your father did a great benefit to," said Mrs Atheling, in a breathless hurried whisper. "Charlie, my dear, I never said it before to any creature—that was him."

She paused only a moment to take breath. "It was before we knew how he had behaved to dear little Bride," she continued, still in haste, and in an undertone. "What he did was a forgery—a forgery! people were hanged for it then. It was either a bill, or a cheque, or something, and Mr Reginald had written to it another man's name. It happened when Papa was in the bank, and before old Mr Lombard died—old Mr Lombard had a great kindness for your father, and we had great hopes then—and by good fortune the thing was brought to Papa. Your father was always very quick, Charlie—he found it out in a moment. So he told old Mr Lombard of it in a quiet way, and Mr Lombard consented he should take it back to Mr Reginald, and tell him it was found out, and hush all the business up. If your papa had not been so quick, Charlie, but had paid the money at once, as almost any one else would have done, it all must have been found out, and he would have been hanged, as certain as anything—he, a haughty young gentleman, and a lord's son!"

"And a very good thing, too," exclaimed Charlie; "saved him from doing any more mischief. So, I suppose now, it's all my father's blame."

"This Lord Winterbourne is a bad man," said Mrs Atheling, taking no notice of her son's interruption: "first he was furious to William, and then he cringed and fawned to him; and of course he had it on his conscience then about poor little Bride, though we did not know—and then he raved, and said he was desperate, and did not know what to do for money. Your father came home to me, quite unhappy about him; for he belonged to the same country, and everybody tried to make excuses for Mr Reginald, being a young man, and the heir. So William made it up in his own mind to go and tell the old lord, who was in London then. The old lord was a just man, but very proud. He did not take it kind of William, and he had no regard for Mr Reginald; but for the honour of the family he sent him away. Then we lost sight of him long, and Aunt Bridget took a dislike to us, and poor little Bride was dead, and we never heard anything of the Lodge or the Hall for many a year; but the old lord died abroad, and Mr Reginald came home Lord Winterbourne. That was all we ever knew. I thought your father had quite forgiven him, Charlie—we had other things to think of than keeping up old grudges—when all at once it came to be in the newspapers that Lord Winterbourne was a political man, that he was making speeches everywhere, and that he was to be one of the ministry. When your father saw that, he blazed up into such an anger! I said all I could, but William never minded me. He never was so bitter before, not even when we heard of little Bride. He said, Such a man to govern us and all the people!—a forger! a liar!—and sometimes, I think, he thought he would expose the whole story, and let everybody know."

"Time enough for that," said Charlie, who had listened to all this without comment, but with the closest attention. "What he did once he'll do again, mother; but we're close at his heels this time, and he won't get off now. I'm going to Oxford now to get some books. I say, mother, you'll be sure, upon your honour, not to tell the girls?"

"No, Charlie," said Mrs Atheling, with a somewhat faint affirmation; "but, my dear, I can't believe in it. It can't be true. Charlie, boy! if this was coming true, our Marian—your sister, Charlie!—why, Marian would be Lady Winterbourne!"

Charlie did not say a word in return; he only took down his little travelling-bag, laid it at his mother's feet to be packed, and left her to that business and her own meditations; but after he had left the room, the lad returned again and thrust in his shaggy head at the door. "Take care of Marian, mother," said Charlie, in a parting adjuration; "remember my father's little sister Bride."

So he went away, leaving Mrs Atheling a good deal disquieted. She had got over the first excitement of Miss Anastasia's great intelligence and the sudden preparations of Charlie. She had scarcely time enough, indeed, to give a thought to these things, when her son demanded this history from her, and sent her mind away into quite a different channel. Now she sat still in Charlie's room, pondering painfully, with the travelling-bag lying quite unheeded at her feet. At one moment she pronounced the whole matter perfectly impossible—at the next, triumphantly inconsequent, she leaped to the full consummation of the hope, and saw her own pretty Marian—dazzling vision!—the lady of Winterbourne! and again the heart of the good mother fell, and she remembered little Bride. Louis, as he was now, having no greater friends than their own simple family, and no pretensions whatever either to birth or fortune, was a very different person from that other Louis who might be heir of lands and lordship and the family pride of the Riverses. Much perplexed, in great uncertainty and pain, mused Mrs Atheling, half-resentful of that grand discovery of Miss Anastasia, which might plunge them all into renewed trouble; while Charlie trudged into Oxford for his Italian grammar—and Louis and Marian wandered through the enchanted wood, drawing homeward—and Rachel sang to the children—and Agnes wondered by herself over the secret which was to be confided only to Mamma.

CHAPTER II

A CRISIS

That night Charlie had need of all his diplomatic talents. Before he returned from Oxford, his mother, by way of precaution lest Agnes should betray the sudden and mysterious visit of Miss Anastasia to Marian, contrived to let her elder daughter know mysteriously, something of the scope and object of the sudden journey for which it was necessary to prepare her brother, driving Agnes, as was to be supposed, into a very fever of suppressed excitement, joy, triumph, and anxiety. Mrs Atheling, conscious, hurried, and studying deeply not to betray herself—and Agnes, watching every one, stopping questions, and guarding off suspicions with prudence much too visible—were quite enough of themselves to rouse every other member of the little company to lively pursuit after the secret. Charlie was assailed by every shape and form of question: Where was he going—what was he to do? He showed no cleverness, we are bound to acknowledge, in evading these multitudinous interrogations; he turned an impenetrable front upon them, and made the most commonplace answers, making vast incursions all the time into Hannah's cakes and Mamma's bread-and-butter.

"He had to go back immediately to the office; he believed he had got a new client for old Foggo," said Charlie, with the utmost coolness; "making no secret of it at all," according to Mamma's indignant commentary.

"To the office!—are you only going home, after all?" cried Marian.

"I'll see when I get there," answered Charlie; "there's something to be done abroad. I shouldn't wonder if they sent me. I say, I wish you'd all come home at once, and make things comfortable. There's my poor father fighting it out with Susan. I should not stand it if it was me."

"Hold your peace, Charlie, and don't be rude," said Mrs Atheling. "But, indeed, I wish we were at home, and out of everybody's way."

"Who is everybody?" said Louis. "I, who am going myself, can wish quite sincerely that we were all at home; but the addition is mysterious—who is in anybody's way?"

"Mamma means to wish us all out of reach of the Evil Eye," said Agnes, a little romantically.

"No such thing, my dear. I daresay we could do him a great deal more harm than he can do us," said Mrs Atheling, with sudden importance and dignity; then she paused with a certain solemnity, so that everybody could perceive the grave self-restraint of the excellent mother, and that she could say a great deal more if she chose.

"But no one thinks what I am to do when you are all gone," said Rachel; and her tearful face happily diverted her companions from investigating and from concealing the secret. There remained among them all, however, a certain degree of excitement. Charlie was returning home to-morrow—specially called home on business!—perhaps to go abroad upon the same! The fact stirred all those young hearts with something not unlike envy. This boy seemed to have suddenly leaped in one day into a man.

And it was natural enough that, hearing of this, the mind of Louis should burn and chafe with fierce impatience. Charlie, who was perfectly undemonstrative of his thoughts and imaginations, was a very boy to Louis—yet there was need and occasion for Charlie in the crowd of life, when no one thought upon this fiery and eager young man. It was late that night when Louis left this only home and haven which he had ever known; and though he would fain have left Rachel there, his little sister would not remain behind him, but clung to his arm with a strange presentiment of something about to happen, which she could not explain. Louis scarcely answered a word to the quiet talk of Rachel as they went upon their way to the Hall. With difficulty, and even with impatience, he curbed his rapid stride to her timid little footsteps, and hurried her along without a glance at the surrounding scene, memorable and striking as it was. The broad moonlight flooded over the noble park of Winterbourne. The long white-columned front of the house—which was a great Grecian house, pallid, vast, and imposing—shone in the white light like a screen of marble; and on the great lawn immediately before it were several groups of people, dwarfed into minute miraculous figures by the great space and silence, and the intense illumination, which was far more striking and particular than the broader light of day. The chances were that Louis did not see them, as he plunged on, in the blindness of preoccupation, keeping no path, through light and shadow, through the trees and underwood, and across the broad unshaded greensward, where no one could fail to perceive him. His little sister clung to his arm in an agony of fear, grief, and confidence—trembling for something about to happen with an overpowering tremor—yet holding a vague faith in her brother, strange and absorbing. She said, "Louis, Louis!" in her tone of appeal and entreaty. He did not hear her, but struck across the broad visible park, in the full stream of the moonlight, looking neither to the right hand nor to the left. As they approached, Rachel could not even hear any conversation among the groups on the lawn; and it was impossible to suppose that they had not been seen. Louis's abrupt direct course, over the turf and through the brushwood, must have attracted the notice of bystanders even in the daylight; it was still more remarkable now, when noiseless and rapid, through the intense white radiance and the perfect stillness, the stately figure of the young man, and his timid, graceful little sister, came directly forward in face of the spectators. These spectators were all silent, looking on with a certain fascination, and Rachel could not tell whether Louis was even conscious that any one was there.

But before they could turn aside into the road which led to the Hall door—a road to which Rachel most anxiously endeavoured to guide her brother—they were suddenly arrested by the voice of Lord Winterbourne. "I must put a stop to this," said his lordship suddenly and loudly, with so evident a reference to themselves, that even Rachel stopped without knowing it. "Here, young fellow, stop and give an account of yourself—what do you mean by wandering about my park at midnight, eh? I know your poaching practices. Setting snares, I suppose, and dragging about this girl as a protection. Get into your kennel, you mean dog; is this how you repay the shelter I have given you all your life?"

"It would be a fit return," said Louis. He did not speak so loud, but with a tremble of scorn and bitterness and intense youthful feeling in his voice, before which the echo of his persecutor's went out and died, like an ignoble thing. "If I were, as you say," repeated the young man, "setting snares for your game, or for your wealth, or for your life, you know it would be a fit return."

"Yes, I live a peaceful life with this villanous young incendiary under my roof!" said Lord Winterbourne. "I'll tell you what, you young ruffian, if nothing better can restrain you, locks and bars shall. Oh, no chance of appealing to my pity, with that fool of a girl upon your arm! You think you can defy me, year after year, because I have given charity to your base blood. My lad, you shall learn to know me better before another week is over our heads. Why, gentlemen, you perceive, by his own confession, I stand in danger of my life."

"Winterbourne," said some one over his shoulder, in a reproving tone, "you should be the last man in the world to taunt this unfortunate lad with his base blood."

Lord Winterbourne turned upon his heel with a laugh of insult which sent the wild blood dancing in an agony of shame, indignation, and rage even into Rachel's woman's face. "Well," said the voice of their tyrant, "I have supported the hound—what more would you have? His mother was a pretty fool, but she had her day. There's more of her conditions in the young villain than mine. I have no idea of playing the romantic father to such a son—not I!"

Louis did not know that he threw his sister off his arm before he sprang into the midst of these half-dozen gentlemen. She did not know herself, as she stood behind clenching her small fingers together painfully, with all the burning vehemence of a woman's passion. The young man sprang forward with the bound of a young tiger. His voice was hoarse with passion, not to be restrained. "It is a lie—a wilful, abominable lie!" cried Louis fiercely, confronting as close as a wrestler the ghastly face of his tyrant, who shrank before him. "I am no son of yours—you know I am no son of yours! I owe you the hateful bread I have been compelled to eat—nothing more. I am without a name—I may be of base blood—but I warn you for your life, if you dare repeat this last insult. It is a lie! I tell every one who condescends to call you friend; and I appeal to God, who knows that you know it is a lie! I may be the son of any other wretch under heaven, but I am not yours. I disown it with loathing and horror. Do you hear me?—you know the truth in your heart, and so do I!"

Lord Winterbourne fell back, step by step, before the young man, who pressed upon him close and rapid, with eyes which flamed and burned with a light which he could not bear. The insulting smile upon his bloodless face had not passed from it yet. His eyes, shifting, restless, and uneasy, expressed nothing. He was not a coward, and he was sufficiently quick-witted on ordinary occasions, but he had nothing whatever to answer to this vehement and unexpected accusation. He made an unintelligible appeal with his hand to his companions, and lifted up his face to the moonlight like a spectre, but he did not answer by a single word.

"Young man," said the gentleman who had spoken before, "I acknowledge your painful position, and that you have been addressed in a most unseemly manner—but no provocation should make you forget your natural duty. Lord Winterbourne must have had a motive for maintaining you as he has done. I put it to you calmly, dispassionately—what motive could he possibly have had, except one?"

"Ah!" said Louis, with a sudden and violent start, "he must have had a motive—it is true; he would not waste his cruel powers, even for cruelty's sake. If any man can tell me what child it was his interest to bastardise and defame, there may be hope and a name for me yet."

At these words, Lord Winterbourne advanced suddenly with a singular eagerness. "Let us have done with this foolery," he said, in a voice which was certainly less steady than usual; "I presume we can all be better employed than listening to the vapourings of this foolish boy. Go in, my lad, and learn a lesson by your folly to-night. I pass it over, simply because you have shown yourself to be a fool."

"I, however, do not pass it over, my lord," said Louis, who had calmed down after the most miraculous fashion, to the utter amazement of his sister. "Thank you for the provision you have given us, such as it is. Some time we may settle scores upon that subject. My sister and I must find another shelter to-night."

The bystanders were half disposed to smile at the young man's heroical withdrawal—but they were all somewhat amazed to find that Lord Winterbourne was as far as possible from sharing their amusement. He called out immediately in an access of passion to stop the young ruffian, incendiary, mischief-maker;—called loudly upon the servants, who began to appear at the open door—ordered Louis to his own apartment with the most unreasonable vehemence, and finally turned upon Rachel, calling her to give up the young villain's arm, and for her life to go home.

But Rachel was wound to the fever point as well as her brother. "No, no, it is all true he has said," cried Rachel. "I know it, like Louis; we are not your children—you dare not call us so now. I never believed you were our father—never all my life."

She exclaimed these words hastily in her low eager voice, as Louis drew her arm through his, and hurried her away. The young man struck again across the broad park and through the moonlight, while behind, Lord Winterbourne called to his servants to go after the fugitives—to bring that fellow back. The men only stared at their master, looked helplessly at each other, and went off on vain pretended searches, with no better intention than to keep out of Louis's way, until prudence came to the aid of Lord Winterbourne. "I shall scarcely think my life in safety while that young fool wanders wild about the country," he said to his friends, as he returned within doors; but his friends, one and all, thought this a very odd scene.

Meanwhile Louis made his rapid way with his little sister on his arm out over the glorious moonlit park of Winterbourne, away from the only home he had ever known—out to the night and to the world. Rachel, leaning closely upon him, scarcely so much as looked up, as her faltering footstep toiled to keep up with her brother. He, holding his proud young head high, neither turned nor glanced aside, but pressed on straight forward, as if to some visionary certain end before his eye. Then they came out at last to the white silent road, lying ghostlike under the excess of light—the quiet road which led through the village where all the houses slept and everything was still, not a curl of smoke in the moonlight, nor a house-dog's bark in the silence. It was midnight, vast and still, a great desolate uninhabited world. There was not a door open to them, nor a place where they could rest. But on pressed Louis, with the rapid step and unhesitating course of one who hastened to some definite conclusion. "Where are we going—where shall we go?" said poor little Rachel, drooping on his shoulder. Her brother did not hear her. He was not selfish, but he had not that superhuman consideration for others which might have broken the fiery inspiration of his own momentous thoughts, and made him think of the desolate midnight, and the houseless and outcast condition which were alone present to the mind of Rachel. He did not see a vast homeless solitude—a vagabond and disgraceful wandering, in this midnight walk. He saw a new world before him, such as had never glanced before across his fancy. "He must have had a motive," he muttered to himself. Rachel heard him sadly, and took the words as a matter of course. "Where are we to go?"—that was a more immediately important question to the simple mind of Rachel.

The Old Wood Lodge was as deep asleep as any house in the village. They paused, reluctant, both of them, to awake their friends within, and went back, pacing rapidly between the house of the Athelings and that of the Rector. The September night was cold, and Rachel was timid of that strange midnight world out of doors. They seemed to have nothing for it but pacing up and down upon the grassy road, where they were at least within sight of a friendly habitation, till morning came.

There was one light in one window of the Old Wood House; Rachel's eye went wandering to it wistfully, unawares: If the Rector knew—the Rector, who once would have been kind if Louis would have let him. But, as if in very response to her thoughts, the Rector, when they came back to this point again, was standing, like themselves, in the moonlight, looking over the low wall. He called to them rather authoritatively, asking what they did there—but started, and changed his tone into one of wondering interest and compassion when Rachel lifted her pale face to him, with the tears in her eyes. He hastened to the gate at once, and called them to enter. "Nay, nay, no hesitation—come in at once, that she may have rest and shelter," said the Rector in a peremptory tone, which, for the first time in his life, Louis had no thought of resenting. He went in without a word, leading his little sister. Perhaps it was the first great thing that ever had been done in all her life for Rachel's sake—for the sake of the delicate girl, who was half a child though a woman in years,—for sake of her tenderness, her delicate frame, her privilege of weakness. The two haughty young men went in silently together into this secluded house, which never opened its doors to any guest. It was an invalid's home, and some one was always at hand for its ailing mistress. By-and-by Rachel, in the exhaustion of great excitement, fell asleep in a little quiet room looking over that moonlit park of Winterbourne. Louis, who was in no mood for sleep, watched below, full of eager and unquiet thoughts. They had left Winterbourne Hall suddenly; the Rector asked no further questions, expressed no wonder, and left the young man who had repelled him once, with a lofty and dignified hospitality, to his meditations or repose.

CHAPTER III

CHARLIE'S PREPARATIONS

Charlie Atheling was not at all of an imaginative or fanciful turn of mind. His slumbers were not disturbed by castle-building—he wasted none of his available time in making fancy sketches of the people, or the circumstances, among which he was likely to be thrown. He was not without the power of comprehending at a glance the various features of his mission; but by much the most remarkable point of Charlie's character was his capacity for doing his immediate business, whatever that might be, with undivided attention, and with his full powers. On this early September morning he neither occupied himself with anticipations of his interview with Miss Anastasia, nor his hurried journey. He did not suffer his mind to stray to difficult questions of evidence, nor wander off into speculations concerning what he might have to do when he reached the real scene of his investigation. What he had to do at the moment he did like a man, bending upon his serious business all the faculties of his mind, and all the furrows of his brow. He got up at six o'clock, not because he particularly liked it, but because these early morning hours had become his habitual time for extra work of every kind, and sat upon Hannah's bench in the garden, close by the kitchen door, with the early sun and the early wind playing hide-and-seek among his elf-locks, learning his Italian grammar, as if this was the real business for which he came into the world.

"Whatsoever thy hand findeth to do"—that was Charlie's secret of success. He had only a grammar, a dictionary, and a little New Testament in Italian—and he had not at this moment the slightest ambition to read Dante in the original; but with steady energy he chased those unknown verbs into the deep caverns of his memory—a memory which was prodigious, and lost nothing committed to it. The three books accompanied him when he went in to breakfast, and marched off in his pocket to Oxford when it was time to keep his appointment with Miss Anastasia. Meanwhile the much-delayed travelling-bag only now began to get packed, and Mrs Atheling, silently toiling at this business, felt convinced that Susan would mislay all the things most important for Charlie's comfort, and very much yearned in her heart to accompany her son home. They were to meet him at the railway, whence he would depart immediately, after his interview with Miss Rivers; and Charlie's secret commission made a considerable deal of excitement in the quiet little house.

Miss Anastasia, who was much too eager and impetuous to be punctual, had been waiting for some time, when her young agent made his appearance at the office of her solicitor. After she had charged him with being too late, and herself suffered conviction as being too early, the old lady proceeded at once to business; they were in Mr Temple's own room, but they were alone.

"I have made copies of everything that seemed to throw light upon my late father's wanderings," said Miss Anastasia—"not much to speak of—see! These papers must have been carefully weeded before they came to my hands. Here is an old guide-book marked with notes, and here a letter dated from the place where he died. It is on the borders of Italy—at the foot of the Alps—on the way to Milan, and not very far from there. You will make all speed, young Atheling; I trust to your prudence—betray nothing—do not say a word about these children until you find some certain clue. It is more than twenty years—nearly one-and-twenty years—since my father died; but a rich Englishman, who married among them, was not like to be forgotten in such a village. Find out who this Giulietta was—if you can discover the family, they might know something. My father had an attendant, a sort of courier, who was with us often—Jean Monte, half a Frenchman half an Italian. I have never heard of him since that time; he might be heard of on the way, and he might know—but I cannot direct you, boy—I trust to your own spirit, your own foresight, your own prudence. Make haste, as if it was life and death; yet if time will avail you, take time. Now, young Atheling, I trust you!—bring clear evidence—legal evidence—what will stand in a court of law—and as sure as you live your fortune is made!"

Charlie did not make a single protestation in answer to this address. He folded up carefully those fragments of paper copied out in Miss Anastasia's careful old-fashioned lady's hand, and placed them in the big old pocket-book which he carried for lack of a better.

"I don't know much of the route," said Charlie,—"over the Alps, I suppose," and for once his cheek flushed with the youthful excitement of the travel. "I shall find out all about that immediately when I get to town; and there is a passport to be seen after. When I am ready to start—which will be just as soon as the thing can be done—I shall let you know how I am to travel, and write immediately when I arrive there;—I know what you mean me to do."

Then Miss Anastasia gave him—(a very important part of the business)—two ten-pound notes, which was a very large sum to Charlie, and directed him to go to the banking-house with which she kept an account in London, and get from them a letter of credit on a banker in Milan, on whom he could draw, according to his occasions. "You are very young, young Atheling," said Miss Rivers; "many a father would hesitate to trust his son as I trust you; but I'm a woman and an optimist, and have my notions: you are only a boy, but I believe in you—forget how young you are while you are about my business—plenty of time after this for enjoying yourself—and I tell you again, if you do your duty, your fortune is made."

The old lady and the youth went out together, to where the little carriage and the grey ponies stood at the solicitor's door. Charlie, in his present development, was not at all the man to hand a lady with a grace to her carriage; nor was this stately gentlewoman, in her brown pelisse, at all the person to be so escorted; but they were a remarkable pair enough, as they stood upon the broad pavement of one of the noblest streets of Christendom. Miss Anastasia held out her hand with a parting command and warning, as she took her seat and the reins.—"Young Atheling, remember! it is life and death!"

She was less cautious at that moment than she had been during all their interview. The words full upon another ear than his to whom they were addressed. Lord Winterbourne was making his way at the moment with some newly-arrived guests of his, and under the conduct of a learned pundit from one of the colleges, along this same picturesque High Street; and, in the midst of exclamations of rapture and of interest, his suspicious and alarmed eye caught the familiar equipage and well-known figure of Miss Anastasia. Her face was turned in the opposite direction,—she did not see him,—but a single step brought him near enough to hear her words. "Young Atheling!" Lord Winterbourne had not forgotten his former connection with the name, but the remembrance had long lain dormant in a breast which was used to potent excitements. William Atheling, though he once saved a reckless young criminal, could do no harm with his remote unbelievable story to a peer of the realm,—a man who had sat in the councils of the State. Lord Winterbourne had begun his suit for the Old Wood Lodge with the most contemptuous indifference to all that could be said of him by any one of this family; yet somehow it struck him strangely to hear so sudden a naming of this name. "Young Atheling!" He could not help looking at the youth,—meeting the stormy gleam in the eyes of Charlie, whose sudden enmity sprung up anew in an instant. Lord Winterbourne was sufficiently disturbed already by the departure of Louis, and with the quick observation of alarm remarked everything. He could understand no natural connection whatever between this lad and Miss Anastasia. His startled imagination suggested instantly that it bore some reference to Louis, and what interpretation was it possible to give to so strange an adjuration—"It is life and death!"

CHAPTER IV

GOING AWAY

"Charlie, my dear boy," said Mrs Atheling, with a slight tremble in her voice, "I suppose it may be months before we see you again."

"I can't tell, mother; but it will not be a day longer than I can help," said Charlie, who had the grace to be serious at the moment of parting. "There's only one thing, you know,—I must do my business before I come home."

"And take care of yourself," said Mrs Atheling; "take great care when you are going over those mountains, and among those people where bandits are—you know what stories we have read about such robbers, Charlie,—and remember, though I should be very glad to hear good news about Louis, Louis is not my own very boy, like you."

"Hush, mother—no need for naming him," said Charlie; "he is of more moment than me, however, this time—for that's my business. Never fear—thieves may be fools there as well as at home, but they're none such fools as to meddle with me. Now, mother, promise me, the last thing,—Agnes, do you hear?—don't tell Marian a word, nor him. I'll tell old Foggo the whole story, and Foggo will do what he can for him when he gets to London; but don't you go and delude him, telling him of this, for it would just be as good as ruin if I don't succeed; and it all may come to nothing, as like as not. I say, Agnes, do you hear?"

"Yes, I hear, very well; but I am not given to telling secrets," said Agnes, with a little dignity.

Charlie only laughed as he arranged himself in the corner of the second-class carriage, and drew forth his grammar; there was no time for anything more, save entreaties that he would write, and take care of himself; and the train flashed away, leaving them somewhat dull and blank in the reaction of past excitement, looking at each other, and half reluctant to turn their faces homeward. Their minds hurried forth, faster than either steam or electricity, to the end of Charlie's journey. They went back with very slow steps and very abstracted minds. What a new world of change and sudden revolution might open upon them at Charlie's return!

Mrs Atheling had some business in the town, and the mother and daughter pursued their way silently to that same noble High Street where Charlie had seen Lord Winterbourne, and where Lord Winterbourne and his party were still to be caught sight of, appearing and reappearing by glimpses as they "did" the halls and colleges. While her mother managed some needful business in a shop, Agnes stood rather dreamily looking down the stately street; its strange old-world mixture of the present and the past; its union of all kinds of buildings; the trim classic pillars and toy cupolas of the eighteenth century—the grim crumbling front of elder days—the gleams of green grass and waving trees through college gateways—the black-gowned figures interrupting the sunshine—the beautiful spire striking up into it as into its natural element,—a noble hyacinthine stem of immortal flowers. Agnes did not know much about artistic effect, nor anything about orders of architecture, but the scene seized upon her imagination, as was its natural right. Her thoughts were astray among hopes and chances far enough out of the common way—but any dream of romance could make itself real in an atmosphere like this.

She was pale,—she was somewhat of an abstracted and musing aspect. When one took into consideration her misfortune of authorship, she was in quite a sentimental pose and attitude—so thought her American acquaintance, who had managed to secure an invitation to the Hall, and was one of Lord Winterbourne's party. But Mr Endicott had "done" all the colleges before, and he could afford to let his attention be distracted by the appearance of the literary sister of the lady of his love.

"I am not surprised at your abstraction," said Mr Endicott. "In this, indeed, I do not hesitate to confess, my country is not equal to your Island. What an effect of sunshine! what a breadth of shade! I cannot profess to have any preference, in respect to Art, for the past, picturesque though it be—a poet of these days, Miss Atheling, has not to deal with facts, but feelings; but I have no doubt, before I interrupted you, the whole panorama of History glided before your meditative eye."

"No, indeed; I was thinking more of the future than of the past," said Agnes hurriedly.

"The future of this nation is obscure and mysterious," said Mr Endicott, gathering his eyebrows solemnly. "Some man must arise to lead you—to glory—or to perdition! I see nothing but chaos and darkness; but why should I prophesy? A past generation had leisure to watch the signs of the times; but for us 'Art is long and time is fleeting,' and happy is the man who can snatch one burning experience from the brilliant mirage of life."

Agnes, a little puzzled by this mixture of images, did not attempt any answer. Mr Endicott went on.

"I had begun to observe, with a great deal of interest, two remarkable young minds placed in a singular position. They were not to be met, of course, at the table of Lord Winterbourne," said the American with dignity; "but in my walks about the park I sometimes encountered them, and always endeavoured to draw them into conversation. So remarkable, in fact, did they seem to me, that they found a place in my Letters from England; studies of character entirely new to my consciousness. I believe, Miss Atheling, I had once the pleasure of seeing them in your company. They stand—um—unfortunately in a—a—an equivocal relationship to my noble host."

"Ah! what of them?" cried Agnes quickly, and with a crimsoned cheek. She felt already how difficult it was to hear them spoken of, and not proclaim at once her superior knowledge.

"A singular event, I understand, happened last night," continued Mr Endicott. "Viscount Winterbourne, on his own lawn, was attacked and insulted by the young man, who afterwards left the house under very remarkable circumstances. My noble friend, who is an admirable example of an old English nobleman, was at one time in actual danger, and I believe has been advised to put this fiery youth—"

"Do you mean Louis?" cried Agnes, interrupting him anxiously. "Louis!—do you mean that he has left the Hall?"

"I am greatly interested, I assure you, in tracing out this romance of real life," said Mr Endicott. "He left the Hall, I understand, last evening—and my noble friend is advised to take measures for his apprehension. I look upon the whole history with the utmost interest. How interesting to trace the motives of this young mind, perhaps the strife of passions—gratitude mixing with a sense of injury! If he is secured, I shall certainly visit him: I know no nobler subject for a drama of passion; and dramas of the passions are what we want to ennoble this modern time."

"Mother!" cried Agnes, "mother, come; we have no time to lose—Mr Endicott has told me—Mamma, leave these things to another time. Marian is alone; there is no one to support her. Oh, mother, mother! make haste! We must go home!"

She scarcely gave a glance to Mr Endicott as he stood somewhat surprised, making a study of the young author's excitable temperament for his next "letter from England"—but hastened her mother homeward, explaining, as she went, though not very coherently, that Louis had attacked Lord Winterbourne—that he had left the Hall—that he had done something for which he might be apprehended. The terror of disgrace—that most dread of all fears to people in their class—overwhelmed both mother and daughter, as they hastened, at a very unusual pace, along the road, terrified to meet himself in custody, or some one coming to tell them of his crime. And Marian, their poor beautiful flower, on whom this storm would fall so heavily—Marian was alone!

CHAPTER V

THE OLD WOOD HOUSE

Louis passed the night in the Rector's library. He had no inclination for sleep; indeed, he was almost scornful of the idea that he could sleep under his new and strange circumstances; and it was not until he roused himself, with a start, to see that the pale sheen of the moonlight had been succeeded by the rosy dawn of morning, that he knew of the sudden, deep slumber, that had fallen upon him. It was morning, but it was still a long time till day; except the birds among the trees there was nothing astir, not even the earliest labourer, and he could not hear a sound in the house. All the events of the previous night returned upon Louis's mind with all the revived freshness of a sudden awaking. A great change had passed upon him in a few hours. He started now at once out of the indefinite musings, the flush of vain ambition, the bitter brooding over wrong which had been familiar to his mind. He began to think with the earnest precision of a man who has attained to a purpose. Formerly it had been hard enough for his proud undisciplined spirit, prescient of something greater, to resolve upon a plan of tedious labour for daily bread, or to be content with such a fortune as had fallen to such a man as Mr Atheling. Even with love to bear him out, and his beautiful Marian to inspire him, it was hard, out of all the proud possibilities of youth, to plunge into such a lot as this. Now he considered it warily, with the full awakened consciousness of a man. Up to this time his bitter dislike and opposition to Lord Winterbourne had been carried on by fits and starts, as youths do contend with older people under whose sway they have been all their life. He took no reason with him when he decided that he was not the son of the man who opposed him. He never entered into the question how he came to the Hall, or what was the motive of its master. He had contented himself with a mere unreasoning conviction that Lord Winterbourne was not his father; but only one word was wanted to awaken the slumbering mind of the youth, and that word had been spoken last night. Now a clear and evident purpose became visible before him. What was Lord Winterbourne's reason for keeping him all his life under so killing a bondage? What child was there in the world whom it was Lord Winterbourne's interest to call illegitimate and keep in obscurity? His heart swelled—the colour rose in his face. He did not see how hopeless was the search—how entirely without grounds, without information, he was. He did not perceive how vain, to every reasonable individual, would seem the fabric he had built upon a mere conviction of his own. In his own eager perception everything was possible to that courage, and perseverance indomitable, which he felt to be in him; and, for the first time in his life, Louis came down from the unreasonable and bitter pride which had shut his heart against all overtures of friendship. Friendship—help—advice—the aid of those who knew the world better than he did—these were things to be sought for, and solicited now. He sat in the Rector's chair, leaning upon the Rector's writing-table; it was not without a struggle that he overcame his old repugnance, his former haughtiness. It was not without a pang that he remembered the obligation under which this stranger had laid him. It was his first effort in self-control, and it was not an easy one; he resolved at last to ask counsel from the Rector, and lay fully before him the strange circumstances in which he stood.

The Rector was a man of capricious hours, and uncertain likings. He was sometimes abroad as early as the earliest ploughman; to-day it was late in the forenoon before he made his appearance. Breakfast had been brought to Louis, by himself, in the library; in this house they were used to solitary meals at all hours—and he had already asked several times for the Rector, when Mr Rivers at last entered the room, and saluted him with stately courtesy. "My sister, I find, has detained your sister," said the Rector. "I hope you have not been anxious—they tell me the young lady will join us presently."

Then there was a pause; and then Mr Rivers began an extremely polite and edifying conversation, which must have reminded any spectator of the courtly amity of a couple of Don Quixotes preparing for the duello. The Rector himself conducted it with the most solemn gravity imaginable. This Lionel Rivers, dissatisfied and self-devouring, was not a true man. Supposing himself to be under a melancholy necessity of disbelieving on pain of conscience, he yet submitted to an innumerable amount of practical shams, with which his conscience took no concern. In spite of his great talents, and of a character full of natural nobleness, when you came to its foundations, a false tone, an artificial strain of conversation, an unreal and insincere expression, were unhappily familiar enough to the dissatisfied clergyman, who vainly tried to anchor himself upon the authority of the Church. Louis, on the contrary, knew nothing of talk which was a mere veil and concealment of meaning; he could not use vain words when his heart burned within him; he had no patience for those conversations which were merely intended to occupy time, and which meant and led to nothing. Yet it was very difficult for him, young, proud, and inexperienced as he was, without any invitation or assistance from his companion, to enter upon his explanation. He changed colour, he became uneasy, he scarcely answered the indifferent remarks addressed to him. At length, seeing nothing better for it, he plunged suddenly and without comment into his own tale.

"We have left Winterbourne Hall," said Louis, reddening to his temples as he spoke. "I have long been aware how unsuitable a home it was for me. I am going to London immediately. I cannot thank you enough for your hospitality to my sister, and to myself, last night."

"That is nothing," said the Rector, with a motion of his hand. "Some time since I had the pleasure of saying to your friends in the Lodge that it would gratify me to be able to serve you. I do not desire to pry into your plans; but if I can help you in town, let me know without hesitation."

"So far from prying," said Louis, eagerly, interrupting him, "I desire nothing more than to explain them. All my life," and once again the red blood rushed to the young man's face,—"all my life I have occupied the most humiliating of positions—you know it. I am not a meek man by nature; what excuse I have had if a bitter pride has sometimes taken possession of me, you know—"

The Rector bowed gravely, but did not speak. Louis continued in haste, and with growing agitation, "I am not the son of Lord Winterbourne—I am not a disgraced offshoot of your family—I can speak to you without feeling shame and abasement in the very sound of your name. This has been my conviction since ever I was capable of knowing anything—but Heaven knows how subtly the snare was woven—it seemed impossible, until now when we have done it, to disengage our feet."

"Have you made any discovery, then? What has happened?" said the Rector, roused into an eager curiosity. Here, at the very outset, lay Louis's difficulty—and he had never perceived it before.

"No; I have made no discovery," he said, with a momentary disconcertment. "I have only left the Hall—I have only told Lord Winterbourne what he knows well, and I have known long, that I am not his son."

"Exactly—but how did you discover that?" said the Rector.

"I have discovered nothing—but I am as sure of it as that I breathe," answered Louis.

The Rector looked at him—looked at a portrait which hung directly above Louis's head upon the wall, smiled, and shook his head. "It is quite natural," he said; "I can sympathise with any effort you make to gain a more honourable position, and to disown Lord Winterbourne—but it is vain, where there are pictures of the Riverses, to deny your connection with my family. George Rivers himself, my lord's heir, the future head of the family, has not a tithe as much of the looks and bearing of the blood as you."

Louis could not find a word to say in face of such an argument—he looked eagerly yet blankly into the face of the Rector—felt all his pulses throbbing with fiery impatience of the doubt thus cast upon him—yet knew nothing to advance against so subtle and unexpected a charge of kindred, and could only repeat, in a passionate undertone, "I am not Lord Winterbourne's son."

"I do not know," said the Rector, "I have no information which is not common to all the neighbourhood—yet I beg you to guard against delusion. Lord Winterbourne brought you here while you were an infant—since then you have remained at the Hall—he has owned you, I suppose, as much as a man ever owns an illegitimate child. Pardon me, I am obliged to use the common words. Lord Winterbourne is not a man of extended benevolence, neither is he one to take upon himself the responsibility or blame of another. If you are not his son, why did he bring you here?"

Louis raised his face from his hands which had covered it—he was very pale, haggard, almost ghastly. "If you can tell me of any youth—of any child—of any man's son, whom it was his interest to disgrace and remove out of the way," said the young man with his parched lips, "I will tell you why I am here."

The Rector could not quite restrain a start of emotion—not for what the youth said, for that was madness to the man of the world—but for the extreme passion, almost despair, in his face. He thought it best to soothe rather than to excite him.

"I know nothing more than all the world knows," said Mr Rivers; "but, though I warn you against delusions, I will not say you are wrong when you are so firmly persuaded that you are right. What do you mean to do in London—can I help you there?"

Louis felt with no small pang this giving up of the argument—as if it were useless to discuss anything so visionary—but he roused himself to answer the question: "The first thing I have to do," he said quickly, "is to maintain my sister and myself."

The Rector bowed again, very solemnly and gravely—perhaps not without a passing thought that the same duty imposed chains more galling than iron upon himself.

"That done, I will pursue my inquiries as I can," said Louis; "you think them vain—but time will prove that. I thank you now, for my sister's sake, for receiving us—and now we must go on our way."

"Not yet," said the Rector. "You are without means, of course—what, do you think it a disgrace, that you blush for it?—or would you have me suppose that you had taken money from Lord Winterbourne, while you deny that you are his son? For this once suppose me your friend; I will supply you with what you are certain to need; and you can repay me—oh, with double interest if you please!—only do not go to London unprovided—for that is the maddest method of anticipating a heartbreak; your sister is young, almost a child, tender and delicate—let it be, for her sake."

"Thank you; I will take it as you give it," said Louis. "I am not so ungenerous as you suppose."

There was a certain likeness between them, different as they were—there was a likeness in both to these family portraits on the walls. Before such silent witnesses Louis's passionate disclaimer, sincere though it was, was unbelievable. For no one could believe that he was not an offshoot of the house of Rivers, who looked from his face and the Rector's to those calm ancient faces on the walls.

CHAPTER VI

AN ADVENTURER

"They have left the Hall."

That was all Marian said when she came to the door to meet her mother and sister, who paused in the porch, overcome with fatigue, haste, and anxiety. Mrs Atheling was obliged to pause and sit down, not caring immediately to see the young culprit who was within.

"And what has happened, Marian,—what has happened? My poor child, did he tell you?" asked Mrs Atheling.

"Nothing has happened, mamma," said Marian, with a little petulant haste; "only Louis has quarrelled with Lord Winterbourne; but, indeed, I wish you would speak to him. Oh, Agnes, go and talk to Louis; he says he will go to London to-day."

"And so he should; there is not a moment to be lost," said Agnes,—"I will go and tell him; we can walk in with him to Oxford, and see him safely away. Tell Hannah to make haste, Marian,—he must not waste an hour."

"What does she mean,—what is the matter? Oh, what have you heard, mamma?" said Marian, growing very pale.

"Hush, dear; I daresay it was not him,—it was Mr Endicott, who is sure to hate him, poor boy; he said Lord Winterbourne would put him in prison, Marian. Oh," said Mrs Atheling, getting up hurriedly, "he ought to go at once to Papa."

But they found Louis, whom they all surrounded immediately with terror, sympathy, and encouragement, entirely unappalled by the threatened vengeance of Lord Winterbourne.

"There is nothing to charge me with; he can bring no accusation against me; if he did ever say it, it must have been a mere piece of bravado," said Louis; "but it is better I should go at once without losing an hour, as Agnes says. Will you let Rachel stay? and you, who are the kindest mother in the world, when will you have compassion on us and come home?"

"Indeed, I wish we were going now," said Mrs Atheling; and she said it with genuine feeling, and a sigh of anxiety. "You must tell Papa we will not stay very long; but I suppose we must see about this lawsuit first; and I am sure I cannot tell who is to manage it now, since Charlie is gone."

"Shall you go to Papa at once, Louis?" asked Marian, who was very anxious to conceal from every one the tears in her downcast eyes.

"Surely, at once," said Louis. "We are in different circumstances now; I have a great deal to ask any one who knows the family of Rivers. Do you know it never before occurred to me that Lord Winterbourne must have had some powerful inducement for keeping me here, knowing as well as I do that I am not his son."

Mrs Atheling and Agnes turned a sudden guilty look upon each other; but neither had betrayed the secret;—what did he mean?

"Unless it was his interest in some way—unless it was for his evident advantage to disgrace and disable me," said Louis, groping in the dark, when they knew one possible solution of the mystery so well, "I am convinced he never would have kept me as he has done at the Hall."

He spoke in a tone different to that which he had used to the Rector, and very naturally different—for Louis here was triumphant in the faith of his audience, and did not hesitate to say all he felt, nor fear too close an investigation into the grounds of his belief. He spoke fervently; and Marian and Rachel looked at him with the faith of enthusiasm, and Mrs Atheling and Agnes with wonder, agitation, and embarrassment. But, as he went on, it became too much for the self-control of the good mother. She hurried out on pretence of superintending Hannah, and was very soon followed by Agnes. "I durst not stay, I should have told him," said Mrs Atheling, in a hurried whisper. "Who could put so much into his head, Agnes? who could lead him so near the truth?—only God! My dear child, I believe in it all now."

Agnes had believed in it all from the first moment of hearing it, but so singular a strain was upon the minds of both mother and daughter, knowing this extraordinary secret which the others did not know, that it was not wonderful they should give a weight much beyond their desert to the queries of Louis. Yet, indeed, Louis's queries took a wonderfully correct direction, and came very near the truth.

It was a day of extreme agitation to them all, and not until Louis, who had no travelling-bag to pack, had been accompanied once more to the railway, and seen safely away, with many a lingering farewell, was any one able to listen to, or understand, Rachel's version of the events of last night. When he was quite gone—when it was no longer possible to wave a hand to him in the distance, or even to see the flying white plume of the miraculous horseman who bounded along with all that line of carriages, the three girls came home together through the quiet evening road—the disenchanted road, weary and unlovely, which Marian marvelled much any one could prefer to Bellevue. They walked very close together, with Marian in the midst, comforting her in an implied, sympathetic, girlish fashion—for Rachel, though Louis had belonged to her so very much longer, and was her sole authority, law-giver, and hero, instinctively kept her own feelings out of sight, and took care of Marian. These girls were very loyal to their own visionary ideas of the mysterious magician who had not come to either of them yet, but whose coming both anticipated some time, with awe and with smiles.

And then Rachel told them how it had fared with her on the previous night. Rachel had very little to say about the Rector; she had given him up conscientiously to Agnes, and with a distant and reverent admiration of his loftiness, contemplated him afar off, too great a person for her friendship. "But in the morning the maid came and took me to Miss Rivers—did you ever see Miss Rivers?—she is very pale—and pretty, though she is old, and a very, very great invalid," said Rachel. "Some one has to sit up with her every night, and she has so many troubles—headaches, and pains in her side, and coughs, and every sort of thing! She told me all about them as she lay on the sofa in her pretty white dressing-gown, and in such a soft voice as if she was quite used to them, and did not mind. Do you think you could be a nurse to any one who was ill, Agnes?"

"She has been a nurse to all of us when we were ill," said Marian, rousing herself for the effort, and immediately subsiding into the pensiveness which the sad little beauty would not suffer herself to break, even though she began in secret to be considerably interested about the interior of the mysterious Wood House, and the invisible Miss Rivers. Marian thought Louis would not be pleased if he could imagine her thinking of any one but him, so soon after he had gone away.

"But I don't mean at home—I mean a stranger," said Rachel, "one whom you did not love. I think it must be rather hard sometimes; but do you know I was very nearly offering to be nurse to Miss Rivers, she spoke so kindly to me? And then Louis will have to work," continued the faithful little sister, with tears in her eyes; "you must tell me what I can do, Agnes, not to be a burden upon Louis. Oh, do you think any one would give me money for singing now?"

CHAPTER VII

LORD WINTERBOURNE

Lord Winterbourne, all his life, had been a man of guile; he was so long experienced in it, that dissimulation became easy enough to him, when he was not startled or thrown suddenly off his guard. Already every one around him supposed he had quite forgiven and forgotten the wild escapade of Louis. He had no confidant whatever, not even a valet or a steward, and his most intimate associate knew nothing of his dark and secret counsels. When any one mentioned the ungovernable youth who had fled from the Hall, Lord Winterbourne said, "Pooh, pooh—he will soon discover his mistake," and smiled his pale and sinister smile. Such a face as his could not well look benign; but people were accustomed to his face, and thought it his misfortune—and everybody set him down as, in this instance at least, of a very forgiving and indulgent spirit, willing that the lad should find out his weakness by experiment, but not at all disposed to inflict any punishment upon his unruly son.

The fact was, however, that Lord Winterbourne was considerably excited and uneasy. He spent hours in a little private library among his papers—carefully went over them, collating and arranging again and again—destroyed some, and filled the private drawers of his cabinet with others. He sent orders to his agent to prosecute with all the energy possible his suit against the Athelings. He had his letters brought to him in his own room, where he was alone, and looked over them with eager haste and something like apprehension. Servants, always sufficiently quick-witted under such circumstances, concluded that my lord expected something, and the expectation descended accordingly through all the grades of the great house; but this did not by any means diminish the number of his guests, or the splendour of his hospitality. New arrivals came constantly to the Hall—and very great people indeed, on their way to Scotland and the moors, looked in upon the disappointed statesman by way of solace. He had made an unspeakable failure in his attempt at statesmanship; but still he had a certain amount of influence, and merited a certain degree of consideration. The quiet country brightened under the shower of noble sportsmen and fair ladies. All Banburyshire crowded to pay its homage. Mrs Edgerley brought her own private menagerie, the newest lion who could be heard of; and herself fell into the wildest fever of architecturalism—fitted up an oratory under the directions of a Fellow of Merton—set up an Ecclesiological Society in the darkest of her drawing-rooms—made drawings of "severe saints," and purchased casts of the finest "examples"—began to embroider an altar-cloth from the designs of one of the most renowned connoisseurs in the ecclesiological city, and talked of nothing but Early English, and Middle Pointed. Politics, literature, and the fine arts, sport, flirtation, and festivity, kept in unusual excitement the whole spectator county of Banbury, and the busy occupants of Winterbourne Hall.

In the midst of all this, the Lord of Winterbourne spent solitary hours in his library among his papers, took solitary rides towards Abingford, moodily courted a meeting with Miss Anastasia, even addressed her when they met, and did all that one unassisted man could do to gain information of her proceedings. He was in a state of restless expectation, not easy to account for. He knew that Louis was in London, but not who had given him the means to go there; and he could find no pretence for bringing back the youth, or asserting authority over him. He waited in well-concealed but frightfully-felt excitement for something, watching with a stealthy but perpetual observation the humble house of the Athelings and the Priory at Abingford. He did not say to himself what it was he apprehended, nor indeed that he apprehended anything; but with that strange certainty which criminals always seem to retain, that fate must come some time, waited in the midst of his gay, busy, frivolous guests, sharing all the occupations round him, like a man in a dream,—waited as the world waits in a pause of deadly silence for the thunderclap. It would rouse him when it came.

It came, but not as he looked for it. Oh blind, vain, guilty soul, with but one honest thought among all its crafts and falsehoods! It came not like the rousing tumult of the thunder, but like an avalanche from the hills; he fell under it with a groan of mortal agony; there was nothing in heaven or earth to defend him from the misery of this sudden blow. All his schemes, all his endeavours, what were they good for now?

CHAPTER VIII

THE NEW HEIR

They had heard from Charlie, who had already set out upon his journey; they had heard from Louis, whom Mr Foggo desired to take into his office in Charlie's place in the mean time; they had heard again and again from Miss Anastasia's solicitor, touching their threatened property; and to this whole family of women everything around seemed going on with a singular speed and bustle, while they, unwillingly detained among the waning September trees, were, by themselves, so lonely and so still. The only one among them who was not eager to go home was Agnes. Bellevue and Islington, though they were kindly enough in their way, were not meet nurses for a poetic child;—this time of mountainous clouds, of wistful winds, of falling leaves, was like a new life to Agnes. She came out to stand in the edge of the wood alone, to do nothing but listen to the sweep of the wild minstrel in those thinning trees, or look upon the big masses of cloud breaking up into vast shapes of windy gloom over the spires of the city and the mazes of the river. The great space before and around—the great amphitheatre at her feet—the breeze that came in her face fresh and chill, and touched with rain—the miracles of tiny moss and herbage lying low beneath those fallen leaves—the pale autumn sky, so dark and stormy—the autumn winds, which wailed o' nights—the picturesque and many-featured change which stole over everything—carried a new and strange delight to the mind of Agnes. She alone cared to wander by herself through the wood, with its crushed ferns, its piled faggots of firewood, its yellow leaves, which every breeze stripped down. She was busy with the new book, too, which was very like to be wanted before it came; for all these expenses, and the license which their supposed wealth had given them, had already very much reduced the little store of five-pound notes, kept for safety in Papa's desk.

One afternoon during this time of suspense and uncertainty, the Rector repeated his call at the Lodge. The Rector had never forgiven Agnes that unfortunate revelation of her authorship; yet he had looked to her notwithstanding through those strange sermons of his, with a constantly-increasing appeal to her attention. She was almost disposed to fancy sometimes that he made special fiery defences of himself and his sentiments, which seemed addressed to her only; and Agnes fled from the idea with distress and embarrassment, thinking it a vanity of her own. On this day, however, the Rector was a different man—the cloud was off his brow—the apparent restraint, uneasy and galling, under which he had seemed to hold himself, was removed; a flash of aroused spirit was in his eye—his very step was eager, and sounded with a bolder ring upon the gravel of the garden path—there was no longer the parochial bow, the clergymanly address, or the restless consciousness of something unreal in both, which once characterised him; he entered among them almost abruptly, and did not say a word of his parishioners, but instead, asked for Louis—told Rachel his sister wished to see her—and, glancing with unconcealed dislike at poor Agnes's blotting-book, wished to know if Miss Atheling was writing now.

"Mr Rivers does not think it right, mamma," said Agnes. She blushed a little under her consciousness of his look of displeasure, but smiled also with a kind of challenge as she met his eye.

"No," said the young clergyman abruptly; "I admire, above all things, understanding and intelligence. I can suppose no appreciation so quick and entire as a woman's; but she fails of her natural standing to me, when I come to hear of her productions, and am constituted a critic—that is a false relationship between a woman and a man."

And Mr Rivers looked at Agnes with an answering flash of pique and offence, which was as much as to say, "I am very much annoyed; I had thought of very different relationships; and it is all owing to you."

"Many very good critics," said Mrs Atheling, piqued in her turn—"a great many people, I assure you, who know about such things, have been very much pleased with Agnes's book."

The Rector made no answer—did not even make a pause—but as if all this was merely irrelevant and an interruption to his real business, said rapidly, yet with some solemnity, and without a word of preface, "Lord Winterbourne's son is dead."

"Who?" said Agnes, whom, unconsciously, he was addressing—and they all turned to him with a little anxiety. Rachel became very pale, and even Marian, who was not thinking at all of what Mr Rivers said, drew a little nearer the table, and looked up at him wistfully, with her beautiful eyes.

"Lord Winterbourne's son, George Rivers, the heir of the family—he who has been abroad so long; a young man, I hear, whom every one esteemed," said the Rector, bending down his head, as if he exacted from himself a certain sadness, and did indeed endeavour to see how sad it was—"he is dead."

Mrs Atheling rose, greatly moved. "Oh, Mr Rivers!—did you say his son? his only son? a young man? Oh, I pray God have pity upon him! It will kill him;—it will be more than he can bear!"

The Rector looked up at the grief in the good mother's face, with a look and gesture of surprise. "I never heard any one give Lord Winterbourne credit for so much feeling," he said, looking at her with some suspicion; "and surely he has not shown much of it to you."

"Oh, feeling! don't speak of feeling!" cried Mrs Atheling. "It is not that I am thinking of. You know a great many things, Mr Rivers, but you never lost a child."

"No," he said; and then, after a pause, he added, in a lower tone, "in the whole matter, certainly, I never before thought of Lord Winterbourne."

And there was nobody nigh to point out to him what a world beyond and above his philosophy was this simple woman's burst of nature. Yet in his own mind he caught a moment's glimpse of it; for the instant he was abashed, and bent his lofty head with involuntary self-humiliation; but looking up, saw his own thought still clearer in the eye of Agnes, and turned defiant upon her, as if it had been a spoken reproof.

"Well!" he said, turning to her, "was I to blame for thinking little of the possibility of grief in such a man?"

"I did not say so," said Agnes, simply; but she looked awed and grave, as the others did. They had no personal interest at all in the matter; they thought in an instant of the vacant places in their own family, and stood silent and sorrowful, looking at the great calamity which made another house desolate. They never thought of Lord Winterbourne, who was their enemy; they only thought of a father who had lost his son.

And Rachel, who remembered George Rivers, and thought in the tenderness of the moment that he had been rather kind to her, wept a few tears silently.

All these things disconcerted the Rector. He was impatient of excess of sympathy—ebullitions of feeling; he was conscious of a restrained, yet intense spring of new hope and vigour in his own life. He had endeavoured conscientiously to regret his cousin; but it was impossible to banish from his own mind the thought that he was free—that a new world opened to his ambition—that he was the heir!

And he had come, unaware of his own motive, to share this overpowering and triumphant thought with Agnes Atheling, a girl who was no mate for him, as inferior in family fortune and breeding as it was possible to imagine—and now stood abashed and reproved to see that all his simple auditors thought at once, not of him and his altered position, but of those grand and primitive realities—Death and Grief. He went away hastily and with impatience, displeased with them and with himself—went away on a rapid walk for miles out of his way, striding along the quiet country roads as if for a race; and a race it was, with his own thoughts, which still were fastest, and not to be overtaken. He knew the truths of philosophy, the limited lines and parallels of human logic and reason; but he had not been trained among the great original truths of nature; he knew only what was true to the mind,—not what was true to the heart.

CHAPTER IX

"Come down, Agnes, make haste; mamma wants you—and Miss Anastasia's carriage is just driving up to the door."

So said Marian, coming languidly into their sleeping-room, and quite indifferent to Miss Anastasia. She was rather glad indeed to hasten Agnes away, to make an excuse for herself, and gain a half-hour of solitude to read over again Louis's letter. It was worth while to get letters like those of Louis. Marian sat down on one of Miss Bridget's old-fashioned chairs, and leaned her beautiful head against its high unyielding angular back. The cover on it was of an ancient blue-striped tabinet, faded, yet still retaining some of its colour, which answered very well to relieve those beautiful half-curled, half-braided locks of Marian's hair, which had such a tendency to escape from all kinds of bondage. She lay there half reclining upon this stiff uneasy piece of furniture, not at all disturbed by its angularity, her pretty cheek flushing, her pretty lips trembling into half-conscious smiles, reading over again Louis's letter, which she held after an embracing fashion in both her hands.

And Rachel, with great diffidence, yet by the Rector's invitation, had gone to visit Miss Rivers at the Old Wood House. When the other Miss Rivers, chief of the name, entered the little parlour of the Lodge, she found the mother and daughter, who were both acquainted with her secret, awaiting her very anxiously. She came in with a grave face and deliberate step. She had not changed her dress in any particular, except the colour of her bonnet, which was black, and had some woeful decorations of crape; but it was evident that she too had been greatly moved and impressed by her young cousin's death.

"He is dead," she said, almost as abruptly as the Rector, when she had taken her usual place. "Yes, poor young George Rivers, who was the heir of the house—it was very well for him that he should die."

"Oh, Miss Rivers!" said Mrs Atheling, "I am very, very sorry for poor Lord Winterbourne."

"Are you?" said Miss Anastasia;—"perhaps you are right,—he will feel this, I dare say, as much as he can feel anything—but I was sorry for the boy. Young people think it hard to die—fools!—they don't know the blessing that lies in it. Living long enough to come to the crown of youth, and dying in its blossom—that's a lot fit for an angel. Agnes Atheling, never look through your tears at me."

But Agnes could not help looking at the old lady wistfully, with her young inquiring eyes.

"What does the Rector do here?—they tell me he comes often," said Miss Rivers. "Do you know that now, so far as people understand, he comes to be heir of Winterbourne?"

"He came to tell us yesterday of the poor young gentleman's death," said Mrs Atheling, "and I thought he seemed a little excited. Agnes, I am sure you observed it as well as I."

"No, mamma," said Agnes, turning away hastily. She went to get some work, that no one might observe her own looks, with a sudden nervous tremor and impatience upon her. The Rector had been very kind to Louis, had done a brother's part to him—far more than any one else in the world had ever done to this friendless youth—yet Louis's friends were labouring with all their might, working in darkness like evil-doers, to undermine the supposed right of Lionel—that right which made his breast expand and his brow clear, and freed him from an uncongenial fate. Agnes sat down trembling, with a sudden nervous access of vexation, disappointment, annoyance, which she could not explain. She had been accustomed for a long time now to follow him with interest and sympathy, and to read his thoughts in those wild public self-revelations of his, which no one penetrated but herself; but she felt actually guilty, a plotter, and concerned against him now.

"I am sorry for Lionel," said Miss Rivers, who had not lost a single fluctuation of colour on Agnes's cheek, nor tremble of emotion in her hurried hands—"but it would have been more grievous for poor George had he lived. There will be only disappointment—not disgrace—for any other heir."

She paused awhile, still watching Agnes, who bent over her work, greatly disposed to cry, and in a very agitated condition of mind. Then she said as suddenly as before, "I forget my proper errand—I have come for the girls. You are to go up with me to the Priory. Go, make haste—put on your bonnet—I never wait, even for young ladies; call your sister, and make ready to go."

Agnes rose, startled and unwilling, and cast an inquiring look at Mamma. Mrs Atheling was startled too, but she was not insensible to the pride and glory of seeing her two daughters drive off to Abingford Priory in the well-known carriage of Miss Anastasia. "Since Miss Rivers is so good, make haste, my dear," said Mrs Atheling; and Agnes had no alternative but to obey.

When she was gone, Miss Rivers looked round the room inquisitively. Rachel was no great needlewoman, nor much instructed in ordinary feminine pursuits; there were no visible traces of the presence of a third young lady in the little dim parlour. "Where is the girl?" said Miss Anastasia, cautiously,—"I was told she was here."

"The Rector asked her to go and see his sister—she is at the Old Wood House," said Mrs Atheling. "I am very sorry—but we never thought of you coming to-day."

"I might come any day," said Miss Rivers, abruptly—"but that is not the question—I prefer not to see her—she is a frightened little dove of a girl—she is not in my way. Is she good for anything?—you ought to know."

"She is a very sweet, amiable girl," said Mrs Atheling, warmly—"and she sings as I never heard any one sing, all my life."

"Ah!" said Miss Rivers, with a look of gratification, "it belongs to the family—music is a tradition among us—yes, yes! You remember my great-grandfather, the fourth lord—he was a great composer." Miss Anastasia was perfectly destitute of the faculty herself, and more than half of the Riverses wanted that humblest of all musical qualifications, "an ear"—yet it was amusing to mark the eagerness of the old lady to find a family precedent for every quality known as belonging to Louis or his sister. "I recollect," added Miss Rivers, bending her brows darkly, "they wanted to make a singer of her—the more disgrace the better—Oh, I understand their tactics! You are sorry for him?—look at the devilish plans he made."

Mrs Atheling shook her head, but did not reply; she only knew that she would have been sorry for the vilest criminal in the world, had he lost his only son.

"I have heard from your boy," said Miss Rivers. "He is gone now, I suppose. What does Will Atheling think of his son? If he does but as I expect he will, the boy's fortune is made; he shall never repent that he did this service for me."

"But it is a great undertaking," said Mrs Atheling. "I know Charlie will do his best—he is a very good boy, Miss Rivers; but he may not succeed after all."

"He will succeed," said the old lady; "but even if he does not—which I cannot believe—so long as he does all he can, it will not alter me."

The mother's heart swelled high with gratification and pleasure; yet there was a drawback. All this time—since the first day when she heard of it, before she made her discovery—Miss Anastasia had never referred to the engagement between Louis and Marian. Did she desire to discourage it? Was she likely to perceive a difference in this respect between Louis nameless and without friends, and Louis the heir of Winterbourne?

But Mrs Atheling's utmost penetration could not tell. Miss Rivers began to pull down the books, to look at them, to strike her riding-whip on the floor, and call out good-humouredly in her loud voice, which every one in the house could hear, that she was not to be kept waiting by a parcel of girls. Finally the girls made their appearance in their best dresses; their new patroness hurried them into her carriage, and drove instantly away.

CHAPTER X

MARIAN ON TRIAL

Miss Anastasia "preferred not to see" Rachel—yet, with a wayward inclination still, was moved to drive by a circuitous road in front of the Old Wood House, where the girl was. The little vehicle went heavily along the grassy road, cutting the turf, but making little sound as it rolled past the windows of the invalid. There was the velvet lawn, the trim flower-plots, the tall autumnal flowers, the straight and well-kept garden-paths, lying vacant and shadowless beneath the sun—but there was nothing to be discovered under the closed blinds of this shut-up and secluded house.

"Why do they keep their blinds down?" said Miss Anastasia; "all the house surely is not one invalid's room? Lucy was a little fool always. I do not believe there is anything the matter with her. She had what these soft creatures call a disappointment in love—words have different meanings, child. And why does this girl go to see Lucy Rivers? I suppose because she is such a one herself."

"It is because Miss Rivers was kind to her," said Agnes; "and the Rector asked her to go—"

"The Rector? Do you mean to tell me," said Miss Anastasia, turning quickly upon her companion, "that when Lionel Rivers comes to the Lodge it is for her he comes?"

"I do not know," said Agnes. She was provoked to feel how her face burned under the old lady's gaze. She could not help showing something of the anger and vexation she felt. She looked up hastily, with a glance of resentment. "He has been very much interested in Louis—he has been very kind to him," said Agnes, not at all indisposed, for the sake of the Rector, whom every one plotted against, to throw down her glove to Miss Anastasia. "I believe, indeed, it has been to inquire about Louis, that he ever came to the Lodge."

Miss Anastasia touched her ponies with her whip, and said, "Humph!" "Both of them! odd enough," said the old lady. Agnes, who was considerably offended, and not at all in an amicable state of mind, did not choose to inquire who Miss Anastasia meant by "both of them," nor what it was that was "odd enough."

Marian occupied the seat behind. She liked it very well, though she would rather have written her letter to Louis. She did not quite hear the conversation before her, and did not much care about it. Marian recognised the old lady only as Agnes's friend, and had never connected her in any way with her own fortunes. She was shy of speaking in that stately presence; she was even resentful sometimes of the remarks of Miss Anastasia; and the lofty old gentlewoman had formed but an indifferent idea yet of the little beauty. She was amused with the pretty pout of Marian's lip, the sparkle, sometimes of fun, sometimes of petulance, in her eye; but Marian would have been extremely dismayed to-day had she known that she, and not Agnes, was the principal object of Miss Anastasia's visit, and was, indeed, about to be put upon her trial, to see if she was good for anything. At all events, she was quite at ease and unalarmed now.

They drove along in silence for some time after this—passing through the village and past the Park gates. Then Miss Anastasia took a road quite unfamiliar to the girls—a grass-grown unfrequented path, lying under the shadow of the trees of Winterbourne. She did not say a word till they came to a sudden break in the trees, when she stopped her ponies abruptly, and fixed a sorrowful gaze upon the Hall, which was visible, and close at hand. The white, broad, majestic front of the great house was not unlike a funeral pile at any time; now, with white curtains drawn close over all its scarcely perceptible windows, still veiled in the pomp of mourning, without a gleam of light or colour, in its blind, grand aspect, turning its back upon the sun—there was something very sadly imposing in the desolated house. No one was to be seen about it—not even a servant: it looked like a vast mausoleum, sacred to the dead. "It was very well for him," said Miss Anastasia with a sigh, "very well. If it were not so pitiful a thing to think of, children, I could thank God."

But as the old lady spoke, the tears stood heavy in her eyes.

This was very dreadful, very mysterious, altogether beyond comprehension to Marian. She was glad to turn her eyes away from the house with dislike and terror—it had been Louis's prison and place of suffering, and not a single hope connected with the Hall of Winterbourne was in Marian's mind. She drew back from Miss Rivers with a shudder—she thought it was the most frightful thing in existence to thank God because this young man had died.

The Priory opened its doors wide to its mistress and her young guests. She led them herself to her favourite room, a very strange place, indeed, to their inexperienced eyes. It was a long narrow room, built over the archway which crossed the entrance to the town of Abingford. This of itself was peculiarity enough; and the walls were of stone, wainscoted to half their height with oak, and the roof was ribbed with strong old oaken rafters, and of course unceiled. Windows on either side, plain lattice-windows, with thick mullions of stone, admitted the light in strips between heavy bars of shadow, and commanded a full sight of every one who entered the town of Abingford. On the country side was a long country road, some trees, and the pale convolutions of the river; on the other, there was a glimpse of the market-place of the town, even now astir with a leisurely amount of business, in the centre of which rose an extraordinary building with a piazza, while round it were the best shops of Abingford, and the farmers' inns, which were full on market days. A little old church, rich with the same rude Saxon ornament which decorated the church of Winterbourne, stood modestly among the houses at the corner of the market-place. A few leisurely figures, such as belong to country towns, stood at the doors, or lounged about the pavement; and market-carts came and went slowly under the arch. Marian brightened into positive amusement; she thought it very funny indeed to watch the people and the vehicles slowly disappearing beneath her, and laughed to herself, and thought it a very odd fancy of Miss Anastasia, to choose her favourite sitting-room here.

The old lady came and stood beside her, somewhat to the embarrassment of Marian. She bade the girl take off her bonnet, which produced its unfailing result, of throwing into a little picturesque confusion those soft, silken, half-curled tresses of Marian's hair. Marian looked out of the window somewhat nervously, a little afraid of Miss Rivers. The old lady looked at her with a keen scrutiny. She was stooping her pretty shoulders in an attitude which might have been awkward in a form less elastic, dimpling her cheek with the fingers which supported it, conscious of Miss Anastasia's gaze, somewhat alarmed, and very shy. In spite of the shrinking, the alarm, and the embarrassment, Miss Rivers looked steadily down upon her with a serious inspection. But even the cloud which began to steal over Marian's brow could not disenchant the eyes that gazed upon her—Miss Anastasia began to smile as everybody else; to feel herself moved to affection, tenderness, regard; to own the fascination which no one resisted. "My dear, you are very pretty," said the old lady, entirely forgetting any prudent precautions on the score of making Marian vain; "many people would tell you, that, with a face like that, you need no other attraction. But I was once pretty myself, and I know it does not last for ever; do you ever think about anything, you lovely little child?"

Marian glanced up with an indignant blush and frown; but the look she met was so kind, that it was not possible to answer as she intended. So the pretty head sank down again upon the hand which supported it. She took a little time to compose herself, and then, with some humility, spoke the truth: "I am afraid, not a great deal."

"What do you suppose I do here, all by myself?" said Miss Anastasia, suddenly.

Marian turned her face towards her, looked round the room, and then turned a wistful gaze to Miss Rivers. "Indeed, I do not know," said Marian, in a very low and troubled tone: it was youth, with awe and gravity and pity, looking out of its bright world upon the loneliness and poverty of age.

That answer and that look brought the examination to a very hasty and sudden conclusion. The old lady looked at her for an instant with a startled glance, stooped over her, kissed her forehead and hurried away. Marian could not tell what she had done, nor why Miss Anastasia's face changed so strangely. She could not comprehend the full force of the contrast, nor how her own simple wonder and pity struck like a sudden arrow to the old lady's heart.

Agnes was puzzled too, and could not help her sister to an explanation. They remained by themselves for some time, rather timidly looking at everything. There were a few portraits hanging high upon the walls, portraits which they knew to be of the family, but could not recognise; and there was one picture of a very strange kind, which all their combined ingenuity could not interpret. It was like one of those old Dyptichs used to preserve some rare and precious altarpiece. What was within could not be seen, but on the closed leaves without were painted two solemn angels, with a silvery surrounding of wings, and flowers in their hands. If Miss Anastasia had been a Catholic—even if she had been a dilettante or extreme High Churchwoman, it might have been a little private shrine: perhaps it was so: there was a portrait within, which no eyes but her own ever saw. Between the windows the walls were lined with book-cases; that ancient joke of poor Aunt Bridget's, her own initials underneath her pupil's name—the B. A., which conferred a degree upon Anastasia Rivers—turned out to be an intentional thing after all.

The girls gazed in awe at Miss Anastasia's book-shelves. She was a great scholar, this old lady. She might have been one of the Heads of Houses in the learned city, but for the unfortunate femininity which debarred her. All by herself among these tomes of grey antiquity—all by herself with her pictures, the sole remnant of another time—it was not wonderful that the two girls paused, looking out from the sunshine of their youth with reverence, yet with compassion. They honoured her with natural humility, feeling their own ignorance, but notwithstanding, were very sorry for Miss Anastasia, all by herself—more sorry than there was occasion to be—for Miss Anastasia was used to be all by herself, and found enjoyment in it now.

When Miss Anastasia came back she took them to see her garden, and the state-apartments of her great stately house. When they were a little familiar she let them stray on before her, and followed watching. Agnes, perhaps, was still her own favourite of the two; but all her observation was given to Marian. As her eyes followed this beautiful figure, her look became more and more satisfied; and while Marian wandered with her sister about the garden, altogether unconscious of the great possibilities which awaited her, Miss Anastasia's fancy clothed her in robes of state, and covered her with jewels. "He might have married a duke's daughter," she said to herself, turning away with a pleased eye—"but he might never have found such a beautiful fairy as this: she is a good little child too, with no harm in her; and a face for a fairy queen!"

CHAPTER XI

DISCONTENT

No one knew the real effect of the blow which had just fallen upon Lord Winterbourne. The guests, of whom his house was full, dispersed as if by magic. Even Mrs Edgerley, in the most fashionable sables, with mourning liveries, and the blinds of her carriage solemnly let down, went forth, as soon as decency would permit, from the melancholy Hall. After all the bustle and all the gaiety of recent days, the place fell into a pause of deadly stillness. Lord Winterbourne sought comfort from no one—showed grief to no one; he made a sudden pause, like a man stunned, and then, with increased impetus, and with a force and resolution unusual to him, resumed his ancient way once more, and rushed forward with exaggerated activity. Instead of subduing him, this event seemed to have roused all his faculties into a feverish and busy malevolence, as if the man had said, "I have no one to come after me—I will do all the harm I can while my time lasts." All the other gentry of the midland counties, put together, did not bring so many poachers to "justice" as were brought by Lord Winterbourne. It was with difficulty his solicitor persuaded him to pass over the pettiest trespass upon his property. He shut up pathways privileged from time immemorial, ejected poor tenants, encroached upon the village rights, and oppressed the village patriarchs; and animated as he was by this spirit of ill-will to every one, it was not wonderful that he endeavoured, with all his might, to press on the suit against the Athelings for the recovery of the Old Wood Lodge.

Mrs Atheling and her daughters, unwilling, embarrassed, and totally ignorant of their real means of defence, remained in their house at the pleasure of the lawyer, and much against their own inclination. Mrs Atheling herself, though with a spark of native spirit she had seconded her husband's resolution not to give up his little inheritance, was entirely worried out with the task of defending it, now that Charlie was gone, and winter was approaching, and her heart yearned to her husband and her forsaken house in Bellevue. When she wrote to Mr Atheling, or when she consulted with Agnes, the good mother expressed her opinion very strongly. "If it turns out a mistake about Louis, none of us will care for this place," said Mrs Atheling; "we shall have the expense of keeping it up, and unless we were living in it ourselves, I do not suppose it is worth ten pounds a-year; and if it should turn out true about Louis, of course he would restore it to us, and settle it so that there could be no doubt upon the subject; and indeed, Agnes, my dear, the only sensible plan that I can think of, would be to give it up at once, and go home. I do think it is quite an unfortunate house for the Athelings; there was your father's poor little sister got her death in it; and it is easy to see how much trouble and anxiety have come into our family since we came here."

"But trouble and anxiety might come anywhere, mamma," said Agnes.

"Yes, my dear, that is very true; but we should have known exactly what we had to look for, if Marian had been engaged to some one in Bellevue."

Mamma's counsels, accordingly, were of a very timid and compromising character. She began to be extremely afraid that the Old Wood Lodge, being so near the trees, would be damp after all the autumn rains, and that something might possibly happen to Bell and Beau; and, with all her heart, and without any dispute, she longed exceedingly to be at home. Then there was the pretty pensive Marian, a little love-sick, and pining much for the society of her betrothed. She was a quiet but potent influence, doing what she could to aggravate the discontent of Mamma; and Agnes had to keep up the family courage, and develop the family patience, single-handed. Agnes, in her own private heart, though she did not acknowledge, nor even know it, was not at all desirous to go away.

The conflict accordingly, about this small disputed possession, lay a great deal more between Lord Winterbourne and Miss Anastasia than between that unfriendly nobleman and the house of Atheling. Miss Anastasia came frequently on errands of encouragement to fortify the sinking heart of Mrs Atheling. "My great object is to defer the trial of this matter for six months," said the old lady significantly. "Let it come on, and we will turn the tables then."

She spoke in the presence of Marian, before whom nothing could be said plainly—in the presence of Rachel even, whom it was impossible to avoid seeing, but who always kept timidly in the background—and she spoke with a certain exultation which somewhat puzzled her auditors. Charlie, though he had done nothing yet, had arrived at the scene of his labours. Assured of this fact, the courage of his patroness rose. She was a woman and an optimist, as she confessed. She had the gift of leaping to a conclusion, equal to any girl in the kingdom, and at the present moment was not disturbed by any doubts of success.

"Six months!" cried Mrs Atheling, in dismay and horror; "and do you mean that we must stay here all that time—all the winter, Miss Rivers? It is quite impossible—indeed I could not do it. My husband is all by himself, and I know how much I am wanted at home."

"It is necessary some one should be in possession," said Miss Rivers. "Eh? What does Will Atheling say?—I daresay he thinks it hard enough to be left alone."

Mrs Atheling was very near "giving away." Vexation and anxiety for the moment almost overpowered her self-command. She knew all the buttons must be off Papa's shirts, and stood in grievous fear of a fabulous amount of broken crockery; besides, she had never been so long parted from her husband since their marriage, and very seriously longed for home.

"Of course it is very dreary for him," she said, with a sigh.

"Mr Temple is making application to defer the trial on the score of an important witness who cannot reach this country in time," said Miss Rivers. "Of course my lord will oppose that with all his power; he has a natural terror of witnesses from abroad. When the question is decided, I do not see, for my part, why you should remain. This little one pines to go home, I see—but you, Agnes Atheling, you had better come and stay at the Priory—you love the country, child!"

Both the sisters blushed under the scrutinising eye of Miss Anastasia; but Agnes was not yet reconciled to the old lady. "We are all anxious to go home," she said with spirit, and with considerably more earnestness than the case at all demanded. Miss Rivers smiled a little. She thought she could read a whole romance in the fluctuating colour and troubled glance of Agnes; but she was wrong, as far-seeing people are so often. The girl was disturbed, uneasy, self-conscious, in a startled and impatient condition of mind; but the romance, even if it were on the way, had not yet definitely begun.

CHAPTER XII

A CONVERSATION

Agnes's rambles out of doors had now almost always to be made alone. Rachel was much engrossed with the invalid of the Old Wood House, who had "taken a fancy" to the gentle little girl. The hypochondriac Miss Rivers was glad of any one so tender and respectful; and half in natural pity for the sufferings which Rachel could not believe to be fanciful, half from a natural vocation for kindly help and tendance, the girl was glad to respond to the partly selfish affection of her new friend, who told Rachel countless stories of the family, and the whole chronicle in every particular of her own early "disappointment in love." In return, Rachel, by snatches, conveyed to her invalid friend—in whom, after all, she found some points of interest and congeniality—a very exalted ideal picture of the Athelings, the genius of Agnes, and the love-story of Marian. Marian and Agnes occupied a very prominent place indeed in the talk of that shadowy dressing-room, with all its invalid contrivances—its closed green blinds, its soft mossy carpets, on which no footstep was ever audible, its easy little couches, which you could move with a finger; the luxury, and the stillness, and the gossip, were not at all unpleasant to Rachel; and she read Hope Hazlewood to her companion in little bits, with pauses of talk between. Hope Hazlewood was not nearly romantic enough for the pretty faded invalid reposing among her pillows in her white dressing-gown, whom Time seemed to have forgotten there, and who had no recollection for her own part that she was growing old; but she took all the delight of a girl in hearing of Louis and Marian—how much attached to each other, and how handsome they both were.

And Marian Atheling did not care half so much as she used to do for the long rambles with her sister, which were once such a pleasure to both the girls. Marian rather now preferred sitting by herself over her needlework, or lingering alone at the window, in an entire sweet idleness, full of all those charmed visions with which the very name of Louis peopled all the fairy future. Not the wisest, or the wittiest, or the most brilliant conversation in the world could have half equalled to Marian the dreamy pleasure of her own meditations. So Agnes had to go out alone.

Agnes did not suffer very much from this necessity. She wandered along the skirts of the wood, with a vague sense of freedom and enjoyment not easy to explain in words. No dreamy trance of magic influence had come upon Agnes; her mind, and her heart, and her thoughts, were quickened by a certain thrill of expectation, which was not to be referred to the strange romance now going on in the family—to Charlie's mission, nor Louis's prospects, nor anything else which was definite and ascertained. She knew that her heart rose, that her mind brightened, that her thoughts were restless and light, and not to be controlled; but she could not tell the reason why. She went about exploring all the country byways, and finding little tracks among the brushwood undiscoverable to the common eye; and she was not cogitating anything, scarcely was thinking, but somehow felt within her whole nature a silent growth and increase not to be explained.

She was pondering along, with her eyes upon the wide panorama at her feet, when it chanced to Agnes, suddenly and without preparation, to encounter the Rector. These two young people, who were mutually attracted to each other, had at the present moment a mutual occasion of embarrassment and apparent offence. The Rector could not forget how very much humbled in his own opinion he himself had been on his late visit to the Lodge; he had not yet recovered the singular check given to his own unconscious selfishness, by the natural sympathy of these simple people with the grander primitive afflictions and sufferings of life: and he was not without an idea that Agnes looked upon him now with a somewhat disdainful eye. Agnes, on her part, was greatly oppressed by the secret sense of being concerned against the Rector; in his presence she felt like a culprit—a secret plotter against the hope which brightened his eye, and expanded his mind. A look of trouble came at once into her face; her brow clouded—she thought it was not quite honest to make a show of friendship, while she retained her secret knowledge of the inquiry which might change into all the bitterness of disappointment his sudden and unlooked-for hope.

He had been going in the opposite direction, but, though he was not at all reconciled to her, he was not willing either to part with Agnes. He turned, only half consciously, only half willingly, yet by an irresistible compulsion. He tried indifferent conversation, and so did she; but, in spite of himself, Lionel Rivers was a truer man with Agnes Atheling than he was with any other person in the world. He who had never cared for sympathy from any one, somehow or other felt a necessity for hers, and had a certain imperious disappointment and impatience when it was withheld from him, which was entirely unreasonable, and not to be accounted for. He broke off abruptly from the talk about nothing, to speak of some intended movements of his own.

"I am going to town," said Mr Rivers. "I am somewhat unsettled at present in my intentions; after that, probably, I may spend some time abroad."

"All because he is the heir!" thought Agnes to herself; and again she coloured with distress and vexation. It was impossible to keep something of this from her tone; when she spoke, it was in a voice subdued a little out of its usual tenor; but all that she asked was a casual question, meaning nothing—"If Mr Mead would have the duty while the Rector was away?"

"Yes," said the Rector; "he is very much better fitted for it than I am. Here I have been cramping my wings these three years. Fathers and mothers are bitterly to blame; they bind a man to what his soul loathes, because it is his best method of earning some paltry pittance—so much a-year!"

After this exclamation the young clergyman made a pause, and so did his diffident and uneasy auditor, who "did not like" either to ask his meaning, or to make any comment upon it. After a few minutes he resumed again—

"I suppose it must constantly be so where we dare to think for ourselves," he said, in a tone of self-conversation. "A man who thinks must come to conclusions different from those which are taught to him—different, perhaps, from all that has been concluded truest in the ages that are past. What shall we say? Woe be to me if I do not follow out my reasoning, to whatever length it may lead!"

"When Paul says, Woe be to him, it is, if he does not preach the Gospel," said Agnes.

Mr Rivers smiled. "Be glad of your own happy exemption," he said, turning to her, with the air of a man who knows by heart all the old arguments—all the feminine family arguments against scepticism and dangerous speculations. "I will leave you in possession of your beautiful Gospel—your pure faith. I shall not attempt to disturb your mind—do not fear."

"You could not!" said Agnes, in a sudden and rash defiance. She turned to him in her turn, beginning to tremble a little with the excitement of controversy. She was a young polemic, rather more graceful in its manifestation, but quite as strong in the spirit of the conflict as any Mause Headrigg—which is to say, that, after her eager girlish fashion, she believed with her whole heart, and did not know what toleration meant.

Mr Rivers smiled once more. "I will not try," he said. "I remember what Christ said, and endeavour to have charity even for those who condemn me."

"Oh, Mr Rivers!" cried Agnes suddenly, and with trembling, "do not speak so coldly—do not say Christ; it sounds as if you did not care for Him—as if you thought He was no friend to you."

The Rector paused, somewhat startled: it was an objection which never had occurred to him—one of those subtle touches concerning the spirit and not the letter, which, being perfectly sudden, and quite simple, had some chance of coming to the heart.

"What do you say?" he asked with a little interest.

Agnes's voice was low, and trembled with reverence and with emotion. She was not thinking of him, in his maze of intellectual trifling—she was thinking of that Other, whom she knew so much better, and whose name she spoke. She answered with an involuntary bending of her head—"Our Lord."

It was no conviction that struck the mind of the young man—conviction was not like to come readily to him—and he was far too familiar with all the formal arguments, to be moved by the reasonings of a polemic, or the fervour of an enthusiast. But he who professed so much anxiety about truth, and contemplated himself as a moral martyr, woefully following his principles, though they led him to ever so dark a desolation, had lived all his life among an infinite number of shams, and willingly enough had yielded to many of them. Perhaps this was the first time in his life in which he had been brought into immediate contact with people who were simply true in their feelings and their actions—whose opinions were without controversy—whose settled place in life, humble as it was, shut them out from secondary emulations and ambitions—and who were swayed by the primitive rule of human existence—the labour and the rest, the affliction and the prosperity, which were real things, and not creations of the brain. He paused a little over the words of Agnes Atheling. He did not want her to think as he did: he was content to believe that the old boundaries were suitable and seemly for a woman; and he was rather pleased than otherwise, by the horror, interest, and regret which such opinions as his generally met with. He paused upon her words, with the air of a spectator, and said in a meditative fashion, "It is a glorious faith."

Now Agnes, who was not at all satisfied with this contemplative approval, was entirely ready and eager for controversy; prepared to plunge into it with the utmost rashness, utterly unaccoutred and ignorant as she was. She trembled with suppressed fervour and excitement over all her frame. She was as little a match for the Rector in the argument which she would fain have entered into, as any child in the village; but she was far too strong in the truth of her cause to feel any fear.

"Do you ever meet with great trouble?" said Agnes.

It was quite an unexpected question. The Rector looked at her inquiringly, without the least perception what she meant.

"And when you meet with it," continued the eager young champion, "what do you say?"

Now this was rather a difficult point with the Rector; it was not naturally his vocation to administer comfort to "great trouble"—in reality, when he was brought face to face with it, he had nothing to say. He paused a little, really embarrassed—that was the curate's share of the business. Mr Rivers was very sorry for the poor people, but had, in fact, no consolation to give, and thought it much more important to play with his own mind and faculties in this solemn and conscientious trifling of his, than to attend to the griefs of others. He answered, after some hesitation: "There are different minds, of course, and different influences applicable to them. Every man consoles himself after his own fashion; for some there are the sublime consolations of Philosophy, for others the rites of the Church."

"Some time," said Agnes suddenly, turning upon him with earnest eyes,—"some time, when you come upon great sorrow, will you try the name of our Lord?"

The young man was startled again, and made no answer. He was struck by the singular conviction that this girl, inferior to himself in every point, had a certain real and sublime acquaintance with that wonderful Person of whom she spoke; that this was by no means belief in a doctrine, but knowledge of a glorious and extraordinary Individual, whose history no unbeliever in the world has been able to divest of its original majesty. The idea was altogether new to him; it found an unaccustomed way to the heart of the speculatist—that dormant power which scarcely any one all his life had tried to reach to. "I do not quite understand you," he said somewhat moodily; but he did not attend to what she said afterwards. He pondered upon the problem by himself, and could not make anything of it. Arguments about doctrines and beliefs were patent enough to the young man. He was quite at home among dogmas and opinions—but, somehow, this personal view of the question had a strange advantage over him. He was not prepared for it; its entire and obvious simplicity took away the ground from under his feet. It might be easy enough to persuade a man out of conviction of a doctrine which he believed, but it was a different matter to disturb the identity of a person whom he knew.

CHAPTER XIII

In the mean time, immediate interest in their own occupations had pretty nearly departed from the inhabitants of the Old Wood Lodge. Agnes went on with her writing, Mamma with her work-basket, Marian with her dreams; but desk, and needle, and meditations were all alike abandoned in prospect of the postman, who was to be seen making his approach for a very long way, and was watched every day with universal anxiety. What Louis was doing, what Charlie was doing, the progress of the lawsuit, and the plans of Miss Anastasia, continually drew the thoughts of the household away from themselves. Even Rachel's constant report of the unseen invalid, Miss Lucy, added to the general withdrawal of interest from the world within to the world without. They seemed to have nothing to do themselves in their feminine quietness. Mamma sat pondering over her work—about her husband, who was alone, and did not like his solitude—about Charlie, who was intrusted with so great a commission—about "all the children"—every one of whom seemed to be getting afloat on a separate current of life. Agnes mused over her business with impatient thoughts about the Rector, with visions of Rachel and Miss Lucy in the invalid chamber, and vain attempts to look into the future and see what was to come. As for Marian, the charmed tenor of her fancies knew no alteration; she floated on, without interruption, in a sweet vision, full of a thousand consistencies, and wilder than any romance. Their conversation ran no longer in the ancient household channel, and was no more about their own daily occupations; they were spectators eagerly looking from the windows at nearly a dozen different conflicts, earnestly concerned, and deeply sympathetic, but not in the strife themselves.

Louis had entered Mr Foggo's office; it seemed a strange destination for the young man. He did not tell any one how small a remuneration he received for his labours, nor how he contrived to live in the little room, in the second floor of one of those Islington houses. He succeeded in existing—that was enough; and Louis did not chafe at his restrained and narrow life, by reason of having all his faculties engaged and urgent in a somewhat fanciful mode, of securing the knowledge which he longed for concerning his own birth and derivation. He had ascertained from Mr Atheling every particular concerning the Rivers family which he knew. He had even managed to seek out some old servants once at the Hall, and with a keen and intense patience had listened to every word of a hundred aimless and inconclusive stories from these respectable authorities. He was compiling, indeed, neither more nor less than a life of Lord Winterbourne—a history which he endeavoured to verify in every particular as he went on, and which was written with the sternest impartiality—a plain and clear record of events. Perhaps a more remarkable manuscript than that of Louis never existed; and he pursued his tale with all the zest, and much more than the excitement, of a romancer. It was a true story, of which he laboured to find out every episode; and there was a powerful unity and constructive force in the one sole unvarying interest of the tale. Mr Atheling had been moved to tell the eager youth all the particulars of his early acquaintance with Lord Winterbourne—and still the story grew—the object of the whole being to discover, as Louis himself said, "what child there was whom it was his interest to disgrace and defame." The young man followed hotly upon this clue. His thoughts had not been directed yet to anything resembling the discovery of Miss Anastasia; it had never occurred to him that his disinheritance might be absolutely the foundation of all Lord Winterbourne's greatness; but he hovered about the question with a singular pertinacity, and gave his full attention to it. Inspired by this, he did not consider his meagre meal, his means so narrow that it was the hardest matter in the world to eat daily bread. He pursued his story with a concentration of purpose which the greatest poet in existence might have envied. He was a great deal too much in earnest to think about the sentences in which he recorded what he learnt. The consequence was, that this memoir of Lord Winterbourne was a model of terse and pithy English—an unexampled piece of biography. Louis did not say a word about it to any one, but pursued his labour and his inquiry together, vainly endeavouring to find out a trace of some one whom he could identify with himself.

Meanwhile, Papa began to complain grievously of his long abandonment, and moved by Louis on one side, and by his own discomfort on the other, became very decided in his conviction that there was no due occasion for the absence of his family. There was great discontent in Number Ten, Bellevue, and there was an equal discontent, rather more overpowering, and quite as genuine, in the Old Wood Lodge, where Mamma and Marian vied with each other in anxiety, and thought no cause sufficiently important to keep them any longer from home. Agnes expressed no opinion either on one side or the other; she was herself somewhat disturbed and unsettled, thinking a great deal more about the Rector than was at all convenient, or to her advantage. After that piece of controversy, the Rector began to come rather often to the Lodge. He never said a word again touching that one brief breath of warfare, yet they eyed each other distrustfully, with a mutual consciousness of what had occurred, and might occur again. It was not a very lover-like point of union, yet it was a secret link of which no one else knew. Unconsciously it drew Agnes into inferences and implications, which were spoken at the Rector; and unconsciously it drew him to more sympathy with common trials, and a singular inclination to experiment, as Agnes had bidden him, with her sublime talisman—that sole Name given under heaven, which has power to touch into universal brotherhood the whole universal heart of man.

CHAPTER XIV

NEWS

While the Lodge remained in this ferment of suspense and uncertainty, Miss Anastasia had taken her measures for its defence and preservation. It was wearing now towards the end of October, and winter was setting in darkly. There was no more than a single rose at a time now upon the porch, and these roses looked so pale, pathetic, and solitary, that it was rather sad than pleasant to see the lonely flowers. On one of the darkest days of the month, when they were all rather more listless than usual, Miss Anastasia's well-known equipage drew up at the gate. They all hailed it with some pleasure. It was an event in the dull day and discouraging atmosphere. She came in with her loud cheerful voice, her firm step, her energetic bearing—and even the pretty fiancée Marian raised her pretty stooping shoulders, and woke up from her fascinated musing. Rachel alone drew shyly towards the door; she had not overcome a timidity very nearly approaching fear, which she always felt in presence of Miss Anastasia. She was the only person who ever entered this house who made Rachel remember again her life at the Hall.

"I came to show you a letter from your boy; read it while I talk to the children," said Miss Rivers. Mrs Atheling took the letter with some nervousness; she was a little fluttered, and lost the sense of many of the expressions; yet lingered over it, notwithstanding, with pride and exultation. She longed very much to have an opportunity of showing it to Agnes; but that was not possible; so Mrs Atheling made a virtuous attempt to preserve in her memory every word that her son said. This was Charlie's letter to his patroness:—

"MADAM,—I have not made very much progress yet. The courier, Jean Monte, is to be heard of as you suggested; but it is only known on the road that he lives in Switzerland, and keeps some sort of inn in one of the mountain villages. No more as yet; but I will find him out. I have to be very cautious at present, because I am not yet well up in the language. The town is a ruinous place, and I cannot get the parish registers examined as one might do in England. There are several families of decayed nobles in the immediate neighbourhood, and, so far as I can hear, Giulietta is a very common name. Travelling Englishmen, too, are so frequent that there is a good deal of difficulty. I am rather inclined to fix upon the villa Remori, where there are said to have been several English marriages. It has been an extensive place, but is now broken down, decayed, and neglected; the family have a title, and are said to be very handsome, but are evidently very poor. There is a mother and a number of daughters, only one or two grown up; I try to make acquaintance with the children. The father died early, and had no brothers. I think possibly this might be the house of Giulietta, as there is no one surviving to look after the rights of her children, did she really belong to this family. Of course, any relatives she had, with any discretion, would have inquired out her son in England; so I incline to think she may have belonged to the villa Remori, as there are only women there.

"I have to be very slow on account of my Italian—this, however, remedies itself every day. I shall not think of looking for Monte till I have finished my business here, and am on my way home. The place is unprosperous and unhealthy, but it is pretty, and rather out of the way—few travellers came, they tell me, till within ten years ago; but I have not met with any one yet whose memory carried back at all clearly for twenty years. A good way out of the town, near the lake, there is a kind of mausoleum which interests me a little, not at all unlike the family tomb at Winterbourne; there is no name upon it; it lies quite out of the way, and I cannot ascertain that any one has ever been buried there; but something may be learned about it, perhaps, by-and-by.

"When I ascertain anything of the least importance, I shall write again.

"Madam,

"Your Obedient Servant,

"Charles Atheling."

Charlie had never written to a lady before; he was a little embarrassed about it the first time, but this was his second epistle, and he had become a little more at his ease. The odd thing about the correspondence was, that Charlie did not express either hopes or opinions; he did not say what he expected, or what were his chances of success—he only reported what he was doing; any speculation upon the subject, more especially at this crisis, would have been out of Charlie's way.

"What do you call your brother when you write to him?" asked Miss Anastasia abruptly, addressing Rachel.

Rachel coloured violently; she had so nearly forgotten her old system—her old representative character—that she was scarcely prepared to answer such a question. With a mixture of her natural manner and her assumed one, she answered at last, in considerable confusion, "We call him Louis; he has no other name."

"Then he will not take the name of Rivers?" said Miss Anastasia, looking earnestly at the shrinking girl.

"We have no right to the name of Rivers," said Rachel, drawing herself up with her old dignity, like a little queen. "My brother is inquiring who we are. We never belonged to Lord Winterbourne."

"Your brother is inquiring? So!" said Miss Anastasia; "and he is perfectly right. Listen, child—tell him this from me—do you know what Atheling means? It means noble, illustrious, royally born. In the old Saxon days the princes were called Atheling. Tell your brother that Anastasia Rivers bids him bear this name."

This address entirely confused Rachel, who remained gazing at Miss Rivers blankly, unable to say anything. Marian stirred upon her chair with sudden eagerness, and put down her needlework, gazing also, but after quite a different fashion, in Miss Anastasia's face. The old lady caught the look of both, but only replied to the last.

"You are startled, are you, little beauty? Did you never hear the story of Margaret Atheling, who was an exile, and a saint, and a queen? My child, I should be very glad to make sure that you were a true Atheling too."

Marian was not to be diverted from her curiosity by any such observation. She cast a quick look from Miss Rivers to her mother, who was pondering over Charlie's letter, and from Mrs Atheling to Agnes, who had not been startled by the strange words of Miss Anastasia; and suspicion, vague and unexplainable, began to dawn in Marian's mind.

"The autumn assizes begin to-day," said Miss Anastasia with a little triumph; "too soon, as Mr Temple managed it, for your case to have a hearing; it must stand over till the spring now—six months—by that time, please God; we shall be ready for them. Agnes Atheling, how long is it since you began to be deaf and blind?"

Agnes started with a little confusion, and made a hurried inarticulate answer. There was a little quiet quarrel all this time going on between Agnes and Miss Rivers; neither the elder lady nor the younger was quite satisfied—Agnes feeling herself something like a conspirator, and Miss Anastasia a little suspicious of her, as a disaffected person in the interest of the enemy. But Mamma by this time had come to an end of Charlie's letter, and, folding it up very slowly, gave it back to its proprietor. The good mother did not feel it at all comfortable to keep this information altogether to herself.

"It is not to be tried till spring!" said Mrs Atheling, who had caught this observation. "Then, I think, indeed, Miss Rivers, we must go home."

And, to Mamma's great comfort, Miss Anastasia made no objection. She said kindly that she should miss her pleasant neighbours. "But what may be in the future, girls, no one knows," said Miss Rivers, getting up abruptly. "Now, however, before this storm comes on, I am going home."

CHAPTER XV

GOING HOME

After this the family made immediate preparations for their return. Upon this matter Rachel was extremely uncomfortable, and much divided in her wishes. Miss Lucy, who had been greatly solaced by the gentle ministrations of this mild little girl, insisted very much that Rachel should remain with her until her friends returned in spring, or till her brother had "established himself." Rachel herself did not know what to do; and her mind was in a very doubtful condition, full of self-arguments. She did not think Louis would be pleased—that was the dark side. The favourable view was, that she was of use to the invalid, and remaining with her would be "no burden to any one." Rachel pondered, wept, and consulted over it with much sincerity. From the society of these young companions, whom the simple girl loved, and who were so near her own age; from Louis, her lifelong ruler and example; from the kindly fireside, to which she had looked forward so long—it was hard enough to turn to the invalid chambers, the old four-volume novels, and poor pretty old Miss Lucy's "disappointment in love." "And if afterwards I had to sing or give lessons, I should forget all my music there," said Rachel. Mrs Atheling kindly stepped in and decided for her. "It might be a very good thing for you, my dear, if you had no friends," said Mrs Atheling. Rachel did not know whether to be most puzzled or grateful; but to keep a certain conscious solemnity out of her tone—a certain mysterious intimation of something great in the future—was out of the power of Mamma.

Accordingly, they all began their preparations with zeal and energy, the only indifferent member of the party being Agnes, who began to feel herself a good deal alone, and to suspect that she was indeed in the enemy's interest, and not so anxious about the success of Louis as she ought to have been. A few days after Miss Anastasia's visit, the Rector came to find them in all the bustle of preparation. He appeared among them with a certain solemnity, looking haughty and offended, and received Mrs Atheling's intimation of their departure with a grave and punctilious bow. He had evidently known it before, and he looked upon it, quite as evidently, as something done to thwart him—a personal offence to himself.

"Miss Atheling perhaps has literary occupation to call her to town," suggested Mr Rivers, returning to his original ground of displeasure, and trying to get up a little quarrel with Agnes. She did not reply to him, but her mother did, on her behalf.

"Indeed, Mr Rivers, it does not make any difference to Agnes; she can write anywhere," said Mrs Atheling. "I often wonder how she gets on amongst us all; but my husband has been left so long by himself—and now that the trial does not come on till spring, we are all so thankful to get home."

"The trial comes on in spring?—I shall endeavour to be at home," said the Rector, "if I can be of any service. I am myself going to town; I am somewhat unsettled in my plans at present—but my friends whom I esteem most are in London—people of scientific and philosophical pursuits, who cannot afford to be fashionable. Shall I have your permission to call on you when we are all there?"

"I am sure we shall all be very much pleased," said Mrs Atheling, flattered by his tone—"you know what simple people we are, and we do not keep any company; but we shall be very pleased, and honoured too, to see you as we have seen you here."

Agnes was a little annoyed by her mother's speech. She looked up with a flash of indignation, and met, not the eyes of Mrs Atheling, but those of Mr Rivers, who was looking at her. The eyes had a smile in them, but there was perfect gravity upon the face. She was confused by the look, though she did not know why. The words upon her lip were checked—she looked down again, and began to arrange her papers with a rising colour. The Rector's look wandered from her face, because he perceived that he embarrassed her, but went no further than her hands, which were pretty hands enough, yet nothing half so exquisite as those rose-tipped fairy fingers with which Marian folded up her embroidery. The Rector had no eyes at all for Marian; but he watched the arrangement of Agnes's papers with a quite involuntary interest—detected in an instant when she misplaced one, and was very much disposed to offer his own assistance, relenting towards her. What he meant by it—he who was really the heir of Lord Winterbourne, and by no means unaware of his own advantages—Mrs Atheling, looking on with quick-witted maternal observation, could not tell.

Then quite abruptly—after he had watched all Agnes's papers into the pockets of her writing-book—he rose to go away; then he lingered over the ceremony of shaking hands with her, and held hers longer than there was any occasion for. "Some time I hope to resume our argument," said Mr Rivers. He paused till she answered him: "I do not know about argument," said Agnes, looking up with a flash of spirit—"I should be foolish to try it against you. I know only what I trust in—that is not argument—I never meant it so."

He made no reply save by a bow, and went away leaving her rather excited, a little angry, a little moved. Then they began to plague her with questions—What did Mr Rivers mean? There was nothing in the world which Agnes knew less of than what Mr Rivers meant. She tried to explain, in a general way, the conversation she had with him before, but made an extremely lame explanation, which no one was satisfied with, and escaped to her own room in a very nervous condition, quite disturbed out of her self-command. Agnes did not at all know what to make of her anomalous feelings. She was vexed to the heart to feel how much she was interested, while she disapproved so much, and with petulant annoyance exclaimed to herself, that she wanted no more argument if he would but let her alone!

And then came the consideration of Lionel's false hope—the hope which some of these days would be taken from him in a moment. If she could only let him know what she knew, her conscience would be easy. As she thought of this, she remembered how people have been told in fables secrets as important; the idea flashed into her mind with a certain relief—then came the pleasure of creation, the gleam of life among her maze of thoughts; the fancy brightened into shape and graceful fashion—she began unconsciously to hang about it the shining garments of genius—and so she rose and went about her homely business, putting together the little frocks of Bell and Beau, ready to be packed, with the vision growing and brightening before her eyes. Then the definite and immediate purpose of it gave way to a pure native delight in the beautiful thing which began to grow and expand in her thoughts. She went down again, forgetting her vexation. If it did no other good in the world, there was the brightest stream of practical relief and consolation in Agnes Atheling's gift.

CHAPTER XVI

NEW INFLUENCES

Once more the Old Wood Lodge stood solitary under the darkening wintry skies, with no bright faces at its windows, nor gleam of household firelight in the dim little parlour, where Miss Bridget's shadow came back to dwell among the silence, a visionary inhabitant. Once more Hannah sat solitary in her kitchen, lamenting that it was "lonesomer nor ever," and pining for the voices of the children. Hannah would have almost been content to leave her native place and her own people to accompany the family to London; but that was out of the question; and, spite of all Mamma's alarms, Susan had really conducted herself in a very creditable manner under her great responsibility as housekeeper at Bellevue.

The journey home was not a very eventful one. They were met by Papa and Louis on their arrival, and conducted in triumph to their own little house, which did not look so attractive, by any means, as it used to do. Then they settled down without more ado into the family use and wont. With so great a change in all their prospects and intentions—so strange an enlargement of their horizon and extension of their hopes—it was remarkable how little change befell the outward life and customs of the family. Marian, it was true, was "engaged;" but Marian might have been engaged to poor Harry Oswald without any great variation of circumstances; and that was always a possibility lying under everybody's eyes. It did not yet disturb the habits of the family; but this new life which they began to enter—this life of separated and individual interest—took no small degree of heart and spirit out of those joint family pleasures and occupations into which Marian constantly brought a reference to Louis, which Agnes passed through with a preoccupied and abstracted mind, and from which Charlie was far away. The stream widened, the sky grew broader, yet every one had his or her separate and peculiar firmament. A maturer, perhaps, and more complete existence was opening upon them; but the first effect was by no means to increase the happiness of the family. They loved each other as well as ever; but they were not so entirely identical. It was a disturbing influence, foreign and unusual; it was not the quiet, assured, undoubting family happiness of the days which were gone.

Then there were other unaccordant elements. Rachel, whom Mrs Atheling insisted upon retaining with them, and who was extremely eager on her own part to find something to do, and terrified to think herself a burden upon her friends; and Louis, who contented himself with his pittance of income, but only did his mere duty at the office, and gave all his thoughts and all his powers to the investigation which engrossed him. Mrs Atheling was very much concerned about Louis. If all this came to nothing, as was quite probable, she asked her husband eagerly what was to become of these young people—what were they to do? For at present, instead of trying to get on, Louis, who had no suspicion of the truth, gave his whole attention to a visionary pursuit, and was content to have the barest enough which he could exist upon. Mr Atheling shook his head, and could not make any satisfactory reply. "There was no disposition to idleness about the boy," Papa said, with approval. "He was working very hard, though he might make nothing by it; and when this state of uncertainty was put an end to, then they should see."

And Marian of late had become actively suspicious and observant. Marian attacked her mother boldly, and without concealment. "Mamma, it is something about Louis that Charlie has gone abroad for!" she said, in an unexpected sally, which took the garrison by surprise.

"My dear, how could you think of such a thing?" cried the prudent Mrs Atheling. "What could Miss Anastasia have to do with Louis? Why, she never so much as saw him, you know. You must, by no means, take foolish fancies into your head. I daresay, after all, he must belong to Lord Winterbourne."

Marian asked no more; but she did not fail to communicate her suspicions to Louis at the earliest opportunity. "I am quite sure," said Marian, not scrupling even to express her convictions in presence of Agnes and Rachel, "that Charlie has gone abroad for something about you."

"Something about me!" Louis was considerably startled; he was even indignant for a moment. He did not relish the idea of having secret enterprises undertaken for him, or to know less about himself than Marian's young brother did. "You must be mistaken," he said, with a momentary haughtiness. "Charlie is a very acute fellow, but I do not see that he is likely to trouble himself about me."

"Oh, but it was Miss Anastasia," said Marian, eagerly.

Then Louis coloured, and drew himself up. His first idea was that Miss Anastasia looked for evidence to prove him the son of Lord Winterbourne; and he resented, with natural vehemence, the interference of the old lady. "We are come to a miserable pass, indeed," he said, with bitterness, "when people investigate privately to prove this wretched lie against us."

"But you do not understand," cried Rachel. "Oh, Louis, I never told you what Miss Anastasia said. She said you were to take the name of Atheling, because it meant illustrious, and because the exiled princes were named so. Both Marian and Agnes heard her. She is a friend, Louis. Oh, I am sure, if she is inquiring anything, it is all for our good!"

The colour rose still higher upon Louis's cheek. He did not quite comprehend at the moment this strange, sudden side-light which glanced down upon the question which was so important to him. He did not pause to follow, nor see to what it might lead; but it struck him as a clue to something, though he was unable to discover what that something was. Atheling! the youth's imagination flashed back in a moment upon those disinherited descendants of Alfred, the Edgars and Margarets, who, instead of princely titles, bore only that addition to their name. He was as near the truth at that moment as people wandering in profound darkness are often near the light. Another step would have brought him to it; but Louis did not take that step, and was not enlightened. His heart rose, however, with the burning impatience of one who comes within sight of the goal. He started involuntarily with haste and eagerness. He was jealous that even friendly investigations should be the first to find out the mystery. He felt as if he would have a better right to anything which might be awaiting him, if he discovered it himself.

Upon all this tumult of thought and feeling, Agnes looked on, saying nothing—looked on, by no means enjoying her spectatorship and superior knowledge. It was a "situation" which might have pleased Mr Endicott, but it terribly embarrassed Agnes, who found it no pleasure at all to be so much wiser than her neighbours. She dared not confide the secret to Louis any more than she could to the Rector; and she would have been extremely unhappy between them, but for the relief and comfort of that fable, which was quickly growing into shape and form. It had passed out of her controlling hands already, and began to exercise over her the sway which a real created thing always exercises over the mind even of its author: it had ceased to be the direct personal affair she had intended to make it; it told its story, but after a more delicate process, and Agnes expended all her graceful fancy upon its perfection. She thought now that Louis might find it out as well as the Rector. It was an eloquent appeal, heart-warm and touching to them both.

CHAPTER XVII

RACHEL'S DOUBTS

After Louis, the most urgent business in the house of the Athelings was that of Rachel, who was so pertinaciously anxious to be employed, that her friends found it very difficult to evade her constant entreaties. Rachel's education—or rather Rachel's want of education—had been very different from that of Marian and Agnes. She had no traditions of respectability to deter her from anything she could do; and she had been accustomed to sing to the guests at Winterbourne, and concluded that it would make very little difference to her, whether her performance was in a public concert-room or a private assembly. "No one would care at all for me; no one would ever think of me or look at me," said Rachel.

"If I sang well, that would be all that any one thought of; and we need not tell Louis—and I would not mind myself—and no one would ever know."

"But I have great objections to it, my dear," said Mrs Atheling, with some solemnity. "I should rather a hundred times take in work myself, or do anything with my own hands, than let my girls do this. It is not respectable for a young girl. A public appearance! I should be grieved and ashamed beyond anything. I should indeed, my dear."

"I am very sorry, Mrs Atheling," said Rachel, wistfully; "but it is not anything wrong."

"Not wrong—but not at all respectable," said Mrs Atheling, "and unfeminine, and very dangerous indeed, and a discreditable position for a young girl."

Rachel blushed, and was very much disconcerted, but still did not give up the point. "I thought it so when they tried to force me," she said in a low tone; "but now, no one need know; and people, perhaps, might have me at their houses; ladies sing in company. You would not mind me doing that, Mrs Atheling? Or I could give lessons. Perhaps you think it is all vanity; but indeed they used to think me a very good singer, long ago. Oh, Agnes, do you remember that old gentleman at the Willow? that very old gentleman who used to talk to you? I think he could help me if you would only speak to him."

"Mr Agar? I think he could," said Agnes; "but, Rachel, mamma says you must not think of it. Marian does not do anything, and why should you?"

"I am no one's daughter," said Rachel, sadly. "You are all very kind; but Louis has only a very little money; and I will not—indeed I will not—be a burden upon you."

"Rachel, my dear," said Mrs Atheling, "do not speak so foolishly; but I will tell you what we can do. Agnes shall write down all about it to Miss Anastasia, and ask her advice, and whether she consents to it; and if she consents, I will not object any more. I promise I shall not stand in the way at all, if Miss Anastasia decides for you."

Rachel looked up with a little wonder. "But Miss Anastasia has nothing to do with us," said the astonished girl. "I would rather obey you than Miss Rivers, a great deal. Why should we consult her?"

"My dear," said Mrs Atheling, with importance, "you must not ask any questions at present. I have my reasons. Miss Anastasia takes a great interest in you, and I have a very good reason for what I say."

This made an end of the argument; but Rachel was extremely puzzled, and could not understand it. She was not very quick-witted, this gentle little girl; she began to have a certain awe of Miss Anastasia, and to suppose that it must be her superior wisdom which made every one ask her opinion. Rachel could not conclude upon any other reason, and accordingly awaited with a little solemnity the decision of Miss Rivers. They were in a singular harmony, all these young people; not one of them but had some great question hanging in the balance, which they themselves were not sufficient to conclude upon—something that might change and colour the whole course of their lives.

Another event occurring just at this time, made Rachel for a time the heroine of the family. Charlie wrote home with great regularity, like a good son as he was. His letters were very short, and not at all explanatory; but they satisfied his mother that he had not taken a fever, nor fallen into the hands of robbers, and that was so far well. In one of these epistles, however, the young gentleman extended his brief report a little, to describe to them a family with which he had formed acquaintance. There were a lot of girls, Charlie said; and one of them, called Giulia Remori, was strangely like "Miss Rachel;" "not exactly like," wrote Charlie,—"not like Agnes and Marian" (who, by the way, had only a very vague resemblance to each other). "You would not suppose them to be sisters; but I always think of Miss Rachel when I see this Signora Giulia. They say, too, she has a great genius for music, and I heard her sing once myself, like—; well, I cannot say what it was like. The most glorious music, I believe, under the skies."

"Mamma, that cannot be Charlie!" said the girls simultaneously; but it was Charlie, without any dispute, and Marian clapped her hands in triumph, and exclaimed that he must be in love; and there stood Rachel, very much interested, wistful, and smiling. The tender-hearted girl had the greatest propensity to make friendships. She received the idea of this foreign Giulia into her heart in a moment, and ran forth eagerly at the time of Louis's usual evening visit to meet him at the gate, and tell him this little bit of romance. It moved Louis a great deal more deeply than it moved Rachel. This time his eye flashed to the truth like lightning. He began to give serious thought to what Marian had said of Charlie's object, and of Miss Anastasia. "Hush, Rachel," he said, with sudden gravity. "Hush, I see it; this is some one belonging to our mother."

"Our mother!" The two orphans stood together at the little gate, silenced by the name. They had never speculated much upon this parent. It was one of the miseries of their cruel position, that the very idea of a dead mother, which is to most minds the most saintlike and holy imagination under heaven, brought to them their bitterest pang of disgrace and humiliation. Yet now Louis stood silent, pondering it with the deepest eagerness. A burning impatience possessed the young man; a violent colour rose over his face. He could not tolerate the idea of an unconcerned inquirer into matters so instantly momentous to himself. He was not at all amiable in his impulses; his immediate and wild fancy was to rush away, on foot and penniless, as he was; to turn off Charlie summarily from his mission, if he had one; and without a clue, or a guide, or a morsel of information which pointed in that direction, by sheer force of energy and desperation to find it out himself. It was misery to go in quietly to the quiet house, even to the presence of Marian, with such a fancy burning in his mind. He left Rachel abruptly, without a word of explanation, and went off to make inquiries about travelling. It was perfectly vain, but it was some satisfaction to the fever of his mind. Louis's defection made Marian very angry; when he came next day they had their first quarrel, and parted in great distraction and misery, mutually convinced of the treachery and wretchedness of this world; but made it up again very shortly after, to the satisfaction of every one concerned. With these things happening day by day, with their impatient and fiery Orlando, always in some degree inflaming the house, it is not necessary to say how wonderful a revolution had been wrought upon the quiet habitudes of this little house in Bellevue.

CHAPTER XVIII

AGNES

Yet the household felt, in spite of itself, a difference by no means agreeable between the Old Wood Lodge and Bellevue. The dull brick wall of Laurel House was not nearly so pleasant to look upon as that great amphitheatre with its maze of wan waters and willow-trees, where the sunshine flashed among the spires of Oxford; neither was Miss Willsie, kind and amusing as she was, at all a good substitute for

Miss Anastasia. They had Louis, it was true, but Louis was in love, and belonged to Marian; and no one within their range was at all to be compared to the Rector. Accustomed to have their interest fixed, after their own cottage, upon the Old Wood House and Winterbourne Hall, they were a little dismayed, in spite of themselves, to see the meagreness and small dimensions even of Killiecrankie Lodge. It was a different world altogether—and they did not know at the first glance how to make the two compatible. The little house in the country, now that they had left it, grew more and more agreeable by comparison. Mrs Atheling forgot that she had thought it damp, and all of them, Mamma herself among the rest, began to think of their return in spring.

And as the winter went on, Agnes made progress with her fable. She did not write it carefully, but she did write it with fervour, and the haste of a mind concerned and in earnest. The story had altered considerably since she first thought of it. There was in it a real heir whom nobody knew, and a supposed heir, who was the true hero of the book. The real heir had a love-story, and the prettiest fiancée in the world; but about her hero Agnes was timid, presenting a grand vague outline of him, and describing him in sublime general terms; for she was not at all an experienced young lady, though she was an author, but herself regarded her hero with a certain awe and respect and imperfect understanding, as young men and young women of poetic conditions are wont to regard each other. From this cause it resulted that you were not very clear about the Sir Charles Grandison of the young novelist. Her pretty heroine was as clear as a sunbeam; and even the Louis of her story was definable, and might be recognised; but the other lay half visible, sometimes shining out in a sudden gleam of somewhat tremulous light, but for the most part enveloped in shadow: everybody else in the tale spoke of him, thought of him, and were marvellously influenced by him; but his real appearances were by no means equal to the importance he had acquired.

The sole plot of the story was connected with the means by which the unsuspected heir came to a knowledge of his rights, and gained his true place; and there was something considerably exciting to Agnes in her present exercise of the privilege of fiction, and the steps she took to make the title of her imaginary Louis clear. She used to pause, and wonder in the midst of it, whether such chances as these would befall the true Louis, and how far the means of her invention would resemble the real means. It was a very odd occupation, and interested her strangely. It was not very much of a story, neither was it written with that full perfection of style which comes by experience and the progress of years; but it had something in its faulty grace, and earnestness, and simplicity, which was perhaps more attractive than the matured perfectness of a style which had been carefully formed, and "left nothing to desire." It was sparkling with youth, and it was warm from the heart. It went into no greater bulk than one small volume, which Mr Burlington put into glowing red cloth, embellished with two engravings, and ornamented with plenty of gilding. It came out, a wintry Christmas flower, making no such excitement in the house as Hope Hazlewood had done; and Agnes had the satisfaction of handing over to Papa, to lock up in his desk in the office, a delightfully crisp, crackling, newly-issued fifty-pound note.

And Christmas had just given way to the New Year when the Rector made his appearance at Bellevue. He was still more eager, animated, and hopeful than he had been when they saw him last. His extreme high-church clerical costume was entirely abandoned; he still wore black, but it was not very professional, and he appeared in these unknown parts with books in his hands and smiles on his face. When he came into the little parlour, he did not seem at all to notice its limited dimensions, but greeted them all with an effusion of pleasure and kindness, which greatly touched the heart of Agnes, and moved her mother, in her extreme gratification and pride, to something very like tears. Mr Rivers inquired at once for Louis, with great gravity and interest, but shook his head when he heard what his present occupation was.

"This will not do; will he come and see me, or shall I wait upon him?" said the Rector with a subdued smile, as he remembered the youthful haughtiness of Louis. "I should be glad to speak to him about his prospects—here is my card—will you kindly ask him to dine with me to-night, alone? He is a young man of great powers; something better may surely be found for him than this lawyer's office."

Mrs Atheling was a little piqued in spite of herself. "My son, when he is at home, is there," said the good mother; and her visitor did not fail to see the significance of the tone.

"He is not at home now—where is he?" said the Rector.

There was a moment's hesitation. Agnes turned to look at him, her colour rising violently, and Mrs Atheling faltered in her reply.

"He has gone abroad to —to make some inquiries," said Mrs Atheling; "though he is so very young, people have great confidence in him; and—and it may turn out very important indeed, what he has gone about."

Once more Agnes cast a troubled glance upon the Rector—he heard of it with such perfect unconcern—this inquiry which in a moment might strike his ambition to the dust.

He ceased at once speaking on this subject, which did not interest him. He said, turning to her, that he had brought some books about which he wanted Miss Atheling's opinion. Agnes shrank back immediately in natural diffidence, but revived again, before she was aware, in all her old impulse of opposition. "If it is wrong to write books, is it right to form opinions upon them?" said Agnes. Mr Rivers imperceptibly grew a little loftier and statelier as she spoke.

"I think I have explained my sentiments on that point," said the Rector; "there is no one whose appreciation I should set so high a value on as that of an intelligent woman."

It was Agnes's turn to blush and say nothing, as she met his eye. When Mr Rivers said "an intelligent woman," he meant, though the expression was not romantic, his own ideal; and there lay his books upon the table, evidences of his choice of a critic. She began to busy herself with them, looking quite vacantly at the title-pages; wondering if there was anything besides books, and controversies, and opinions, to be found in the Rector's heart.

When Mrs Atheling, in her natural pride and satisfaction, bethought her of that pretty little book with its two illustrations, and its cover in crimson and gold, she brought a copy to the table immediately. "My dear, perhaps Mr Rivers might like to look at this?" said Mrs Atheling. "It has only been a week published, but people speak very well of it already. It is a very pretty story. I think you would like it—Agnes, my love, write Mr Rivers' name."

"No, no, mamma!" cried Agnes hurriedly; she put away the red book from her, and went away from the table in haste and agitation. Very true, it was written almost for him—but she was dismayed at the idea of being called to write in it Lionel Rivers' name.

He took up the book, however, and looked at it in the gravest silence. The Heir;—he read the title aloud, and it seemed to strike him; then without another word he put the little volume safely in his pocket, repeated his message to Louis, and a few minutes afterwards, somewhat grave and abstracted, took his leave of them, and hastened away.

CHAPTER XIX

LIONEL

The Rector became a very frequent visitor during the few following weeks at Bellevue. Louis had gone to see him, as he desired, and Mr Rivers anxiously endeavoured to persuade the youth to suffer himself to be "assisted." Louis as strenuously resisted every proposal of the kind; he was toiling on in pursuit of himself, through his memoir of Lord Winterbourne—still eager, and full of expectation—still proud, and refusing to be indebted to any one. The Rector argued with him like an elder brother. "Let us grant that you are successful," said Mr Rivers; "let us suppose that you make an unquestionable discovery, what position are you in to pursue it? Your sister, even—recollect your sister—you cannot provide for her."

His sister was Louis's grand difficulty; he bit his lip, and the fiery glow of shame came to his face. "I cannot provide for her, it is true. I am bitterly ashamed of it; but, at least, she is among friends."

"You do me small credit," said the Rector; "but I will not ask, on any terms, for a friendship which is refused to me. You are not even in the way of advancement; and to lose your time after this fashion is madness. Let me see you articled to these people whom you are with now; that is, at least, a chance, though not a great one. If I can accomplish it, will you consent to this?"

Louis paused a little, grateful in his heart, though his tongue was slow to utter his sentiments. "You are trying to do me a great service," said the young man; "you think me a churl, and ungrateful, but you endeavour to benefit me against my will—is it not true? I am just in such a position that no miracle in the world would seem wonderful to me; it is possible, in the chances of the future, that we two may be set up against each other. I cannot accept this service from you—from you, or from any other. I must wait."

The Rector turned away almost with impatience. "Do you suppose you can spend your life in this fashion—your life?" he exclaimed, with some heat.

"My life!" said Louis. He was a little startled with this conclusion. "I thank you," he added abruptly, "for your help, for your advice, for your reproof—I thank you heartily, but I have no more to say."

That was how the conversation ended. Lionel, grieved for the folly of the boy, smiling to himself at Louis's strange delusion that he, who was the very beau-ideal of the race of Rivers, belonged to another house, went to his rest, with a mind disturbed, full of difficulties, and of ambition, working out one solemn problem, and touched with tender dreams; yet always remembering, with a pleasure which he could not restrain, the great change in his position, and that he was now, not merely the Rector, but the heir of Winterbourne. Louis, on his part, went home to his dark little lodging, with the swell and tumult of excitement in his mind, and could not sleep. He seemed to be dizzied with the rushing shadows of a crowd of coming events. He was not well; his abstinence, his studiousness, his change of place and life, had weakened his young frame; these rushing wings seemed to tingle in his ears, and his temples throbbed as if they kept time. He rose in the middle of the night, in the deep wintry silence and moonlight, to open his window, and feel the cold air upon his brow. There he saw the moonbeams falling softly, not on any imposing scene, but on the humble roof underneath whose shelter sweet voices and young hearts, devout and guileless, prayed for him every night; the thought calmed him into sudden humility and quietness; and, in his poverty, and hope, and youth, he returned to his humble bed, and slept. Lionel was waking too; but he did not know of any one who prayed for him in all this cold-hearted world.

But the Rector became a very frequent visitor in Bellevue. He had read the little book—read it with a kind of startled consciousness, the first time, that it looked like a true story, and seemed somehow familiar to himself. But by-and-by he began to keep it by him, and, not for the sake of the story, to take it up idly when he was doing nothing else, and refer to it as a kind of companion. It was not, in any degree whatever, an intellectual display; he by no means felt himself pitted against the author of it, or entering into any kind of rivalship with her. The stream sparkled and flashed to the sunshine as it ran; but it flowed with a sweet spontaneous readiness, and bore no trace of artificial force and effort. It wanted a great many of the qualities which critics praise. There was no great visible strain of power, no forcible evidence of difficulties overcome. The reader knew very well that he could not have done this, nor anything like it, yet his intellectual pride was not roused. It was genius solacing itself with its own romaunt, singing by the way; it was not talent getting up an exhibition for the astonishment, or the enlightenment, or the instruction of others. Agnes defeated her own purpose by the very means she had taken to procure it. The Rector forgot all about the story, thinking of the writer of it; he became indifferent to what she had to tell, but dwelt and lingered—not like a critic—like something very different—upon the cadence of her voice.

To tell the truth, between his visits to Bellevue, and his musings thereafter—his study of this little fable of Agnes's, and his vague mental excursions into the future, Lionel Rivers, had he yielded to the fascination, would have found very near enough to do. But he was manful enough to resist this trance of fairyland. He was beginning to be "in love;" nobody could dispute it; it was visible enough to wake the most entire sympathy in the breasts of Marian and Rachel, and to make for the mother of the family wakeful nights, and a most uneasy pillow; but he was far from being at ease or in peace. His friends in London were of a class as different as possible from these humble people who were rapidly growing nearer than friends. They were all men of great intelligence, of great powers, scholars, philosophers, authorities—men who belonged, and professed to belong, to the ruling class of intellect, prophets and apostles of a new generation. They were not much given to believing anything, though some among them had a weakness for mesmerism or spiritual manifestations. They investigated all beliefs and faculties of believing, and received all marvellous stories, from the Catholic legends of the saints to the miracles of the New Testament, on one general ground of indulgence, charitable and tender, as mythical stories which meant something in their day. Most of them wrote an admirable style—most of them occasionally said very profound things which nobody could understand; all of them were scholars and gentlemen, as blameless in their lives as they were superior in their powers; and all of them lived upon a kind of intellectual platform, philosophical demigods, sufficient for themselves, and looking down with a good deal of curiosity, a little contempt, and a little pity, upon the crowds who thronged below of common men.

These were the people to whom Lionel Rivers, in the first flush of his emancipation, had hastened from his high-churchism, and his country pulpit—some of them had been his companions at College—some had inspired him by their books, or pleased him by their eloquence. They were a brotherhood of men of great cultivation—his equals, and sometimes his superiors. He had yearned for their society when he was quite removed from it; but he was of a perverse and unconforming mind. What did he do now?

He took the strange fancy suddenly, and telling no man, of wandering through those frightful regions of crime and darkness, which we hide behind our great London streets. He went about through the miserable thoroughfares, looking at the miserable creatures there. What was the benefit to them of these polluted lives of theirs? They had their enjoyments, people said—their enjoyments! Their sorrows, like the sorrows of all humanity, were worthy human tears, consolation, and sympathy,—their hardships and endurances were things to move the universal heart; but their enjoyments—Heaven save us!—the pleasures of St Giles's, the delights and amusements of those squalid groups at the street corners! If they were to have nothing more than that, what a frightful fate was theirs!

And there came upon the spectator, as he went among them in silence, a sudden eagerness to try that talisman which Agnes Atheling had bidden him use. It was vain to try philosophy there, where no one knew what it meant—vain to offer the rites of the Church to those who were fatally beyond its pale. Was it possible, after all, that the one word in the world, which could stir something human—something of heaven—in these degraded breasts, was that one sole unrivalled Name?

He could not withdraw himself from the wretched scene before him. He went on from street to street with something of the consciousness of a man who carries a hidden remedy through a plague-stricken city, but hides his knowledge in his own mind, and does not apply it. A strange sense of guilt—a strange oppression by reason of this grand secret—an overpowering passionate impulse to try the solemn experiment, and withal a fascinated watchfulness which kept him silent—possessed the mind of the young man.

He walked about the streets like a man doing penance; then he began to notice other passengers not so idle as himself. There were people here who were trying to break into the mass of misery, and make a footing for purity and light among it. They were not like his people;—sometimes they were poor city missionaries, men of very bad taste, not perfect in their grammar, and with no great amount of discretion. Even the people of higher class were very limited people often to the perception of Mr Rivers; but they were at work, while the demigods slept upon their platform. It would be very hard to make philosophers of the wretched population here. Philosophy did not break its heart over the impossibility, but calmly left the untasteful city missionaries, the clergymen, High Church and Low Church, who happened to be in earnest, and some few dissenting ministers of the neighbourhood, labouring upon a forlorn hope to make them men.

All this moved in the young man's heart as he pursued his way among these squalid streets. Every one of these little stirrings in this frightful pool of stagnant life was made in the name of Him whom Lionel Rivers once named with cold irreverence, and whom Agnes Atheling, with a tender awe and appropriation, called "Our Lord." This was the problem he was busy with while he remained in London. It was not one much discussed, either in libraries or drawing-rooms, among his friends; he discussed it by himself as he wandered through St Giles's—silent—watching—with the great Name which he himself did not know, but began to cling to as a talisman, burning at his heart.

CHAPTER XX

AN ARRIVAL

While the Athelings at home were going on quietly, but with anxiety and disturbance of mind in this way, they were startled one afternoon by a sudden din and tumult out of doors, nearly as great as that which, not much short of a year ago, had announced the first call of Mrs Edgerley. It was not, however, a magnificent equipage like that of the fashionable patroness of literature which drew up at the door now. It was an antique job carriage, not a very great deal better to look at than that venerable fly of Islington, which was still regarded with respect by Agnes and Marian. In this vehicle there were two horses, tall brown bony old hacks, worthy the equipage they drew—an old coachman in a very ancient livery, and an active youth, fresh, rural, and ruddy, who sprang down from the creaking coach-box to assault, but in a moderate country fashion, the door of the Athelings. Rachel, who was peeping from the window, uttered an exclamation of surprise—"Oh, Agnes, look! it is Miss Anastasia's man."

It was so beyond dispute, and Miss Anastasia herself immediately descended from the creaking vehicle, swinging heavily upon its antiquated springs; she had a large cloak over her brown pelisse, and a great muff of rich sables, big enough to have covered from head to foot, like a case, either little Bell or little Beau. She was so entirely like herself in spite of those additions to her characteristic costume, and withal so unlike other people, that they could have supposed she had driven here direct from the Priory, had that been possible, without any commonplace intervention of railway or locomotive by the way. As the girls came to the door to meet her, she took the face—first of Agnes, then of Marian, and lastly of Rachel, who was a good deal dismayed by the honour—between her hands, thrusting the big muff, like a prodigious bracelet, up upon her arm the while, and kissed them with a cordial heartiness. Then she went into the little parlour to Mrs Atheling, who in the mean time had been gathering together the scattered pieces of work, and laying them, after an orderly fashion, in her basket. Then Papa's easy-chair was wheeled to the fire for the old lady, and Marian stooped to find a footstool for her, and Agnes helped to loose the big cloak from her shoulders. Miss Anastasia's heart was touched by the attentions of the young people. She laid her large hand caressingly on Marian's head, and patted the cheek of Agnes. "Good children—eh? I missed them," she said, turning to Mamma, and Mamma brightened with pleasure and pride as she whispered something to Agnes about the fire in the best room. Then, when she had held a little conversation with the girls, Miss Rivers began to look uneasy. She glanced at Mrs Atheling with a clear intention of making some telegraphic communication; she glanced at the girls and at the door, and back again at Mamma, with a look full of meaning. Mrs Atheling was not generally so dull of comprehension, but she was so full of the idea that Miss Anastasia's real visit was to the girls, and so proud of the attraction which even this dignified old lady could not resist, that she could not at all consent to believe that Miss Rivers desired to be left alone with herself.

"There's a hamper from the Priory," said Miss Anastasia at last, abruptly; "among other country things there's some flowers in it, children—make haste all of you and get it unpacked, and tell me what you think of my camellias! Make haste, girls!"

It was a most moving argument; but it distracted Mrs Atheling's attention almost as much as that of her daughters, for the hamper doubtless contained something else than flowers. Mamma, however, remained decorously with her guest, despite the risk of breakage to the precious country eggs; and the girls, partly deceived, partly suspecting their visitor's motive, obeyed her injunction, and hastened away. Then Miss Rivers caught Mrs Atheling by the sleeve, and drew her close towards her. "Have you heard from your boy?" said Miss Anastasia.

"No," said Mrs Atheling with a sudden momentary alarm, "not for a week—has anything happened to Charlie?"

"Nonsense—what could happen to him?" cried the old lady, with a little impatience, "here is a note I had this morning—read it—he is coming home."

Mrs Atheling took the letter with great eagerness. It was a very brief one:—

MADAM,—I have come to it at last—suddenly. I have only time to tell you so. I shall leave to-day with an important witness. I have not even had leisure to write to my mother; but will push on to the Priory whenever I have bestowed my witness safely in Bellevue. In great haste.—Your obedient servant,

C. ATHELING.

Charlie's mother trembled all over with agitation and joy. She had to grasp by the mantel-shelf to keep herself quite steady. She exclaimed, "My own boy!" half-crying and wholly exultant, and would have liked to have hurried out forthwith upon the road and met him half-way, had that been possible. She kept the letter in her hand looking at it, and quite forgetting that it belonged to Miss Anastasia. He had justified the trust put in him—he had crowned himself with honour—he was coming home! Not much wonder that the good mother was weeping-ripe, and could have sobbed aloud for very joy.

"Ay," said Miss Anastasia, with something like a sigh, "you're a rich woman. I have not rested since this came to me, nor can I rest till I hear all your boy has to say."

At this moment Mrs Atheling started with a little alarm, catching from the window a glimpse of the coach, with its two horses and its antiquated coachman, slowly turning round and driving away. Miss Anastasia followed her glance with a subdued smile.

"Do you mean then to—to stay in London, Miss Rivers?" asked Mrs Atheling.

"Tut! the boy will be home directly—to-night," said Miss Anastasia; "I meant to wait here until he came."

Mrs Atheling started again in great and evident perturbation. You could perceive that she repeated "to wait here!" within herself with a great many points of admiration; but she was too well-bred to express her dismay. She cast, however, an embarrassed look round her, said she should be very proud, and Miss Rivers would do them honour, but she was afraid the accommodation was not equal—and here Mrs Atheling paused much distressed.

"I have been calculating all the way up when he can be here," interrupted Miss Anastasia. "I should say about twelve o'clock to-night. Agnes, when she comes back again, shall revise it for me. Never mind accommodation. Give him an hour's grace—say he comes at one o'clock—then a couple of hours later—by that time it will be three in the morning. Then I am sure one of the girls will not grudge me her bed till six. We'll get on very well; and when Will Atheling comes home, if you have anything to say to him, I can easily step out of the way. Well, am I an intruder? If I am not, don't say anything more about it. I cannot rest till I see the boy."

When the news became diffused through the house that Charlie was coming home to-night, and that Miss Anastasia was to wait for him, a very great stir and bustle immediately ensued. The best room was hastily put in order, and Mrs Atheling's own bedchamber immediately revised and beautified for the reception of Miss Anastasia. It was with a little difficulty, however, that the old lady was persuaded to leave the family parlour for the best room. She resisted energetically all unusual attentions, and did not hesitate to declare, even in the presence of Rachel, that her object was to see Charlie, and that for his arrival she was content to wait all night. A great anxiety immediately took possession of the household. They too were ready and eager to wait all night; and even Susan became vaguely impressed with a solemn sense of some great approaching event. Charlie was not to be alone either. The excitement rose to a quite overpowering pitch—who was coming with him? What news did he bring? These questions prolonged to the most insufferable tediousness the long slow darksome hours of the March night.

CHAPTER XXI

CHARLIE'S RETURN

The girls could not be persuaded to go to rest, let Mamma say what she would. Rachel, the only one who had no pretence, nor could find any excuse for sitting up, was the only one who showed the least sign of obedience; she went up-stairs with a meek unwillingness, lingered as long as she could before lying down, and when she extinguished her light at last, lay very broad awake looking into the midnight darkness, and listening anxiously to every sound below. Marian, in the parlour on a footstool, sat leaning both her arms on her mother's knee, and her head upon her arms, and in that position had various little sleeps, and half-a-dozen times in half-a-dozen dreams welcomed Charlie home. Agnes kept Miss Anastasia company in the best room, and Papa, who was not used to late hours, went between the two rooms with very wide open eyes, very anxious for his son's return. Into the midnight darkness and solemnity of Bellevue, the windows of Number Ten blazed with a cheerful light; the fires were studiously kept up, the hearths swept, everything looking its brightest for Charlie; and a pair of splendid capons, part produce of Miss Anastasia's hamper, were slowly cooking themselves into perfection, under the sleepy superintendence of Susan, before the great kitchen-fire—for even Susan would not go to bed.

Miss Anastasia sat very upright in an easy-chair, scorning so much as a suspicion of drowsiness. She did not talk very much; she was thinking over a hundred forgotten things, and tracing back step by step the story of the past. The old lady almost felt as if her father himself was coming from his foreign grave to bear witness to the truth. Her heart was stirred as she sat gazing into the ruddy firelight, hearing not a sound except now and then the ashes falling softly on the hearth, or the softer breath of Agnes by her side. As she sat in this unfamiliar little room, her mind flew back over half her life. She thought of her father as she had seen him last; she thought of the dreary blank of her own youthful desolation, a widowhood almost deeper than the widowhood of a wife—how she did not heed even the solemn pathos of her father's farewell—could not rouse herself from her lethargy even to be moved by the last parting from that last and closest friend, and desired nothing but to be left in her dreary self-seclusion obstinately mourning her dead—her murdered bridegroom! The old lady's eyes glittered, tearless, looking into the gleaming shadowy depths of the little mirror over the mantelpiece. It was scarcely in human nature to look back upon that dreadful tragedy, to anticipate the arrival to-night of the witnesses of another deadly wrong, and not to be stirred with a solemn and overwhelming indignation like that of an avenger of blood. Miss Anastasia started suddenly from her reverie, as she caught a long-drawn anxious sigh from her young companion; she drew her shawl close round her with a shudder. "God forgive me!" cried the vehement old lady; "did you ever have an enemy, child?"

In this house it was a very easy question. "No," said Agnes, looking at her wistfully.

"Nor I, perhaps, when I was your age." Miss Anastasia made a long pause. It was a long time ago, and she scarcely could recollect anything of her youth now, except that agony with which it ended. Then in the silence there seemed to be a noise in the street, which roused all the watchers. Mr Atheling went to the door to look out. It was very cold, clear, and calm, the air so sharp with frost, and so still with sleep, that it carried every passing sound far more distinctly than usual. Into this hushed and anxious house, through the open door came ringing the chorus of a street ballad, strangely familiar and out of unison with the excited feelings of the auditors, and the loud, noisy, echoing footsteps of some late merry-makers. They were all singularly disturbed by these uncongenial sounds; they raised a certain vague terror in the breasts of the father and mother, and a doubtful uneasiness among the other watchers. Under that veil of night, and silence, and distance, who could tell what their dearest and most trusted was doing? The old people could have told each other tales, like Jessica, of "such a night;" and the breathless silence, and the jar and discord of those rude voices, stirred memories and presentiments of pain even in the younger hearts.

It was now the middle of the night, two or three hours later than Miss Anastasia had anticipated, and the old lady rose from her chair, shook off her thoughtful mood, and began to walk about the room, and to criticise it briskly to Agnes. Then by way of diversifying her vigil, she made an incursion into the other parlour, where Papa was nursing the fire, and Mamma sitting very still, not to disturb Marian, who slept with her beautiful head upon her mother's knee. The old lady was suddenly overcome by the sight of that fair figure, with its folded arms and bowed head, and long beautiful locks falling down on Mrs Atheling's dark gown, like a stream of sunshine. She laid her hand very tenderly upon the sleeper's head. "She does not know," said Miss Anastasia—"she would not believe what a fairy fortune is coming to her, the sleeping beauty—God bless them all!"

The words had scarcely left her lips, the tears were still shining in her eyes, when Marian started up, called out of her dream by a sound which none of them besides had been quick enough to hear. "There! there! I hear him," cried Marian, shaking back her loose curls; and they all heard the far-off rapid rumble of a vehicle, gradually invading all the echoes of this quietness. It came along steadily—nearer—nearer—waking every one to the most overpowering excitement. Miss Anastasia marched through the little parlour, with an echoing step, throwing her tall shadow on the blind, clasping her fingers tight. Mr Atheling rushed to the door; Marian ran to the kitchen to wake up Susan, and see that the tray was ready for Charlie's refreshment; Mamma stirred the fire, and made it blaze; Agnes drew the blind aside, and looked out into the darkness from the window. Yes, there could be no mistake; on came the rumbling wheels, closer and closer. Then the cab became absolutely visible, opposite the door—some one leapt out—was it Charlie?—but he had to wait, to help some one else, very slow and uncertain, out of the vehicle. They all crowded to the door, the mother and sisters for the moment half forgetting Miss Anastasia; and there stood a most indisputable Charlie, very near six feet high, with a travelling-cap and a rough overcoat, bringing home the most extraordinary guest imaginable to his amazed parental home.

It was a woman, enveloped from head to foot in a great cloak, but unbonneted, and with an amazing head-dress; and after her stumbled forth a boy, of precisely the same genus and appearance as the Italian boys with hurdy-gurdies and with images, familiar enough in Bellevue. Charlie hurried forward, paying the greatest possible attention to his charge, who was somewhat peevish. He scarcely left her hand when he plunged among all those anxious people at the door. "All safe—all well, mother; how did you know I was coming?—how d'ye do, papa? Let her in, let her in, girls!—she's tired to death, and doesn't know a word of English. Let's have her disposed of first of all—she's worth her weight in gold—Miss Rivers!"

The young man fell back in extreme amazement. "Who is she, young Atheling?" cried Miss Anastasia, towering high in the background over everybody's head.

Charlie took off his cap with a visible improvement of "manners." "The nurse that brought them home," he answered, in the concisest and most satisfactory fashion; and, grasping the hand of every one as he passed, with real pleasure glowing on his bronzed face, Charlie steered his charge in—seeing there was light in it—to the best room. Arrived there, he fairly turned his back to the wall, and harangued his anxious audience.

"It's all right," said Charlie; "she tells her story as clearly as possible when she's not out of humour, and the doctor's on his way. I've made sure of everything of importance; and now, mother, if you can manage it, and Miss Rivers does not object, let us have something to eat, and get her off to bed, and then you shall hear all the rest."

Marian went off instantly to call Susan, and all the way Marian repeated under her breath, "All the rest! all the rest of what? Oh, Louis! but I'll find out what they mean."

CHAPTER XXII.

CHARLIE'S REPORT

It was far from an easy achievement to get her safely conveyed up the stairs. She turned round and delivered addresses to them in most lively and oratorical Italian, eloquent on the subject of her sufferings by the way; she was disposed to be out of temper when no one answered her but Charlie, and fairly wound up, and stimulated with Miss Anastasia's capon and Mrs Atheling's wine, was not half so much disposed to be sent off to bed as her entertainers were to send her. These entertainers were in the oddest state of amaze and excitement possible. It was beginning to draw near the wintry morning of another day, and this strange figure in the strange dress, which did not look half so pretty in its actual reality, and upon this hard-featured peasant woman, as it did in pictures and romance—the voluble foreign tongue of which they did not know a word—the emphatic gestures; the change in the appearance of Charlie, and the entire suddenness of the whole scene, confused the minds of the lookers-on. Then a pale face in a white cap, a little shrinking white-robed figure, trembling and anxious, was perceptible to Mrs Atheling at the top of the stair, looking down upon it with terror. So Mamma peremptorily sent Charlie back beside Miss Anastasia, and resumed into her own hands the management of affairs. Under her guidance the woman and the boy were comfortably disposed of, no one being able to speak a word to them, in the room which had been Charlie's. Rachel was comforted and sent back to bed, and then Mrs Atheling turned suddenly upon her own girls. "My dears," said Mamma, "you are not wanted down stairs. I don't suppose Papa and I are wanted either; Miss Anastasia must talk over her business with Charlie—it is not our business you know, Marian, my darling; go to sleep."

"Go to sleep!—people cannot go to sleep just when they choose at five o'clock in the morning, mamma!" cried the aggrieved and indignant Marian; but Agnes, though quite as curious as her sister, was wise enough to lend her assistance in the cause of subordination. Marian was under very strong temptation. She thought she could almost like to steal down in the dark and listen; but honour, we are glad to say, prevailed over curiosity, and sleep over both. When her pretty young head touched the pillow, there was no eavesdropping possible to Marian; and in the entirest privacy and silence, after all this tumult, in the presence of Mamma and Mr Atheling, and addressing himself to Miss Anastasia, Charlie told his tale. He took out his pocket-book from his pocket—the same old-fashioned big pocket-book which he had carried away with him, and gave his evidences one by one into Miss Anastasia's hands as he spoke.

But the old lady's fingers trembled: she had restrained herself as well as she could, feeling it only just that he should be welcomed by his own, and even half diverted out of her anxiety by the excited Tyrolese; but now her restrained feelings rushed back upon her heart. The papers rustled in her hand; she did not hear him as he began, in order, and deliberately, his report. "Information! I cannot receive information, I am too far gone for that," cried the old lady, with a hysterical break in her voice. "Give me no facts, Charlie, Charlie!—I am not able to put them together—tell me once in a word—is it true?"

"It is true," said Charlie, eagerly—"not only true, but proved—certain, so clear that nobody can deny it. Listen, Miss Rivers, I could be content to go by myself with these evidences in my hand, before any court in England, against the ablest pleader that ever held a brief. Don't mind the proofs to-night; trust my assurance, as you trusted me. It is true to the letter, to the word, everything that you supposed. Giulietta was his wife. Louis is his lawful son."

Miss Anastasia did not say a word; she bowed down her face upon her hands—that face over which an ashy paleness came slowly stealing like a cloud. Mrs Atheling hastened forward, thinking she was about to faint, but was put aside by a gesture. Then the colour came back, and Miss Anastasia rose up, herself again, with all her old energy.

"You are perfectly right, young Atheling—quite right—as you have always been," said Miss Rivers; "and, of course, you have told me in your letters the most part of what you could tell me now. But your boy is born for the law, Will Atheling," she said, turning suddenly to Charlie's pleased and admiring father. "He wrote to me as if I were a lawyer instead of a woman: all facts and no opinion; that was scant measure for me. Shake hands, boy. I'll see everything in the morning, and then we'll think of beginning the campaign. I have it in my head already—please Heaven! Charlie, we'll chase them from the field."

So saying, Miss Anastasia marched with an exultant and jubilant step, following Mrs Atheling up the narrow stairs. She was considerably shaken out of her usual composure—swells of great triumph, suddenly calmed by the motion of a moved heart, passed over the spirit of this brave old gentlewoman like sun and wind; and her self-appointed charge of the rights of her father's children, who might have been her own children so far as age was concerned, had a very singular effect upon her. Mrs Atheling did not linger a minute longer than she could help with her distinguished guest. She was proud of Miss Anastasia, but far prouder of Charlie,—Charlie, who had been a boy a little while ago, but who had come back a man.

"Come here and sit down, mother," said Charlie; "now we're by ourselves, if you will not tell the girls, I'll tell you everything. First, there's the marriage. That she belonged to the family I wrote of—the family Remori—I got at after a long time. She was an only daughter, and had no one to look after her. I have a certificate of the marriage, and a witness coming who was present—old Doctor Serrano—one of your patriots who is always in mischief; besides that, what do you think is my evidence for the marriage?"

"Indeed, Charlie, I could not guess," cried Mrs Atheling.

"There's a kind of tomb near the town, a thing as like the mausoleum at Winterbourne as possible, and quite as ugly. There is this good in ugliness," said Charlie, "that one remarks it, especially in Italy. I thought no one but an Englishman could have put up such an affair as that, and I could not make out one way or another who it belonged to, or what it was. The priests are very strong out there. They would not let a heretic lie in consecrated ground, and no one cared to go near this grave, if it was a grave. They wouldn't allow even that. You know what the Winterbourne tomb is—a great open canopied affair, with that vast flat stone below. There was a flat stone in the other one too, not half so big, and it looked to me as if it would lift easily enough. So what do you think I did? I made friends with some wild fellows about, and got hold of one young Englishman, and as soon as it was dark we got picks and tools and went off to the grave."

"Oh, Charlie!" Mrs Atheling turned very pale.

"After a lot of work we got it open," said Charlie, going on with great zest and animation. "Then the young fellow and I got down into the vault—a regular vault, where there had been a lamp suspended. It, I suppose, had gone out many a year ago; and there we found upon the two coffin-lids—well, it's very pitiful, mother, it is indeed—but we wanted it for evidence—on one of the coffins was this inscription:—'Giulietta Rivers, Lady Winterbourne, née Remori, died January 1822, aged twenty years.' If it had been a diamond mine it would not have given so much pleasure to me."

"Pleasure! oh Charlie!" cried Mrs Atheling faintly.

"But they might say you put it there, Charlie, and that it was not true," said Mr Atheling, who rather piqued himself upon his caution.

"That was what I had the other young fellow for," said Charlie quietly; "and that was what made me quite sure she belonged to the Remoris; it was easy enough after that—and I want only one link now, that is, to make sure of their identity. Father, do you remember anything about the children when they came to the Hall?"

Mr Atheling shook his head. "Your aunt Bridget, if she had been alive, would have been sure to know," said Mamma meditatively; "but Louis found out some old servant lately that had been about Winterbourne long ago."

"Louis! does he know?" cried Charlie.

"He is doing something on his own account, inquiring everything he can about Lord Winterbourne. He does not know, but guesses every possible kind of thing, except the truth," said Mr Atheling; "how long he may be of lighting upon that, it is impossible to say."

"Now Charlie, my dear boy, you can ask all about Louis to-morrow," said Mrs Atheling. "Louis! Dear me, William, to think of us calling him Louis, and treating him like any common young man, and he Lord Winterbourne all the time! and all through Charlie!—and oh, my Marian! when I think of it all, it bewilders me! But, Charlie, my dear, you must not be fatigued too much. Do not ask him any more questions to-night, papa; consider how important his health is; he must lie down directly. I'll make him all comfortable; and, William, do you go to the parlour—bid him good-night."

Papa obeyed, as dutiful papas are wont to obey, and Charlie laughed, but submitted, as his mother, with her own kind unwearying hands, arranged for him the sofa in the best room; for the Tyrolese and Miss Anastasia occupied all the available bedrooms in the house. Then she bade him good-night, drawing back his dark elf-locks, and kissing his forehead tenderly, and with a certain respect for the big boy who was a boy no longer; and then the good mother went away to arrange her husband similarly on the other sofa, and to take possession, last of all, of the easy-chair. "I can sleep in the day if I am disposed," said Mrs Atheling, who never was disposed for any such indulgence; and she leaned back in the big chair, with a mind disturbed and glowing, agitated with grand fancies. Marian! was it possible? But then, Agnes—after all, what a maze of splendid uncertainty it was!

CHAPTER XXIII

PROCRASTINATION

"You may say what you like, young Atheling," said Miss Rivers, "you've a very good right to your own opinion; but I'm not a lawyer, nor bound by rule and precedent, mind. This is the middle of March; it comes on in April; we must wait for that; and you're not up with all your evidence, you dilatory boy."

"But I might happen to be up with it in a day," said Charlie, "and at all events an ejectment should be served, and the first step taken in the case without delay."

"That is all very well," said the old lady, "but I don't suppose it would advance the business very much, besides rousing him at once to use every means possible, and perhaps buy off that poor old Serrano, or get hold of Monte. Why did you not look for Monte, young Atheling? The chances are that he was present too?"

"One witness was as much as I could manage," said Charlie, shrugging his shoulders at the recollection; "but the most important question of all—Louis—I mean—your brother—the heir—"

"My brother—the heir." Miss Rivers coloured suddenly. It was a different thing thinking of him in private, and hearing him spoken of so. "I tell you he is not the heir, young Atheling; he is Lord Winterbourne: but I will not see him yet, not till the day; it would be a terrible time of suspense for the poor boy."

"Then, if it is your pleasure, he must go away," said Charlie, firmly—"he cannot come here to this agitated house of ours without discovering a good deal of the truth; and if he discovered it so, he would have just grounds to complain. If he is not told at once, he ought to have some commission such as I have had, and be sent away."

Miss Rivers coloured still more, all her liking for Charlie and his family scarcely sufficing to reconcile her to the "sending away" of the young heir, on the same footing as she had sent young Atheling. She hesitated and faltered visibly, seeing reason enough in it, but extremely repugnant. "If you think so," she said at last, with a slightly averted face, "ah—another time we can speak of that."

Then came further consultations, and Charlie had to tell his story over bit by bit, and incident by incident, illustrating every point of it by his documents. Miss Anastasia was particularly anxious about the young Englishman whose name was signed with Charlie's own, in certification of the inscription on the coffin. Miss Anastasia marvelled much whether he belonged to the Hillarys of Lincolnshire, or the Hillarys of Yorkshire, and pursued his shadow through half-a-dozen counties. Charlie was not particularly given to genealogy. He had the young man's card, with his address at the Albany, and the time of his possible return home. That was quite enough for the matter in hand, and Charlie was very much more concerned about the one link wanting in his evidence—the person who received the children from the care of Leonore the Tyrolese.

As it chanced, in this strange maze of circumstance, the Rector chose this day for one of his visits. He was very much amazed to encounter Miss Anastasia; it struck him evidently as something which needed to be accounted for, for she was known and noted as a dweller at home. She received him at first with a certain triumphant satisfaction, but by-and-by a little confusion appeared even in the looks of Miss Anastasia. She began to glance from the stately young man to the pale face and drooping eyelids of Agnes. She began to see the strange mixture of trouble and hardship in this extraordinary revolution, and her heart was touched for the heir deposed, as well as for the heir discovered. Lionel was "in trouble" himself, after an odd enough fashion. Some one had just instituted an action against him in the ecclesiastical courts touching the furniture of his altar, and the form in which he conducted the services. It was a strange poetic justice to bring this against him now, when he himself had cast off his high-churchism, and was luxuriating in his new freedom. But the Curate grew perfectly inspired under the infliction, and rose to the highest altitude of satisfaction and happiness, declaring this to be the testing-touch of persecution, which constantly distinguishes the true faith. It was on Miss Anastasia's lips to speak of this, and to ask the young clergyman why he was so long away from home at so critical a juncture, but her heart was touched with compunction. From looking at Lionel, she turned suddenly to Agnes, and asked, with a strange abruptness, a question which had no connection with the previous conversation—"That little book of yours, Agnes Atheling, that you sent to me, what do you mean by that story, child?—eh?—what put that into your idle little brain? It is not like fiction; it is quite as strange and out of the way as if it had been life."

Involuntarily Agnes lifted her heavy eyelids, and cast a shy look of distress and sympathy upon the unconscious Rector, who never missed any look of hers, but could not tell what this meant. "I do not know," said Agnes; but the question did not wake the shadow of a smile upon her face—it rather made her resentful. She thought it cruel of Miss Anastasia, now that all doubt was over, and Lionel was certainly disinherited. Disinherited!—he had never possessed anything actual, and nothing was taken from him; whereas Louis had been defrauded of his rights all his life; but Agnes instinctively took the part of the present sufferer—the unwitting sufferer, who suspected no evil.

But the Rector was startled in his turn by the question of Miss Anastasia. It revived in his own mind the momentary conviction of reality with which he had read the little book. When Miss Anastasia turned away for a moment, he addressed Agnes quietly aside, making a kind of appeal. "Had you, then, a real foundation—is it a true tale?" he said, looking at her with a little anxiety. She glanced up at him again, with her eyes so full of distress, anxiety, warning—then looked down with a visible paleness and trembling, faltered very much in her answer, and at last only said, expressing herself with difficulty, "It is not all real—only something like a story I have heard."

But Agnes could not bear his inquiring look; she hastily withdrew to the other side of the room, eager to be out of reach of the eyes which followed her everywhere. For his part, Lionel's first idea was of some distress of hers, which he instinctively claimed the right to soothe; but the thing remained in his mind, and gave him a certain vague uneasiness; he read the book over again when he went home, to make it out if he could, but fell so soon into thought of the writer, and consideration of that sweet youthful voice of hers, that there was no coming to any light in the matter. He not only gave it up, but forgot it again, only marvelling what was the mystery which looked so sorrowful and so bright out of Agnes Atheling's eyes.

They all waited with some little apprehension that night for the visit of Louis. He was very late; the evening wore away, and Miss Anastasia had long ago departed, taking with her, to the satisfaction of every one, the voluble Tyrolese; but Louis was not to be seen nor heard of. Very late, as they were all preparing for rest, some one came to the door. The knock raised a sudden colour on the cheeks of Marian, which had grown very pale for an hour or two. But it was not Louis; it was, however, a note from him, which Marian ran up-stairs to read. She came down again a moment after, with a pale face, painfully keeping in two big tears. "Oh, mamma, he has gone away," said Marian. She did not want to cry, and it was impossible to speak without crying; and yet she did not like to confide to any one the lover's letter. At last the tears fell, and Marian found her voice. He had just heard suddenly something very important, had seen Mr Foggo about it, and had hurried off to the country; he would not be detained long, he was sure; he had not a moment to explain anything, but would write whenever he got there. "He does not even say where," said Marian, sadly; and Rachel came close up to her, and cried without any restraint, as Marian very much wished, but did not quite like to do before her father and her brother. Mrs Atheling took them both into a corner, and scolded them after a fashion she had. "My dears, do you think you cannot trust Louis?" said Mamma—"nonsense!—we shall hear to-morrow morning. Why, he has spoken to Mr Foggo, and you may be quite sure everything is right, and that it was the most sensible thing he could do."

But it was very odd certainly, not at all explainable, and withal the most seasonable thing in the world. "I should think it quite a providence," said Mrs Atheling, "if we only heard where he was."

CHAPTER XXIV

THE FOGGOS

The first thing to be done in the morning, before it was time even for the postman, was to hasten to Killiecrankie Lodge, and ascertain all that could be ascertained concerning Louis from Mr Foggo. This mission was confided to Agnes. It was a soft spring-like morning, and the first of Miss Willsie's wallflowers were beginning to blow. Miss Willsie herself was walking in her little garden, scattering crumbs upon the gravel-path for the poor dingy town-sparrows, and the stray robin whom some unlucky wind had blown to Bellevue. But Miss Willsie was disturbed out of her usual equanimity; she looked a little heated, as if she had come here to recover herself, and rather frightened her little feathered acquaintances by the vehemence with which she threw them her daily dole. She smoothed her brow a little at sight of Agnes. "And what may you be wanting at such an hour as this?" said Miss Willsie; "if there is one thing I cannot bide, it is to see young folk wandering about, without any errand, at all the hours of the day!"

"But I have an errand," said Agnes. "I want to ask Mr Foggo about—about Mr Louis—if he knows where he has gone!"

Mr Louis—his surname, as everybody supposed—was the name by which Louis was known in Bellevue.

Miss Willsie's brow puckered with a momentary anger. "I would like to know," said Miss Willsie, "why that monkey could not content herself with a kindly lad at home: but my brother's in the parlour; you'll find him there, Agnes. Keep my patience!—Foggie's there too—the lad from America. If there's one thing in this world I cannot endure, it's just a young man like yon!"

Miss Willsie, however, reluctantly followed her young visitor into the breakfast parlour, from which the old lady had lately made an indignant and unceremonious exit. It was a very comfortable breakfast-table, fully deserving the paragraph it obtained in those "Letters from England," which are so interesting to all the readers of the Mississippi Gazette. There was a Scottish prodigality of creature comforts, and the fine ancient table-linen was white as snow, and there was a very unusual abundance, for a house of this class, of heavy old plate. Mr Foggo was getting through his breakfast methodically, with the Times erected before him, and forming a screen between himself and his worshipful nephew; while Mr Foggo S. Endicott, seated with a due regard to his profile, at such an angle with the light as to exhibit fitly that noble outline, conveyed his teacup a very long way up from the table, at dignified intervals, to his handsome and expressive mouth.

Agnes hastened to the elder gentleman at once, and drew him aside to make her inquiries. Mr Foggo smiled, and took a pinch of snuff. "All quite true," said Mr Foggo; "he came to me yesterday with a paper in his hand—a long story about next of kin wanted somewhere, and of two children belonging to some poor widow woman, who had been lost sight of a long time ago, one of whom was named Louis. That's the story; it's a mare's nest, Agnes, if you know what that is; but I thought it might divert the boy; so instead of opposing, I furnished him for his journey, and let him go without delay. No reason why the lad should not do his endeavour for his own hand. It's good for him, though it's sure to be a failure. He has told you perfectly true."

"And where has he gone?" asked Agnes anxiously.

"It's in one of the midland counties—somewhere beyond Birmingham—at this moment I do not remember the place," said Mr Foggo; "but I took a note of it, and you'll hear from him to-morrow. We've been hearing news ourselves, Agnes. Did you tell her, Willsie, what fortune has come to you and me?"

"No," said Miss Willsie. She was turning her back upon her dutiful nephew, and frowning darkly upon the teapot. The American had no chance with his offended aunt.

"A far-away cousin of ours," said Mr Foggo, who was very bland, and in a gracious humour, "has taken it into his head to die; and a very bonny place indeed, in the north country—a cosy little estate and a good house—comes to me."

"I am very glad," said Agnes, brightening in sympathy; "that is good news for everybody. Oh, Miss Willsie, how pleased Mr Foggo must be!"

Miss Willsie did not say a word—Mr Foggo smiled. "Then you think a cosy estate a good thing, Agnes?" said the old gentleman. "I am rather afraid, though you write books, you are not poetical; for that is not the view of the subject taken by my nephew here."

"I despise wealth," said Mr Endicott. "An estate, sir, is so much dirty soil. The mind is the true riches; a spark of genius is worth all the inheritances in the world!"

"And that's just so much the better for you, Foggie, my man," cried Miss Willsie suddenly; "seeing the inheritances of this world are very little like to come to your share. If there's one thing I hate, it's a lee!"

Mr Endicott took no notice of this abstract deliverance. "A very great estate—the ancient feudal domain—the glens and the gorges of the Highland chief, I respect, sir," said the elevated Yankee; "but a man who can influence a thousand minds—a man whose course is followed eagerly by the eyes of half a nation—such a man is not likely to be tempted to envy by a mile of indifferent territory. My book, by which I can move a world, is my lever of Archimedes; this broadsheet"—and he laid his hand upon the pages of the Mississippi Gazette—"is my kingdom! Miss Atheling, I shall have the honour of paying my respects to your family to-day. I shall soon take leave of Europe. I have learned much—I have experienced much—I am rejoiced to think I have been able to throw some light upon the manners and customs of your people; and henceforward I intend to devote myself to the elucidation of my own."

"We shall be very glad to see you, Mr Endicott," said Agnes, who was rather disposed to take his part, seeing he stood alone. "Now I must hasten home and tell them. We were all very anxious; but every one will be glad, Mr Foggo, to hear of you. We shall feel as if the good fortune had come to ourselves."

"Ay, Agnes, and so it might, if Marian, silly monkey, had kept a thought for one that liked her well," said Miss Willsie, as she went with her young visitor. "Poor Harry! his uncle's heart yearns to him; our gear will never go the airt of a fool like yon!" said Miss Willsie, growing very Scotch and very emphatic, as she inclined her head in the direction of Mr Endicott; "but Harry will be little heeding who gets the siller now."

Poor Harry! since he had heard of it—since he had known of Marian's engagement, he had never had the heart to make a single appearance in Bellevue.

Mr Endicott remembered his promise; he went forth in state, as soon after noon as he could go, with a due regard to the proper hour for a morning call. Mr Endicott, though he had endured certain exquisite pangs of jealousy, was not afraid of Louis; he could not suppose that any one was so blind, having his claims fairly placed before them, as to continue to prefer another; such an extent of human perversity did not enter into the calculations of Mr Endicott. And he was really "in love," like the rest of these young people. All the readers of the Mississippi Gazette knew of a certain lovely face, which brightened the imagination of their "representative man," and it was popularly expected on the other side of the water, in those refined circles familiar with Mr Endicott, that he was about to bring his bride home. He had an additional stimulus from this expectation, and went forth to-day with the determination of securing Marian Atheling. He was a little nervous, because there was a good deal of real emotion lying at the bottom of his heart; but, after all, was more doubtful of getting an opportunity than of the answer which should follow when the opportunity was gained.

To his extreme amazement, he found Marian alone. He understood it in a moment—they had left her on purpose—they comprehended his intentions! She was pale, her beautiful eyes glistened, and were wet and dewy. Perhaps she, too, had an intuition of what was coming. He thought her subdued manner, the tremble in her voice, the eyes, which were cast down so often, and did not care to meet his full gaze, were all signs of that maiden consciousness about which he had written many a time. In the full thought of this, the eloquent young American dispensed with all preamble. He came to her side with the delightful benevolence of a lover who could put this beautiful victim of his fascinations out of her suspense at once. He addressed her by her name—he added the most endearing words he could think of—he took her hand. The young beauty started from him absolutely with violence. "What do you mean, sir?" said Marian. Then she stood erect at a little distance, her eyes flashing, her cheek burning, holding her hands tight together, with an air of petulant and angry defiance. Mr Endicott was thunderstruck. "Did you not expect me—do you not understand me?" said the lover, not yet daunted. "Pardon me; I have shocked your delicate feelings. You cannot think I mean to do it, Marian, sweet British rose? You know me too well for that; you know my mind—you appreciate my feelings. You were born to be a poet's bride—I come to offer you a poet's heart!"

Before he had concluded, Marian recovered herself; into the dewy eyes, that had been musing upon Louis, the old light of girlish mischief came arch and sweet. "I did not quite understand you, Mr Endicott," said Marian, demurely. "You alarmed me a little; but I am very much obliged, and you are very good; only, I—I am sorry. I suppose you do not know I—I am engaged!"

She said this with a bright blush, casting down her eyes. She thought, after all, it was the honestest and the easiest fashion of dismissing her new lover.

"Engaged! Marian, you did not know of me—you were not acquainted with my sentiments," cried the American. "Oh, for a miserable dream of honour, will you blight my life and your own? You were not aware of my love—you were ignorant of my devotion. Beautiful Mayflower! you are free of what you did in ignorance—you are free for me!"

Marian snatched away her hand again with resentment. "I suppose you do not mean to be very impertinent, Mr Endicott, but you are so," cried the indignant little beauty. "I do not like you—I never did like you. I am very sorry, indeed, if you really cared for me. If I were free a hundred times over—if I never had seen any one," cried Marian vehemently, blushing with sudden passion, and feeling disposed to cry, "I never could have had anything to say to you. Mamma—oh, I am sure it is very cruel!—Mamma, will you speak to Mr Endicott? He has been very rude to me!"

Mamma, who came in at the moment out of the garden, started with amazement to see the flushed cheeks of Marian, and Mr Endicott, who stood in an appealing attitude, with the most crestfallen and astonished face. Marian ran from the room in an instant, scarcely able to restrain her tears of vexation and annoyance, till she was out of sight. Mrs Atheling placed a chair for her daughter's suitor very solemnly. "What has happened?—what have you been saying, Mr Endicott?" said the indignant mother.

"I have only been offering to your daughter's acceptance all that a man has to offer," said the American, with a little real dignity. "It is over; the young lady has made her own election—she rejects me! It is well! it is but another depth of human suffering opening to his feet who must tread them all! But I have nothing to apologise for. Madam, farewell!"

"Oh, stay a moment! I am very sorry—she is so young. I am sure she did not mean to offend you," said Mrs Atheling, with distress. "She is engaged, Mr Endicott. Miss Willsie knew of it. I am sure I am grieved if the foolish child has answered you unkindly; but she is engaged."

"So I am aware, madam," said Mr Endicott, gloomily; "may it be for her happiness—may no poetic retribution attend her! As for me, my art is my lifelong consolation. This, even, is for the benefit of the world; do not concern yourself for me."

But Mrs Atheling hastened up-stairs when he was gone, to reprove her daughter. To her surprise, Marian defended herself with spirit. "He was impertinent, mamma," said Marian; "he said if I had known he cared for me, I would not have been engaged. He! when everybody knows I never would speak to him. It was he who insulted me!"

So Mr Endicott's English romance ended, after all, in a paragraph which, when the time comes, we shall feel a melancholy pleasure in transcribing from the eloquent pages of the Mississippi Gazette.

CHAPTER XXV

GOOD FORTUNE

This evening was extremely quiet, and something dull, to the inhabitants of Bellevue. Though everybody knew of the little adventure of Mr Endicott, the young people were all too reverential of the romance of youth themselves to laugh very freely at the disappointed lover. Charlie sat by himself in the best room, sedulously making out his case. Charlie had risen into a person of great importance at the office since his return, and, youth as he was, was trusted so far, under Mr Foggo's superintendence, as to draw up the brief for the counsel who was to conduct this great case; so they had not even his presence to enliven the family circle, which was very dull without Louis. Then Agnes, for her part, had grown daily more self-occupied; Mrs Atheling pondered over this, half understood it, and did not ask a question on the subject. She glanced very often at the side-table, where her elder daughter sat writing. This was not a common evening occupation with Agnes; but she found a solace in that making of fables, and was forth again, appealing earnestly, with all the power and privilege of her art, not so much to her universal audience as to one among them, who by-and-by might find out the second meaning—the more fervent personal voice.

As for Marian and Rachel, they both sat at work somewhat melancholy, whispering to each other now and then, speaking low when they spoke to any one else. Papa was at his newspaper, reading little bits of news to them; but even Papa was cloudy, and there was a certain shade of dulness and melancholy over all the house.

Some one came to the door when the evening was far advanced, and held a long parley with Susan; the issue of which was, that Susan made her appearance in the parlour to ask information. "A man, ma'am, that Mr Louis appointed to come to him to-night," said Susan, "and he wants to know, please, when Mr Louis is coming home."

Mrs Atheling went to the door to answer the inquiry; then, having become somewhat of a plotter herself by force of example, she bethought her of calling Charlie. The man was brought into the best room; he was an ordinary-looking elderly man, like a small shopkeeper. He stated what he wanted slowly, without any of the town sharpness. He said the young gentleman was making out some account—as he understood—about Lord Winterbourne, and hearing that he had been once about the Hall in his young days, had come to him to ask some questions. He was a likely young gentleman, and summat in his own mind told the speaker he had seen his face afore, whether it were about the Hall, or where it were, deponent did not know; but thinking upon it, just bethought him at this moment that he was mortal like the old lord. Now the young gentleman—as he heard—had gone sudden away to the country, and the lady of the house where he lived had sent the perplexed caller here.

"I know very well about that quarter myself," said Mrs Atheling. "Do you know the Old Wood Lodge? that belongs to us; and if you have friends in the village, I daresay I shall know your name."

The man put up his hand to his forehead respectfully. "I knowed the old lady at the Lodge many a year ago," said he. "My name's John Morrall. I was no more nor a helper at the stables in my day; and a sister of mine had charge of some children about the Hall."

"Some children—who were they?" said Charlie. "Perhaps Lord Winterbourne's children; but that would be very long ago."

"Well, sir," said the man with a little confusion, glancing aside at Mrs Atheling, "saving the lady's presence, I'd be bold to say that they was my lord's, but in a sort of an—unlawful way; two poor little morsels of twins, that never had nothing like other children. He wasn't any way kind to them, wasn't my lord."

"I think I know the children you mean," said Charlie, to the surprise and admiration of his mother, who checked accordingly the exclamation on her own lips. "Do you know where they came from?—were you there when they were brought to the Hall?"

"Ay, sir, I know—no man better," said Morrall. "Sally was the woman—all along of my lord's man that she was keeping company with the same time, little knowing, poor soul, what she was to come to—that brought them unfortunate babbies out of London. I don't know no more. Sally's opinion was, they came out o' foreign parts afore that; for the nurse they had with them, Sally said, was some outlandish kind of a Portugee."

"A Portuguese!" exclaimed both the listeners in dismay—but Charlie added immediately, "What made your sister suppose she was a Portuguese?"

"Well, sir, she was one of them foreign kind of folks—but noways like my lady's French maid, Sally said—so taking thought what she was, a cousin of ours that's a sailor made no doubt but she was a Portugee—so she gave up the little things to Sally, not one of them able to say a word to each other; for the foreign woman, poor soul, knew no English, and Sally brought down the babbies to the Hall."

"Does your sister live at Winterbourne?" asked Charlie.

"What, Sally, sir? poor soul!" said John Morrall, "to her grief she married my lord's man, again all we could say, and he went pure to the bad, as was to be seen of him, and listed—and now she's off in Ireland with the regiment, a poor creature as you could see—five children, ma'am, alive, and she's had ten; always striving to do her best, but never able, poor soul, to keep a decent gown to her back."

"Will you tell me where she is?" said Charlie, while his mother went hospitably away to bring a glass of wine, a rare and unusual dainty, for the refreshment of this most welcome visitor—"there is an inquiry going on at present, and her evidence might be of great value: it will be good for her, don't fear. Let me know where she is."

While Charlie took down the address, his mother, with her own hand, served Mr John Morrall with a slice of cake and a comfortable glass of port-wine. "But I am sure you are comfortable yourself—you look so, at least."

"I am in the green-grocery trade," said their visitor, putting up his hand again with "his respects," "and got a good wife and three as likely childer as a man could desire. It ain't just as easy as it might be keeping all things square, but we always get on; and lord! if folks had no crosses, they'd ne'er know they were born. Look at Sally, there's a picture!—and after that, says I, it don't become such like as us to complain."

Finally, having finished his refreshment, and left his own address with a supplementary note, and touch of the forehead—"It ain't very far off; glad to serve you, ma'am"—Mr John Morrall withdrew. Then Charlie returned to his papers, but not quite so composedly as usual. "Put up my travelling-bag, mother," said Charlie, after a few ineffectual attempts to resume; "I'll not write any more to-night; it's just nine o'clock. I'll step over and see old Foggo, and be off to Ireland to-morrow, without delay."

CHAPTER XXVI

THE OXFORD ASSIZES

April, as cloudless and almost as warm as summer, a day when all the spring was swelling sweet in all the young buds and primroses, and the broad dewy country smiled and glistened under the rising of that sun, which day by day shone warmer and fuller on the woods and on the fields. But the point of interest was not the country; it was not a spring festival which drew so many interested faces along the high-road. An expectation not half so amiable was abroad among the gentry of Banburyshire—a great many people, quite an unusual crowd, took their way to the spring assizes to listen to a trial which was not at all important on its own account. The defendants were not even known among the county people, nor was there much curiosity about them. It was a family quarrel which roused the kind and amiable expectations of all these excellent people,—The Honourable Anastasia Rivers against Lord Winterbourne. It was popularly anticipated that Miss Anastasia herself was to appear in the witness-box, and everybody who knew the belligerents, delighted at the prospect of mischief, hastened to be present at the fight.

And there was a universal gathering, besides, of all the people more immediately interested in this beginning of the war. Lord Winterbourne himself, with a certain ghastly levity in his demeanour, which sat ill upon his bloodless face, and accorded still worse with the mourner's dress which he wore, graced the bench. Charlie Atheling sat in his proper place below, as agent for the defendant, within reach of the counsel for the same. His mother and sisters were with Miss Anastasia, in a very favourable place for seeing and hearing; the Rector was not far from them, very much interested, but exceedingly surprised at the unchanging paleness of Agnes, and the obstinacy with which she refused to meet his eye; for that she avoided him, and seemed overwhelmed by some secret and uncommunicated mystery, which no one else, even in her own family, shared, was clear enough to a perception quickened by the extreme "interest" which Lionel Rivers felt in Agnes Atheling. Even Rachel had been brought thither in the train of Miss Anastasia; and though rather disturbed by her position, and by the disagreeable and somewhat terrifying consciousness of being observed by Lord Winterbourne, in whose presence she had not been before, since the time she left the Hall—Rachel, with her veil over her face, had a certain timid enjoyment of the bustle and novelty of the scene. Louis, too, was there, sent down on the previous night with a commission from Mr Foggo; there was no one wanting. The two or three who knew the tactics of the day, awaited their disclosure with great secret excitement, speculating upon their effect; and those who did not, looked on eagerly with interest and anxiety and hope.

Only Agnes sat drawing back from them, between her mother and sister, letting her veil hang with a pitiful unconcern in thick double folds half over her pale face. She did not care to lift her eyes; she looked heavy, wretched, spiritless; she could not keep her thoughts upon the smiling side of the picture; she thought only of the sudden blow about to fall—of the bitter sense of deception and craftiness, of the overwhelming disappointment which this day must bring forth.

The case commenced. Lord Winterbourne's counsel stated the plea of his noble client; it did not occupy a very long time, for no one supposed it very important. The statement was, that Miss Bridget Atheling had been presented by the late Lord Winterbourne with a life-interest in the little property involved; that the Old Wood Lodge, the only property in the immediate neighbourhood which was not in the peaceful possession of Lord Winterbourne, had never been separated or alienated from the estate; that, in fact, the gift to Miss Bridget was a mere tenant's claim upon the house during her lifetime, with no power of bequest whatever; and the present Lord Winterbourne's toleration of its brief occupancy by the persons in possession, was merely a good-humoured carelessness on the part of his lordship of a matter not sufficiently important to occupy his thoughts. The only evidence offered was the distinct enumeration of the Old Wood Lodge along with the Old Wood House, and the cottages in the village of Winterbourne, as in possession of the family at the accession of the late lord; and the learned gentleman concluded his case by declaring that he confidently challenged his opponent to produce any deed or document whatever which so much as implied that the property had been bestowed upon Bridget Atheling. No deed of gift—no conveyance—nothing whatever in the shape of title-deeds, he was confident, existed to support the claim of the defendant; a claim which, if it was not a direct attempt to profit by the inadvertence of his noble client, was certainly a very ugly and startling mistake.

So far everything was brief enough, and conclusive enough, as it appeared. The audience was decidedly disappointed: if the answer was after this style, there was no "fun" to be expected, and it had been an entire hoax which seduced the Banburyshire notabilities to waste the April afternoon in a crowded court-house. But Miss Anastasia, swelling with anxiety and yet with triumph, was visible to every one; visible also to one eye was something very different—Agnes, pale, shrinking, closing her eyes, looking as if she would faint. The Rector made his way behind, and spoke to her anxiously. He was afraid she was ill; could he assist her through the crowd? Agnes turned her face to him for a moment, and her eyes, which looked so dilated and pitiful, but only said "No, no," in a hurried whisper, and turned again. The counsel on the other side had risen, and was about to begin the defence.

"My learned brother is correct, and doubtless knows himself to be so," said the advocate of the Athelings. "We have no deed to produce, though we have something nearly as good; but, my lord, I am instructed suddenly to change the entire ground of my plea. Certain information which has come to the knowledge of my clients, but which it was not their wish to make public at present, has been now communicated to me; and I beg to object at once to the further progress of the suit, on a ground which your lordship will at once acknowledge to be just and forcible. I assert that the present bearer of the title is not the true Lord Winterbourne."

There rose immediately a hum and murmur of the strangest character—not applause, not disapproval—simple consternation, so extreme that no one could restrain its utterance. People rose up and stared at the speaker, as if he had been seized with sudden madness in their presence; then there ensued a scene of much tumult and agitation. The judges on the bench interposed indignantly. The counsel for Lord Winterbourne sprang to his feet, appealing with excitement to their lordships—was this to be permitted? Even the audience, Lord Winterbourne's neighbours, who had no love for him, pressed forward as if to support him in this crisis, and with resentment and disapproval looked upon Miss Anastasia, to whom every one turned instinctively, as to a conspirator who had overshot the mark. It was scarcely possible for the daring speaker to gain himself a hearing. When he did so, at last, it was rather as a culprit than an accuser. But even the frown of a chief-justice did not appal a man who held Charlie Atheling's papers in his hands; he was heard again, declaring, with force and dignity, that he was incapable of making such a statement without proofs in his possession which put it beyond controversy. He begged but a moment's patience, in justice to himself and to his client, while he placed an abstract of the case and the evidence in their lordships' hands.

Then to the sudden hum and stir, which the officials of the court had not been able to put down, succeeded that total, strange, almost appalling stillness of a crowd, which is so very impressive at all times. While the judges consulted together, looking keenly over these mysterious papers, almost every eye among the spectators was riveted upon them. No one noticed even Lord Winterbourne, who stood up in his place unconsciously, overlooking them all, quite unaware of the prominence and singularity of his position, gazing before him with a motionless blank stare, like a man looking into the face of Fate. The auditors waited almost breathless for the decision of the law. That anything so wild and startling could ever be taken into consideration by those grave authorities was of itself extraordinary; and as the consultation was prolonged, the anxiety grew gradually greater. Could there be reality in it? could it be true?

At last the elder judge broke the silence. "This is a very serious statement," he said: "of course, it involves issues much more important than the present question. As further proceedings will doubtless be grounded on these documents, it is our opinion that the hearing of this case had better be adjourned."

Lord Winterbourne seated himself when he heard the voice—it broke the spell; but not so Louis, who stood beneath, alone, looking straight up at the speaker in his judicial throne. The truth flashed to the mind of Louis like a gleam of lightning. He did not ask a question, though Charlie was close by him; he did not turn his head, though Miss Anastasia was within reach of his eye; his whole brain seemed to burn and glow; the veins swelled upon his forehead; he raised up his head for air, for breath, like a man overwhelmed; he did not see how the gaze of half the assembly began to be attracted to himself. In this sudden pause he stood still, following out the conviction which burst upon him—this conviction, which suddenly, like a sunbeam, made all things clear. Wrong as he had been in the details, his imagination was true as the most unerring judgment. For what child in the world was it so much this man's interest to disgrace and disable as the child whose rights he usurped—his brother's lawful heir? This silence was like a lifetime to Louis, but it ended in a moment. Some confused talking followed—objections on the part of Lord Winterbourne's representative, which were overruled; and then another case was called—a common little contest touching mere lands and houses—and every one awoke, as at the touch of a disenchanting rod, to the common pale daylight and common controversy, as from a dream.

Then the people streamed out in agitated groups, some retaining their first impulse of contradiction and resentment; others giving up at once, and receiving the decision of the judges as final. Then Agnes looked back, with a sick and trembling anxiety, for the Rector. The Rector was gone; and they all followed one after another, silent in the great tremor of their excitement. When they came to the open air, Marian began to ask questions eagerly, and Rachel to cry behind her veil, and cast woeful wistful looks at Miss Anastasia. What was it? what was the matter? was it anything about Louis? who was Lord Winterbourne?

CHAPTER XXVII

THE TRUE HEIR

"I do not know how he takes it, mother," said Charlie. "I do not know if he takes it at all; he has not spoken a single word all the way home."

He did not seem disposed to speak many now; he went into Miss Bridget's dusky little parlour, lingering a moment at the door, and bending forward in reflection from the little sloping mirror on the wall. The young man was greatly moved, silent with inexpressible emotion; he went up to Marian first, and, in the presence of them all, kissed her little trembling hand and her white cheek; then he drew her forward with him, holding her up with his own arm, which trembled too, and came direct to Miss Anastasia, who was seated, pale, and making gigantic efforts to command herself, in old Miss Bridget's chair. "This is my bride," said Louis firmly, yet with quivering lips. "What are we to call you?"

The old lady looked at him for a moment, vainly endeavouring to retain her self-possession—then sprang up suddenly, grasped him in her arms, and broke forth into such a cry of weeping as never had been heard before under this peaceful roof. "What you will! what you will! my boy, my heir, my father's son!" cried Miss Anastasia, lifting up her voice. No one moved, or spoke a word—it was like one of those old agonies of thanksgiving in the old Scriptures, when a Joseph or a Jacob, parted for half a patriarch's lifetime, "fell upon his neck and wept."

When this moment of extreme agitation was over, the principal actors in the family drama came again into a moderate degree of calmness: Louis was almost solemn in his extreme youthful gravity. The young man was changed in a moment, as, perhaps, nothing but this overwhelming flood of honour and prosperity could have changed him. He desired to see the evidence and investigate his own claims thoroughly, as it was natural he should; then he asked Charlie to go out with him, for there was not a great deal of room in this little house, for private conference. The two young men went forth together through those quiet well-known lanes, upon which Louis gazed with a giddy eye. "This should have come to me in some place where I was a stranger," he said with excitement; "it might have seemed more credible, more reasonable, in a less familiar place. Here, where I have been an outcast and dishonoured all my life—here!"

"Your own property," said Charlie. "I'm not a poetical man, you know—it is no use trying—but I'd come to a little sentiment, I confess, if I were you."

"In the mean time there are other people concerned," said Louis, taking Charlie's arm, and turning him somewhat hurriedly away from the edge of the wood, which at this epoch of his fortunes, the scene of so many despairing fancies, was rather more than he chose to experiment upon. "You are not poetical, Charlie. I do not suppose it has come to your turn yet—but we do not want poetry to-night; there are other people concerned. So far as I can see, your case—I scarcely can call it mine, who have had no hand in it—is clear as daylight—indisputable. Is it so?—you know better than me."

"Indisputable," said Charlie, authoritatively.

"Then it should never come to a trial—for the honour of the house—for pity," said the heir. "A bad man taken in the toils is a very miserable thing to look at, Charlie; let us spare him if we can. I should like you to get some one who is to be trusted—say Mr Foggo, with some well-known man along with him—to wait upon Lord Winterbourne. Let them go into the case fully, and show him everything: say that I am quite willing that the world should think he had done it in ignorance—and persuade him—that is, if he is convinced, and they have perfect confidence in the case. The story need not be publicly known. Is it practicable?—tell me at once."

"It's practicable if he'll do it," said Charlie; "but he'll not do it, that's all."

"How do you know he'll not do it?—it is to save himself," said Louis.

"If he had not known it all along, he'd have given in," said Charlie, "and taken your offer, of course; but he has known it all along—it's been his ghost for years. He has his plans all prepared and ready, you may be perfectly sure. It is generous of you to suggest such a thing, but he would suppose it a sign of weakness. Never mind that—it's not of the least importance what he supposes; if you desire it, we can try."

"I do desire it," said Louis; "and then, Charlie, there is the Rector."

Charlie shook his head regretfully. "I am sorry for him myself," said the young lawyer; "but what can you do?"

"He has been extremely kind to me," said Louis, with a slight trembling in his voice—"kinder than any one in the world, except your own family. There is his house—I see what to do; let us go at once and explain everything to him to-night."

"To-night! that's premature—showing your hand," said Charlie, startled in his professional caution: "never mind, you can stand it; he's a fine fellow, though he is the other line. If you like it, I don't object; but what shall you say?"

"He ought to have his share," said Louis—"don't interrupt me, Charlie; it is more generous in our case to receive than to give. He ought, if I represent the elder branch, to have the younger's share: he ought to permit me to do as much for him as he would have done for me. Ah, he bade me look at the pictures to see that I was a Rivers. I did not suppose any miracle on earth could make me proud of the name."

They went on hastily together in the early gathering darkness. The Old Wood House stood blank and dull as usual, with all its closed blinds; but the gracious young Curate, meditating his sermon, and much elated by his persecution, was straying about the well-kept paths. Mr Mead hastened to tell them that Mr Rivers had left home—"hastened away instantly to appear in our own case," said the young clergyman. "The powers of this world are in array against us—we suffer persecution, as becomes the true church. The Rector left hurriedly to appear in person. He is a devoted man, a noble Anglican. I smile myself at the reproaches of our adversary; I have no fear."

"We may see him in town," said Louis, turning away with disappointment. "If you write, will you mention that I have been here to-night, to beg his counsel and friendship—I, Louis Rivers—" A sudden colour flushed over the young man's face; he pronounced the name with a nervous firmness; it was the first time he had called himself by any save his baptismal name all his life.

As they turned and walked home again, Louis relapsed into his first agitated consciousness, and did not care to say a word. Louis Rivers! lawful heir and only son of a noble English peer and an unsullied mother. It was little wonder if the young man's heart swelled within him, too high for a word or a thought. He blotted out the past with a generous haste, unwilling to remember a single wrong done to him in the time of his humiliation, and looked out upon the future as upon a glorious vision, almost too wonderful to be realised: it was best to rest in this agitated moment of strange triumph, humility, and power, to convince himself that this was real, and to project his anticipations forward only with a generous anxiety for the concerns of others, with no question, when all questions were so overwhelming and incredible, after this extraordinary fortune of his own.

CHAPTER XXVIII

AT HOME

It would not be easy to describe the state of mind of the feminine portion of this family which remained at home. Marian, in a strange and overpowering tumult—Marian, who was the first and most intimately concerned, her cheek burning still under the touch of her lover's trembling lip in that second and more solemn betrothal, sat on a stool, half hidden by Miss Anastasia's big chair and ample skirts, supporting her flushed cheeks on those pretty rose-tipped hands, to which the flush seemed to have extended, her beautiful hair drooping down among her fingers, her eyes cast down, her heart leaping like a bird against her breast. Her own vague suspicions, keen and eager as they were, had never pointed half so far as this. If it did not "turn her head" altogether, it was more because the little head was giddy with amaze and confusion, than from any virtue on the part of Marian. She was quite beyond the power of thinking; a strange brilliant extraordinary panorama glided before her—Louis in Bellevue—Louis at the Old Wood Lodge—Louis, the lord of all he looked upon, in Winterbourne Hall!

Rachel, for her part, was to be found, now in one corner, now in another, crying very heartily, and with a general vague impulse of kissing every one in the present little company with thanks and gratitude, and being caressed and sympathised with in turn. The only one here, indeed, who seemed in her full senses was Agnes, who kept them all in a certain degree of self-possession. It was all over, at last, after so long a time of suspense and mystery; Agnes was relieved of her secret knowledge. She was grave, but she did not refuse to participate in the confused joy and thankfulness of the house. Now that the secret was revealed, her mind returned to its usual tone. Though she had so much "interest" in Lionel—almost as much as he felt in her—she had too high a mind herself to suppose him overwhelmed by the single fact that his inheritance had passed away from him. When all was told, she breathed freely. She had all the confidence in him which one high heart has in another. After the first shock, she prophesied proudly, within her own mind, how soon his noble spirit would recover itself. Perhaps she anticipated other scenes in that undeveloped future, which might touch her own heart with a stronger thrill than even the marvellous change which was now working; perhaps the faint dawn of colour on her pale cheek came from an imagination far more immediate and personal than any dream which ever before had flushed the maiden firmament of Agnes Atheling's meditations. However that might be, she said not a single word upon the subject: she assumed to herself quietly the post of universal ministration, attended to the household wants as much as the little party, all excited and sublimed out of any recollection of ordinary necessities, would permit her; and lacking nothing in sympathy, yet quieter than any one else, insensibly to herself, formed the link between this little agitated world of private history and the larger world, not at all moved from its everyday balance, which lay calm and great without.

"I sign a universal amnesty," said Miss Anastasia abruptly, after a long silence—"himself, if he would consult his own interest, I could pass over his faults to-day."

"Poor Mr Reginald!" said Mrs Atheling, wiping her eyes. "I beg your pardon, Miss Rivers; he has done a great deal of wrong, but I am very sorry for him: I was so when he lost his son; ah, no doubt he thinks this is a very small matter after that."

"Hush, child, the man is guilty," said Miss Anastasia, with strong emphasis. "Young George Rivers went to his grave in peace. Whom the gods love die young; it was very well. I forgive his father if he withdraws; he will, if he has a spark of honour. The only person whom I am grieved for is Lionel—he, indeed, might have cause to complain. Agnes Atheling, do you know where he has gone?"

"No." Agnes affected no surprise that the question should be asked her, and did not even show any emotion. Marian, with a sudden impulse of generosity, got up instantly, and came to her sister. "Oh, Agnes, I am very sorry," said the little beauty, with her palpitating heart; and Marian put her pretty arms round Agnes's neck to console and comfort her, as Agnes might have done to Marian had Louis been in distress instead of joy.

Agnes drew herself instinctively out of her sister's embrace. She had no right to be looked upon as the representative of Lionel, yet she could not help speaking, in her confidence and pride in him, with a kindling cheek and rising heart. "I am not sorry for Mr Rivers now," said Agnes, firmly; "I was so while this secret was kept from him—while he was deceived; but I think no one who does him due credit can venture to pity him now."

Miss Anastasia roused herself a little at sound of the voice. This pride, which sounded a little like defiance, stirred the old lady's heart like the sound of a trumpet; she had more pleasure in it than she had felt in anything, save her first welcome of Louis a few hours ago. She looked steadily into the eyes of Agnes, who met her gaze without shrinking, though with a rapid variation of colour. Whatever imputations she herself might be subject to in consequence, Agnes could not sit by silent, and hear him either pitied or belied.

"I wonder, may I go and see Miss Rivers? would it be proper?" asked Rachel timidly, making a sudden diversion, as she had rather a habit of doing; "she wanted me to stay with her once; she was very kind to me."

"I suppose we must not call you the Honourable Rachel Rivers just yet—eh, little girl?" said Miss Anastasia, turning upon her; "and you, Marian, you little beauty, how shall you like to be Lady Winterbourne?"

"Lady Winterbourne! I always said she was to be for Louis," cried Rachel—"always—the first time I saw her; you know I did, Agnes; and often I wondered why she should be so pretty—she who did not want it, who was happy enough to have been ugly, if she had liked; but I see it now—I see the reason now!"

"Don't hide your head, little one; it is quite true," said Miss Anastasia, once more a little touched at her heart to see the beautiful little figure, fain to glide out of everybody's sight, stealing away in a moment into the natural refuge, the mother's shadow; while the mother, smiling and sobbing, had entirely given up all attempt at any show of self-command. "Agnes has something else to do in this hard-fighting world. You are the flower that must know neither winds nor storms. I don't speak to make you vain, you beautiful child. God gave you your lovely looks, as well as your strange fortune; and Agnes, child, lift up your head! the contest and the trial are for you; but not, God forbid it! as they came to me."

CHAPTER XXIX

THE RIVAL HEIRS

Louis and Rachel returned that night with Miss Anastasia to the Priory, which, the old lady said proudly—the family jointure house for four or five generations—should be their home till the young heir took possession of his paternal house. The time which followed was too busy, rapid, and exciting for a slow and detailed history. The first legal steps were taken instantly in the case, and proper notices served upon Lord Winterbourne. In Miss Anastasia's animated and anxious house dwelt the Tyrolese, painfully acquiring some scant morsels of English, very well contented with her present quarters, and only anxious to secure some extravagant preferment for her son. Mrs Atheling and her daughters had returned home, and Louis came and went constantly to town, actively engaged himself in all the arrangements, full of anxious plans and undertakings for the ease and benefit of the other parties concerned. Miss Anastasia, with a little reluctance, had given her consent to the young man's plan of a compromise, by which his uncle, unattacked and undisgraced, might retire from his usurped possessions with a sufficient and suitable income. The ideas of Louis were magnificent and princely. He would have been content to mulct himself of half the revenues of his inheritance, and scarcely would listen to the prudent cautions of his advisers. He was even reluctant that the first formal steps should be taken, before Mr Foggo and an eminent and well-known solicitor, personally acquainted with his uncle, had waited upon Lord Winterbourne. He was overruled; but this solemn deputation lost no time in proceeding on its mission. Speedy as they were, however, they were too late for the alarmed and startled peer. He had left home, they ascertained, very shortly after the late trial—had gone abroad, as it was supposed, leaving no information as to the time of his return. The only thing which could be done in the circumstances was hastened by the eager exertions of Louis. The two lawyers wrote a formal letter to Lord Winterbourne, stating their case, and making their offer, and despatched it to the Hall, to be forwarded to him. No answer came, though Louis persuaded his agents to wait for it, and even to delay the legal proceedings. The only notice taken of it was a paragraph in one of the fashionable newspapers, to the effect that the late proceedings at Oxford, impugning the title of a respected nobleman, proved now to be a mere trick of some pettifogging lawyer, entirely unsupported, and extremely likely to call forth proceedings for libel, involving a good deal of romantic family history, and extremely interesting to the public. After this, Louis could no longer restrain the natural progress of the matter. He gave it up, indeed, at once, and did not try; and Miss Anastasia pronounced emphatically one of her antique proverbs, "Whom the gods would destroy, they first make mad."

This was not the only business on the hands of Louis. He had found it impossible, on repeated trials, to see the Rector. At the Old Wood House it was said that Mr Rivers was from home; at his London lodgings he had not been heard of. The suit was given against him in the Ecclesiastical Courts, and Mr

Mead, alone in the discharge of his duty, mourned over a stripped altar and desolated sanctuary, where the tall candles blazed no longer in the religious gloom. When it became evident at last that the Rector did not mean to give his young relative the interview he sought, Louis, strangely transformed as he was, from the petulant youth always ready to take offence, to the long-suffering man, addressed Lionel as his solicitors had addressed his uncle. He wrote a long letter, generous and full of hearty feeling; he reminded his kinsman of the favours he had himself accepted at his hands. He drew a very vivid picture of his own past and present position. He declared, with all a young man's fervour, that he could have no pleasure even in his own extraordinary change of fortune, were it the means of inflicting a vast and unmitigated loss upon his cousin. He threw himself upon Lionel's generosity—he appealed to his natural sense of justice—he used a hundred arguments which were perfectly suitable and in character from him, but which, certainly, no man as proud and as generous as himself could be expected to listen to; and, finally, ended with protesting an unquestionable claim upon Lionel—the claim of a man deeply indebted to, and befriended by him. The letter overflowed with the earnestness and sincerity of the writer; he assumed his case throughout with the most entire honesty, having no doubt whatever upon the subject, and confided his intentions and prospects to Lionel with a complete and anxious confidence, which he had not bestowed upon any other living man.

This letter called forth an answer, written from a country town in a remote part of England. The Rector wrote with an evident effort at cordiality. He declined all Louis's overtures in the most uncompromising terms, but congratulated him upon his altered circumstances. He said he had taken care to examine into the case before leaving London, and was thoroughly convinced of the justice of the new claim. "One thing I will ask of you," said Mr Rivers; "I only wait to resign my living until I can be sure of the next presentation falling into your hands: give it to Mr Mead. The cause of my withdrawal is entirely private and personal. I had resolved upon it months ago, and it has no connection whatever with recent circumstances. I hope no one thinks so meanly of me as to suppose I am dismayed by the substitution of another heir in my room. One thing in this matter has really wounded me, and that is the fact that no one concerned thought me worthy to know a secret so important, and one which it was alike my duty and my right to help to a satisfactory conclusion. I have lost nothing actual, so far as rank or means is concerned; but, more intolerable than any vulgar loss, I find a sudden cloud thrown upon the perfect sincerity and truth of some whom I have been disposed to trust as men trust Heaven."

The letter concluded with good wishes—that was all; there was no response to the confidence, no answer to the effusion of heartfelt and fervent feeling which had been in Louis's letter. The young man was not accustomed to be repulsed; perhaps, in all his life, it was the first time he had asked a favour from any one, and had Louis been poor and without friends, as he was or thought himself six months ago, such a tone would have galled him beyond endurance. But there is a charm in a gracious and relenting fortune. Louis, who had once been the very armadillo of youthful haughtiness, suddenly distinguished himself by the most magnanimous patience, would not take offence, and put away his kinsman's haughty letter, with regret, but without any resentment. Nothing was before him now but the plain course of events, and to them he committed himself frankly, resolved to do what could be done, but addressing no more appeals to the losing side.

Part of the Rector's letter Louis showed to Marian, and Marian repeated it to Agnes. It was cruel—it was unjust of Lionel—and he knew himself that it was. Agnes, it was possible, did not know—at all events, she had no right to betray to him the secrets of another; more than that, he knew the meaning now of the little book which he carried everywhere with him, and felt in his heart that he was the real person addressed. He knew all that quite as well as she did, as she tried, with a quivering lip and a proud wet eye, to fortify herself against the injustice of his reproach, but that did not hinder him from saying it. He was in that condition—known, perhaps, occasionally to most of us—when one feels a certain perverse pleasure in wounding one's dearest. He had no chance of mentioning her, who occupied so much of his thoughts, in any other way, and he would rather put a reproach upon Agnes than leave her alone altogether; perhaps she herself even, after all, at the bottom of her heart, was better satisfied to be referred to thus, than to be left out of his thoughts. They had never spoken to each other a single word which could be called wooing—now they were perhaps separated for ever—yet how strange a link of union, concord, and opposition, was between these two!

CHAPTER XXX

AN ADVENTURE

It was September—the time when all Englishmen of a certain "rank in life" burn with unconquerable longings to get as far away from home as possible—and there was nothing remarkable in the appearance of this solitary traveller pacing along Calais pier—nothing remarkable, except his own personal appearance, which was of a kind not easily overlooked. There was nothing to be read in his embrowned but refined face, nor in his high thoughtful forehead. It was a face of thought, of speculation, of a great and vigorous intellectual activity; but the haughty eyes looked at no one—the lips never moved even to address a child—there was no response to any passing glance of interest or inquiry. His head was turned towards England, over the long sinuous weltering waves of that stormy Channel which to-day pretended to be calm; but if he saw anything, it was something which appeared only in his own imagination—it was neither the far-away gleam, like a floating mist, of the white cliffs, nor the sunbeam coming down out of the heart of a cloud into the dark mid-current of that treacherous sea.

He had no plan of travel—no settled intentions indeed of any kind—but had been roaming about these three months in the restlessness of suspense, waiting for definite intelligence before he decided on his further course. An often-recurring fancy of returning home for a time had brought him to-day to this common highway of all nations from a secluded village among the Pyrenees; but he had not made up his mind to go home—he only lingered within sight of it, chafing his own disturbed spirit, and ready to be swayed by any momentary impulse. Though he had been disturbed for a time out of his study of the deepest secrets of human life, his mind was too eager not to have returned to it. He had come to feel that it would be sacrilege to proclaim again his own labouring and disordered thoughts in a place where he was set to speak of One, the very imagination of whom, if it was an imagination, was so immeasurably exalted above his highest elevation. A strange poetic justice had come upon Lionel Rivers—prosecuted for his extreme views at the time when he ceased to make any show of holding them—separating himself from his profession, and from the very name of a believer, at the moment when it began to dawn upon him that he believed—and thrust asunder with a violent wrench and convulsion from the first and sole human creature who had come into his heart, at the very hour in which he discovered that his heart was no longer in his own power. He saw it all, the strange story of contradictory and perverse chances, and knew himself the greatest and strangest contradiction of the whole.

He gave no attention whatever to what passed round him, yet he heard the foreign voices—the English voices—for there was no lack of his countrymen. It was growing dark rapidly, and the shadowy evening lights and mists were stealing far away to sea. He turned to go back to his hotel, turning his face away from his own country, when at the moment a voice fell upon his ear, speaking his own tongue: "You will abet an impostor—you who know nothing of English law, and are already a marked man." These were the words spoken in a very low, clear, hissing tone, which Lionel heard distinctly only because it was well known to him. The speaker was wrapt in a great cloak, with a travelling-cap over his eyes; and the person he addressed was a little vivacious Italian, with a long olive face, smooth-shaven cheeks, and sparkling lively eyes, who seemed much disconcerted and doubtful what to do. The expression of Lionel's face changed in an instant—he woke out of his moody dream to alert and determined action; he drew back a step to let them pass, and then followed. The discussion was animated and eager between them, sometimes in English, sometimes in Italian, apparently as caprice guided the one or the other. Lionel did not listen to what they said, but he followed them home.

The old Italian parted with his companion at the door of the hotel where Lionel himself was lodged; there the Englishman in the cloak and cap lingered to make an appointment. "At eleven to-morrow," said again that sharp hissing voice. Lionel stepped aside into the shadow as the stranger turned reluctantly away; he did not care for making further investigations to ascertain his identity—it was Lord Winterbourne.

He took the necessary steps immediately. It was easy to find out where the Italian was, in a little room at the top of the house, the key of which he paused to take down before he went up-stairs. Lionel waited again till the old man had made his way to his lofty lodging. He was very well acquainted with all the details of Louis's case; he had, in fact, seen Charlie Atheling a few days before he left London, and satisfied himself of the nature of his young kinsman's claim—it was too important to himself to be forgotten. He remembered perfectly the Italian doctor Serrano who had been present, and could testify to the marriage of the late Lord Winterbourne. Lionel scaled the great staircase half-a-dozen steps at a time, and reached the door immediately after the old man had entered, and before he had struck his light. The Rector knocked softly. With visible perturbation, and in a sharp tone of self-defence, the Italian called out in a very good French to know who was there. Dr Serrano was a patriot and a plotter, and used to domiciliary visitations. Lionel answered him in English, asked if he were Doctor Serrano, and announced himself as a friend of Charles Atheling. Then the door opened slowly, and with some jealousy. Lionel passed into the room without waiting for an invitation. "You are going to England on a matter of the greatest importance," said the Rector, with excitement—"to restore the son of your friend to his inheritance; yet I find you, with the serpent at your ear, listening to Lord Winterbourne."

The Italian started back in amaze. "Are you the devil?" said Doctor Serrano, with a comical perturbation.

"No; instead of that, you have just left him," said Lionel; "but I am a friend, and know all. This man persuades you not to go on—by accident I caught the sound of his voice saying so. He has the most direct personal interest in the case; it is ruin and disgrace to him. Your testimony may be of the greatest importance—why do you linger? why do you listen to him?"

"Really, you are hot-headed; it is so with youth," said Doctor Serrano, "when we will move heaven and earth for one friend. He tells me the child is dead—that this is another. I know not—it may be true."

"It is not true," said Lionel. "I will tell you who I am—the next heir if Lord Winterbourne is the true holder of the title—there is my card. I have the strongest interest in resisting this claim if I did not know it to be true. It can be proved that this is the same boy who was brought from Italy an infant. I can prove it myself; it is known to a whole village. If you choose it, confront me with Lord Winterbourne."

"No; I believe you—you are a gentleman," said Doctor Serrano, turning over the card in his hand—and the old man added with enthusiasm, "and a hero for a friend!"

"You believe me?" said Lionel, who could not restrain the painful smile which crossed his face at the idea of his heroism in the cause of Louis. "Will you stay, then, another hour within reach of Lord Winterbourne?"

The Italian shrugged his shoulders. "I will break with him; he is ever false," said the old man. "What besides can I do?"

"I will tell you," said Lionel. "The boat sails in an hour—come with me at once, let me see you safe in England. I shall attend to your comfort with all my power. There is time for a good English bed at Dover, and an undisturbed rest. Doctor Serrano, for the sake of the oppressed, and because you are a philosopher, and understand the weakness of human nature, will you come with me?"

The Italian glanced lovingly at the couch which invited him—at the slippers and the pipe which waited to make him comfortable—then he glanced up at the dark and resolute countenance of Lionel, who, high in his chivalric honour, was determined rather to sleep at Serrano's door all night than to let him out of his hands. "Excellent young man! you are not a philosopher!" said the rueful Doctor; but he had a quick eye, and was accustomed to judge men. "I will go with you," he added seriously, "and some time, for liberty and Italy, you will do as much for me."

It was a bargain, concluded on the spot. An hour after, almost within sight of Lord Winterbourne, who was pacing the gloomy pier by night in his own gloom of guilty thought, the old man and the young man embarked for England. A few hours later the little Italian slept under an English roof, and the young Englishman looked up at the dizzy cliff, and down at the foaming sea, too much excited to think of rest. The next morning Lionel carried off his prize to London, and left him in the hands of Charlie Atheling. Then, seeing no one, speaking to no one, without lingering an hour in his native country, he turned back and went away. He had made up his mind now to remain at Calais till the matter was entirely decided—then to resign his benefice—and then, with things and not thoughts around him in the actual press and contact of common life, to read, if he could, the grand secret of a true existence, and decide his fate.

CHAPTER XXXI

THE TRIAL

Lord Winterbourne had been in Italy, going over the ground which Charlie Atheling had already examined so carefully. Miss Anastasia's proverb was coming true. He who all his life had been so wary, began to calculate madly, with an insane disregard of all the damning facts against him, on overturning, by one bold stroke, the careful fabric of the young lawyer. He sought out and found the courier Monte, whom he himself had established in his little mountain-inn. Monte was a faithful servant enough to his employer of the time, but he was not scrupulous, and had no great conscience. He undertook, without much objection, for the hire which Lord Winterbourne gave him, to say anything Lord Winterbourne pleased. He had been present at the marriage; and if the old Doctor could have been delayed, or turned back, or even kidnapped—which was in the foiled plotter's scheme, if nothing better would serve—Monte, being the sole witness of the ceremony present, might have made it out a mock marriage, or at least delayed the case, and thrown discredit upon the union. It was enough to show what mad shifts even a wise intriguer might be driven to trust in. He believed it actually possible that judge and jury would ignore all the other testimony, and trust to the unsupported word of his lying witness. He did not pause to think, tampering with truth as he had been all his life, and trusting no man, what an extreme amount of credulity he expected for himself.

But even when Doctor Serrano escaped him—when the trial drew nearer day by day—when Louis's agents came in person, respectful and urgent, to make their statement to him—and when he became aware that his case was naught, and that he had no evidence whatever to depend on save that of Monte, his wild confidence did not yield. He refused with disdain every offer of a compromise; he commanded out of his presence the bearers of that message of forbearance and forgiveness; he looked forward with a blind defiance of his fate miserable to see. He gave orders that preparations should be made at Winterbourne for the celebration of his approaching triumph. That autumn he had invited to his house a larger party than usual; and though few came, and those the least reputable, there was no want of sportsmen in the covers, nor merry-makers at the Hall: he himself was restless, and did not continue there, even for the sake of his guests, but made incessant journeys to London, and kept in constant personal attendance on himself the courier Monte. He was the object of incessant observation, and the gossip of half the county: he had many enemies; and many of those who were disposed to take his part, had heard and been convinced by the story of Louis. Almost every one, indeed, who did hear of it, and remembered the boy in his neglected but noble youth, felt the strange probability and vraisemblance of the tale; and as the time drew nearer, the interest grew. It was known that the new claimant of the title lived in Miss Anastasia's house, and that she was the warmest supporter of his claim. The people of Banburyshire were proud of Miss Anastasia; but she was Lord Winterbourne's enemy. Why? That old tragedy began to be spoken of once more in whispers; other tales crept into circulation; he was a bad man; everybody knew something of him—enough ground to judge him on; and if he was capable of all these, was he not capable of this?

As the public voice grew thus, like the voice of doom, the doomed man went on in his reckless and unreasoning confidence; the warnings of his opponents and of his friends seemed to be alike fruitless. No extent of self-delusion could have justified him at any time in thinking himself popular, yet he seemed to have a certain insane conviction now, that he had but to show himself in the court to produce an immediate reaction in his favour. He even said so, shaken out of all his old self-restrained habits, boasting with a vain braggadocio to his guests at the Hall; and people began, with a new impulse of pity, to wonder if his reason was touched, and to hint vaguely to each other that the shock had unsettled his mind.

The trial came on at the next assize; it was long, elaborate, and painful. On the very eve of this momentous day, Louis himself had addressed an appeal to his uncle, begging him, at the last moment when he could withdraw with honour, to accept the compromise so often and so anxiously proposed to him. Lord Winterbourne tore the letter in two, and put it in his pocket-book. "I shall use it," he said to the messenger, "when this business is over, to light the bonfire on Badgeley Hill."

The trial came on accordingly, without favour or private arrangement—a fair struggle of force against force. The evidence on the side of the prosecutor was laid down clearly, particular by particular; the marriage of the late Lord Winterbourne to the young Italian—the entry in his pocket-book, sworn to by Miss Anastasia—the birth of the children—their journey from Italy to London, from London to Winterbourne—and the identity of the boy Louis with the present claimant of the title—clearly, calmly, deliberately, everything was proved. It took two days to go over the evidence; then came the defence. Without an overwhelming array of witnesses on the other side—without proving perjury on the part of these—what could Lord Winterbourne answer to such a charge as this?

He commenced, through his lawyer, by a vain attempt to brand Louis over again with illegitimacy, to sully the name of his dead brother, and represent him a villanous deceiver. It was allowed, without controversy, that Louis was the son of the old lord; and then Monte was placed in the witness-box to prove that the marriage was a mock marriage, so skilfully performed as to cheat herself, her family, the old quick-witted Serrano, whose testimony had pleased every one—all the people present, in short, except his own acute and philosophical self.

The fellow was bold, clever, and scrupulous, but he was not prepared for such an ordeal. His attention distracted by the furious contradictory gestures of Doctor Serrano, whose cane could scarcely be kept out of action—by the stern, steady glance of Miss Anastasia, whom he recognised—he was no match for the skilful cross-examiners who had him in hand. He hesitated, prevaricated, altered his testimony. He held, with a grim obstinacy, to unimportant trifles, and made admissions at the same moment which struck at the very root of his own credibility as a witness. He was finally ordered to sit down by the voice of the judge himself, which rung in the fellow's ears like thunder. That was all the case for the defence! Even Lord Winterbourne's counsel coloured for shame as he made the miserable admission. The jury scarcely left the court; there was no doubt remaining on the mind of the audience. The verdict was pronounced solemnly, like a passionless voice of justice, as it was, for the plaintiff. There was no applause—no exultation—a universal human horror and disgust at the strange depravity they had just witnessed, put down every demonstration of feeling. People drew away from the neighbourhood of Lord Winterbourne as from a man in a pestilence. He left the court almost immediately, with his hat over his eyes—his witness following as he best could; then came a sudden revulsion of feeling. The best men in the county hurried towards Louis, who sat, pale and excited, by the side of his elder and his younger sister. Congratulatory good wishes poured upon him on every side. As they left the court slowly, a guard of honour surrounded this heir and hero of romance; and as he emerged into the street the air rang with a cheer for the new Lord Winterbourne. They called him "My lord," as he stood on the step of Miss Anastasia's carriage, which she herself entered as if it had been a car of triumph. She called him "My lord," making a proud obeisance to him, as a mother might have done to her son, a new-made king; and they drove off slowly, with riders in their train, amid the eager observation of all the passengers—the new Lord Winterbourne!

The old one hastened home on foot, no one observing him—followed far off, like a shadow, by his attendant villain—unobserved, and almost unheeded, entered the Hall; thrust with his own hand some necessaries into his travelling-bag, gathered his cloak around him, and was gone. Winterbourne Hall that night was left in the custody of the strangers who had been his guests, an uneasy and troubled company, all occupied with projects of departure to-morrow. Once more the broad chill moonlight fell on the noble park, as when Louis and his sister, desolate and friendless, passed out from its lordly gates into midnight and the vacant world. Scarcely a year! but what a change upon all the actors and all the passions of that moonlight October night!

CHAPTER XXXII

ESPOUSALS

It was winter, but the heavens were bright—a halcyon day among the December glooms. All the winds lay still among the withered ferns, making a sighing chorus in the underground of Badgeley Wood; but the white clouds, thinner than the clouds of summer, lay becalmed upon the chill blue sky, and the sun shone warm under the hedgerows, and deluded birds were perching out upon the hawthorn bows; the green grass brightened under the morning light; the wan waters shone; the trees which had no leaves clustered their branches together, with a certain pathos in their nakedness, and made a trellised shadow here and there over the wintry stream; and, noble as in the broadest summer, in the sheen of the December sunshine lay Oxford, jewelled like a bride, gleaming out upon the tower of Maudlin, flashing abroad into the firmament from fair St Mary, twinkling with innumerable gem-points from all the lesser cupolas and spires. In the midst of all, this sunshine retreated in pure defeat and failure, from that sombre old heathen, with his heavy dome—but only brightened all the more upon those responsive and human inhabitants dwelling there from the olden ages, and native to the soil. There was a fresh breath from the broad country, a hum of life in the air, a twitter of hardy birds among the trees. It was one of those days which belong to no season, but come, like single blessings, one by one, throwing a gleam across the darker half of the year. Though it was in December instead of May, it was as fair "a bridal of the earth and sky" as poet could have wished to see; but the season yielded no flowers to strew upon the grassy footpath between the Old Wood Lodge and the little church of Winterbourne; they did not need them who trod that road to-day.

Hush, they are coming home—seeing nothing but an indefinite splendour in the earth and in the sky—sweet in the dews of their youth—touched to the heart—to that very depth and centre where lie all ecstasies and tears. Walking together arm in arm, in their young humility—scarcely aware of the bridal train behind them—in an enchantment of their own; now coming back to that old little room, with its pensive old memories of hermit life and solitude—this quiet old place, which never before was lighted up with such a gleam of splendid fortune and happy hope.

You would say it was Marian Atheling, "with the smile on her lip, and the tear in her eye"—the very same lovely vision whom the lad Louis saw some eighteen months ago at the garden gate. But you would be mistaken; for it is not Marian—it is the young Lady Winterbourne. This one is quite as beautiful for a consolation—almost more so in her bridal blush, and sunshine, and tears—and for a whole hour by the village clock has been a peeress of the realm.

This is what it has come to, after all—what they must all come to, those innocent young people—even Rachel, who is as wild as a child, in her first genuine and unalarmed outburst of youthful jubilation—even Agnes, who through all this joy carries a certain thoughtful remembrance in her dark eyes—possibly even Charlie, who fears no man, but is a little shy of every womankind younger than Miss Anastasia. There are only one or two strangers; but the party almost overflows Miss Bridget's parlour, where the old walls smile with flowers, and the old apartment, like an ancient handmaid, receives them with a prim and antique grace—a little doubtful, yet half hysterical with joy.

But it does not last very long, this crowning festival. By-and-by the hero and the heroine go away; then the guests one by one; then the family, a little languid, a little moved with the first inroad among them, disperse to their own apartments, or to a meditative ramble out of doors; and when the twilight falls, you could almost suppose Miss Bridget, musing too over the story of another generation, sitting before the fire in her great old chair, with no companion but the flowers.

This new event seemed somehow to consolidate and make certain that wonderful fortune of Louis, which until then had looked almost too much like a romance to be realised. His uncle had made various efforts to question and set aside the verdict which transferred to the true heir his name and inheritance—efforts in which even the lawyers whom he had employed at the trial, and who were not over-scrupulous, had refused any share. The attempt was entirely fruitless—an insane resistance to the law, which was irresistible; and the Honourable Reginald Rivers, whom some old sycophants who came in his way still flattered with his old title, was now at Baden, a great man enough in his own circle, rich in the allowance from his nephew, which he was no longer too proud to accept. He alone of all men expressed any disapprobation of Louis's marriage—he whose high sense of family honour revolted from the idea of a mesalliance—and one other individual, who had something of a more reasonable argument. We hasten to extract, according to a former promise, the following pathetic paragraph from the pages of the Mississippi Gazette:—

"I have just heard of the marriage of the young Lord W— with the beautiful M— A—. Well!—is that so wonderful? Oh, visionary dream! That thou shouldst pause to comment upon a common British bargain—the most ordinary arrangement of this conventional and rotten life? What is a heart in comparison with a title?—true love in the balance of a coronet? Oh, my country, thou hast not come to this! But for these mercenary and heartless parents—but for the young mind dazzled with the splendid cheat of rank—oh heaven, what true felicity—what poetic rapture—what a home thou mightst have seen! For she was beautiful as the day when it breaks upon the rivers and the mountains of my native land! It is enough—a poet's fate would have been all incomplete without this fiery trial. Farewell, M—! Farewell, lovely deluded victim of a false society! Some time out of your hollow splendour you will think of a true heart and weep!"

CHAPTER XXXIII

AN OLD FRIEND

"The Winterbournes" had been for some time at home—they were now in London, and Marian had appeared at court in the full splendour of that young beauty of hers; which never had dazzled any one at home as it dazzled every one now. She and her handsome young husband were the lions of the season, eagerly sought after in "the best society." Their story had got abroad, as stories which are at all remarkable have such a wonderful faculty of getting; and strangers whom Marian had never seen before, were delighted to make her acquaintance—charmed to know her sister, who had so much genius, and wrote such delightful books, and, most extraordinary of all, extremely curious and interested about Charlie, the wonderful young brother who had found out the mystery. At one of the fashionable assemblies, where Louis and Marian, Rachel and Agnes, were pointed out eagerly on all sides, and commented upon as "such fresh unsophisticated young creatures—such a group! so picturesque, so interesting!" they became aware, all of them, with different degrees of embarrassment and pain, that Mrs Edgerley was in the company. Louis found her out last of all. She could not possibly fail to notice them; and the young man, anxious to save her pain, made up his mind at once to be the first to address her. He went forward gravely, with more than usual deference in his manner. She recognised him in a moment, started with a little surprise and a momentary shock, but immediately rushed forward with her most charming air of enthusiasm, caught his hand, and overwhelmed him with congratulations. "Oh, I should be so shocked if you supposed that I entertained any prejudice because of poor dear papa!" cried Mrs Edgerley. "Of course he meant no harm; of course he did not know any better. I am so charmed to see you! I am sure we shall make most capital cousins and firm allies. Positively you look quite grave at me. Oh, I assure you, family feuds are entirely out of fashion, and no one ever quarrels with me! I am dying to see those sweet girls!"

And very much amazed, and filled with great perturbation, those sweet girls were, when Mrs Edgerley came up to them, leaning upon Louis's arm, bestowed upon them all a shower of those light perfumy kisses which Marian and Agnes remembered so well, and, declaring Lady Winterbourne far too young for a chaperone, took her place among them. Amazed as they were at this sudden renewal of old friendship, none of them desired to resist it; and before they were well aware, they found themselves engaged, the whole party, to Mrs Edgerley's next "reception," when "every one would be so charmed to see them!" "Positively, my love, you are looking quite lovely," whispered the fine lady into the shrinking ear of Marian. "I always said so. I constantly told every one you were the most perfect little beauty in the world; and then that charming book of Miss Atheling's, which every one was wild about! and your brother—now, do you know, I wish so very much to know your brother. Oh, I am sure you could persuade him to come to my Thursday. Tell him every one comes; no one ever refuses me! I shall send him a card to-morrow. Now, may I leave my cause in your hands?"

"We will try," said Marian, who, though she bore her new dignities with extraordinary self-possession on the whole, was undeniably shy of Agnes's first fashionable patroness. The invitation was taken up as very good fun indeed, by all the others. They resolved to make a general assault upon Charlie, and went home in great glee with their undertaking. Nor was Charlie, after all, so hard to be moved as they expected. He twisted the pretty note in his big fingers with somewhat grim amusement, and said he did not mind. With this result Mrs Atheling showed the greatest delight, for the good mother began to speculate upon a wife for Charlie, and to be rather afraid of some humble beauty catching her boy's eye before he had "seen the world."

With almost the feeling of people in a dream, Agnes and Marian entered once more those well-remembered rooms of Mrs Edgerley, in which they had gained their first glimpse of the world; and Charlie, less demonstrative of his feelings, but not without a remembrance of the past, entered these same portals where he had exchanged that first glance of instinctive enmity with the former Lord Winterbourne. The change was almost too extraordinary to be realised even by the persons principally concerned. Marian, who had been but Agnes Atheling's pretty and shy sister, came in now first of the party, the wife of the head of her former patroness's family. Agnes, a diffident young genius then, full of visionary ideas of fame, had now her own known and acknowledged place, but had gone far beyond it, in the heart which did not palpitate any longer with the glorious young fancies of a visionary ambition; and Charlie, last of all—Charlie, who had tumbled out of the Islington fly to take charge of his sisters—a big boy, clumsy and manful, whom Lord Winterbourne smiled at, as he passed, with his ungenial smile—Charlie, almost single-handed, had thrust the usurper from his seat, and placed the true heir in his room. No wonder that the Athelings were somewhat dizzy with recollections when they came among all the fashionable people who were charmed to see them, and found their way at last to the boudoir where Agnes and Marian had looked at the faces and the diamonds, on that old Thursday of Mrs Edgerley's, which sparkled still in their recollection, the beginning of their fate.

But though Louis and Marian, and Agnes and Rachel, were all extremely attractive, had more or less share in the romance, and were all more or less handsome, Charlie was without dispute the lion of the night. Mrs Edgerley fluttered about with him, holding his great arm with her pretty hand, and introducing him to every one; and with a smile, rueful, comical, half embarrassed, half ludicrous, Charlie, who continued to be very shy of ladies, suffered himself to be dragged about by the fashionable enchantress. He had very little to say—he was such a big fellow, so unmanageable in a delicate crowd of fine ladies, with draperies like gossamer, and, to do him justice, very much afraid of the dangerous steering; but Charlie's "manners," though they would have overwhelmed with distress his anxious mother, rather added to his "success." "It was he who conducted the whole case." "I do not wonder! Look, what a noble head! What a self-absorbed expression! What a power of concentration!" were the sweet and audible whispers which rang around him; and the more sensible observers of the scene, who saw the secret humour in Charlie's upper-lip, slightly curved with amusement, acute, but not unkindly, and caught now and then a gleam of his keen eye, which, when it met with a response, always made a momentary brightening of the smile—were disposed to give him full credit for all the power imputed to him. Mrs Edgerley was in the highest delight—he was a perfect success for a lion. Lions, as this patroness of the fine arts knew by experience, were sadly apt to betray themselves, to be thrown off their balance, to talk nonsense. But Charlie, who was not given to talking, who was still so delightfully clumsy, and made such a wonderful bow, was perfectly charming; Mrs Edgerley declared she was quite in love with him. After all, natural feeling put out of the question, she had no extraordinary occasion to identify herself with the resentments or enmities of that ruined plotter at Baden; and he must have been a worthy father, indeed, who had moved Mrs Edgerley to shut her heart or her house to the handsome young couple, whom everybody delighted to honour, or to the hero of a fashionable romance, which was spoken of everywhere. She had no thought of any such sacrifice; she established the most friendly relations instantly with her charming young cousins. She extended the kindly title, with the most fascinating amiability, to Agnes and Charlie. She overwhelmed the young lawyer with compliments and invitations. He had a much stronger hold upon her fickle fancy than the author of Hope Hazlewood. Mrs Edgerley was delighted to speak to all her acquaintances of Mr Atheling, "who conducted all the case against poor dear papa—did everything himself, I assure you—and such a charming modesty of genius, such a wonderful force and character! Oh, any one may be jealous who pleases; I cannot help it. I quite adore that clever young man."

Charlie took it all very quietly; he concerned himself as little about the adoration of Mrs Edgerley, as he did about the secret scrutiny of his mother concerning every young woman who chanced to cross the path of her son. Young women were the only created things whom Charlie was afraid of, and what his own secret thoughts might be upon this important question, nobody could tell.

CHAPTER XXXIV

SETTLING DOWN

Many lesser changes had been involved in the great revolution which made the nameless Louis head of the family, and conferred upon him the estates and title of Lord Winterbourne: scarcely any one, indeed, in the immediate circle of the two families of Rivers and Atheling, the great people and the small, remained uninfluenced by the change of sovereignty, except Miss Anastasia, whose heart and household charities were manifestly widened, but to whom no other change except the last, and grand one, was like to come. The Rector kept his word; as soon as he heard of the definite settlement of that great question of Louis's claim, he himself resigned his benefice; and one of the first acts of the new Lord Winterbourne was to answer the only request of Lionel, by conferring it upon Mr Mead. After that, Lionel made a settlement upon his sister of all the property which belonged to them, enough to make a modest maidenly income for the gentle invalid, and keep her in possession of all the little luxuries which seemed essential to her life. For himself, he retained a legacy of a thousand pounds which had been left to him several years before. This was the last that was known of the Rector—he disappeared into entire gloom and obscurity after he had made this final arrangement. It was sometimes possible to hear of him, for English travellers, journeying through unfamiliar routes, did not fail to note the wandering English gentleman who seemed to travel for something else than pleasure, and whose motives and objects no one knew; but where to look for him next, or what his occupations were, neither Louis nor his friends, in spite of all their anxious inquiries, could ever ascertain.

And Mr Mead was now the rector, and reigned in Lionel's stead. A new rectory, all gabled and pinnacled, more "correct" than the model it followed, and truer to its period than the truest original in Christendom, rose rapidly between the village and the Hall; and Mr Mead, whose altar had been made bare by the iconoclastic hands of authority, began to exhibit some little alteration in his opinions as he grew older, held modified views as to the priesthood, and cast an eye of visible kindness upon the Honourable Rachel Rivers. The sentiment, however, was not at all reciprocal; no one believed that Rachel was really as old as Louis—older than the pretty matron Marian, older even than Agnes. She had never been a girl until now—and Rachel cared a great deal more for the invalid Lucy in her noiseless shadowy chamber in the Old Wood House, than for all the rectors and all the curates in the world. She was fancy free, and promised to remain so; and Marian had already begun with a little horror to entertain the idea that Rachel possibly might never marry at all.

The parent Athelings themselves were not unmoved by the changes of their children. Charlie was to be received as a partner into the firm which Mr Foggo, by dint of habit, still clung to, as soon as he had attained his one-and-twentieth year. Agnes, as these quiet days went on, grew both in reputation and in riches, girl though she still was; and the youngest of them was Lady Winterbourne! All these great considerations somewhat dazzled the eyes of the confidential clerk of Messrs Cash, Ledger, & Co., as he turned over his books upon that desk where he had once placed Agnes's fifty-pound notes, the beginning of the family fortune. Bellevue came to be mightily out of the way when Louis and Marian were in town living in so different a quarter; and Mr Atheling wearied of the City, and Mamma concluded that the country air would be a great deal better for Bell and Beau. So Mr Atheling accepted a retiring allowance, the half of his previous income, from the employers whom he had served so long. The whole little household, even including Susan, removed to the country, where Marian had been delighting herself in the superintendence of the two or three additional rooms built to the Old Wood Lodge, which were so great a surprise to Mamma when she found them, risen as at the touch of a fairy's wand. The family settled there at once in unpretending comfort, taking farewell affectionately of Miss Willsie and Mr Foggo, but not forgetting Bellevue.

And here Agnes pursued her vocation, making very little demonstration of it, the main pillar for the mean time, and crowning glory of her father's house. Her own mind and imagination had been profoundly impressed, almost in spite of herself, by that last known act of Lionel's—his hasty journey to London with Doctor Serrano. It was the kind of act beyond all others to win upon a temperament so generous and sensitive, which a more ostentatious generosity might have disgusted and repelled; and perhaps the very uncertainty in which they remained concerning him kept up the lurking "interest" in Agnes Atheling's heart. It was possible that he might appear any day at their very doors; it was possible that he never might be seen again. It was not easy to avoid speculating upon him—what he was thinking, where he was?—and when, in that spontaneous delight of her young genius, which yet had suffered no diminution, Agnes's thoughts glided into impersonation, and fairy figures gathered round her, and one by one her fables grew, in the midst of the thread of story—in the midst of what people called, to the young author's amusement, "an elaborate development of character, the result of great study and observation"—thoughts came to her mind, and words to her lip, which she supposed no one could thoroughly understand save one. Almost unconsciously she shadowed his circumstances and his story in many a bright imagination of her own; and contrasted with the real one half-a-dozen imaginary Lionels, yet always ending in finding him the noblest type of action in that great crisis of his career. It blended somehow strangely with all that was most serious in her work; for when Agnes had to speak of faith, she spoke of it with the fervour with which one addresses an individual, opening her heart to show the One great Name enshrined in it to another, who, woe for him, in his wanderings so sadly friendless, knew not that Lord.

So the voice of the woman who dwelt at home went out over the world; it charmed multitudes who thought of nothing but the story it told, delighted some more who recognised that sweet faulty grace of youth, that generous young directness and simplicity which made the fable truth. If it ever reached to one who felt himself addressed in it, who knew the words, the allusions, that noble craft of genius, which, addressing all, had still a private voice for one—if there was such a man somewhere, in the desert or among the mountains far away, wandering where he seldom heard the tongue of his country, and never saw a face he recognised, Agnes never knew.

But after this fashion time went on with them all. Then there came a second heir, another Louis to the Hall at Winterbourne—and it was very hard to say whether this young gentleman's old aunt or his young aunt, the Honourable Rachel, or the Honourable Anastasia, was most completely out of her wits at this glorious epoch in the history of the House. Another event of the most startling and extraordinary description took place very shortly after the christening of Marian's miraculous baby. Charlie was one-and-twenty; he was admitted into the firm, and the young man, who was one of the most "rising young men" in his profession, took to himself a holiday, and went abroad without any one knowing much about it. No harm in that; but when Charlie returned, he brought with him a certain Signora Giulia, a very amazing companion indeed for this taciturn hero, who was afraid of young ladies. He took her down at once to Winterbourne, to present her to his mother and sisters. He had the grace to blush, but really was not half so much ashamed of himself as he ought to have been. For the pretty young Italian turned out to be cousin to Louis and Rachel—a delicate little beauty, extremely proud of the big young lover, who had carried her off from her mother's house six weeks ago: and we are grieved to acknowledge that Charlie henceforth showed no fear whatever, scarcely even the proper awe of a dutiful husband, in the presence of Mrs Charles Atheling.

CHAPTER XXXV

THE END

Agnes Atheling was alone in old Miss Bridget's parlour; it was a fervent day of July, and all the country lay in a hush and stillness of exceeding sunshine, which reduced all the common sounds of life, far and near, to a drowsy and languid hum—the midsummer's luxurious voice. The little house was perfectly still. Mrs Atheling was at the Hall, Papa in Oxford, and Hannah, whose sole beatific duty it was to take care of the children, and who envied no one in the world save the new nurse to the new baby, had taken out Bell and Beau. The door was open in the fearless fashion and license of the country. Perhaps Susan was dozing in the kitchen, or on the sunny outside bench by the kitchen door. There was not a sound about the house save the deep dreamy hum of the bees among the roses—those roses which clustered thick round the old porch and on the wall. Agnes sat by the open window, in a very familiar old occupation, making a frock for little Bell, who was six years old now, and appreciated pretty things.

Agnes was not quite so young as she used to be—four years, with a great many events in them, had enlarged the maiden mind, which still was as fresh as a child's. She was changed otherwise: the ease which those only have who are used to the company of people of refinement, had added another charm to her natural grace. As she sat with her work on her knee, in her feminine attitude and occupation, making a meditative pause, bowing her head upon her hand, thinking of something, with those quiet walls of home around her—the open door, the open window, and no one else visible in the serene and peaceful house, she made, in her fair and thoughtful young womanhood, as sweet a type as one could desire of the serene and happy confidence of a quiet English home.

She did not observe any one passing; she was not thinking, perhaps, of any one hereabout who was like to pass—but she heard a step entering at the door. She scarcely looked up, thinking it some member of the family—scarcely moved even when the door of the parlour opened wider, and the step came in. Then she looked up—started up—let her work drop out of her hands, and, gazing with eagerness in the bronzed face of the stranger, uttered a wondering exclamation. He hastened to her, holding out his hand. "Mr Rivers?" cried Agnes, in extreme surprise and agitation—"is it you?"

What he said was some hasty faltering expressions of delight in seeing her, and they gazed at each other with their mutual "interest," glad, yet constrained. "We have tried often to find out where you were," said Agnes—"I mean Louis; he has been very anxious. Have you seen him? When did you come home?"

"I have seen no one save you."

"But Louis has been very anxious," said Agnes, with a little confusion. "We have all tried to discover where you were. Is it wrong to ask where you have been?"

But Lionel did not at all attend to her questions. He was less self-possessed than she was; he seemed to have only one idea at the present moment, so far as was visible, and that he simply expressed over again—"I am very glad—happy—to see you here and alone."

"Oh!" said Agnes with a nervous tremor—"I—I was asking, Mr Rivers, where you had been?"

This time he began to attend to her. "I have been everywhere," he said, "except where pleasure was. I have been on fields of battles—in places of wretchedness. I have come to tell you something—you only. Do you remember our conversation once by Badgeley Wood?"

"Yes."

"You gave me a talisman, Agnes," said the speaker, growing more excited; "I have carried it all over the world."

"Well," said Agnes as he paused. She looked at him very earnestly, without even a blush at the sound of her own name.

"Well—better than well!" cried Lionel; "wonderful—invincible—divine! I went to try your spell—I who trusted nothing—at the moment when everything had failed me—even you. I put yonder sublime Friend of yours to the experiment—I dared to do it! I took his name to the sorrowful, as you bade me. I cast out devils with his name, as the sorcerers tried to do. I put all the hope I could have in life upon the trial. Now I come to tell you the issue; it is fit that you should know."

Agnes leaned forward towards him, listening eagerly; she could not quite tell what she expected—a confession of faith.

"I am a man of ambition," said Lionel, turning in a moment from the high and solemn excitement of his former speech, with a sudden smile like a gleam of sunshine. "You remember my projects when I was heir of Winterbourne. You knew them, though I did not tell you; now I have found a cave in a wild mining district among a race of giants. I am Vicar of Botallach, among the Cornish men—have been for four-and-twenty hours—that is the end."

Agnes had put out her hand to him in the first impulse of joy and congratulation; a second thought, more subtle, made her pause, and blush, and draw back. Lionel was not so foolish as to wait the end of this self-controversy. He left his seat, came to her side, took the hand firmly into his own, which she half gave, and half withdrew—did not blush, but grew pale, with the quiet concern of a man who was about deciding the happiness of his life. "The end, but the beginning too," said Lionel, with a tremor in his voice. "Agnes hear me still—I have something more to say."

She did not answer a word; she lifted her eyes to his face with one hurried, agitated momentary glance. Something more! but the whole tale was in the look. They did not know very well what words followed, and neither do we.

Margaret Oliphant – A Short Biography

Margaret Oliphant Wilson was born on April 4th, 1828 to Francis W. Wilson, a clerk, and Margaret Oliphant, at Wallyford, near Musselburgh, East Lothian.

She spent her childhood at Lasswade, near Dalkeith, Glasgow before moving to Liverpool.

Her youth was spent in establishing a writing style so much so that, in 1849, she had her first novel published: Passages in the Life of Mrs. Margaret Maitland based on the Scottish Free Church movement. It met with some success and was a good start to her career.

Two years later, in 1851, her third book Caleb Field was published. It was also now that she met the publisher William Blackwood in Edinburgh and was asked to contribute to his well-received Blackwood's Magazine. It was to be a lifelong endeavor. Over the course of the relationship she would have well over 100 articles published.

In May 1852, Margaret married her cousin, Frank Wilson Oliphant, at Birkenhead, and they settled at Harrington Square, Camden, London. He was an artist working primarily in stained glass. With the marriage she became Margaret Oliphant Wilson Oliphant.

Their marriage produced six children but three tragically died in infancy.

When her husband developed signs of the dreaded consumption (tuberculosis) they moved, on the advice of doctors, to warmer climes. In January 1859 it was to Florence, and then to Rome where, sadly, he died.

Margaret was naturally devastated but was also now left without support and only her income from her writing. She returned to England and took up the task of supporting her three remaining children by her literary activity.

By now she was being published both as an established novelist and regularly in Blackwood's Magazine, amongst several others. Her incredible and prolific work rate increased both her commercial reputation and the size of her reading audience.

Against this her domestic life continued to be tragic, full of sorrow and disappointment.

In January 1864 her only remaining daughter, Maggie, died and was buried in her father's grave in Rome. Her brother, who had emigrated to Canada, was shortly afterwards involved in financial ruin. Margaret generously offered a home to him and his children, adding another demand to her already heavy responsibilities.

In 1866 she settled at Windsor to be closer to her sons, who were being educated at near-by Eton School. That year, her second cousin, Annie Louisa Walker, came to live with her as a companion-housekeeper. Windsor was now to be her home for the rest of her life.

Her literary career for three decades was one of constant delivery and success. Whether she wrote historical works or across several genres in fiction: domestic realism, historical, romance or supernatural she was successful.

For more than thirty years she pursued a varied literary career but family life continued to bring problems.

The literary ambitions she wished for her sons were unfulfilled. Cyril Francis, the eldest, died in 1890, leaving a Life of Alfred de Musset, which was later incorporated in his mother's Foreign Classics for English Readers. The younger, Francis, who she nicknamed 'Cecco', collaborated with her in the Victorian Age of English Literature and won a position at the British Museum, but was rejected by Sir Andrew Clark, a famous physician. Cecco died in 1894.

With the last of her children now lost to her, she had but little further interest in life. Her health steadily and inexorably declined.

Margaret Oliphant Wilson Oliphant died at the age of 69 in Wimbledon on 20th June 1897. She is buried in Eton beside her sons.

At her death, Margaret was still working on Annals of a Publishing House, a record of Blackwood's Magazine with which she had enjoyed such a successful relationship.

Her Autobiography and Letters, which present a thoughtful picture of her domestic anxieties, was published in 1899. Only parts were written with a wider audience in mind: she had originally intended the Autobiography for her son, but he died before she could finish it.

Opinions on Oliphant's work are split, with some critics seeing her as a 'domestic novelist', while others recognize her work as influential and important to the Victorian literature canon. Critical reception from her contemporaries is also divided. John Skelton took the view that Oliphant wrote too much and too quickly. Writing a Blackwood's article called 'A Little Chat About Mrs. Oliphant', he asked, "Had Mrs. Oliphant concentrated her powers, what might she not have done? We might have had another Charlotte Brontë or another George Eliot." However not all of the contemporary reception was negative. The esteemed M. R. James admired Oliphant's supernatural fiction, concluding that "the religious ghost story, as it may be called, was never done better than by Mrs. Oliphant in 'The Open Door' and 'A Beleaguered City'. Mary Butts lavished praise on Oliphant's ghost story 'The Library Window', describing it as "one masterpiece of sober loveliness".

More modern critics of Oliphant's work include Virginia Woolf, who asked in 'Three Guineas' whether Oliphant's autobiography does not lead the reader "to deplore the fact that Mrs. Oliphant sold her brain, her very admirable brain, prostituted her culture and enslaved her intellectual liberty in order that she might earn her living and educate her children."

Whatever the merits of their cases Margaret Oliphant has been shamefully neglected in modern years. She is now becoming more widely recognised as a leading writer of her day.

Margaret Oliphant – A Concise Bibliography

A canon of more than 120 works, including novels, travel books, histories, and volumes of literary criticism.

Novels
Margaret Maitland (1849)
Merkland (1850)
Caleb Field (1851)
John Drayton (1851)
Adam Graeme (1852)
The Melvilles (1852)
Katie Stewart (1852)
Harry Muir (1853)
Ailieford (1853)
The Quiet Heart (1854)
Magdalen Hepburn (1854)
Zaidee (1855)
Lilliesleaf (1855)
Christian Melville (1855)
The Athelings (1857)
The Days of My Life (1857)
Orphans (1858)
The Laird of Norlaw (1858)
Agnes Hopetoun's Schools and Holidays (1859)
Lucy Crofton (1860)
The House on the Moor (1861)
The Last of the Mortimers (1862)
Heart and Cross (1863)

Salem Chapel (1863)
The Rector (1863)
Doctor's Family (1863)
The Perpetual Curate (1864)
Miss Marjoribanks (1866)
Phoebe Junior (1876)
A Son of the Soil (1865)
Agnes (1866)
Madonna Mary (1867)
Brownlows (1868)
The Minister's Wife (1869)
The Three Brothers (1870)
John: A Love Story (1870)
Squire Arden (1871)
At his Gates (1872)
Ombra (1872
May (1873)
Innocent (1873)
The Story of Valentine and His Brother (1875)
A Rose in June (1874)
For Love and Life (1874)
Whiteladies (1875)
An Odd Couple (1875)
The Curate in Charge (1876)
Carità (1877)
Young Musgrave (1877)
Mrs. Arthur (1877)
The Primrose Path (1878)
Within the Precincts (1879)
The Fugitives (1879)
A Beleaguered City (1879)
The Greatest Heiress in England (1880)
He That Will Not When He May (1880)
In Trust (1881)
Harry Joscelyn (1881)
Lady Jane (1882)
A Little Pilgrim in the Unseen (1882)
The Lady Lindores (1883)
Sir Tom (1883)
Hester (1883)
It Was a Lover and his Lass (1883)
The Lady's Walk (1883)
The Wizard's Son (1884)
Madam (1884)
The Prodigals and Their Inheritance (1885)
Oliver's Bride (1885)
A Country Gentleman and His Family (1886)
A House Divided Against Itself (1886)

Effie Ogilvie (1886)
A Poor Gentleman (1886)
The Son of His Father (1886)
Joyce (1888)
Cousin Mary (1888)
The Land of Darkness (1888)
Lady Car (1889)
Kirsteen (1890)
The Mystery of Mrs. Biencarrow (1890)
Sons and Daughters (1890)
The Railway Man and His Children (1891)
The Heir Presumptive and the Heir Apparent (1891)
The Marriage of Elinor (1891)
Janet (1891)
The Cuckoo in the Nest (1892)
Diana Trelawny (1892)
The Sorceress (1893)
A House in Bloomsbury (1894)
Sir Robert's Fortune (1894)
Who Was Lost and is Found (1894)
Lady William (1894)
Two Strangers (1895)
Old Mr. Tredgold (1895)
The Unjust Steward (1896)
The Ways of Life (1897)

Short stories
Neighbours on the Green (1889)
A Widow's Tale and Other Stories (1898)
That Little Cutty (1898)
The Open Door (1918)

Selected Articles
Mary Russel Mitford (Blackwood's Magazine, Vol. 75, 1854)
Evelin and Pepys (Blackwood's Magazine, Vol. 76, 1854)
The Holy Land (Blackwood's Magazine, Vol. 76, 1854)
Mr. Thackeray and his Novels (Blackwood's Magazine, Vol. 77, 1855)
Bulwer (Blackwood's Magazine, Vol. 77, 1855)
Charles Dickens (Blackwood's Magazine, Vol. 77, 1855)
Modern Novelists—Great and Small (Blackwood's Magazine, Vol. 77, 1855)
Modern Light Literature: Poetry (Blackwood's Magazine, Vol. 79, 1856)
Religion in Common Life (Blackwood's Magazine, Vol. 79, 1856)
Sydney Smith (Blackwood's Magazine, Vol. 79, 1856)
The Laws Concerning Women (Blackwood's Magazine, Vol. 79, 1856)
The Art of Caviling (Blackwood's Magazine, Vol. 80, 1856)
Béranger (Blackwood's Magazine, Vol. 83, 1858)

The Condition of Women (Blackwood's Magazine, Vol. 83, 1858)
The Missionary Explorer (Blackwood's Magazine, Vol. 83, 1858)
Religious Memoirs (Blackwood's Magazine, Vol. 83, 1858)
Social Science (Blackwood's Magazine, Vol. 88, 1860)
Scotland and her Accusers (Blackwood's Magazine, Vol. 90, 1861)
The Chronicles of Carlingford (Blackwood's Magazine 1862–1865)
Girolamo Savonarola (Blackwood's Magazine, Vol. 93, 1863)
The Life of Jesus (Blackwood's Magazine, Vol. 96, 1864)
Giacomo Leopardi (Blackwood's Magazine, Vol. 98, 1865)
The Great Unrepresented (Blackwood's Magazine, Vol. 100, 1866)
Mill on the Subjection of Women (The Edinburgh Review, Vol. 130, 1869)
The Opium-Eater (Blackwood's Magazine, Vol. 122, 1877)
Russian and Nihilism in the Novels of I. Tourgeniéf (Blackwood's Magazine, Vol. 127, 1880)
School and College (Blackwood's Magazine, Vol. 128, 1880)
The Grievances of Women (Fraser's Magazine, New Series, Vol. 21, 1880)
Mrs. Carlyle (The Contemporary Review, Vol. 43, May 1883)
The Ethics of Biography (The Contemporary Review, July 1883)
Victor Hugo (The Contemporary Review, Vol. 48, July/December 1885)
A Venetian Dynasty (The Contemporary Review, Vol. 50, August 1886)
Laurence Oliphant (Blackwood's Magazine, Vol. 145, 1889)
Tennyson (Blackwood's Magazine, Vol. 152, 1892)
Addison, the Humorist (Century Magazine, Vol. 48, 1894)
The Anti-Marriage League (Blackwood's Magazine, Vol. 159, 1896)

Biographies
Edward Irving (1862)
Francis of Assisi (1871)
Count de Montalembert (1872)
Dante (1877)
Cervantes (1880)
Life of Sheridan in the English Men of Letters series (1883)
John Tulloch (1888)
Laurence Oliphant (1892)

Historical & Critical Works
Historical Sketches of the Reign of George II (1869)
The Makers of Florence (1876)
A Literary History of England from 1760 to 1825 (1882)
The Makers of Venice (1887)
Royal Edinburgh (1890)
Jerusalem (1891)
The Makers of Modern Rome (1895)
William Blackwood and his Sons (1897)
The Sisters Brontë. In: Women Novelists of Queen Victoria's Reign (1897)